THE LONGEST WINTER

THE LONGEST WINTER

Julie Harris

ROBERT HALE · LONDON

ISBN 0 7090 7890 0

Robert Hale Limited
Clerkenwell House
Clerkenwell Green
London EC1R 0HT

2 4 6 8 10 9 7 5 3 1

Printed in Great Britain by
St Edmundsbury Press Limited, Bury St Edmunds, Suffolk.
Bound by Woolnough Bookbinding Limited.

In memory of my dad, Denis, and Viv,
who are now flying in a brighter sky.

Thanks to Dr. Lowry Ware, Anne G. Clarke,
Louise and Carroll Ferguson,
and to Mary, who introduced us.

T H E events of this story take place during several decades early in this century, and are centered on the "memoirs" of a man marooned on an island off the mainland of Alaska. During his seventeen years on this island, John Robert Shaw's only companions were its Native American inhabitants. Shaw, like most people of the time, was completely unaware that any distinctions existed among the groups of people that he refers to as "Indians" and "Eskimos." Today we are more informed and we refer to various cultures in the terms that they choose for themselves. But this is a historical work, not unlike Defoe's *Robinson Crusoe,* and as such must be taken in the light of its time. The usage of terms considered incorrect today is not intended as a slight to any group: It is simply the way things were done in an earlier and, perhaps, less enlightened era.

I N 1911, a boy from Abbeville, South Carolina, had his first taste of flying. In 1926, two years after the death of his best friend, John Robert Shaw, age twenty-four, attempted a solo flight record in a refitted 1923 Curtiss Jenny. Sponsored by a Miami newspaper, he made it to Anchorage on April 23, 1926, half the solo complete. On April 27, he was caught in a storm, went down, and for seventeen years was listed as missing, presumed dead, until the evacuation of the Aleutian Islands in May 1943.

This is his story.

PROLOGUE

━━━━━━━━

I first met John in May 1943, when he came in with a boat-load of Aleut evacuees from the Andreanof Islands. As far as I could determine, no one knew that island was charted or inhabited until the seaplanes flew their first missions.

I spent many weeks in Anchorage Hospital listening to John tell me his story. He would have told anyone who had time to listen. Not many did. We were at war, or so was the excuse.

His story emerged in pieces. Sometimes he could talk for hours on end. On his worst days, he would simply stare at the wall as if he was longing for something he couldn't have.

He had written down most of what had happened, but, like his storytelling, nothing came in any order.

It took me eight years to make some sense of it all, to recall the missing pieces he told me so long ago.

Betty-Sue Llewellyn
Anchorage, Alaska
1957

ONE

━◦━◦━◦━◦━◦━◦━

T H E sun was almost shining the day he woke and knew his name. He almost remembered how he'd gotten there; what he didn't remember was why or when.

For a while, he was convinced he was somewhere southeast of Anchorage. All he vaguely recalled was the storm building. Half an hour out and heading home before the 120-knot head wind, which became a crosswind, then a tailwind, shattered any futile hope he had concerning futures. Nothing existed at that time except spewing fuel, hemorrhaging oil lines, and when the Jenny finally, inevitably died, all was replaced by a blanket of dark, prickly calm until he saw the cliff face, the frozen sea. And there were seconds of hour-long duration before the final impact.

Images came in waking dream states, frail, torn, faded, intangible, and too often confusing because it seemed that they belonged to someone else, not to him.

Mostly, his mind spiraled from repetitive, screaming nightmares of the crash. He'd wake to the sounds of children at play, to foreign, happy voices singing. The echo of the tambours always chased the demons away until he closed his eyes again.

The woman was ever-present—the soft, soothing voice, the touch of the gloved hand. The occasional curious, fur-lined faces of the others peeked in, probably to see if he was still alive, or not. He'd be there, on his back, immobile, watching them.

Sometimes he'd smile at those faces, but mostly he wished they'd go away and leave him be, and take the godforsaken wind with them.

Then one day when the fog had lifted enough to show him traces of a beach beyond the cliff, when the narrow opening on that unreal world of incessant cold was opened by a touch of summer, the woman came back in carrying a heavy bundle. She pulled the skins down and obliterated his view. It was no use asking her to open the door again, let some fresh air in. Whenever he spoke, she just smiled.

"What you got this time?" he asked.

She heaved the pack to the raised earth table, turned to him, and grinned.

It was a package wrapped in sealskin. She opened it, smiling constantly, as if knowing that seeing this would break his pain. She held up his all-weather bag, the catches rusted, broken. From inside, the items appeared—curiosities to her, but they weren't to him. A pilot's log, pencils, maps. A compass, a can opener. His Bowie knife. Forks, spoons. One rusted tin of beans. One frozen orange, underwear, and his spare cap.

Most of all, there was paper—a wad of brittle, water-damaged yellow paper.

Perhaps it was then he began to remember, truly remember. He took the logbook first; most of the pages had stuck together from the seawater. Some tore at the slightest touch. The ink had run, but here and there was a word he recognized. Especially the last entry:

April 23, '26. 0700. Left Anchorage. Supplies and fuel enough for Vancouver. Northeaster, 30 knots. Hell of a storm building back on the NW horizon. Should make it to . . .

John sighed. Anchorage. He remembered trying to call his sister from Alaska—collect. He remembered Mrs. Johnson telling him no one was answering; could he try again? She'd lived all her simple life in Abbeville, South Carolina. Maybe she thought Anchorage was in Kentucky, or Georgia. So he left the message with Mrs. Johnson—"Tell Meg I'm coming home"—and as he disconnected the call, he knew that Meg would never get the message.

John looked at the woman. She was studying the Bowie knife, then the silver spoon engraved BHS—it had been in the Shaw family since the Boston Tea Party. She wanted it, that much he knew, so he nodded and the smile she gave in return was contagious.

She found a nest for her new toy and came back, this time with the two bentwood bowls, one containing four mouthfuls of warmed seal blood and the other the thick black ointment she used on him on the hour, every hour—or so it seemed.

He didn't fight it anymore. It did no good. The blood didn't nauseate him now as it had at first, and he drank it quickly, with the grace of a child downing castor oil.

John guessed the ointment was an Eskimo equivalent to antiseptic. Whatever it was, it relieved some of the pain. He sat quietly while she rubbed some on his face. He sat quietly while she removed his parka and rubbed it into his chest. But he turned his face the other way as he always did when the black ointment was dabbed with gentle care and attention on the stump of his left arm. Then, as routine decreed, he lay down, picked up the logbook, and tried to concentrate on the words while the woman took hold of his left foot and exercised his left leg. He didn't see too many words—the sharp, hot pains overrode everything until the numbness set in. He'd been badly injured in the crash—lost the arm, almost lost the leg. He'd broken his left collarbone, some ribs, had hurt his head, too. Some days when his vision was impaired and his equilibrium shot, he dared do nothing but lie entirely still, for one simple movement was agony. Those days, though, were less and less common. He was getting better, and it was all due to the woman.

When she was done, she left him alone, but this time he didn't sleep. He reached into that all-weather bag, fumbled blindly for a pencil, one objective in mind.

Maybe, he thought, I'll never get out of here alive, but perhaps one day someone might find this and my family will know I didn't die. I might be thought of as lost, I might even be presumed dead, but I don't want anyone thinking I died like Bobby.

His mother's greatest fear, almost a reality.

John sat as best he could on the bed, his back to the driftwood upright. Two of the woman's cook pots hung over his left shoulder; the fur of her outdoor parka hem tickled his neck. It was more comfortable raising his right leg so that the logbook rested on it, but using his right hand for the pencil seemed alien and nearly impossible.

And no words would come. Hadn't it always been that way? He drew a plane instead. The lines weren't entirely correct, but it was the 1923 Jenny he'd been flying since ... February? Was that when he'd left Miami?

He had only partial use of his thumb and index finger— enough to write. He hadn't used that hand since he was nine years old, and to John, who for so long had strained to remember his name, childhood came flooding back. So he wrote it down as quickly as he could in case it all disappeared again and was lost forever, like he was.

It was June 14, 1911. We lived near an airfield at Abbeville, South Carolina, although I can't call it an airfield, because back then it was just a field and in those days anywhere flat and treeless was a place to put down. And five hundred yards was all Billy Taylor ever needed.

Billy Taylor flew my dream, and every day at five after four, my mother would try hard to swallow her temper as he roared right over our house. She'd mumble about newfangled inventions and curse to herself because the chickens hadn't laid eggs for six weeks.

4

But I didn't care about the chickens.

There always was this boy balancing on the fence post, watching his hero land a machine that coughed and spluttered and roared, and I never moved an inch until Billy Taylor shut it down and climbed on out.

I used to make deals with God. I'd say, God, if you let me fly just like Billy Taylor, I'll volunteer to go to Sunday school. That'll sure surprise Ma, won't it, God? You, too, I guess. Sir.

Well, God must have heard me, but nothing ever went as I thought it would.

Billy Taylor never saw me balancing on that fence post, or at least that's what I thought, until that day in June when he came down over our house a little too low.

I fell off the fence post and broke my arm.

Happy birthday, John Robert Shaw. I was nine that day.

Mom heard me screaming. I guess Billy Taylor did, too. All the neighbors came out for a look, wondering what the noise was.

Her favorite expression was, I told you so! And as she carried me into town, she must have said it two thousand times. The doc was away delivering a baby, so his old nurse jammed the bones back into place. The most I remember is screaming a lot more, and when I woke, I was in my bed at home.

My arm was never the same again. But I didn't need to hold a pencil to know what it was I had to do. I had to fly, and a busted arm wasn't going to stop me.

My father had gone off to find work in Alabama in 1909 and he never came home. So my mother was left alone with two kids, me and my little sister. But I never really knew how important those chicken eggs were in terms of our survival, because for me there was nothing more important than watching Billy Taylor landing that machine of his every day at five after four.

Until June 15, 1911.

My mother heaved me off the fence by my good arm and said, "We gonna show Mr. Billy Goddamned Taylor just what it is

5

he's done, ruining us!" In her hand was the empty egg basket, and I'd never heard her curse before, not when I was around at least.

Ruin. I'd heard that word a lot—a lump of beef ruined by too much salt; spilling catsup on my one and only best shirt so I wouldn't have to go to Sunday school, unless I knew for sure there was somebody there I could torment. So I didn't know what she meant by "ruining us," and I didn't care, either. All I knew was that we were heading across the field toward Billy Taylor's shed, and the closer we came, the bigger the plane got.

I never heard my mother as angry at anyone before. And she was the one who'd always tell me to take a deep breath, count to ten, and that by the time you'd made it to eight, you shouldn't be angry anymore. Maybe that day she'd forgotten what came after five.

By the time she had yelled Billy Taylor's name and he turned, she was crying with rage. And when my mother cried with rage, the best place to be was anywhere but close to her, but she had a good tight grip on my hand and there was no way out. All I could do was look at my feet, not at Billy Taylor's face. I'd never been so ashamed in all my life. I'd dreamed a hundred ways to meet my hero, and this wasn't one of them. Now and then, I'd sneak a glance, but he was always looking at me when I did. I felt stupid, standing there barefoot, nine years old and holding my mother's hand. It was about the only time I ever pretended she'd just found me on the wayside.

Up close, Billy Taylor looked about as old as my father was when he went away—about thirty-five. Either he was polite or he knew it was no use trying, because he let my mother have her way with words till nothing more came. He'd say, "I'm sorry, Mrs. Shaw," and that would start her off again.

Then he looked at me when I was looking at him and he smiled. And the smile grew so big, it was catching, like somebody yawning in class.

I think I loved Billy Taylor from the moment we shared that smile. He was too much like my daddy—the same twinkling gaze was about all I could remember except for the way he said, "Yes, Mrs. Shaw," the same way my daddy had said, "Yes, honey."

My father had been a hell of a tall man; I couldn't recall ever having seen past his thigh unless he was sitting down, and Billy Taylor seemed nearly as tall, standing there in his leather coat and his boots and his cap. I started dreaming again about how I'd look just like him one day.

After awhile, both of us never heard my mother's voice. I saw her poke the empty egg basket under his nose, and I think he said he'd pay. To that, Mom said she was angry on principle, whatever that meant. He assured her that the chickens would get used to the noise, and she swore they wouldn't. Then I heard that he'd bought the airfield, had his own flying school. This was the only place on the outskirts of town that suited and he couldn't move on. He was here to stay.

I wondered how many times you can make a deal with God.

Billy Taylor looked at me again, and he must have recognized something lingering there in my eyes—hope, excitement, something. He looked over at his plane and so did I, and he said, "Go look, son, but don't touch."

So I looked, but *don't* was a word that never fit in my dictionary. *Don't* meant "Why can't I?"

Her name was *Gloria*.

She sat with her tail on the ground. She still smelled hot. Her wooden propeller was twice as long as I was, and it was sleek and shiny except for a blotch or two of some kind of squashed bug. I turned back. Billy Taylor wasn't looking, and Mom had stopped crying. Whatever he was saying was working.

I touched the wing. The cover felt like cloth, maybe linen. I tapped it. It felt hollow. I touched. Stroked it like the dog I used to have. She liked me. *Gloria* liked me. I nearly heard her whispering, Come on, climb in. Let's play make-believe awhile.

I looked back to the shed, to the words on the sign, and I stuttered to myself, trying to read, to sound out the letters. The last word was easy enough: *School*. Billy Taylor's Flying School.

Joyrides. Five dollars for fifteen minutes.

If I could have hocked my soul for five dollars, I would have.

Billy Taylor's Flying School.

My kind of school.

I heard Billy Taylor's voice. "Ten cents an hour, every day after school, four hours on weekends."

That added up to nearly a dollar a week, which was as much as my mother got for selling her eggs, or so she said as she held my hand and we walked home across the airfield. I held the wire apart so she could get through and she did the same for me.

"Do you understand, John Robert?" she asked.

I said nothing; I hadn't been listening. She didn't need a dumb boy as well as a dancing daughter, an absent husband, and hens that didn't lay eggs anymore.

"John Robert, have you been hearing a word I said?"

"Yeah, Ma, course I have," I said, hoping she'd say more so I could take it from there.

"John Robert, you have a job."

"Where, Ma?"

"At Billy Taylor's Flying School. John Robert, you haven't been listening."

But she didn't cuff my ear; instead, she took my hand again.

That evening as Meg was pretending to be a ballet star across the porch, I thought about that day. How I'd never gotten very close to God before, till then. Till my mother grabbed me, lifted me high, and planted a kiss on my cheek.

I had a job.

"Fell off the fence, huh?" Billy Taylor asked the next afternoon at twenty after four.

"Yes, sir, I sure did."

"Hurt much?"

"I broke my arm, Mr. Taylor, sir."

"Hurt much?" he asked again.

8

"Nope," I lied, and tried to hide the purple fingers on my right hand.

He grinned at me awhile, as if he'd been watching me watch him every day for the past six weeks. "I used to have a boy about as old as you."

"That so, Mr. Taylor?" I asked, not knowing what else to say, using my mother's words when she was stuck. Always worked for her.

"Aha. Died with his mother in a fire. Going on seven years now."

"Sorry to hear that, Mr. Taylor, sir. Real sorry to hear that."

"Your mother's got a good mind of her own."

"You like her, Mr. Taylor, sir? You think she's pretty?"

He said nothing to that. I was getting paid ten cents an hour to work, not talk about my mother, even if I hoped he'd marry her. I could do with a new father, especially one like him.

"Want to fly, boy?" he asked.

"Oh, yes, sir. I sure do."

"Why?"

I never expected he'd ask me that. Why did I want to fly? It was like asking me why the earth was round, when for as far as you looked it was flat. It just stretched forever. I always had trouble putting feelings into words others could understand, and right then I had a dead spot in my brain about the size of the Appalachians. I always had dead spots, especially when Mrs. Moriarty asked me a question in class. I always knew the answer, but nothing ever came out right.

"I asked you why, boy."

"I don't know, Mr. Taylor, sir. I don't. But I've been watching and wondering things and I see the birds flying and I see you flying and I think, I can do that, too. I guess. Sir."

He handed me a bucket and a rag and he said, "You get up there and you clean the puke, boy. And if you still want to fly . . ."

I heard nothing else. My brain stopped on the word *puke*.

Puke. Me? Me cleaning up puke?

I looked up into Billy Taylor's eyes and I knew then that some things were worth anything, even cleaning puke for. I just hoped my mother never heard about it. Was this how God worked his deals?

"You're a man now, John Robert. Do me proud." My mother had given me a list of dos and don'ts a mile long, and I don't know what she was thinking of when she patted my butt and watched me walk off toward the airfield and the flying school, but I knew if she'd seen me cleaning the puke off the front seat of Billy Taylor's biplane, with my eyes closed and my cheeks puffed out like a bullfrog in spring, she would have thought I wasn't much of a man to do anyone proud—that's after she stopped laughing, of course.

When I'd done and my lunch had finally stopped coming back to meet me, I discovered I didn't need to hock my soul for five dollars. "You got a coat?" he asked as he inspected the front seat of his plane, no puke anywhere.

"No, sir." It was June. It was hot. I didn't need a coat. I didn't say I didn't have one; maybe he guessed. He came out of his Billy Taylor's Flying School shed and over his arm was a black leather coat with fur at the collar. It smelled of puke. Or maybe it was me.

I put it on. I felt like a flier with my feet on the ground and swarm of wild bees in my belly.

And when I climbed into the backseat, I was too short to see much over the side, but it sure beat standing on a fence post dreaming about what it'd be like.

"I want you to help me, son," Billy Taylor said, but I was too busy looking at the gauges, switches, and other things to pull on the shiny wood panel right in front of me. "Main switch on," he said. I looked for the main switch. Pulled it over to on. Then off. Then on. Throttle clearance? What the hell was that? He showed me. Choke on, choke off...

I wanted to fly? How would I remember all of this?

Prop clear?

What was that? No one was about to get their heads chopped off, except Billy maybe.

Choke off?

Contact.

I pulled the switch from off to on.

Throttle open?

It sure was.

And he pulled down on the propeller and leapt back. The plane roared to life. The entire machine shook. I nearly wet my pants. My knuckles were already white, my eyes popping. I thought I was going to die. Sure I'd seen it land; I'd even seen it take off. But I was here, now, in it. Different story.

And Billy Taylor made me sit in the front seat. All I could see was the circle of gray mist; all I could feel was the machine shaking in anticipation.

When the hand grabbed my shoulder, I thought I'd die. He didn't hear my yell. I never heard it myself. I tried to remember everything I'd never paid attention to at Sunday school, but the only thing that would come was my mother's voice before supper: "For what we are about to receive . . ."

Billy Taylor didn't hear my scream as we hurtled down the grass toward the fence. If he heard it, he ignored it. And he didn't hear my scream when suddenly the ground was not there, either. Up at an angle, like climbing the apple tree and then slipping down and clinging, banking to the left . . . I just prayed my stomach would stay in one place long enough for me to open my eyes.

A hand on my shoulder again. Then I knew why there was puke. Billy Taylor scared it out of his passengers.

He yelled something I never heard and I opened my frozen eyes and followed his pointing finger. Away in the distance, Abbeville. It looked different from up in the air. It looked neat, tidy. Closer was my house. Jesus, I prayed, don't let me puke on our roof.

There was the rusty iron; the guttering falling down; the yellow bramble roses out back; Meg coming out of the outhouse. I

11

recognized her red hair. My mother was bending to go into the henhouse. My vegetable patch looked so neat from up there.

Billy Taylor circled the house twice, then took us out southwest. Land spread out as far as I could see—we were on the edges of Sumter Forest one minute, then looking down over the falls at Calhoun another, and just when I thought we were going to come down near Antreville, we banked right real hard—so hard, I thought I was going to fall right out.

When I opened my eyes again, I saw Abbeville. But we were heading straight for Main Street and going down, and down—so low, I thought he was going to land right outside the bank. And before I knew it, we were up again, just missing the monument, banking to the left and coming down—so close to the fence, I thought we'd knock it down.

No wonder I'd fallen off. And I knew then that I'd been seen—the kid on a fence post, standing there every day at five after four. I knew this aviator had seen me fall off and break my arm.

I think my heart beat again when the wheels touched the ground and finally stayed there after a few good bounces. Then next to the shed, the propeller stopped. She coughed, farted, and then there was nothing. I could hardly move my fingers on my left hand; my muscles had locked tight.

Billy Taylor helped me down and kept me upright while my knees tried to lock.

It was amazing, but I didn't puke, and I didn't wet my pants, either. I felt so alive, I wanted to cry.

"Well, boy, still want to fly?"

"I sure do, Mr. Taylor, sir. I sure do." I pretended it was the wind making my eyes water.

Billy Taylor gave me ten cents and told me he'd see me the next day.

And as I walked home, I thought it was about the only day in a whole year that I missed my daddy. He would have listened to my story. He mightn't have said much, but he would have listened.

It wasn't ballet, so Meg didn't want to know. She'd only listen if I tied her hands to her feet out back of the outhouse, but that afternoon I was too happy inside to have her spit on me. I just said, "I been flying" as I bounced up the stairs. Meg pulled a face and kept spinning about on her toes.

I gave my mother the money I'd earned—still couldn't figure why I'd been paid to fly—and she put it in the cookie jar. But my mother was like my sister—she didn't want to know, either. "I went flying," I said, hoping she'd say something, anything.

"That's good, John Robert. Fetch me three potatoes."

It wasn't what I had in mind, but I never knew what either of them would say next, anyway. So I went out back to the sack and brought in three potatoes. "It was great up there, Ma."

She gave me a look I'd never forget. She looked at stray, hungry dogs the same way.

"It's really great up there."

I couldn't explain the sense of freedom in any other way. Mostly I can't explain myself in any way. Some folks are good speakers; some folks are good writers. If there's ever going to be a war with words, I guess I'd just surrender right away.

"I'm sure it's good up there, John Robert, but I like my feet on the ground. No place for people in the sky. If people was meant to fly, we'd be born with wings, and don't you forget it."

I thought about what she'd said. Maybe that was why God decided to let someone invent airplanes so people could fly.

No one at school believed me, either. It didn't matter. I finally had something real to live for—it made for waking up to a whole new world. I'd greet the day with a heart that beat fast in anticipation. I even tried to pay attention to Mrs. Moriarty, and my mother wondered what was wrong when I didn't try to avoid Sunday school. I only went because it made Sunday mornings go faster, but I think she realized that after awhile, too.

Billy Taylor became my hero for a while, till one day he told me about a Frenchman who had flown across the English Channel. That took my attention, because Billy just flew around the Old 96 country. So I asked my mother where Frenchmen lived, because I wanted to ask the Frenchman what it had felt like, and she showed me France and the rest of the world in a book the next day when we went to town.

The book we looked at covered a lot more territory than South Carolina, or even the United States. I looked her in the eye and told her that one day I'd fly all around the world. And I'd start with the USA.

My mother's favorite words changed from then on. There was no more "I told you so"; now it was, "That's nice, John Robert."

But she never really lost that look in her eye, the one she kept for stray, hungry dogs.

Most of what he'd scribbled was illegible. His writing had never been that good, plus he had to use a hand that had disobeyed orders since he was nine years old. Here and there was a word that seemed a key to the overall meaning. He felt like a secretary who could decipher her boss's handwriting only by the loops in a consonant.

Not a lot was making sense. It was difficult to think in the cold, nearly impossible to hold a pencil. The fingers on his invisible hand ached, too. There was pain all over.

It felt as if his life to date—all twenty-four years of it—had been just a dream, grasped from the fringes, intangible. It wasn't writing on that paper. It was a jumbled mass of hieroglyphics, translatable from memory alone. And all the memory he had left was that of a nine-year-old boy—clear, clean, innocent.

But he couldn't remember what had happened yesterday. And he couldn't remember his mother's name, either. One of the most important people in his life stood there so clearly in his mind's eye, but her name remained too elusive to grasp.

Meg was there, though, in the tattered ballet tutu someone had given her. Five steps to the end of the porch, turn, five steps back. The bare wood polished to a deep shine from the constant glide of stockinged feet. Meg, front teeth gone, long straggly red hair, bright green eyes. Meg the ballerina. Stars of a different kind in her eyes.

There were clean, sharp memories of viewing a house from fifty feet. And memories of a friend—Bobby Sullivan, the prankster, the joker, the one whose face was enough to turn any girl's head more than once.

I was fifteen when I first went to Florida with Billy Taylor. Mama stood on the train platform, holding Meg by the shoulders, keeping her still, lifting her hand as the train pulled away. I didn't understand why she was crying; I was only going away for a week.

A week in Florida with Billy Taylor, tagging along for company while he bought himself a new plane. He'd ditched his into the water hole south of the airfield when he'd lost power on takeoff. I'd run over, thinking he was dead—hell, he had to be—but he climbed on out, walked sideways awhile, and gave the machine a good kick. Now we were off to Florida for a Jenny, he called it. A Curtiss Jenny. One hundred horses, thirty-six-foot wingspan, nearly thirty foot long. Seventy-five mph cruise, 225 mile range. He talked of her as if he wanted to marry her. I'd known Billy Taylor for six years now and never gave up hoping he'd marry my mother. But it almost worked my way—he was my pretend father and I played along being his pretend son.

Like the one he lost in the house fire. And he'd never tell me about it. Now and then, I'd think he might—some days he was quiet and looked at me funny—but he never did.

It was in Florida, where I met Bobby Sullivan at an airfield outside of Miami. "Wish my old man owned an airplane," was the first thing he ever said to me.

I didn't say Billy Taylor was my boss, not my father. I said nothing except, "Guess I'll sit right here awhile, sir," and after

Billy walked off to inspect his new plane, I watched Bobby do what I did, clean the machines. He didn't talk much, but neither did I. But Bobby grinned when I said the only job I hated to death was cleaning up someone's puke. I guess he'd had his share of that, too.

I saw his bike; it looked like it'd been born from a hundred mothers in a dump. It had. Bobby Sullivan was poorer than we were. I didn't feel so bad. "Built it myself," he said, pride or shame in his voice; I couldn't tell.

I liked Bobby Sullivan. Where I didn't have a father, he didn't have a mother, and that was about all we had in common except our dreams. "What happened to her?" I asked.

"She just died. Pa don't talk about her. Too busy drinking."

My mother used to talk about my father, usually when I'd done something wrong, and it was mostly, "John Robert, if your daddy was alive, he'd turn in his grave to see what you just done!"

She never made much sense. Maybe it was because she had hardly anyone her own age to talk to—except Billy Taylor, and all he talked about was flying circuses, and she had no interest in that. I think it scared her. As for Meg, she only cared about dancing. My mother talked to the chickens a lot.

Bobby Sullivan listened to all I had to say. I don't think I'd talked so much to anyone for a long time except maybe one of my cousins, but I hardly ever saw him after my dad went away.

Bobby didn't go to school. Said he tried it once. If he was going to sit cramped like cattle, he'd visit the slaughter yards instead and learn more there. "Ever see a cow what's gonna die?"

"Nope," I said.

"They know, you know. They know. It's fear in them big black eyes. It's fear."

Bobby had dark eyes, too. I'd never seen eyes as dark on anyone. For a while, I thought he was an Indian, an Apache warrior like those in a book I'd read once. Cowboys, cavalry, killing the Indians. I told him the story; he listened, and when I'd finished, he said, "Pa said Ma was from Cuba. She weren't no Indian. Died a week after I was born, she did. That's all I ever hear. How I killed my ma."

I didn't like the look in his eyes. "Oh," was all I could think of to say for a while. "So what do they pay you in Florida?" I asked.

"What do they pay you wherever you come from?" he asked.

"A dollar seventy-five a week."

"I gets five."

It never occurred to me to ask Billy Taylor for more than a quarter a day, now that the chickens were used to the noise and had laid again. Mom wasn't worrying as much and we were eating okay.

"And I'm gonna be an aviator," Bobby said as I sat under the wing of a 1916 Jenny. "I'm saving my money to buy my own machine."

I couldn't say much to that. "Did you know the Wright brothers tossed a coin? The one who lost flew first. Did you know that?" I asked, trying to outdo him, ready to explain what Billy Taylor had told me a long time ago.

"Course I know that," Bobby said. "Where you from, anyway?"

I told him.

Well, he'd been there to South Carolina, but no, he hadn't got to see Abbeville. But he'd heard of it, with the Confederates and Yankees and all. All told, he'd been to New York, and Minnesota, and once he stayed in Cheyenne, and Washington State was real pretty. The girls were real pretty there, too. He showed me on a map all the places he'd been. Maybe he thought it was safe to lie, made him feel good. I was from South Carolina and would probably never see him again.

But some folks have a habit of reappearing in your life when you never expect them to. Bobby Sullivan was about the best friend I ever had.

And as Billy Taylor came back from inspecting the Jenny he was going to buy, Bobby said, "I'm gonna fly right up to the North Pole one day."

"Yeah?" I said, and got up, dusted off. "I'm gonna fly right around the world."

Bobby Sullivan never made it out of Atlanta, Georgia. I watched him die in 1924.

John balked and dropped the pencil. The woman looked up at him, curious, if not concerned. She smiled and he tried to return it.

Hers was the first face he remembered seeing clearly and hers had been the constant one since, always smiling, but, like his mother, she never hid that look kept for stray, hungry dogs. She didn't know what he was, or why he was. But they had one thing in common: Each understood the meaning of a smile.

"I'm starting to remember some more things."

He showed her what he'd written, but she didn't understand what he was saying, what he was doing. She continued her chore—unpacking her share of the stores. He watched from habit alone. Another pot of grease—grease from the medicine man—rank, thick. And she unpacked enough raw fish to keep them eating for another week. He would have sold his soul for the taste of an apple, a strawberry ice cream soda, a hot potato baked in its skin.

He'd eaten the can of beans and paid severely for his greed. He'd offered her some, but the look and smell alone was enough to make her recoil. The sight of raw fish always turned his stomach circle. "Jesus," he moaned.

She mimicked, "Jesus," and smiled. She sat down next to him, looked into his eyes. He knew she liked his eyes. He knew she liked his hair. She was forever touching it as if to make sure it was real. Then she'd burst into hysterical laughter.

She looked down again at what lay across his legs and asked what it was.

Eskimos didn't write.

But John knew a question when he heard one, even if he didn't understand the language yet.

18

"Memories," was all he said, and he put his good arm around her, pulled her close for a while.

She liked it when he did that.

But his Eskimo woman liked it when he did anything.

TWO

●━●━●━●━●━●━●

KIOKI talks a lot. It's as if she's trying to teach me Eskimo. She thinks that because I finally managed to repeat her name as best I could, there's hope.

She'll hold up an object, give me four words to describe it, and when I try to imitate the strange noise they use as a language, she's overcome by hysterics. I can't see what's so funny, but I guess if you have to live in this frozen hellhole you'd be happy to grab the chance, any chance, to laugh, too.

I don't laugh at her when she can't say John properly.

The day I decided to explore a little farther beyond the confines of this snow house (I don't know what else to call it), I hobbled out, using a whalebone for a walking stick. I took it out of the wall and the place didn't fall down, although I was expecting it to.

Kioki didn't want me to go. I don't know exactly why I did either, because the outside temperature was enough to freeze my breath midair and the howling wind blew it straight back into my face. I didn't know my cheek was cut till the numbness went away.

Now I know what that old Anchorage prospector meant when he said to me that night, "Sonny, when you can't feel any pain, you're in trouble." At the time, I thought he was drunk.

Even my eyeballs nearly froze. I've never known glare like it. For as far as I could see, the sea was flat and gray. Through the wind, I could hear the cracks, rumbles, and tears as the ice parted. There were men out there on that ice, about eight of them, all huddled around a hole as if waiting. How could they do that? I was in the open only a few minutes and already I was numb all over.

I couldn't tell which way was north, south, east, or west, but to my right a black-and-gray blanket was chasing the thickest fog I have ever seen. It was rolling in quicker than any summer storm off the Florida Keys, but none of the hunters out there took much notice—I suppose they've lived with this weather longer than I have.

So I turned back, was hit by an eighty-knot blast, lost my footing, and stepped into four feet of snow. I heard the snap of bone long before I felt the agony. But I know the scream was enough to wake the dead. What followed is another blur. Kioki was calling, "Asuluk! Asuluk!" and I think, although I'm not sure, that two people carried me back inside.

The medicine man, Asuluk, came running, stripped me naked from the waist down and chanted to himself. Kioki had hold of my head, and cold hands suddenly jammed the bones back into place.

I remember sitting up and right-hooking what I considered the village quack half a second before I threw up all over him. Kioki was screaming and so was I. She forced something down my throat. It was bitter, stinging, and hot. The world spun three times faster than a spiral dive from eight hundred feet. I don't remember pulling out.

But when I woke, I was covered in thick, warm skins and Kioki was napping beside me. My leg felt heavy, dead except for an unscratchable itch, and I couldn't move it. I took a look. They'd splinted me to my walking stick.

My only thought was, Another six weeks before I can walk. Another six weeks before I can figure a way out of here.

I felt Kioki's warm body very close. I felt her breathing and I waited to feel the pain I'd become accustomed to. There was nothing much except her smell. God, I remember thinking. Oh,

God, why can't she be Sally? But God never answered me when I needed an answer the most. Kioki rolled over and cuddled into me, closer. She opened her eyes and smiled at me and I knew what lay in her eyes, too. So I smiled back and I held her tighter for a moment. Then I closed my eyes, and it wasn't Kioki I was holding tightly. It was Sally—Sally with no other name because I never took the time to ask.

It's not the first time I've daydreamed of her and I know it won't be the last. Memory might retrace old footsteps, but daydreams sure put in a few detours.

If anything, I guess I know for certain that not all my hydraulics were lost in that crash.

But wanting someone you knew only for a couple of hours doesn't help much. Because she's not here. I know I'll never see her again.

Damn it. If only I'd reached Prince Rupert, then Vancouver, and finally Seattle, I could have stayed with Sally for as long as I wanted to this time. I might even have gotten to know her name.

I remember the storm well—another storm, which blew me off course, set me back a day getting to Seattle. Zero visibility, fog so thick that I could barely see the wingtips. Through luck more than good flying, I glimpsed a bare patch of mountainside; actually, I'd skimmed it by fifteen feet when there was a sudden break in the fog.

There was a road through the forest, too narrow to put down. My legs were cramped from cold, so I started praying. I always did that when there was no other option. Then I saw it, two acres with barely a tree stump visible, a site only God could have made especially for me.

I put down, forgot about God, and considered my next course of action.

I took a mile walk on a narrow, muddy road and I remember thinking that I should have turned back then. I remembered saying, No more, no way. I was going to call Miami, tell Sam I was coming home. I rehearsed every damned word.

Then I saw the trading post, smoke churning from a chimney. Smoke, fire, warmth. Ten years of flying had taught me that folks living far away from others are grateful for any company.

I didn't realize how grateful some could be.

The store had four steps up. An old wooden Indian chief who'd stood there since time began guarded the door. He had sunset paint on his face as cracked as my lips. The defeated expression in his eyes followed each move I made. I was hungry, wet, cold, and those four stairs felt like Everest.

The store had a bell that fell off when the northeaster pushed me inside. I'd have put more than a faded PLEASE CLOSE THE DOOR sign there. I leaned against the door and pushed till it shut, then picked up the bell and tried to see where it fit.

It wasn't unusual; I was forever breaking things for other people.

"It sure is windy out there," a soft girlish voice said, taking me by surprise.

She had green eyes and hair as red as Meg's. She was barely five two; she took the bell from my hand, climbed on a ladder, and put it back in place. She didn't have to do that. I could have reached. But I guess I never had to worry about reaching things others couldn't. I was six four and a half—my father had given me all except that extra half inch of height. Before I left Florida, my mother made me promise I'd return. Said she looked at me and saw my daddy.

That made me wonder again if he had run out, not died.

Well, Mom, I thought to myself, I am coming back. You got your way after all.

"On your way to Seattle or Vancouver?" the red-haired girl asked.

"No. The Pole," I said. I was getting tired of people asking me where I was going and why when no one gave a damn, anyway. As if this across-the-country run was only important to me. The luster was wearing off this personal trophy the Miami newspaper was paying for.

"The Pole?" she asked.

Was it a town she hadn't heard of? A new logging camp? "I put down because of the storm."

"Was that you buzzing around awhile ago?"

"I guess so." It had taken two hours to walk this far in a blistering head wind, pelting sleet icy enough to stun a cougar, and now it was snowing. It was spring and it was snowing. I suppose it's right to say I was almighty pissed off. But I looked into her eyes and my anger melted away. I smiled. I was still able to. It seemed a miracle.

My mother used to say there was something about the way I could look at a girl and smile and give her the flushes. This one was no exception, but at the time I was too cold and too pissed to notice.

"What's it like?" she asked.

"What?" I asked, my teeth chattering a mile a minute.

"Up there in the sky."

"Okay for folks who wanted to be born with feathers, I guess." It was my standard answer to the standard question.

"Where's the Pole?" she asked.

"It's the top of the world, the Arctic." I was going to say I was only joking, that I was flying from Florida, overland to San Francisco, Seattle, Anchorage, across to Maine, back to Florida, and too many places in between, but she beat me to the draw.

"There's nothing but ice up there."

Nothing but ice. I was getting closer to it each day. I was wet; I was cold. All I wanted was something hot to drink and a telephone to use before I died of cold and exposure, before my wet clothes snap-froze. I could think of better places to die, and, Miami was first on my list.

"You gonna buy something, mister?"

I couldn't see a telephone anywhere, just shelves on walls in the dark store—shelves with a few cans, bottles, tins of tobacco—and that old Indian still staring at me, even though I couldn't see him. "What you got?"

She blushed again. I didn't know why she giggled. Bobby Sul-

24

livan always said it was a good sign. It might have worked for
him, but I was too cold to care. Cold, upset, pissed.

"Got anything hot?"

"Sure. You better dry off before you die. Ground's still too
muddy to bury you. It's been a long winter." She said it with a
smile and led me out back of the store into a small log room with
a table, two chairs, shelves on the wall, and two cots. What took
my attention first was the roaring fire. It drew me like a bug to a
light.

She made me a coffee—hot, strong, and sweet—and I sat near
the fire in a tiny kitchen and watched while she continued doing
what she'd been doing when I, the tall stranger, came in out of
the blizzard. She was cooking dinner and it smelled like some
kind of stew. It smelled fantastic.

"Papa's gone to Seattle," she said. "I'm here on my own."

If she'd said it any other way, I'd have been alarmed.

"Take them clothes off. Some clothes here might fit you." She
took a shirt that looked five sizes too big and a lumber jacket
from hooks behind the door, and she scrounged in a box under
one of the beds until she pulled out a pair of trousers. She went
back to making her dinner and ignored me while I took off the
wet clothes and laid them across the chair near the fire. My feet
were blue. She kicked a huge pair of moccasins across the floor.

I dressed, put the slippers on, and sat on a wooden box near
the fire. She reminded me of Meg when she was younger, but
Meg never was all that beautiful—not that I could see at least.
This girl had the same offhand manner. Would hardly blink if
the roof crashed in. Here she was, sheltering me—some stranger—from a storm. Hell, I could have been anybody. Anybody.

She wore a faded red dress with a torn black lace collar, a car-
digan; her legs were bare from her knees to her ankles. On her
feet, a pair of moccasins.

"Where's your airplane?" she asked, just like Meg. Straight to
the point.

"A mile south."

"A mile south . . . that'd be Johnson's farm?"

Johnson's farm. I'd seen a deserted shack near that stretch of cleared ground and decided I'd keep drier if I slept under the Jenny. "Guess so."

"What you going to do tonight, then?"

"I'll figure something."

"Log camp's closed down."

Yes, I'd walked right by it.

"No one comes around here much no more. That's why Papa's in Seattle. He comes home on Fridays, though."

I figured it was Wednesday. But maybe when you're alone in a place like this, it's easy to lose track of days.

She picked up the pot and stood it on the old wood burner. There weren't many logs left in the stack under the fire. She bent over, took a lump of wood, and threw it into the fire. She had nice legs.

"Storm might last two or three days. Things you could do here if I fed you and kept a roof."

She had the same look in her eyes as my mother had whenever she saw Billy Taylor, whenever he'd come to dinner and fix something for her. But he never fixed the heart that needed repair. So I said, "Sounds fine. My name's John Robert Shaw."

"I'm Sally. You like stew, John Robert Shaw?"

Stew? Hell yes. I'd been eating cold beans for four days. But the stew wasn't ready, so we went out back in the snow to the woodshed.

I was wondering if I'd been the only customer that day when she said, "It used to be a trading post," as she sheltered from the snow with me and watched me chop wood.

It was late by then; the wind wasn't howling as much, but the hail hitting the roof sounded like baseballs falling from the sky. She held the lamp while I chopped. I remember thinking how lucky I was to have found this place. I even wondered what the odds were.

"Papa took over the post when his pa died. Just me and him here these days." She was huddled in a corner, freezing, trying to make polite conversation.

I told her to go inside, no sense in both of us dying of cold, but she wouldn't, not until I'd finished. By the time I'd cut enough wood for her, I'd raised a sweat, and it was good to feel it, too.

We dashed the fifty yards back to the trading post. The snow hadn't eased up. "You're not from here, are you?" she said while my coat and boots dried by the fire.

"No, I'm from Florida. South Carolina originally."

"Is that far away?"

I guessed she'd never been to a school but recognized enough words and knew numbers enough to get by. So I took one of my maps from the bag and spread it out on the floor and showed her where Seattle was, then South Carolina and Florida. I pointed to all the places I'd been so far as she crouched beside me on the floor. The map meant nothing. I could feel her watching me when she thought I wasn't looking, but I had to do something, say something. So I told her how many weeks it had taken to get this far, tried to explain how far the airplane could fly before refueling.

"But why?"

I folded the map. "Why what?" I asked, and looked at her and saw again just how pretty she was.

"Why are you flying around the country like this? All on your own?"

I suppose that was a good question, considering I was beginning to question the logic of it myself. Why *was* I doing this? Did I really want to be some kind of quickly forgotten hero? Was it worth getting my picture in the Miami news? This girl didn't even know where Miami was. Hell, I should have been in Seattle yesterday; now there'd be no newspapermen waiting at the airfield for me. "Me and a friend, we'd been planning this since we were kids. Florida to Florida. But he died New Year's '24. That's why I'm on my own."

"Sorry. I really am sorry. I know what it's like when someone dies."

I looked at her while she stepped away. And I knew her father wasn't in Seattle, nor did he come home on Fridays.

27

"What was your friend's name?"

"Bobby."

"Hurts, don't it? Hurts bad. Seen him die, didn't you?"

More than that, I thought. Mine was the last face he ever saw.

"Hurts you bad."

With every moment that passed, I expected her father to come in cold and angry from Seattle, even though I knew he wouldn't. I expected to be thrown out into the rain, even though I knew I wouldn't be.

She ruffled my hair, kept her fingers in it too long. "Wish mine was this color."

I looked at her hair and tried to smile. "Nothing wrong with yours, Sally." I was used to saying that to red-haired girls. But this time I wanted to touch, feel how soft it was.

She gave me another coffee instead, then climbed on a box and took a photo album from the shelf over the fire. She put it on the table, her time for show-and-tell. Black pages of memories were turned, someone else's memories, because she recognized none of the people in last century's dress. I could tell because I looked at her more than the photos. Then she pointed to a wedding photograph and I had to look.

It was taken before smiles were invented. A bearded, dark-haired man in a three-piece suit and his fair-haired bride, a pretty lady with frightened eyes who looked to me as if she'd blow away in a stiff breeze.

"That's my mother," she said. "Papa says I look just like her."

So I did as expected. I looked at her face, at the photo. "No. You're better-looking than your mother."

I hadn't ever seen a smile like it. "Papa says she was crazy, but I think this place sent her crazy. She was from Washington, you know. Washington, D.C."

Bullshit, I thought, but maybe fantasy was all she had left.

"Pa told me all about her. I don't remember much except the day I found her hanging in the woodshed. All swelled up. I think I was five. That's how I know how it feels, see, when someone you love goes and dies. Papa said she was crazy, but I think she was lonely."

I didn't know what to say. I nearly told her about Bobby, but I knew if I started, I'd never stop and I'd get no sleep. Remembering. I needed sleep bad.

But Sally needed company more.

"If you want to wash, there's hot water. Papa washes there," she said, pointing to the other end of the kitchen. "And I wash here."

"Oh. Right. I can go outside awhile—"

"What for? It's too cold out there. Hell, you got nothin' I ain't already seen."

She filled two bowls with hot water and she went to one end of the room, I to the other. I took off my shirt and hung it on a peg and had the quickest wash in history. "You can sleep in Papa's bed."

I wondered how she knew what I was thinking.

She came over to me, pulling the plaits out of her hair as she walked, and drew back the covers on the cot. "Sheets is clean."

"Thanks, Sally."

And her hair fell like a cloud over bare white arms. I took a deep breath; even my breath was shaking. She went back to her corner. I touched the sheets. Clean. I hadn't touched clean sheets since Wyoming. I looked back to her corner. She was stepping out of that faded dress.

So I looked at the wall while I stripped and dived into the cot. There was a hot-water bottle in the bed.

She knew I was going to stay—either that or she hoped it was Friday.

From the corner of my eye, I watched her reach for a night-gown on a peg. She looked as though her skin had never been touched by sunshine. I looked again, just a quick glance from the corner of my eye—the worst way to peek. You see things that aren't really there, or things you wished to God were. So I stared up at the ceiling, the rafters, and wondered if that fair-

29

haired lady with the frightened eyes had hung herself in this room and not the woodshed.

"How come you never talk much?" she asked. I turned to her, figured it was safe to look now she was talking to me. She was sitting on the other cot across the room, her head down between her knees, brushing her long red hair. I'd have liked to have done that for her, but I folded my hands under my head instead. It'd be a miracle if I slept at all.

"Maybe I only talk when I have to. That way, people don't get wrong ideas."

"Papa never says much except, 'What you cooking, girl? How long's it gonna be? You washed them socks yet, girl?' " I smiled. She was a good imitator. "Try to talk, get told, 'No girl needs know that. Just you cook. You wash. Is all you need know.' "

I wondered what else it was he felt she needed to know. All sorts of things were running around in my brain. I didn't know what to say; I knew I shouldn't be thinking these kind of thoughts, but I'd seen that photograph. I'd known he was a mean old bastard and she was probably the only female for miles.

"Know what I did?" she asked quietly.

"No, I don't," I said, wondering if she took a shotgun and blew her father's head off one night. Lord. I sure needed sleep bad. My mind was running over again. "What'd you do?"

"I taught myself to read. Got in trouble for reading and not working. That's how come I know there's nothing but ice up there at the Pole. What you think of that?"

I smiled. And I wondered what anyone else would have done if they'd been me. Billy Taylor used to say women heard words you never said, saw things you never saw. Believed they'd do anything if they felt they were being loved, or wanted to be loved. That there was a difference between motive and intent. Women's motive was to be loved and man's intent to love. Sometimes they met in the middle.

I felt we were going to meet very soon, and the thought scared me more than the first time I flew.

"And I read that if you brushed your hair a hundred times a night, it makes it grow. Makes it shiny."

She threw that mane back, and I needed something to do, or say. I coughed, then yawned and pretended I was stretching.

"Would you like a whiskey?" she asked. "Sounds like you're getting yourself a cold, John Robert."

She wiped the coffee cup and reached for a bottle of whiskey covered in dust. I hoped, then I didn't, that it'd be moonshine. I'd been stuck in some Kentucky backwoods with Bobby for one and a half days a couple of years before and the folks we stayed with went to town once a year for a new roll of copper line. Bobby and I could have died on that run. Died. Or if we'd been caught by the law . . .

The whiskey she handed me sure smelled like moonshine. "Papa says it's so good, it curls more'n your toes."

I needed something to curl more than my toes. Maybe she didn't know what she was doing, walking about in a nightdress I could see through. I didn't know where to look. Her eyes weren't safe territory, either. Bobby would have given away his airplane for a chance like this. Me, I was squirming.

"Helped Papa sleep," she said after she gave me the whiskey.

I sat up in bed and tried the whiskey. My eyes watered and it burned a trail to my toes. I was back in those Kentucky backwoods with Bobby and that huge family of hillbillies and guns shooting and . . . It all disappeared when she said, "You're nice, John Robert."

How many times had I heard those words? I guess there were worse ways to be remembered. "So are you, Sally."

"You think so?"

"Aha."

"Did you mean it when you said I was prettier than my mother?"

"Why would I lie to you?" I asked.

"Can say a lot to a stranger. A stranger don't know enough about you to judge."

31

"I never judge, and pretty comes in all kinds of ways."

"So does nice. Nice can be pleasant. Nice can be boring. Nice can be a lie, too."

She sat on my bed and inspected her feet. Rubbed her fingers between her toes and looked at me. I wished she wouldn't do that, sit so close, sit like that. Her legs were thin and shapely, and smooth, too. "I always tell folks Papa's coming home soon."

"But he won't."

"No. He died last winter."

I said nothing. When I know I'm right, I like to keep it to myself.

"Want to know how he died?"

"Only if you want to tell me."

"We was having dinner and he starts choking. But he wasn't choking on no food. He grabbed his arm and his chest, like this." And what came next was an imitation of someone having a heart attack. "And he couldn't breathe and his eyes popped. He went sort of blue and just fell backward on the floor. Made some awful strange noises. I didn't know what to do. I just stared at him, lying there. Dead. I didn't feel nothing. Nothing. Know what I thought?"

Jesus, did I have to know?

"I thought, Ground's too muddy. Can't bury him till spring."

She was quiet for awhile.

"Know what he said a couple of minutes before he died? He said we was gonna get a telephone. He'd fix it next time he went to Seattle."

She didn't say anything for a while, nor did I. Till she mentioned it, I'd forgotten about needing to call home.

"That's what you were looking for, wasn't it? A telephone. It's what most folks want if they get lost out here. Not that people come by much."

She was quiet again.

"I didn't want to lie to you, John Robert. Sometimes I got to. Sometimes you just don't know who's gonna come through that door next. You know?"

"I can understand that."

"But I looked at you when you came in and I knew you weren't no logger, no lumberjack always wanting the same thing. And when you spoke, I really knew you was okay."

Maybe she put too much value on first impressions. What did she think I was? Dead from the waist down? I was so scared of what I knew was coming that I was sweating. She didn't notice.

"Things were good till the loggers left. Sometimes I keep hoping they'll come back. They moved somewhere more . . . more—"

"Accessible."

"Yeah. I hear they float the logs downriver now. Saves money, and time. That's all people care about now—money and time. If you got no money, no one has time. And if that's what the world's coming to, then I guess I'm better off living out here on my own. Just me and the dog."

She was quiet again, and I didn't know what was expected of me, so I had another sip of whiskey and wondered if I should tell her the Kentucky story, because I could feel a great black cloud of doom falling over us both.

"But the dog can't talk. I get awful lonely for a body to talk to."

"Everyone does sometimes."

And she turned her head and fixed me to the wall with those green eyes. "Sometimes ain't all the time," she said, and her voice was shaking, too.

Oh God. Oh God, she was going to cry. My mouth went dry. It was a reflex action to touch her hand, and she squeezed the life clean out of it. What'd she want? What was I supposed to do? I knew what I wanted to do. I wanted to pull her close awhile, touch that hair, do what my mother used to do to me when I was little and upset about something only a kid could be upset about. She'd hold me, tell me everything would be fine. But I'd never been in a position like this before, and the most I'd ever done to an upset female was squeeze a hand and run like hell. And with Rosie . . .

Rosie. Rosanna, as she preferred to be called. I only called her Rosie to get her mad. The most I'd ever done to her was kiss a cheek. Touch by accident. One time, I'd tried to squeeze her leg while we were sitting on her daddy's porch swing. Damn, hadn't I paid for that.

"Don't cry, Sally. Something good's gonna happen. Maybe you just have to wait awhile longer."

I held her hand tightly. Then she leaned into me, and before I knew it, I was holding her.

What was I doing? I had a girl back home. Even if she always said no to anything except a kiss good-bye. She wanted a ring on her finger before she'd let me do a damned thing. She wouldn't even let me look. I asked one day; she ran off howling, calling me a perverted wretch—whatever the hell that was.

I'd promised to marry her when I got back, and there I was, holding another girl. And suddenly I knew I only made that promise to stop her nagging me. That when I got back, I'd put her off again, and again. Rosanna never did to me what Sally did. When Rosanna sat close, I felt nothing much—except maybe to wonder what she wanted.

"You're not mad 'coz I lied to you?" Sally asked when she drew away, wiping her eyes on her sleeve.

"No." I offered her my cup.

"No. I can't. Sends me crazy."

"We need crazy now and then."

She took a sip, looked at me awhile. "What's this?" she asked, touching the medal around my neck.

"St. Christopher."

"What's it for?"

"Brings me luck."

"Did Bobby give it to you?" she asked, as if by touching it, she knew.

"Yes, he gave it to me."

"Didn't bring him luck."

It had crossed my mind a thousand times. In my mind, I saw

Bobby lying across my lap, dying. People swarming like bees, taking a look, watching a man die. But I never saw them, never heard them. "Take it, buddy, take it," he'd said. So I took it. . . .

As long as I wore it, Bobby'd be with me. I could feel him close, laughing at me again. Laughing at my shyness. He always said I felt too much.

"Does he talk to you?" she asked.

"He's dead. He can't talk to me."

She smiled a little, as if she knew better, gave the cup back, and said, "I shouldn't drink. Makes me say stupid things. Makes me want to dance."

"Nothing wrong with wanting to dance. Nothing wrong with anything if it makes you feel good." I wondered why I said that. That was a line Bobby would use, not me.

"I can't dance very good."

"Show me. I'll tell you if you can or can't. I spent half my life watching my sister dance, so I should be an expert."

I grinned at her and she grinned back. She poured herself a whiskey and I sat on the bed, my back against the wall. It was easy talking to Sally. Suddenly, it felt like I'd known her forever, not a few hours.

"How old's your sister?" she asked.

Two years younger than I am would make her . . . "She's nearly twenty-two."

"I never had a sister or a brother."

"I would have swapped Meg for a brother any day."

"Meg?"

"Short for Margaret."

Sally drank that whiskey in one hit. Sure, she didn't drink. Sure, she couldn't dance very good. What else would she lie to me about?

She started to move. If there was any music playing, I never heard it. I could pretend, too. I knew I'd better not sing; the dog tied to the woodshed would howl for sure. So I just sat there, warm, calm, fuzzy. She wasn't a stranger anymore. I liked her even if she lied. And with each sip of that whiskey, I liked her some more.

"You laughing at me, John Robert Shaw?"

"No, I'm just happy. First time I've been happy to put down 'cause of a storm."

"Put down?"

"Land the plane."

She started dancing with her imaginary partner. "If it's a good day tomorrow, you'll be leaving."

"I have to."

"The Pole."

"You never know. I might get to Maine via the Pole if this wind keeps up."

"I wish you wouldn't go."

And at that time with my eyes feeding on Sally as she moved around the tiny room, my belly warm from whiskey and clean sheets under me, and a storm raging outside and a different one raging inside me, I didn't particularly want to go, either, until some kind of calm had been restored.

It felt as if something was enticing me to keep my feet on the ground a little while longer. I always was defiant. I always knew better than anyone else. Billy Taylor used to say, "You'll learn, boy. You'll learn, or die trying."

I finished the drink and cut in on her invisible partner. Barefoot in long johns. The top of her head nearly reached my chest. Her hands were half the size of mine. If I held too tightly, I thought that maybe she'd break. But she didn't. I stood on her toes twice, so she stood on mine, and that was how we danced. I led; she followed. And she'd have done anything I asked or wanted, but it was she who asked and both of us who wanted. She could cling to something more real than a memory or a dream for a few hours. Maybe she thought she was the only person left on earth, until I broke her doorbell just in time.

She was sweet. She smelled sweet, and smoky, too. Her skin was paler than mine—I spent a lot of free time on beaches and I had a constant tan. But her skin felt different, too—soft, so soft. When I kissed her, I tasted whiskey. She looked up at me but said nothing. A look like that one didn't need words. She touched my face and tears filled her eyes. "You're gonna go."

And I touched her face and said, "Aha. I'm gonna go."

I just held her tightly, thinking how different she was from Rosanna. "Am I as pretty as her?" she asked after awhile.

Had I thought aloud? So loud that she'd heard? "You're prettier than she is." It was no lie. I kissed her again. Her mouth opened a little. I was afraid she'd kick me, bite me, or slap me, something. But she was touching me, little warm hands sliding over my skin, giving me gooseflesh that had nothing to do with the cold or the storm roaring outside. So I put my hand on her neck, then her shoulder. I let the back of my hand glide over a breast. I looked into her eyes. She smiled a little, kind of shy. "Can I?" I asked, my voice breaking so much, I had to say it twice.

"You never seen a naked girl before?"

Wow, what to say now? I'd seen pictures, sure. Billy Taylor had caught me one day—I was fifteen at the time—looking at some magazines he'd bought in New York. He'd snuck up behind me while I was staring and dreaming and wondering how come I'd never seen ladies with breasts like these in real life before. Meg was thirteen and I'd noticed she was changing, but what lay spread out across that cement floor was incredible.

"John!" he'd yelled. Needless to say, I almost shit. Maybe I did. "What the hell you got there?" I couldn't even think quickly enough to hide them. He saw. Oh God, no. "Where'd you find them, boy?"

"In this magazine, sir."

Well, he tried to hide his smile. And he just told me to put them back when I'd done. And if I wanted to ask anything, I knew where he was. But what would Billy Taylor know? All he did was fly airplanes.

"John?" Sally asked again. "I don't mind if I'm the first girl you've ever seen." She lifted the nightgown over her head. It dropped to the floor. She just stood there, watching me. Then she took my hand. "You can touch."

I would have, too, if I hadn't been frozen all over.

She took both my hands, put them on her breasts, and let me touch. For a while, I thought she was cold, then I realized how hot the fire was making the room. Little rivers of sweat were coming from beads on her forehead. It was my touch making her shiver. And inside I was roaring.

"Does that feel good?" she asked. Before I could answer or even know what to say, she reached up and touched my face. She'd have to stand on tiptoe to reach me, so I bent down, and when she kissed me, her mouth was wide. Like she was hungry, roaring inside, like me. She pulled my undershirt off, and I think it landed on one of the rafters. Her hands were hot. I didn't know how much longer I could take it without exploding. Be worse than gas on hot coals.

"Let's lie down. It's easier lying down."

For the first time in my life, I never stopped to argue. She lay down on the bed and pulled me down on top of her. The old cot creaked bad. I just hoped to hell I could do this right.

"Sally, I haven't . . . I mean, I've never . . ."

She touched my face again, then turned her hand upside down. And she touched me—*all* of me. My mouth went dry. I closed my eyes. "I've never done this—"

"It don't matter. You'll do fine. We both will. Ain't no hurry. . . ."

I didn't hear much else. It soon felt like I'd run a mile in one hell of a crosswind, and I didn't care one bit. Limp, fuzzy, warm, happy, sleepy. She was lying beside me, my shoulder her pillow. Her leg was wrapped over mine and she said she was listening to my heart. Hell, so was I. It was telling me all sorts of things, too.

In my head, I could hear Bobby Sullivan singing the "Hallelujah Chorus." Or maybe it was my imagination.

We stayed in the same little bed all night long. I knew I'd never feel this way about anyone ever again, and for a long time,

I never wanted to leave. I wanted her to lie there cuddled into me forever.

But forever is a hell of a long time.

It was overcast when I woke at dawn—overcast but clearing, damn it. My left arm was numb—I hadn't wanted to move all night in case I woke her. I didn't think of the Jenny waiting in Johnson's field, either. I watched Sally while she slept—the way she breathed, the feel of the soft warmth so close. I wanted to take the feeling with me and make it last for the rest of my life.

Something about her reminded me of Bobby's girl, Bess. Not that Bess and I had ever done anything like this together, even if we'd both maybe thought about it once or twice. . . . I'd walked in on them once in the Miami office. Bobby had his hands full, his mind on other things. Bess saw me, but I walked out just in time. And I couldn't look her in the eye for two years after that day.

Now I finally knew what Bobby had been so happy about— why at times he was late for work and not guilty and why his eyes were sparkling on Saturdays and Thursdays. It finally made sense where he'd been on Friday and Wednesday nights, all night. And that dumb half smile of his . . . If I'd seen a mirror, I knew I'd have seen it on my own face. If I'd listened hard enough, I probably would have heard him say, Hey, buddy, it's about time. Congratulations. God knew, I felt it strongly enough.

I was thinking all kinds of things when Sally finally opened her eyes and saw me looking down at her. "Morning," I said, my voice breaking up again. Damn it.

She climbed on top of me, stretched, and I pushed her hair away from her shoulders. She looked down at me. "You still gonna go?"

"I have to." I pulled her down and kissed her, and she lay on top of me for a while.

"Are you hungry?" she asked in a whisper.

"Aha." But it wasn't food I had in mind.

We had breakfast half an hour later. They were the best pancakes I have ever eaten. But throughout, she never said a word, just looked at me with sad, haunted eyes. If she was trying to make me feel guilty, it was working.

"Sally, I have to go."

"I wish you wouldn't."

"I'd like to stay here with you more than anything—"

"But," she said as if she'd heard it a hundred times already.

She walked with me all the way to Johnson's field, her dog running ahead through the mud. Maybe she thought I'd change my mind, stay another day.

When she saw the Jenny, she came to a dead stop. All the color disappeared from her face. I thought she was going to pass out.

"What's wrong?"

She just stood there, shaking her head, fear in her eyes.

While I ate that morning, I'd offered her a ride because I'd remembered her asking what it was like up there in the sky. She'd said maybe. But that was an hour before, and in one hour on a muddy, slow walk, a lot can happen. "Don't you want a ride?"

"Oh Lord, no. Not in that."

I tried to tell her it wouldn't crash, but something in her eyes told me she knew better. She grabbed my arm and I looked down into her frightened eyes, which were like her mother's in that wedding photograph.

And that same look had been in Meg's eyes when I'd kissed her good-bye at the Miami field, and in my mother's eyes, too. Rosanna never came; she'd said if I flew off to find some dream, it would only turn into a nightmare for us both. If I loved her, I'd stay.

I felt the tight grip on my arm—a grip of fear I already recognized, and I held Sally close. Again I had the feeling that maybe I shouldn't go.

"Stay another day?"

Another day would become another, and another. Too much of Sally, I would never want to go, and I knew there were better places to spend the rest of my life. No. No, I had too much to do to be sidetracked by a frightened, lonely, green-eyed girl. Maybe someone else, just like me, would come along. Maybe he would stay. Maybe she'd find what she so desperately needed. I wasn't the answer to her loneliness, even if for a few hours of one night I'd wanted to be.

"I can't, Sally. I have to go. You know that. You know what I have to do."

"For a dead man."

"No, for me. I have to do something for myself."

I touched her face; I kissed her. But she never kissed me back.

She never said good-bye. She just watched while I took off and headed for Seattle, where I planned to refuel and head northwest again, to Anchorage.

God, I wished she had said good-bye.

THREE

━━━━━━━━

I don't know who heard the plane first—it wouldn't have been engine noise, because I was out of fuel. Perhaps it was the howl of the glide. I was ten feet above the ground before the fog cleared, and I had a choice of a snow-covered cliff half a breath from the right wing or an ice floe. I battled to take her left.

There was a beach of sorts I glimpsed—a beach and, thirty feet out, pack ice. I recall taking one long, deep breath and then a wave of quiet descended. Something deep inside told me, This is it. If I was going to die, I'd die calm. I think I said something stupid to myself—Sally, I love you.

Then I was shearing through a wave of white snow, ice spraying high and hard. There was agony, sudden and strong. I remember feeling nothing after that, because what came next seemed like a dream.

Only it was too real to be a dream.

There was no sound, no light—just a motionless gray vacuum.

Next I knew, I was standing on the ice. I could see the furrow the Jenny had ploughed her way through, the wreck in the distance. There was no tail, no left wing. Or maybe there was and it was submerged. I remember thinking, How'd I get out of that?

I looked around; all I could see were miles and miles of ice to my left, which I guessed must have been south, and bare rocky cliffs to my right—north, or so I thought.

Then I heard a familiar voice calling my name. I looked behind. It was Bobby. Bobby? I'd know him anywhere. Six feet tall, in moleskin pants, boots, the cap in his hand, the flying jacket with our company emblem on the breast. I had it, too. I touched. My jacket was torn.

"Overshot again, huh?" he said. It wasn't even a question. As he came toward me, he never took his hands from his pockets. Definitely Bobby. "You should have stayed at that trading post, John. I tried every damned thing I could think of to get you to stay. This wasn't supposed to happen. I tried everything to get you to stay in Anchorage, too. You sure can make it hard. Some things never change, right?"

He looked out at the view and I could tell by his face that he didn't like it much.

"You can't be here."

"Who says? I've been with you all the way."

"Bullshit. You're dead."

"And you're not?" was all he said.

I looked down at myself. I remembered feeling some kind of pain, something tearing—my left leg, my left arm. My chest felt as if it had been pushing out my ears. But at that moment, I felt as I had walking down that muddy little road with Sally holding my hand. I felt fantastic. Nothing made sense.

"You have to get back into that plane, John."

"You're joking."

"No. It's not your time to come yet. Things to do. You know. I'm not lying to you. Still don't believe me?"

He turned, and coming across the ice was a man I knew from somewhere, but I couldn't work out who he was, not straight away. But as he got closer, something about the way he walked, the way he looked . . . "Dad?"

He stood beside Bobby and he smiled at me. He was exactly as I remembered him the last time I'd seen him, his head out of the train window, waving good-bye to us. He looked just like I

43

did. No, I looked like he did. But he was dead, too. What the hell was going on here? "It's not your time yet, son. It won't be for thirty years. You can't come with us yet."

Bobby and my father looked to the Jenny and so did I, to the person, the man, strapped in there. His head was hanging back at a funny angle. I couldn't see his face for all the blood. He looked dead. He looked strange. Then I realized who the poor bastard was.

It was me.

But I couldn't be in two places at once. It wasn't possible. And I heard Bobby's voice on the edges: "I won't be far away."

Then there was a vacuum sucking me down. I tried to fight it. I couldn't breathe. I was drowning in ice water; I was fighting against it. And I felt giant hands heaving me out of the tangle of wood and metal. I dragged myself onto the ice, numb from the neck down. There was something warm trailing across my face. Blood on the ice. I tried to lift my head; I couldn't move. I couldn't move at all. But I tried. Because I knew if I kept moving, I wouldn't freeze. That was my only thought: I don't want to freeze.

Then there were voices, noise, the crunching of feet on snow. I opened my eyes. The sun was shining so brightly, I couldn't see properly, but I saw enough. Fur boots. A hand reached down to touch, and I heard another voice. Curious. I tried to talk, but started coughing instead.

There was a circle of people around me. I knew what they were. They were Eskimos. And nothing could save me from what came next.

One of them rolled me onto my back. I tried to scream, but nothing came out. They took my leather jacket off. I could see enough to know why I could feel nothing in my left arm. It was almost in two pieces below the elbow; my arm was hanging by threads.

I saw some kind of shiny hatchet and I screamed, but it wasn't my head they were going to take; it was the arm.

If anything else happened, I do not remember.

Just the woman's face, the sound of her voice, the touch of her hands. And warmth. Finally, there was warmth.

I was in and out for a long, long time. I know this because of the hair on my face, my head. It's long now, very long. But I survived, and that alone seems a major miracle.

It takes a long time to get used to this place.

Night, if it exists here, seems to last for a couple of hours, so I guess it's coming on to summer and continual light. It doesn't feel like summer except for the times when Kioki and I are together and alone and the air inside is warm—warm enough to loosen the clothes, anyway.

I never took much notice of white as a color before I found myself here. There's too much of it, broken only by the blue-green water of the sea, or there's an occasional glimpse of blue sky for a while before another storm howls on in.

The storms here blow up from nowhere, very quickly. I watch them when I can. It's been a habit of mine for a long time. I used to watch storms building up when I was a kid. But the storms here aren't like the ones back home—these howling monsters are killers. Like the one that brought me here. So when I watch a storm building, I don't think of home. I either think of the crash or I wonder how many people are stuck out there, dying in it.

Stupid, insignificant things make me think of home. Some things, though, aren't so meaningless.

Today I was out for a short walk, hoping to see some blue sky. I'm not supposed to walk very far, but Kioki was helping with a birthing and what she never knew wouldn't hurt me. I decided I'd look down off the high cliff because today the wind wasn't so bad.

One of the little village boys was down there, waiting for his daddy to come home. Just a solitary kid, standing on a rock, waiting. I knew in my heart that his daddy wouldn't be coming home; that his daddy had died in yesterday's storm. He wouldn't listen to anybody. So I limped on down to where he was standing. I didn't say a word. I was going back into the past, when my mother would find me on the front porch, watching for Daddy to come walking down the road. Maybe I didn't understand the language yet, but I sure knew what that boy was feeling.

He pretended I wasn't there.

So I touched his hand. Not a word was said. He took one long look out to the horizon, then sank to his knees and started crying. I put my hand on his head and he clung to me.

Just like I had clung to my mother the night I finally realized I'd never see my daddy again. That's all she did, too. Put her hand on my head. But it took me a full year before I gave up hoping.

I still don't know how these people feel about death. I know they mourn. They wail and they chant and pretty soon it's over. The vacancy is filled.

I was thirteen when I first saw a man die. I've seen a few since then, but my first will stay with me forever.

A drunk named Ed Maginley skidded his truck sideways around our corner and rolled. He took out the telephone pole, which took out our fence and our porch.

And it woke me up from a good dream.

The noise of the accident had brought out a lot of folks too early that Sunday morning. Most of them were in their nightgowns and long johns. The police deputy, Freddie Larsen, who lived three houses up on the opposite side of the street, came running out, wearing nothing but a towel, shaving soap all over his face. I never remembered seeing him like that, or if I did, I never took any notice. I don't remember much at all except sitting bolt upright in my bed because I thought Billy Taylor had crashed on our roof. The whole house shook. I ran out, halfnaked, to see what the hell had happened. The telephone pole was across the fence and our porch.

I ran out to the street and there it was—Ed Maginley's truck. It had rolled a few times till it came to rest on its side.

I was on my knees, peering in, asking Ed Maginley if he was okay. I asked before I'd seen. He'd been skewered. He turned his head to me and opened his mouth, but all that came out was blood. Then I felt the hand on my pants and I skidded across the dirt on my knees. It was Freddie Larsen telling me to get away, go get the doc, get the sheriff. I couldn't do anything else except throw up, so he yelled at someone else instead.

I can't remember what I felt, because it didn't seem real. My mother came and dragged me home. She didn't want me looking at such things, a boy my age.

I fell up the stairs; my feet wouldn't do what I wanted them to. Next I knew, I was sitting on my bed, watching from my window. I was sweating and shaking, and I knew if Ed Maginley was still alive when he looked at me, he'd have to be dead by now. I guessed he was dead by the time they got him out, by the time a lot of the neighbors put the truck back on its wheels again.

They put him on the road; someone covered him with a horse blanket. I knew he was dead.

Then they put him in the back of another truck and took him away; his truck was towed off by Denny Jones, who had the only tractor in town.

And it was all over.

I lay on my bed and I stared at the balsa-wood model I'd made. It hung from the ceiling on a piece of string and it flew whenever there was a breeze coming through the window. I'd painted it yellow and red and green and used to pretend I'd have a real one of my own one day. But that morning as I looked at my model, I thought, If a truck could crash and do that to a body, what would an airplane do if it skewered into the ground at eighty or a hundred miles an hour?

For a while, I didn't want to know the answer.

Then, I saw the sheriff walking toward my mother, then toward our house. I was sitting on my bed, still staring at the model, when he came into my room without knocking.

"John," he said in his deep, gruff voice, which had scared every kid in Abbeville at one time or another.

"Sir."

"What happened out there, son?"

I looked at him and felt sick again because his shirt was soaked in blood. I shrugged. "I'm sleeping, hear an almighty crash, go out. The porch is wrecked; the fence is down. I see Mr. Maginley's truck on its roof and I run over and I ask, 'You okay, Mr. Maginley?' But he couldn't talk, sir, 'coz he had the gear stick poking all the way through and sticking out his back. Here." I showed the sheriff. "He was alive. I know he was. He had this real funny look in his eyes like he wanted me to do something, and all I did was puke."

My eyes were stinging.

"You didn't see the accident happen?"

"No, sir. Just heard it."

"You were the first there?"

"Yes, sir."

"There was no one else you saw? No other vehicles?"

"No, sir. It's too early for Billy Taylor to come by, sir."

He was quiet for a while, watching me. "You all right, John?" he asked.

Because he had Ed Maginley's blood all over his clothes, I looked at my feet. If the sheriff could be all right after what he'd just done—gotten Ed Maginley off that gear stick—so could I. "I guess I'm all right, sir," I lied.

"You sure about that, son?"

"Yes, sir," I lied again. Damn my voice. It was either high or low, or not at all. Right then, it was just a little squeak. Like those rats I'd chase out of the chicken feed, the ones that'd squeak when I whopped them with the broom.

The sheriff grabbed my chin and just about broke my neck when he lifted my face up so I'd look him in the eye. But I was trying to hold back tears.

I'd heard folks say you couldn't lie to the sheriff, and this was the first time he'd ever spoken to me. I didn't know how he knew my name. And I wondered what made him ruffle my hair, put a hand on my shoulder before he walked out. I wondered what made him look at the airplane model, look back at me,

48

smile a bit, and close the door quietly. I could hear him talking with my mother outside.

I went to work at Billy Taylor's that day, but he got mad at me for not paying attention. "What's the matter with you today, Johnny?"

He was the only person on earth I let call me Johnny. He asked me three times before I cried and didn't think I'd ever stop.

Billy hadn't known about Ed Maginley. He'd ridden his motorcycle a different way to the airfield that day.

He asked if I wanted to talk about what I'd seen and I said no, that I was fine. But he put me on the back of his bike and he rode me home, anyway. Denny Jones was pulling the pole off our fence and phone company workers were putting another pole up. They left the old one on our sidewalk, fixed the phones for those folks in our street who had them, and then they all went away.

The truck wasn't there, but I could still see it every time I closed my eyes.

And I could hear my mother and Billy in the kitchen. I'd never heard her crying before, so I opened the door a little and looked in. Billy was holding her tightly, telling her it'd be okay, that he wanted to help in any way he could.

He lifted her face, but not the way the sheriff had lifted mine, and my heart stopped beating for a moment when he kissed her. I don't know what else might have happened, because she saw me watching and Billy let go very quickly.

He didn't come to our house for weeks after that. It took me a long time to understand why, too.

My mother cried for two whole days, and it wasn't because Ed Maginley had died, either. When I think of her, I see a woman sitting alone in the dark, looking out at nothing. It was always Meg who'd try and climb on her lap, only to hear "Not now. Leave me be awhile. . . ." For two nights in a row, I had to read Meg's bedtime story to her, some stupid story about a dancer. If I tried to skip a word, she'd know. She seemed a baby way too long, then I discovered that bedtime was the only time she had Mom to herself.

Meg had a wall covered in pictures of ballerinas. Her friends collected them for her. And while I looked at my plane, she had her ballet girls. I wondered what Mom had. "She's always crying lately," Meg said that night, and I was surprised she'd even noticed.

"She's missing Pa."

"Why?"

"He'd know what to do. Now shut it; I'm trying to read a story here."

When Meg was finally asleep, I closed her door quietly.

Then I opened my mother's. She didn't turn. She didn't move except to lower her head a little.

She was sitting in my father's rocking chair by the window, but the curtains weren't pulled aside. She looked scared, lonely, and pretty in a funny kind of way. She had long hair she always kept on her head. I didn't see it down very often, but when it was down, it reached her waist. It was down that night, a light brown color that always shone like gold in the sun. She had dark blue eyes that turned black when she was angry, and her nose was little and pointed at the end. One of her front teeth was crooked, and so was her smile.

Maybe that's where mine came from.

She never cried aloud. She was able, somehow, to hide tears behind a smile, and if I asked what was wrong, she'd just say, "Don't be silly. Nothing's wrong." That made me feel worse, as if it was all my fault.

I loved her more than anything else in my life and I hated to see her that way.

"It's late, John Robert."

Everyone else called me John except her. I had my father's first name, and I told myself she said both names so she wouldn't be mistaken.

I walked across the floor of a room I rarely went into and stood beside my mother for a while. I wanted to touch her hair. I needed a hug, too, but she didn't hug me much anymore. Said I was all arms and legs, didn't fit on her lap. So instead of telling her what I needed the most, I asked, "Why do you always sit in the dark?"

"Helps me think."

She put down the pillow she was holding. I looked back to the bed; the pillow on her side was still there. Pa's, I thought. I was right—she was missing him.

"You want me to try to fix the fence for you?" I asked quietly.

"Can't afford the palings, John Robert."

"Maybe Billy Taylor would—"

"No! No, don't you even think it, and don't you dare ask him!"

I flinched away. I hated it when she yelled like that. I was only trying to help, to find a way out of this terrible sadness she was always in lately.

"We can get by without charity."

She looked thin, sick. Her eyes had big black rings under them. Her hands shook when she blew her nose. She was always coughing, too. Could hear her wheezing when I walked past. "You sick, Ma?"

"No, I'll be all right. It's just a cold. Go to bed, son. This is my time to be alone."

I didn't move. I figured she spent too long on her own. Besides, I needed to know something, because every time I closed my eyes, all I saw was Ed Maginley and the gear stick through his chest and sticking out his back. I thought later how maybe he was reaching for something on the floor when the corner came up too quickly. But I didn't want to know any more about Ed Maginley. There was something else on my mind.

"Mom?"

"What—"

"Is my daddy really dead?" I asked.

"Of course he is."

I looked at my feet, not knowing how I'd ask the important part but knowing I'd have to sooner or later.

"How'd he die?" I asked, and my voice was shaking.

She looked at me quickly. I didn't want to cry; I hadn't planned on it. But I couldn't help it. The tears welled up, stung my eyes.

"Did he die like Ed Maginley?"

"John Robert, please go to bed."

"I gotta know."

Till then, I thought I was a man. I was working hard, giving her all the money I earned. My voice was breaking. I was having weird dreams. I was searching for girls to tease. But that night, I felt helpless and confused. Instead of scolding me again, telling me to act my age, my mother grabbed me, pulled me onto her rocker, and held me tightly.

I told her what I'd seen. Maybe I thought my father had died that awful way because she never said a word about him. She always said it was important that we knew how to live, not die. But if it was so important to live, why'd she sit in the dark, crying?

She rocked me like she used to when I was very little. She was soft and warm and she smelled like she always did—lilacs. Her heartbeat was loud against my ear and her voice was very deep because it came from inside her when she said, "Your daddy didn't die like Ed Maginley. He was trying to save three boys in a flooded river at Mobile. He saved two of them, but he and the other boy, they were swept away. Your daddy, he died a hero."

She'd rather have had him alive, though. I would have, too.

"Mobile, Alabama?" I asked.

"He was working there."

"Who told you that he'd died?"

"Police came. The sheriff, Fred Larsen. Reverend Willis. But I knew. I knew. . . ."

"How?"

"I just did. John Robert, your daddy wouldn't want us to keep crying because he's not here."

"But it's all you do."

"I miss him, honey."

"So do I, Mom."

"I know you do."

"He was a good pa."

"And don't you ever forget it." She touched my face, looked down into my eyes. "When I look at you, I see him."

"Are you sure, Mom?"

"Of course I'm sure. You're the image of your daddy."

"No, I mean about . . ."

"He didn't die like Ed Maginley."

I was quiet for a while. "I'd never seen so much blood before."

"I know."

I was quiet. She hadn't told me to get off to bed again. "He looked at me."

"Who did?"

"Ed Maginley. He couldn't talk. He tried to, though."

"What did the sheriff tell you to do?"

"Nothing. Just asked if I was all right."

"What did you say?"

"Said I was. And I am . . . sorta. Just can't stop seeing that face, that's all. Like he wanted me to help him."

She said nothing else except, "I don't think either of us will get much sleep tonight."

When I woke the next day, she was still holding me.

Why is it always the bad things that come back to haunt you? It's never the good. The good things drift in and out, leave you with a smile, then an ache because they're all gone.

I wish there was someone here I could talk to. It wouldn't be so bad if someone could just *try* to understand me. There's so much I could teach these people if only they'd give me a chance.

A while back, I thought a milestone had been reached when I

taught Kioki how to play ticktacktoe. I let her win for a long time, too. Soon she didn't need any help winning. She still doesn't. They all play the game now, especially when the weather stops everything except sleep.

Sometimes I wake hoping my prayers for a deck of cards will be answered.

She watches me write, listens to the one-sided conversations I have with myself. Because I talk as I write. I never used to; maybe I'm afraid of losing the one thing I have left—my language. I'd like to teach her the things I know, tell her about the places I've been so she'll know that there is more than this cold hell. I wonder, though, if she'd even care. She must have eyes to see I'm different. Hell, I arrived out of a storm in some soaring bird from heaven, didn't I?

FOUR

◦◦◦◦◦◦◦◦

R ECENTLY, there was a break in the weather—
sunshine for a whole day. The wind dropped to a mild
ten knots and I was able to go outside, loosen the parka a little,
feel some sun on my face and look out over the thirty-foot cliff.
No little boy there this time, just the ice melting, crumbling in
the open sea. I guessed it was either the Aleutian Trench or the
Bering Sea, I'm finding it extremely difficult to get any kind of
bearing at all here, fine or foul weather. If I go by my feelings,
I'm sure the village faces south. I can't tell by the stars because
the night sky is rarely visible. There's usually only fog so thick,
you can't see your boots, or storm clouds that are any aviator's—or sailor's—nightmare.

But today, there was sunshine, warmer weather; the pack ice
was melting and the good recent catch—seal, walrus, a few gulls
soaring through the wrong airspace at the right time, and baskets full of fish—ensured two things: The entire village would
be able to eat for a long time and there'd be a celebration of the
coming summer.

I'd never been to an Eskimo party before and I didn't know
till later that it heralded the relocation to the summer side of the
island. The celebration was like any party I'd ever attended—
food, jokes, music, dancing. We all moved from one house to the
next, and next, and next. . . . Asuluk, who's been keeping his distance ever since I right-hooked him, kept everyone riveted by
his stories.

But I don't understand what anyone says yet. A word or two, yes.

I'm not treated like the outsider I feel. Either I join in what they believe is fun or I don't. If I'm there, I'm accepted; if I'm not, I am not missed. I still get tired quickly, so I went home for a nap, deciding that if the party was still on when I woke, I'd rejoin it as best I could.

Kioki woke me with her packing. Her pots, bowls, knives, scrapers, skins, clothes. She packed my gear, too: the two parkas she'd made for me, the spare boots, the bundle wrapped in seal hide. I didn't realize till then that we were all relocating. Most of the others had already gone—they could pack up and move on quicker than a troop of Boy Scouts.

A few kids appeared on the beach, collecting driftwood. I bet none of them have ever seen a tree in their lives. They used the driftwood for building, not fuel. I wanted to go down, take a closer look at what the kids were doing down there. I knew I'd get down easily enough; crawling back up the cliff alone was another matter.

I was watching the boys for too long. Someone came and called them to hurry—at least that's what it sounded like, and that's the effect it had. The boys scattered, not wanting to be left behind. Me, too.

Kioki had already left. All I could see of her was the way she waddled as she pulled her private sled, the deep tracks it left in the thawing mud.

It took me a long time to catch up, and for most of the way I hobbled in silence along with a very old lady I'd seen a few times. But we'd never so much as shared a smile before. I don't know who she was, or to which family she belonged. Everyone else took as much notice of her as they did of me. I offered to help her through the mud once we were on the windy flats, but she wouldn't let me.

Kioki was slowing down. Now and then, she'd look back to see where I was and she'd call out. Sound carries almost as well across these flats as it does across water.

56

In my younger days, when I still had a good arm, I could have thrown a baseball across the width of the island, from south shore to north at least. I could have sprinted the distance once. But the walk now felt like a hundred miles. So we left the winter dugout houses behind. And each time I had to stop, take a breather, I wondered what kind of shelters they lived in on the other side. I hadn't walked this far since the crash, and it was getting harder to breathe all the time. I think now that's why Kioki kept looking back. She wasn't worried about the old lady struggling along with me. She was worried about me. I remembered what that old prospector from Anchorage had told me. My feet were wet, but while they still hurt, I knew I was okay.

Then I heard the thump and squelch of something hitting mud close behind me. The old lady had fallen over. I remembered thinking that if she'd let me hold her hand, this wouldn't have happened. She lay there on her face, coughing, wheezing. I called out for help, but no one even looked back. Someone started singing; it was more of a chant, I guess, and it became contagious. I didn't know what was happening. I couldn't leave her there. I tried to get her face out of the mud, tried again to make someone hear me over that damned singing. So I sat in six inches of mud, turned the old lady over, and tried to hold her up so she wouldn't choke. At first, she was angry, and I didn't know why. Then I realized she was dying and this must be the way Eskimos liked to die—alone, without fuss.

I looked down at her old weather-beaten face. I couldn't understand why I was there, not her sons or daughters. She looked up at me, all her anger faded away, and she smiled. She didn't have too many teeth left. Fifty or sixty years of chewing on mukluk would wear anything down. She grabbed for my hand, said something to me, then stopped breathing. I'd had a few lessons in first aid—had to so I could get my license to fly. And I almost started to get her breathing again, but something stopped me. I don't know exactly what it was. I just looked down at her and somehow knew that what I was planning to do was wrong.

That old lady was the second person who'd died in my arms.

You never forget something like that, *never*. She died with this smile on her face, as if she was pleased it was over. And I didn't feel sad. Maybe it was because I never knew her. But she sure picked a good day for it.

I put the old lady back into the mud and looked up. There was a semicircle of Eskimos a hundred yards away, and there was one very loud silence, too. As if each one of them had known the moment she died. Then they all turned away and kept walking, all except Kioki.

She was waiting for me. Again.

It gave me a lot to think about. If that's what happened to their old people when they were of no more use, then why in God's name did they bother saving me? I'm of no great use even if I do what I can, when I can, and when I'm better, I know I'll be expected to go out with the other men and hunt and fish. If I could walk properly, if I had two arms and two good hands, I'd be out there with them now. All these *ifs*.

I just can't trust myself yet. Some days the memory of what happened yesterday is just not there. Some days I lose my name. Some days I don't even know who Kioki is. But I think somehow that watching the way all these people turned and walked on ... well, I will never forget that, ever.

I remember taking hold of Kioki's hand and walking with her, but what happened after that is anyone's guess. By the time we'd made it to the other village, I'd just about forgotten that old lady dead out there in the slush.

I vaguely recall seeing the summer side of the island. Not a lot different from the winter side except that there isn't a beach here. Sea meets rock, and one glance at the water tells me it'd be a long step down. Probably without end. Storm clouds rolled in from the north, and for a while I thought I saw islands out there to the north or north-northeast. But what I think I see often is not the case, but I'll get to that soon enough.

The houses here are much the same as the others; they're dug into the ground and a little bit larger. They're certainly not igloos. These folks can make a shelter in a couple of hours. It's only temporary, used when the hunt takes them miles from home for any great length of time. Maybe some Eskimos farther north live in igloos; all I know is that these folks don't.

Kioki and I live together in a one-room place about fourteen feet in diameter, and the ceiling's high enough for me to stand up straight. I'm probably the tallest man anyone here has ever seen. The bed is another raised platform; the table where we sit and eat is also made of packed, dry mud, raised up. In this house, it gets hot enough with the lamp and body heat to let us discard a few layers of clothing. It's not the warm I'm used to, though.

Speaking of warm, Kioki doesn't call me John. She calls me Floreeda. Maybe I talk about Florida so much that she's mistaken it for my name.

I don't know whose clothes I wear. I watch her sometimes and wonder if she was married and he died on a hunt or in a storm. God knows, the weather here is anyone's worst enemy. I can wonder as much as I like; I'll probably never know very much about this woman. Kioki. It's the closest I can get to the way her name sounds. And I've had to abbreviate it a little, too.

I don't understand why I'm living here with her. One day, I might find a reason for all this. One day.

She can laugh for no reason. Those little eyes come alive. At times, I feel strange because I can't find a reason to share her joy, and when I don't laugh with her, I hurt her feelings. I don't like hurting her feelings, but I never was much of an actor, either.

I spend a lot of time sleeping. When I'm in a lot of pain, it's hard to focus on anything else. She'll give me some of that bitter, hot mix and a minute or so later I fade away.

I still feel the arm they took. My hand itches. I try to scratch, but it isn't there. I try to walk without the whalebone but can't stop my left leg from dragging. I can't bend it at all now. I try, but the agony's enough to make me pass out or throw up, whichever comes first. Most of the time, my head feels as if it's splitting into five pieces. And when it's bad, I can't see at all for the fog that has nothing to do with outside weather.

And when my emotions take a spiral dive, I'm as out of control as that air-show crash that took Bobby Sullivan.

I'll wake sometimes needing an orange so bad, I can smell it. But they only found one in the wreck. And by the time I managed to thaw it out, it was rotten inside. I know I had a bag of oranges in the Jenny. Tinned beans, tinned meat, dry biscuits, clothes, money. I even had a gun, a Colt .45 six-shooter. God knows where that ended up.

My hair's longer now, way past my ears, and I've never had a beard before. I decided to grow one after my face got cut by ice that time. All told, I think I've been here about a year.

Funny how it feels like ten.

I left Anchorage in April. I must have left Miami in February. It's in my logbook, but the first twenty pages are a write-off. I don't know where the plane is; she probably went down in the melt or she's drifted in pack ice and is knocking on the Siberian coastline by now.

The dreams are getting weirder. I can't remember what happened yesterday, but twenty years ago is a breeze, and here I am, with dreams following me all day long. The most frequent one and the one I hate most is of me, standing on pack ice, screaming at a de Havilland flying overhead at eighty feet. I'm never seen. I've lighted fires on the ice. The yellow-and-green Jenny is only out of fuel. I've even cleared a strip for takeoff. I'm screaming for a fuel drop, and the de Havilland banks and disappears.

No one ever sees me.

I wake crying and she's there touching me, holding me.

The dreams are getting so bad, so haunting, I don't want to sleep anymore. But when I fight sleep, my waking mind has dreams all of its own.

I nearly killed Kioki because of what I thought I'd seen. I was still getting used to this new house, the different routine. She came in with some more supplies, mainly raw fish to keep us eating for a couple of days, and she also had a pouch filled with berries the kids had picked. They call it *sue wuk*; they look and taste a little like bilberries to me.

She had something new around her neck. I couldn't see what it was at first, not clearly anyway. And by the door was a sled I'd never seen before, but something about it was familiar.

I looked closer.

The Jenny's propeller had been chopped into two pieces. The prop was now sled tracks.

I never felt anger like it before and I never want to feel it again.

Maybe I had this insane notion or hope that when I could walk more than fifty yards at a time, I'd be able to get to the plane, wherever it was, bring her back to the island, fix her somehow, fly out of here.

I was screaming at Kioki and all she did was look at me, vacant. There was no one home behind those beady, little eyes. I hated it when she had that vacant stare. Then she blinked and started unpacking the stores. She ignored me. That was worse.

I'd suffered anger before but never hate, and I was never violent. There was no room for whys or counting to ten. I saw red, literally.

I'd never hit a woman before, but I couldn't stop. Worse, I didn't want to. And as I went crazier, I could see pieces of my airplane everywhere, pieces of her wing linen now patches on Kioki's coat. There were wing-linen curtains on nonexistent windows. But I think the worst sight was the oil-pressure gauge hanging on plaited strut wire around her neck. I wanted it back, but the damned thing wouldn't come off.

I remember kicking when she went down. I didn't hear her screams—my own were too loud.

She was screaming because I was killing her.

Then the men must have come. It took about three of them to drag me off her, to hold me down. They came from nowhere, like those Arctic storms. The men were short, thickset, and each one seemed younger and twice as strong as I was. And the one who hit me had only one good eye.

It was his punch that stopped the nightmare. I lay on the ground in the rain, wondering what the hell had happened.

The last things I remember about Kioki were her bruised and swollen face, her bleeding nose, black eyes, the red handprint around her throat as Asuluk carried her out.

Then they dragged me away. Right away.

I guess God's punishing me by letting me remember it all, every last detail.

They dragged me into a little place about as big as a dog box—dark, cramped, stinking. The one about as old as I am, the one with one eye, sunk his boot in before he left.

I was alone in the dark for a long, long time before Asuluk came in. They'd beaten me fairly good; the most I could do was lie there, wishing I could die and let it all be over with.

The medicine man sat down, stared at me awhile.

In his hands was a collection of rocks. He chanted, threw the rocks into the air, studied the way they fell, and was silent. He reached down, touched my face. I flinched and so did he. He said something that seemed like, "Keep still. I won't hurt you."

He turned my head and touched the exact spot where the blinding pain overrode sanity. He chanted again.

And I calmed to the sound of his voice, that low, distant hum. He dug in his clothes, found a piece of carved walrus ivory, and rubbed at my head with it.

"Kioki? Where is she?"

He looked at me and said nothing, but I could see in his eyes that he understood every word I had said. But how to prove feelings? I needed an answer. I needed to know. I didn't know if I'd killed her or not. All I wanted was to see her face, to be sure she was okay.

Asuluk said nothing. He chanted again. His voice was low, humming, steadily gaining in pitch, and what I knew of daylight was soon gone.

When I woke, I was still in the dog box, still alone. Maybe this was the Eskimo version of white man's prison.

From the low ceiling hung strips of cloth, roughly woven wool, or fur. Perhaps it was grass.

There was a flame, alive in a tin. I was naked, covered by a bearskin. It was the same skin I'd seen Asuluk wearing, and a circle of stones was on my chest, stuck there by some kind of sticky, dark stuff. But by then, any evil had died its own natural death. I was me again, at least until something else turned me into a demon. If only I knew when it was coming, I could take myself away from these people. I never wanted to hurt anyone in my life. Least of all her.

I called, but no one came. I half-expected no one to come. I sat up. I had bruises all over; my lip was swollen twice its size, split. I looked at the tin awhile, watching the flames feeding on the fat. The tin was blackened from years of use. I moved a little to get a better view and I discerned writing, a word.

It was Russian.

Russian? There'd been others through here? Of course. What was I thinking? Fur traders, last century. The *promyshlennicki*. So how far from the Alaskan mainland was I?

It was dark in the dog box, but I could see that the internal structure of this shelter wasn't just driftwood. There was a four-by-two above my head, machine-planed angles. I reached to touch. It looked and felt like varnished mahogany.

From a plane?

No.

A ship? More likely.

But was there mahogany on a fishing boat? Maybe a whaler? Doubtful.

A steamer? A passenger liner? Maybe even an icebreaker? Probably.

A Russian ship had gone down? Caught in the ice?

Would I ever damned well know?

I tried to stand up, nearly impossible. I was circled by the same stones the medicine man had put on my chest. I wrapped the skin around me as best I could and I went out into the sudden light. It was raining again. My bare feet were numb. I was standing in slush halfway up my calves, hair blowing in my face. If I couldn't cut it soon, I'd have to get someone to plait the damned stuff. My beard was itching. I couldn't see straight. Dizzy.

I called out again. Not a thing. There were sixteen houses like ours, skins and cloth covering the entrances. The entire village was deserted. There were no dogs, no sleds, no kids. No one, no one at all. They'd disappeared. It was one of the worst feelings I'd endured yet—the sudden realization of being very alone, helpless.

I panicked. The last time I'd panicked was when Bobby died, but it was a quiet internal panic turning to a scream of denial when the machine contacted earth. It wasn't panic like this. I called again—I was crying. I called and cried so much, my voice was getting hoarse. And still, no one came.

Sense told me to go back in to the fire, to the dry, that no one had abandoned me. Maybe they'd killed a whale.

Sure. That was it. It had to be. All the village went to a whale kill. Yes, it was a whale. It had to be. They'd taken me in, helped me, fed me, chanted me back from death, tried to communicate, sang to me, told me long stories I never understood but laughed at when everyone else did, so they wouldn't let me down now. They wouldn't abandon me. Hell, they knew who I was, what I was. Just because I went a little crazy now and then . . . they wouldn't do this to me, surely to God? I knew them.

And I knew Kioki. She wouldn't let them leave me, not now.

So I went back in and sat in that circle of stones, replacing the ones I'd kicked aside on my way out, and I wrapped the skin tighter around me.

And I thought.

I thought clearly for once. At least I tried, because in here I felt almost safe. It might have been the circle of stones. It's hard to say; I never was very superstitious.

I looked down at the tin and little by little, warmth returned. But it wasn't the kind of warmth I wanted. What I wanted most, I knew I'd never have again. I wanted someone I knew to walk in the door and tell me it was just a bad dream. I wanted it to be my mother. I wanted to be a kid again. I thought about my family. Hell, right then, if Rosanna had walked in, I'd have run away with her. Why didn't I think about her much? Why did I want some girl I knew for only one night and not the girl I was supposed to marry?

What would Rosanna say if she could see me now? Six words for sure: Oh my Lord, look at you.

Then she'd probably want to show me something else her daddy had bought her. Daddy's little angel. Daddy didn't know her that well. He died before he got the chance.

Her father, the colonel. The little man with the collection of swords and guns, the little man with the steel gray hair and heart as warm as an Alaskan winter.

He was wounded in the Great War and had come home to another. I never knew the full story or why he took up writing for the newspaper at Columbia and made his mark for the KKK before he hung himself in December 1924.

To me, the boy who courted his daughter, he didn't seem like a man to suicide; he seemed like a man who had a lot of enemies. I never knew him; I don't think Rosanna did, either. The daddy she talked of so much seemed a figment of an overactive imagination when compared with the cranky old bastard I knew. Most folks feared him; with fear came respect, but respect born of fear isn't really respect. A lot of people were glad when that coffin was lowered and the volley fired him a fond farewell. It's hard to mourn a stranger; maybe that's why Rosanna never cried.

I wonder if she's crying for me now. I wonder if she even thinks of me.

We'd gone to school together until she was thirteen and was taken to London with her family. I didn't see her again, nor did I miss her for another four years until she returned to the Old 96

65

district with her father; her mother had decided it was better to stay in London. I met her again at Abbeville's café. It was a hot day in July. I'd come in from Alabama—one of a few solo deliveries for Billy Taylor—and I was hot and dry, and Mickey Gill made the best ice cream sodas in four states. I noticed her of course; it was difficult not to. Not many girls dressed the way she did. Her pearls were real ones, her fingernails were long, and she didn't have the drawl most southern girls had—unless she got upset and forgot she was a lady. She used to sit beside me at school and get me into more trouble with the teacher.

A lot can happen in four years. Rosanna was sitting alone in a booth, reading a book when I walked in. I talked to Mickey awhile and turned when I felt her stare. First glance, I knew who she was. I smiled back, wondering why she was smiling at me. I thought she used to hate me.

"Hello, John."

"Rosanna."

"I hear you're flying for Billy Taylor now?"

"I heard you were living in England."

She put her book away and invited me to sit opposite. I needed a bed, I needed to sleep bad, and I needed one of my mother's huge meals first, but there was something in Rosanna's eyes that prompted me to sit down and wallow in her voice for a while.

Catching up on old times.

I saw again just how pretty she'd become—not beautiful, but pretty. I liked her voice; I always had. Her eyes dimmed at something sad, sparkled at something happy. The sodas and four slices of blueberry pie cost me needed sleep and a lot of future worry. I took her for a ten-minute flight over Abbeville, and after that, Rosanna decided I was hers for life—whether I wanted it that way or not.

Rosanna usually got what she wanted, never what she needed.

I never could say no to her; I tried once, and she cried. I could never tell her what I wanted or needed. Maybe I was just too gutless to say what was on my mind. I've never liked hurting people's feelings, even people I don't like much.

I get a little sad when I think of what might have been if I hadn't flown off chasing some wild dream. But what would have been a worse hell? Marrying a girl I never loved or spending the rest of my life freezing my ass off in the snow? The future, one way or another, looks about as bright.

I'd rather be listening to Kioki. I've forgotten what Rosanna's voice sounded like. I've almost forgotten what she looked like. I remember she was about five foot three, had dark curly hair and dark blue eyes. And she was thin. Always dressed spiffy. She used to sing a lot, but she never sang the kinds of stuff I liked. I liked something with a little life to it, not the opera I never understood. Never liked tragedies much. For me there always had to be a happy ending.

I heard the dogs first. I must have been asleep, because I woke with a fright, my heart in my ears. Dogs, kids—the normal sounds I'd convinced myself I'd never hear again.

I went out and I watched them return. Yes, it had been a whale. Thirty-five people, old, young, everyone, had joined in the kill. The women were carrying what the half dozen sleds could not, and everyone stopped and stared when they saw me, the naked white man, standing in knee-deep slush, crying with happiness.

Asuluk came toward me and in his hand was a harpoon. He threw it; it landed two inches from my right foot. He was angry. He pointed to the dog box and I obeyed silently. I was alone again for far too long, but I felt a little better. My mind had come back to normal again; I knew who I was.

I expected Kioki to come in.

But I expected too much.

They sent an old woman instead. She looked like one of Asuluk's wives. She sat down, took out some kind of shaker, and began wailing. Maybe the devil hadn't departed yet. No one here ran about naked in the thaw, no one with half a brain, anyhow.

"Kioki?" I asked. "Is she all right?" She smiled—kind of. "Please, you have to tell me how she is. Please." She didn't understand a word till I asked for Asuluk. I was crying again. I couldn't stop.

The old woman stopped chanting. She put her head to one side and I just lay down, rolled over. It was useless, futile. She shook my shoulder, I put my hand up. Back off. She did. She left.

And Asuluk came in. He nudged me with his fur boot, saw my tears, and a look of utter disgust crossed his face. They simply didn't know what to do with me. Well, they weren't alone.

He threw my clothes at me and barked what meant "come." It was the same word they used to call the dogs. But they called them in a friendlier tone. Jesus, did I need this right now?

I dressed in the clothes Kioki had made for me, and Asuluk was impatient while I tied the boots to my calves, one-handed. I followed him outside; he didn't slow his pace for me. She always did. It was as if no one here gave a damn except her. But I guess if they didn't care, they'd have left me to die all that time ago.

Asuluk came to a stop outside his house and he said something so quickly, I couldn't understand. A few words here and there I was beginning to catch and comprehend. All I understood was the current disgust. He ushered me in, but he stood out there in the cold.

Something aromatic was being burned; it was biting and familiar. It was the smoke Asuluk had blown over me while I was recovering and unable to breathe.

Kioki was lying on a wide bed. I could hardly recognize her. She could barely see, but she turned her head in silence and stared at me and her eyes said, Look what you have done.

I wanted to believe she'd been in some kind of accident.

But I never was a very good liar, even to myself.

Then she said something to the old lady—something that seemed like, Show him, Mother. Show him what he's done.

I froze. I couldn't move an inch in any direction. It was time to make another deal with God.

Old mama pulled back the skins that covered her daughter and let me see what I'd done.

I never knew Kioki was pregnant. To me, she'd always been little and round. There was no mistaking the reason for that swollen belly.

Damned if I could think of a reason to explain the beating, though.

I tried to kneel beside her, but her old mama hit me on the shoulder with a cook pot. "I'm not going to hurt her. I just want, just have . . ." She hit me again, until Kioki raised her hand to the old woman. And she touched my face.

"I didn't mean to. I didn't know what I was doing. I don't even know why. . . ."

The old lady was ready to hit me again, harder this time. I wished she would. I touched Kioki's hand, about the only part of her I could see that wasn't hurt. She touched my face, looked at the tears with detached interest, then went back to sleep.

The old lady shooed me out. I couldn't stay.

Asuluk was still waiting, and he seemed happy to see so much distress in me. He walked off again, wanting me to follow. But I grabbed his arm. It was a mistake touching him. I let go quickly. And I said as best I could in Eskimo, "I didn't know she's your daughter." Which I guess was wrong. But the tears in my eyes were saying more than any language could. He studied me as if I were a new kind of bug he'd never seen before. Then he barked at me to come, and he spat on the ground.

I followed, slowly again, using the bone as a walking stick. He walked me to the other side of the island, the side I was more familiar with, and he pointed into the distance, across a vast expanse of deep blue water to a berg. And on the edge of that berg, frozen into the ice, was my airplane—what was left of it. From his coat, he took out an ancient spyglass—a remnant of the 1800s, or so it seemed—and he gave it to me.

The plane was a skeleton, stripped bare of anything that might have proved useful to these people. They'd have used the wood for building, the steel for weapons, the wire for God knows what. I should have known the plane had resurfaced on an ice floe when Kioki had brought in all that paper, my logbook, the pencils, the few clothes I'd carried with me. Things that had been mine were duly returned. They weren't thieves. I knew something was stopping the plane from plunging God knows how far down, although I sure didn't. Caught on a ledge, I guessed. Now she'd resurfaced, what was left of her.

Asuluk took his telescope back, said something, and left me on my own, staring out at what remained of my life, my love, my plane. A mangled memory so far away.

Asuluk was giving me time to think. Maybe become human. Maybe decide it wasn't worth fighting anymore. I was here. I had to make the most of what little I had left in a place that offered nothing and gave even less, a place where no man was supposed to live, yet these people had resided here for centuries. And they were happy. They were content. Because they knew no better.

And I who did know better . . .

I thought of who I was, what I was, but not of the past or people I'd once known and loved.

I was in another world now.

I looked back to the village on the other side of the island; the wind brought the sounds of youngsters at play. I looked down the cliff to the bloodstains on the beach below—blood from the whale, which would keep us all alive for six more months. I saw some gulls fighting over what little remained.

They'd asked nothing of me, had given me too much. And what had I given in return?

I went back to Kioki's house, gathered up my bed, and took it to Asuluk's. I'd stay there until Kioki was better. I'd nurse her until she got better. I would do for her what she had done for me, or so I thought. So was the plan.

70

Until Kioki saw me standing in the doorway and said two words to me: "Floreeda. No."

And with great pain, she turned her back on me.

So I walked away. I don't know where I was going, even how far I got before I felt the touch to my shoulder and I turned.

It was Asuluk, telling me silently to come back. I shook my head. He nodded. Some of the disgust had melted from his eyes, because what I saw there instead was a kind of curiosity, a gentleness. Maybe it was forgiveness.

Maybe the medicine man knew exactly how I felt, knew exactly what to do.

He took my hand and led me back to the village. And while we walked, he talked. It was another long, long story, but I'm damned if I could understand it.

FIVE

⬤━⬤━⬤━⬤━⬤━⬤━⬤

I T ' S been five days. I've been sitting alone in this empty house, not knowing how she is, trying to understand why I'm like this, trying to come to terms with too much, too soon. I've seen her every day, but no one will let me get too close.

I have too much time to think, and mostly I think of my fears, things I used to be afraid of, things I'd laugh at on the outside but that could tear me apart on the inside. Mainly, I've been thinking about New Year's 1924. I felt then just like I feel now: dead inside.

I remember sitting on a park bench, looking at a garden. It was in Miami—one of those Happy Valley establishments, red-brick, bars on the windows, lawns so immaculate, you'd think the grass had been cut one blade at a time. People were being walked around those gardens, close by where I sat. They were folks who didn't know where they were, who they were, what they were. They just existed—they breathed, they ate, they slept, and not much else happened in between that they knew of. It wasn't life. It wasn't living. They walked with the staff, who had better things to do, better places to be once their shifts were over. Then they could take off their white coats and finally go home, back to the real world.

I couldn't look at those patients and I envied anyone who could work with them, the relations who could visit and pretend nothing was wrong. I guess I was so uncomfortable that deep inside I was afraid, afraid of the strangeness of life, the lack of control, the lack of almost everything that made you human.

Every time someone'd look at me and smile, I'd look down at my boots. I wore the leather coat with the Sullivan and Shaw emblem. And I guess I was waiting for some courage to arrive, lead me on inside so I could tell Bobby's father about the accident.

I didn't want the police to tell him. In a fit of madness, I'd said no, no, I'd tell him myself. Be better that way.

I'd met Bobby's old man once before, and I remember Bobby trying to stop me going into that dark, filthy house on the outskirts of Hialeah. Bobby had only two haunting shames, his father and his origins. I'd known Bob since we were kids. Times now, I think I knew him a lot better than I knew myself. He saw things in me I was blind to and vice versa. He saw things and said things only a true friend could get away with.

I took the call at work. Bob's old man thought I was his son. If it'd been a wrong number, he'd have thought anyone was his son. I went out to Bobby; he was with the mechanic, Sam, working on a fuel block. When I told him his old man needed to see him, Bobby didn't blink.

"Did you hear me?"

"Yeah—"

"I said you'd go."

"That's your problem."

"Bob!"

"What! For Christ's sakes, what!"

He hated being interrupted.

"He needs you." For a while, I thought he was going to punch me in the nose. "He sounds sick."

Bobby looked away. I couldn't understand his reasoning, his lack of concern. Nothing crossed that dark-eyed face.

"Look, I'll go with you. How long can it take?"

I sat on the back of Bobby's motorbike—he had a Harley a year younger than mine—and we rode up to Hialeah. When I'd thought the town ended five minutes ago, Bobby kept riding. It

73

must have taken him an hour or more to ride that old bicycle of his to Miami and back every day when he was a kid.

We went past the stinking slaughter yards, where apparently he'd worked once, only once.

And we were there, parked outside an unpainted wooden house, half the size of mine back in Abbeville. It had a rusted roof; grass and weeds hadn't been cut since we all emerged grunting from caves. An old starving dog met Bobby. It was half-crippled, nearly blind. A bullet between the eyes would have been kinder, but Bobby patted its head, talked to it, stepped over the gate. He gave that old dog more attention than I'd ever seen him give anything except his airplanes and his girls, especially Bess.

And I knew that according to Bess, Bobby Sullivan had no parents. It was safer that way. Now I knew why he threatened to kill me if I ever tripped him on that one lie.

I patted the dog, too, and could still smell it on me hours later. "I don't want you coming in," Bobby said. "No need for you even to be here."

I told him he could have said no in the first place.

"I tried to warn you," was all he said. We followed him inside, the dog and I.

"Where are you?" Bobby called. Maybe a bit of the kindness he'd showed the dog would be better spent on his father, I thought. Bobby was off, searching each obvious room. Nothing. I finally heard "John!" And I didn't like the sound of that call.

Bobby's old man, hard to guess his age, was flat on his face three steps from the outhouse. He hadn't quite made it, in more ways than one. I thought he was dead; maybe I hoped he was. If he was, he'd be someone else's problem. Sure, I'd touch him, providing my hand was on the other end of a long stick.

Bobby had grown up with this kind of thing, and the best way to wake the old man was to throw a bucket of water over him. As far as I could see, it'd be the first time his skin had touched water for weeks, if not months. Maybe even a year.

I went inside, sifted through the crap till I found a tin bucket without holes. I saw plates used over and over and then probably over again. He'd bled, skinned, and gutted rabbits in the kitchen. The place was crawling with maggots.

There were so many empty booze bottles about that I had to kick my way through. God knows how many times old man Sullivan had been arrested; maybe it was habit to throw him into jail for a few days, clean him up, feed him, dry him out, and send him home to the garbage dump so he could start over again.

So when we'd cleaned him up and Bobby put him into bed in a way that he wouldn't choke on his own puke, we attempted to clean up the house. I was wondering where we'd start when Bobby asked, "Got some matches?" I didn't reply. I thought I saw tears in his eyes, so I pretended I was blind. We hardly said a thing to each other. He wanted to be quiet, in case his old man woke.

I never understood till that day why Bobby preferred living on his own in that rented house near the Miami airfield.

For the next two hours, we cleaned the pigsty, fed the old dog. But Bobby wouldn't let me anywhere near his father when the old man woke. I sat on the front stairs, the dog at my feet, and tried not to hear the argument. It was none of my business, yet it hurt listening. And the only way Bobby could escape was to promise he'd come back on the weekend.

I said two words to Casey Sullivan that day. I nodded, said his name. He nodded back, and that was the last I saw of him, leaning on the fence, trying to wave good-bye, turning and throwing up.

I was glad to be out of there, very glad.

My mother would have passed out if she'd seen what I had. I'd taken Bobby home on and off since we were teenagers; she always said he was a joy to have under her roof. He did everything he could and more just to see her smile. Back in those days, I'd run off before she could touch me—it wasn't right getting hugged by a mother—but Bobby would do anything just to feel the touch of her hand on his head. He lied so much about his folks, his house, even I used to believe him—till I knew better. I never told my mother the truth. I loved Bobby too much, I guess. So did she.

Damned if I know why I volunteered to break the news to Bobby's father. Bob put his old man into that funny farm. A last resort, I suppose. A lifetime of overproof alcohol, sometimes straight methylated spirits when nothing else was available, had eaten away at his brain.

As far as I know, he's still alive. Gets taken for a walk once a day. But he doesn't know who he is, or even why he is.

New Year's 1924. I was sitting there on a bench in a nice garden, knowing I had to go in and ask for Casey Sullivan, tell him that his only boy was dead.

I guess I was facing one of my fears. Soon I'd be surrounded by brain-dead people, brain-dead by accident or design.

So I went in, asked for Casey Sullivan.

Was I a relative?

No. But it was important.

"He doesn't speak to anyone, Mr. Shaw."

"He'll talk to me."

The nurse let one of the warders take me upstairs and into a dayroom where big guys in white coats all stood smoking, picking at fingernails, bored. It was a long, narrow room, bare of anything except a gray linoleum floor and bars on the windows. No one really saw me except the warders. Casey Sullivan was pointed out. He was standing by the window, staring at nothing. I walked to him.

"Mr. Sullivan?"

He blinked; maybe that meant he'd heard me.

"Mr. Sullivan, there's something I have to tell you."

He looked at me. He didn't know who I was. He looked at my leather jacket, recognized something about the emblem, and went back to the window.

I didn't know how I'd say it. I supposed the straighter, the better for us both. "It's about Bobby, sir. Bobby was killed on New Year's Eve."

Something crossed his eyes, like the final curtain on a bad

76

one-act play. He said one word, but it took forever to emerge. "Airplane?"

"Yes, sir. An air show at Atlanta."

"At . . . Atlanta?"

"Georgia, sir."

"How?" he asked, not looking at me. He'd spoken a few words, the most offered to anyone for months, apparently.

"He was attempting a double loop, then a spiral dive. He lost it, sir. He lost it."

I suppose the old man could see it happening. I didn't want to say any more. I'd already said too much. Huge tears welled up in the old man's eyes. "Did he die quick?" he asked.

"Yes, sir," I lied. "He wouldn't have known much."

"When?"

"Yesterday, sir. He was buried this morning in Atlanta."

The old man looked me in the eye, and I was trying unsuccessfully to hold back my own tears again.

"He loved you more'n me."

What was left of my heart hit my boots and I reached out to touch the old man's arm, but he pulled away and said one final word—"Git!"—before he slid down the wall and sat there on the floor, weeping.

I ran.

Seems to me it's all I ever do.

I know that my brain got damaged when I crashed. Died. I know I died, and no one will convince me otherwise. I know I saw Bobby; I know I talked to him. I even spoke with my father, and he's been dead a long time. It either happened or I've gone crazy, too. In my heart, I know it happened, because even now, at this moment, I can feel Bobby close.

But there's a craziness I can't control. I turn on and off like a shorting light switch. It doesn't happen as much lately, but when I crack, I have no control. I am no better than Casey Sullivan, who drank his brain dry.

And like Casey, I don't know what to do.

Since she said no.

The only word she understands: *no*. Possibly the worst word in the English language, and it's the one she knows.

I got fed up being miserable, so I took a walk.

I watched from a distance as a dozen men readied to set sail in half a dozen kayaks. Spears, clubs, harpoons. No firearms were visible. They still hunted as their ancestors had, and to me they seemed relatively untouched by the white man. Asuluk was there, so I decided to venture a little closer, hoping I'd be seen, maybe be invited to go along. He saw me, ignored me until the eleven boats were gone. One remained.

I limped on down to the rock. When I said good morning with a smile, he turned to see who I was talking to. "No, you. I'm saying good morning to you, Asuluk."

"You," he repeated.

"You. Me." I pointed. It was the only way to get the message through to Kioki and a few kids, so why would he be any different?

He pealed off an array of tongue-twisting words, ending with Floreeda.

"No, my name's John. Not Florida. I'm *from* Florida."

He looked me up and down, picked up his bow, and pointed to the kayak. After a few moments of irreparable confusion, he shook his head, sighed, and said, "Come. You come."

So he had been listening to me after all. He had picked up a couple of words we could both understand completely.

It was the invitation I'd yearned months for. I nodded and smiled. "About time," I said.

"Ti . . . time?"

"Don't matter."

I never enjoyed the water much except for the occasional skinny-dip on a hot summer's day. I preferred watching the girls on one of the beaches, going out to a couple of the islands off the Keys. When I was a kid, a troop of us had our own swimming hole, with rafts, canoes. . . . I preferred flying to getting wet.

The water was calm until we rounded the tip of the island. I looked for the inevitable storm front, but there was none, not yet at least. After a few moments of dodging rock that I'd never seen when I crash-landed because this entire expanse of sea was covered in ice, I looked back to the island. There wasn't a hint of life anywhere. Not even the roofs of the winter houses were visible.

"Kulowyl," Asuluk said, pointing back to the shore.

"Kulowyl," I repeated, wondering if an island called Kulowyl was charted. I'd go through my maps the moment I got back, and hopefully I'd know exactly where I was, providing the Eskimos and the mapmakers used the same name for the same place.

Five days ago, he'd walked me to the winter side, had shown me the Jenny. Showing me, though, hadn't been enough. He was taking me to it, dodging volcanic rock, drift ice, ignoring a walrus sunbathing and asleep on a rock hardly big enough for it. It hung there, a great wad of blubber, about the dumbest critter I've ever seen in my life. It barely flinched when we paddled by. It was lucky that day, because the stores were already full.

We landed with a heavy thump against the three-foot cliff of ice, thirty yards across by twenty long. Asuluk climbed out first, aided me, and together we pulled the kayak out of the water.

It was hard to believe that I'd landed here over a year before, when the ice was thicker and stretched to the still-water beach of the island Asuluk called Kulowyl.

There she was, as I'd seen her through that ancient spyglass: nose down, tail sheared almost in two, left wing gone. Pieces of rotten linen flapped in the wind, and to my ears she seemed to be crying. I've never liked the sound of wind through metal.

The paint had faded; the frame was rusted. She was only a skeleton.

She stuck out of the ice like some terrible sculptor's nightmare.

Asuluk was watching me, no doubt reading my mind.

I climbed into the wreck. The engine block had relocated to the front seat. What I thought was grease proved to be my own bloodstains on the mangled backseat, but I sat in it anyhow and wondered again how the hell I'd gotten out of this alive.

The Morse radio seemed intact, but the battery had corroded badly.

I remembered as I sat there what I'd felt as I'd taxied out from Miami airfield. All those who'd come to watch, friends, family, everyone. There was no fear that day in February, just expectation, anticipation, excitement. Hell, I hadn't been able to wait to get away.

All I felt now was desolation.

So I kicked it aside before it took over and I felt behind my seat for the tool kit. I reached blindly, touched rotten canvas, and dragged it out. Asuluk by then had climbed up and was having a curious gander. I opened the bag, but it disintegrated. Pliers, spanners, drivers, cutters, a hammer, even a spare razor. And the Colt .45 six-shooter. The bullets were rolling, so I gathered as many as I could reach, stuffed them into my coat, then looked at Asuluk.

He definitely knew what a gun was. We looked at each other a long time and in his eyes was a reminder of what I'd done to his daughter barely a week before. Perhaps it was a flicker of fear there or a reflection of my own, but I handed him the Colt. And he took it. Imitated the sound it made. *Bang*.

I imitated the effect it had. Bull's-eye. You got me.

He thought it was funny, then his laughter died and he looked at me again. I think that was the moment when we became friends.

I didn't trust myself, but I did trust him. I had proved it by giving him that gun.

I spent the good part of an hour stripping the airplane of anything at all that might be handy one day: screws, a couple of bolts—U-bolts—wire, perished rubber. The radio—Kioki might find a use for it. We sat there a short time, the medicine man and I, and he alternated between watching me and the view. Nothing was said for a long time, then he looked to the west.

80

It was time to go. Another storm was on its way. He must have smelled the rain on the wind. The walrus, too, because he'd gone, as well. I didn't feel a lot as we paddled away. No sadness, no loneliness, not even an ache of loss, but I did wonder how long she'd stay like that, frozen in ice, nose trapped on a submerged ledge. God knows how far down she'd go when the ice finally cracked.

Asuluk stopped paddling barely halfway home. He reached for his bow. I looked around, couldn't see a thing apart from that hellish storm rolling in.

It was over so quickly, I barely heard or saw a thing. Just a whack and a gull of some kind hit the water to my left and floated there belly-up; the medicine man's arrow had stopped it midflight. Asuluk paddled over, reached down, grabbed the arrow, and threw the gull at me.

It seemed I came in useful for something. I pulled the arrow out, dipped it into the sea until it was clean, and replaced it in his quiver.

Asuluk talked to himself the rest of the way. He was probably thanking his God or the bird for the timely sacrifice. He'd let the walrus live, had shot the bird I hadn't even seen. Perhaps he felt like a change of diet. I looked at the bird, and instead of feeling sorry for it, I wondered if it'd taste like chicken. Chances of roasting it over an open fire were slim to none. He'd probably eat it raw like everything was eaten. Raw.

We were met by a swarm of excited kids, kids of all ages from about ten to three. They helped us off-load the curious catch of the day, the tools, the wire, the radio. To keep them away from the drivers and screws, I set the Morse down, and the clicking noises it made kept them entertained for a little while.

A little girl came late, running to Asuluk. She used the word I've come to learn means "grandfather." And I could tell she was a favorite, too. She was given the bird and ran off to the village, the dead bird pressed against her mouth. I still can't come to terms with the way these folks can drink blood like that.

Seven kids followed me home. I think Asuluk told them each

to carry something for me. No one left once we arrived. They were all quiet, too quiet, but I guess they hadn't seen me this close up before, either. I invited them inside and I sat on the floor of my house with a semicircle of kids, all staring at me. We looked at each other for a long time, then the girl skidded in, late again. She had a white feather stuck to her face. I reached out and she didn't pull away.

"Feather," I said, holding it up. She tried to repeat the word, eventually did, and I winked at her. She tried to wink back. I was hit with the idea of teaching the kids English, when the eldest, a boy about ten or so, reached out and touched my beard. He touched his own face, then my hair. He had a close look at my eyes.

"Blue," I said. "I have blue eyes; you have brown."

"Blue . . . brown . . ." a few voices tried.

Then came the assault. Small fingers unfastened my parka; little eyes doubled in size at the sight of chest hair. The girl I call Feather broke the line and sat beside me, leaned in very close. She was trying to get a better look at my tooth, the one I'd had capped with gold at age twenty-one.

Having all these kids so close, so curious, so friendly . . .

Well, I think we covered nearly every part of the human body visible, little voices repeating my words, me trying to repeat their words.

Then someone called me Floreeda.

"No. John," I said. "My name is John."

The kids call me John now. To everyone else, I'm still Floreeda. If I'm real lucky, it's Floreeda John.

I can't win.

The kids stayed with me till Asuluk arrived and sent them away. I carried on with what I was doing, plaiting wire into a long handle for Kioki's sled. She'd be able to pull it one-handed and wouldn't have to worry about her rope breaking all the time. I was using my right hand, along with the toes on my left foot, and Asuluk watched me for a long time.

He wanted to talk but, like me, was growing tired of all the

82

charades. I thanked him for taking me out that day anyway, and I think he understood me. He nodded. Then he withdrew the revolver and I searched my pockets for the bullets to give him. He shook his head, offered the gun back to me.

"No, Asuluk. No. It's yours. Yours."

He wanted to give me something for it, but I said no. It was my turn to give something back. He'd have far more use for the gun than I would.

"Come," he said.

"What, now?"

"Come!" he repeated. There was no arguing with that tone. I hurriedly finished what I was doing and followed him out. I decided I could test-run the new handle on the sled while I was at it. Kids came from nowhere, jumped on for a ride.

If I'd thought to, or had been able, I could have made a cart for them from the airplane's wheels, perished rubber tires.

While I was watching two boys drag an assortment of kids around the village, deep in thought about what else I could do, I realized that Asuluk had disappeared. He was probably waiting around a corner for me, getting more impatient by the minute. I was just about to call his name when someone touched my shoulder.

Kioki.

"Show me," she said slowly, almost clearly.

I couldn't believe it. She'd said two words, two words of too many I'd tried to teach her.

"Show you?" I asked.

"Show me. Me." She touched her chest. "Me." She touched me. "You, show me."

What, did she think I was stupid?

Asuluk called out, a disembodied voice. His daughter answered. Whatever he wanted from me could wait. I whistled to the kids and they brought the sled back. She looked at the plaited wire, and at me.

She smiled, nodded, and turned away. She headed for our house.

And I knew what would happen when she saw the state of the place, too.

"I know the place is a mess. I'm sorry."

She grunted at me, started to tidy up.

"No, I'll do it."

She ignored me. She was as house-proud as my own mother. Everything had its place. She was a lot like my mother, Lily. Or maybe I was trying hard to find similarities. I know I was trying hard to find excuses.

"Kioki, I'll do it. It's my mess."

Still she ignored me.

I touched her shoulder and fear lighted her eyes. I let go quickly. Great, now she was scared of me. I'd never be able to touch her again. "You sit down. Sit." I took her hand and sat her down. I kicked my bits and pieces of leather and plaited wire and the hammer, the pliers, cutters, pushed them all into one heap. Then I took a little square of sealskin she used as a mat and I covered it all. I looked at her, grinned, and said, "All done."

She grunted, rose to her feet with the grace of a three-legged elephant, and told me to sit. She fed me first, and I didn't worry about the taste of the fish. What I'd been force-feeding myself just didn't have the same taste as it had when Kioki put it in my bowl. I watched her wrap all my bits and pieces, tie it with thin rope, and put it neatly into a corner. Then she was satisfied. Then she ate. It was so quiet, for a long time we were like strangers.

I asked how she was. She looked at me and said, "Good."

We were like strangers until I reached for her hand and looked her in the eye and told her I was sorry for what I'd done.

She squeezed my hand, smiled a little, and lay down to rest.

I watched her for a long time, wondering how far pregnant she was, whether it was mine. Stupid thought. It had to be mine. And just as I was getting ready to bed myself on the floor, she turned, patted the skins beside her, and faced the wall again.

It seemed I'd been forgiven. The hardest part was forgiving

84

myself. I didn't realize how much I'd missed her until I climbed up beside her, put my arm around her, and held her close. This time, I wasn't thinking of Sally.

I told Kioki I loved her, but I guess she didn't know yet what it meant.

She didn't sleep well, nor did I. She talked a lot, woke herself too many times with a choked scream. And I wondered again just how much damage I'd done. The outer bruises were faded, but the scars I'd left on the inside, the scars on her mind, I wondered if they would ever heal. All I could do was say, "It's okay; it's okay," and make vague promises that it would never happen again. All I could do was hold her like my mother used to hold me—tightly.

I think I even sang to her, a sweet little French lullaby, even though I couldn't sing that well. Maybe it was my heartbeat she needed to hear.

All I know was that she needed to be held.

It was my time to give a little. And I decided then that I'd beat this. I'd beat this dark, searing anger even if it killed me. I'd learn to recognize its presence before it came, before it enveloped me totally. I'd take myself outside, away, far away, because out there, there were only the island, the seals, the occasional walrus, and the birds in summer.

I couldn't hurt anyone if I did that.

SIX

●━●━●━●━●━●━●

T IME, as I once knew it, ceases to be. These people live by sunup and sundown and by the seasons, not by my weeks, days, hours. I never knew till now how much time ruled my life.

I used to be a timetable man. My mother's life ran on time, and Meg and I were dragged along for the ride, willing or not.

"It's time to get out of bed."

"It's time to get off to school now, and don't you be late getting home."

"It's time you went off to work now."

The only time I liked was five after four. My job with Billy Taylor was like my father's rocking chair in a lot of ways—it had always been there, even when he relocated to Davis Field. It just meant that I had an extra walk, was all. And come the fall, Billy would do a lot of joyrides from the fairgrounds. In those days, all I ever did was a lot of running. He seemed to take a number of ladies up there in the air, which sorely pissed off a lot of the other aviators at the time.

I took for granted that my job would never disappear. He taught me to fly. Taught me a hell of a lot. He was always there, and I never believed there'd be a time when he wouldn't be. A week after I got my license, Billy Taylor went off to Europe. Bobby and I kept the company alive while he was gone.

Most folks said he'd never come back. I knew better.

I'd been flying solo since I was sixteen, and the air held a special magic for me, an obsession. Nothing else mattered until my feet were on the ground once more. If something was wrong, I'd escape to the sky. Nothing followed me, nagged me at twelve hundred feet. I was flying deliveries for Taylor's Air from the time I was seventeen—mainly the runs to Alabama, Kentucky, or Florida. Sometimes Georgia. Bobby took that run mostly, and I didn't know till I was eighteen just why he was always itching to take off.

Bess was the reason. She lived in Atlanta.

Bobby was flying a year before I was—he was a year older, twenty years wiser.

Lots of folks thought we were brothers. Damned if I knew how they came to that conclusion. We were as opposite as any two people could ever be.

From the time she was thirteen, my sister, when she was upset over something, would tell me she'd swap me for Bobby any day. But it wasn't a brother she wanted out of Bobby. I guess he knew that from the start, too.

I'd taken Meg for granted all my life, too—until noon on my twentieth birthday, when I finally put down at Tampa.

Bobby was waiting for me. He had the jiggles bad, which meant he had words to say but didn't know how they'd come out. It was a small mystery that he knew where I'd be. At the time, I didn't realize just how many folks had been involved in tracking me down that day. I was supposed to pick up boxes of gator skins and have them in Orlando by nightfall. I was already running late. Seeing Bobby wasn't so good. We were never together for less than three hours at a time, and to us three hours was a quick howdy.

I didn't even have time to say hi. I was climbing down and about to stretch my legs when I heard, "You've got to get home, John."

Everything inside me froze. You know what it's like, how it feels when you hear words you've been expecting for too long. It still comes as a shock.

I knew it was my mother. Lily. My heart hit my boots and stayed there way too long.

Things about her I didn't want to acknowledge, so I pretended I was blind, deaf, and dumb, and nothing could follow me in the sky. She was getting thinner than a walking stick every day. I knew it was that damned cough. One of her brothers had died of tuberculosis. The few times she'd seen the doctor, he'd given her some thick red potion; all it did was make her cough and puke more.

"It's my mother, Jesus, no—" I said, voice shaking.

"No, buddy. It's Meg."

Meg? Meg was dead?

"What?" My voice was a squeak.

Bobby didn't want to say any more but knew he'd better. He knew how long it took to fly home. He knew what a worrier I was over the least thing. "It's polio, buddy."

"Polio? What the hell's that?"

"Look, your mother wants you home. Now."

But I had this delivery to make. . . . Bobby read my mind. "I'll do your run. Just get your ass home." He put a hand on my shoulder and turned me toward his airplane. He'd flown in to meet me here. My mother must have called him in desperation.

I must have trusted Bobby more than I thought. I never let a soul touch my plane. "I gotta, I gotta . . ." My brain was running in circles as I made it to the bathroom, Bobby two steps behind me. "What is it, this polio? What is it?"

"Some kind of bug. Some folks get it, some don't."

"But it's serious, right? If it wasn't—"

"It's serious." Bobby scratched his head. "It cripples some people."

My brain stopped on that word. Cripple? *Meg?* No. Can't be. All she ever wanted was to be a ballerina. She was damned good, too.

Meg. Something shook loose inside me.

One of my first memories was of my daddy lifting me onto his shoulders, letting me look through glass at all these babies in a neat row while a nurse pushed a wire-crate contraption closer to the window. My father told me this was my new sister. I didn't care a hoot about any new sister; all I wanted was my mama back.

This new sister looked as ugly as an old man ready to die. She had peeling skin, a red face. She was screaming. She looked like a skinned rabbit. And I looked at my daddy. He must have thought she was beautiful. Whatever I saw in his eyes that day, I know I never saw again. It flickered once, then disappeared forever.

Next time I saw Meg—I called her Magget, the most I could do with Margaret—she was in my cot, next to my mother's bed.

It was my cot. That was my bed, not hers. Now I had to sleep alone in the dark room out by the porch. Everything changed when she moved in.

I didn't want to touch it, hold it, be nice to it. All it did was scream and suck its hand. Mom spent a lot of time alone in her room with it and I wasn't allowed anywhere near my own mother when that door was closed. When my daddy came home from the gin, it was better. I'd follow him everywhere. I tried hard to ignore this new sister.

It was hard to do. Before I knew it, she was smiling at me a lot. No matter what I did when Mom wasn't looking, she'd still smile at me. She was stupid, but I started to like her. I didn't want to; it just happened. When she started eating by herself, Mom had more time for me, but by then this baby used to crawl after me, everywhere I went, like a dog. Sometimes she smelled worse than a dog.

Now and then, I'd carry her, specially if she got caught at the gate. She'd get to her feet and rattle the fence and scream, like she wanted to come feed the chickens, too. I figured I'd wait till she was old enough to hold the bucket; then she could do all my chores and I could watch.

It never worked that way.

Meg. A little like Dad's rocking chair, too. She was always there. When she was two, Mom would say, "Watch, John Robert. She's trying to dance."

Then it became, "She's such a wonderful dancer."

I wasn't wonderful at anything.

When she was seven, she was given an old ballet tutu for her birthday. After that, the porch was always shiny. Five steps across, turn on her toes, five steps back.

She nearly killed me the day I put tacks in the floorboards. I never knew how fast she could run. She tackled me. I never should have taught her how to tackle. And Mom watched while she beat me up. It didn't hurt. I was laughing so hard, I thought I'd die. The harder I laughed, the harder she punched, kicked, and bit.

Meg never had much to say to anyone about anything. But once she started, she used hundred-dollar words and got at me that way because she knew mine never stretched above fifty cents—total.

I remember looking at Bobby, standing there beside me in that Tampa outhouse. He wanted me to say something, anything. But I couldn't. Everything was blurred; my hands were shaking.

"This can't be happening," I said. "She was fine last time I saw her."

Bobby looked at me—half a squint, one eyebrow raised. The bastard could always see right through me.

Okay, she'd been tired for a long time, but it was school. She was almost eighteen, falling asleep over her books at night. I'd come in around midnight, see the light from under her door. It was habit now to say, "Meg. Hey. Sleep in bed."

And I'd steer her toward her bed. When was it she lay down, said she was sore all over? I told her it was probably a cold, threw the covers over her. She'd yelped; I'd hurt her legs.

I took no notice.

My sister and Mary Jo Batten, her dance partner and best friend, had been straining too many muscles again.

A fair-enough assumption.

Dancing was her life. If she couldn't be a dancer, she'd be a lawyer. A dancing lawyer, she'd say, those green eyes sparkling. She had more brains than I did. Hell, anyone could see that. I was the one who had to leave school, get a job, support the family. I didn't mind. School never did anything for me. Taught me a lot of rubbish that wasn't fit for the real world. I got Daddy's looks; she got his brains. Brains he never used much; otherwise, he wouldn't have tried to stop two Negroes from killing each other down by the mill. If he'd had any brains, he'd be boss of that mill by now. Instead, he lost his job because he tried to stop two blacks from killing each other. Got another job working on the railroad in Alabama, tried to be a hero, and died.

"You okay?" Bobby asked.

"I can't go home. I can't face her, Bob. I can't."

"You have to."

End of story. You have to. I knew it; he knew it. My mother was alone; I didn't know how she'd cope with this. Her children were her life. She'd take on a mountain lion bare-handed if she thought one of us would be hurt by it.

"I talked to Doc Brown. He said there're three kinds of polio. Maybe she's got the mild one. Maybe it's not so bad."

I looked at him. My family never did anything by half measures. "What else did he say?"

"Jesus, John. Would you just go home."

I must have had a terrified look on my face, because he said, "I'll be there tonight, okay? I'll get there somehow."

Knowing he'd be there made it a little easier. But maybe facing a firing squad without a blindfold would have been easier, too.

Meg would like to see him, I knew that. He was her first love. She was nearly thirteen when I first brought Bobby home. I thought nothing of it; he needed a place to sleep. His boss and mine had a few business arrangements from the time I went with Billy on that one-way train ride to Florida.

Mom was in a panic because of the unexpected visitor. It was half past eight when we walked in. "Mind if Bobby stays the night?"

Meg, in her nightgown, was sitting at the kitchen table, cutting up a ballet program someone had given her—all she ever wanted to do was dance at the Opera House in town.

She turned to Bobby; her eyes went wide, like they did when she saw a spider on her wall. Her face went redder than overripe strawberries and she dived under the table.

Bobby was sixteen but looked twenty. He was six feet tall already; he had short dark hair, looks that I noticed girls wanted to see again and again. He sat down and talked only when he was spoken to, which, with my mother, meant he spoke more in half an hour than I'd heard him talk in the time I'd known him.

I didn't say anything about my sister hiding under the table, and neither did Bobby. She was always doing weird things. He was talking to Mom about Hialeah, where he lived, how his Pa wrestled gators for a living. He lied so well, everyone believed him, even me at the start.

And Meg, under the table, had nowhere to go. She stabbed me with her scissors. I gave her a kick and pretended I'd dropped a spoon. She handed me a note. All I saw were Bobby's jiggling legs and her terrified eyes. The note read: "Get my dressing gown."

I smiled at her and stayed where I was.

Then as Mom put the pancakes on the table and took out the jar of syrup kept for special occasions, she said, "Meg, get out from under the table. We have a guest."

Meg stabbed my leg again. She shot out from under the table and took the hall at takeoff speed, and her door slammed until further notice.

Bobby hid his grin all night long.

I showed him the way to the outhouse at midnight and Mom stood beside me by the back door and said, "What a nice young man."

She had stars in her eyes, too.

It wasn't the first time I'd wished I could have some of whatever it was he had.

Bobby slept on the floor in my room, on an old mattress kept under my bed. Last time anyone had slept on that was the night Bawler Johnson stayed, two years before. He pissed the bed. I didn't tell Bobby that. I was nearly asleep when he said, "You've got a nice family." As if I'd been lying. And he meant it, too. I didn't know his father then. I thought he was luckier because he had one.

Meg was up early the next morning, and so was Bobby. I woke to the voices from the porch.

"John tells me you like to dance."

Ah, dance. She won't stop talking now. But she said nothing, and I imagined her face the color of overripe strawberries again. "Have you got any sisters?" she asked, finally, in a shy voice I'd never heard before.

"No."

Maybe he was just trying to know my kid sister, and when she went off to make him breakfast, I knew she was in love. She'd always just say to me, "Get it yourself. I'm busy." And I lay there thinking that if he touched my sister, I'd murder him. I wasn't stupid. I'd seen the way boys kept looking at Meg. I knew what was on their minds, too. I had a mind just the same. But she was my sister. It was different.

When he asked me later how old she was, we were walking through the field toward Taylor's Air. It had long ago replaced the sign FLYING SCHOOL. I told him to keep his hands off—no Cubans allowed in Shaw blood.

He laughed at me. He thought I was joking. He didn't laugh when I said, "She's thirteen." Was it my fault she looked older?

So much ran through my mind while I flew Bobby's plane home—home to Davis Field, where my Harley was waiting for me.

It was nearly eleven when I got to the hospital and they let me in. The place was new—old but new. It used to be a school for black girls till the county bought it. I'd been to school with the nurse who was washing the floor when I got there. I told her someone else would probably arrive about midnight or one.

It must have been the polio ward she led me to.

I don't like hospitals, I never have. I can almost feel everyone's sickness, pain. I broke out into a cold sweat; my belly was turning circles. I didn't know what Meg would look like, or even where she was in this room full of agony.

Then I saw the silhouette of my mother in the semidarkness. This thin woman who looked so old, so old and tired, was sitting by her daughter's bed, stroking a hand, a forehead in turn.

And my feet were stuck to the polished floor. So much for courage. But she turned her head; she always knew when I was there. I looked at her; I looked at my sister. She was asleep. She looked more than sick. She looked as if she was dying.

I turned and ran. I didn't know I was running. My mother, so sick herself, tried to run after me. I didn't stop till I was breathing in Abbeville night air, not hospital stink, sickness, pain. Sickness and pain had no right to smell like antiseptic bottles.

Even when she called me, her voice sounded tired. "John Robert! Where were you going?"

"That's not my sister in there. That's not my sister...."

"John Robert, please—"

"My name is John, and that is not my sister!"

I was staring down at a stranger, a stranger I'd known all my life. I don't know what else I said, or whether I even let thoughts turn to words. Everything that had ever gone wrong had accumulated in a thundercloud around me, and I hit my mother with the lightning.

I think I blamed her for not seeing that Meg was sick. Thought that she could have stopped it or gotten help sooner. What sort of mother was she?

Didn't she know I was twenty years old, not some child anymore? If she couldn't say the name John anymore, maybe it was time to face it that he was dead—yes, my daddy was dead and I was me. I was not him. Never had been, never would be. I had been feeding the family for over ten years, not him. I fed and clothed them. I had paid to put my sister through school and now college so she could waste it all by marrying the first pretty, rich boy who chanced by. So much for buying my own airplane now; it'd all go on medical bills. Who was paying for all this, anyway?

I probably would have said a lot more, too. I would have if she hadn't hit me. She hadn't hit me since I'd tried to light that fire under the house when I was ten. But that night, she did. And for years, I carried the sting like something nasty and ugly wrapped in a handkerchief. So nasty and ugly that even a hole in the ground would spit it back outright.

I couldn't tell her how I felt, so I gave her the anger instead. I couldn't say I loved Meg, or that I'd care about her, for her, till the day I died.

There was nothing but futile, helpless anger. Then she hit me. And all was silent. We both stared at each other. She couldn't believe she'd hit me, this six foot four son of hers; and I couldn't believe I had said what I had.

When she said four words—"You're not my son"—something broke inside me.

The day my sister got polio was the day I learned what an apology was. I tried to hold my mother. She pushed me away. I thought I was tired till I looked down into her eyes.

She saw me cry. For a little while, she let me cry. Then I said I was sorry. It was the only word I could think of, but it wasn't enough. It didn't feel enough, nor did it sound right.

She was about thirty-eight back then. Thirty-eight, and she looked fifty.

I used to be so proud of my pretty, courageous widow of a mother that I'd willingly fight to the death anyone who said different. There was always whispered talk about the widow Shaw—talk from little minds, from people who preyed on anyone else's hardship, pain, misfortune. Most of the talk was about men coming in and out of our house at all hours.

While my mother sat alone in the dark.

Always alone.

The only man I'd ever seen her look at in an odd way was Billy Taylor. She tried to smile the day I told her how he'd written me that he planned on marrying himself a rich English widow. She went into her room and spent hours in there. I guess she was crying.

Now she thought that the other man she loved, her son, had abandoned her, too.

I told her I loved her. I told her I'd do all I could to help, even if there was nothing I could do but use what money I'd put aside for my own airplane. It didn't matter that this would put me three years behind schedule; I'd do what I could, regardless.

Money or the lack of it was not on her mind.

"Sit with her, John."

She called me John.

"She needs you. So do I." And then she leaned against me, as if she was trying too hard to get me to share what she thought I had too much of—strength. Because she'd used up all of hers.

I took her home; maybe she didn't realize she was on the back of that motorcycle she hated. She was always saying that if I didn't die in an airplane, I'd die because of that motorcycle.

I put her to bed. Then I went back to the hospital and sat with my sister and held her hand until she finally woke just before dawn.

She was surprised to see me, I think. It took all she had to say, "You're supposed to be in Florida."

"Yes, I know."

She was upset that Mom had sent for me. She was ashamed, embarrassed, Something. We looked at each other a long time—me sitting there nervous, not knowing what to say, what to do.

"Why me?" she asked finally.

"I don't know. I've been asking that for a full day."

She held my hand tightly and looked into my eyes and said, "Dr. Davis says I'll never dance now."

I looked at the ceiling. I was starting to choke. There was no way in hell I would let my kid sister see me cry. I knew how she felt. I knew how I'd feel if someone said, "You will never fly again." It was like watching her entire life go down the drain and knowing she couldn't get it back, ever. Everything was slipping away.

"Can't move my legs. I can't feel anything from my waist down."

I noticed that the ceiling was ornate. I could see things there that only hospital patients ever saw, hospital patients and maybe some bored black girl a long time gone.

"I didn't want you to know."

"Why?" I asked.

"You have enough to worry about."

As if she wasn't important.

Then we both heard it: Bobby's voice, arguing with one of the nurses. Maybe it was the matron he was arguing with.

"I may as well be a relation, lady!"

"I can't see him. He can't see me like this. He can't."

"Are you going to stop him?" I asked, trying to make a joke. I squeezed her hand and could feel her eyes on me as I walked to the door to meet him. A lot of people were watching.

Bobby came in and the nurse at the table at the end of the ward stared at him the entire time. He leaned against the end of my sister's bed and said, "What have you done to yourself this time?"

He was the one she went to for a bandage on a knee, to pry out a splinter, to fix broken hearts, to ask questions about boys. And they'd go off together for hours on end and all they'd do was talk. I think he might have kissed her once, and it might have been during one of her "I'm so ugly, I hate myself" times, which came with annoying regularity. All I ever did was agree that yes, she was ugly, and yes, she sure should hate herself.

"Come on. What have you done this time?"

She was fine until he sat on the edge of her bed, took both her hands in one of his. Then she cried—finally.

And there they were, my best friend and my only sister, and I was watching her cry.

As far as I was aware, Meg never cried. I could have talked all day and half the next night, giving her hope that maybe she did have a future after all, that there had to be more to life than just dancing.

She'd only have agreed with my lies, these half-truths I could have sprouted. Between us, we could have made a list, a rewrite of those unwritten goals, ambitions, that list that's born with each of us and dies untouched with most of us. I'm glad we never had to make that list. I couldn't think of anything, anything, that a crippled girl could have done in 1922.

She couldn't even go to college. Colleges were designed for complete people, not cripples.

She couldn't even write books. Meg had too much intelligence, not enough imagination. She couldn't see or feel those things that I could. She couldn't pinpoint the cause of sadness behind someone's eyes. She hardly even recognized sadness, except her own. She never saw elephants or dragons in the clouds and she'd look at me as if I were nuts if I said, "Hey, look! There's a witch's face, a horse, a chariot, a great fat bulldog, and now it's a . . ."

Sometimes I find it hard getting all this down on paper. Nothing fits sometimes. What I'm feeling when put into words sounds too barren, too stale, too empty. Something's missing. It's not what I am, what I used to be, but it's the closest I can get to what's happening inside me.

What I was no longer matters. Back in the real world, it was what you did that mattered, how you looked, too, sometimes. Here, what matters is who you are, how you fit, what you are able and willing to do.

I'm willing, but with one right hand near useless since the time I was a kid falling off a fence post, a left hand lying out there somewhere on that ice, a twice-broken leg that hasn't mended, and a brain that snaps when I least expect it to, there's not a lot I can do, willing or able.

I can't even sharpen what's left of my pencils. What I'd do to have some ink.

My father had a quill pen he kept in his drawer, a bottle of ink. The quill pen belonged to his grandfather and was over a century old. It came from England. The feather was hardly ruffled. I was never allowed to touch it. I'd sit across from him at the table, watch him write. He'd let me watch, providing I was quiet. He used to write poetry, read it out to my mother. She said he was good. To me they were fancy, pretty words that made no sense unless it was a funny rhyme about Meg and me.

I wish I could remember the poem he wrote about the snake in the outhouse. That was my favorite. I used to know it by heart. It meant more to me than six times table. Still would, I guess, if I could remember either of them.

I guess that quill pen would have been mine one day. It was meant to follow the eldest sons of the Shaws. The house, too. It was on old place, old for as long as I can remember. Like the willows by the lake, the oaks in the woods that I'd explore, but I wouldn't be me when I did. I'd be leading my own army.

There were six of us. I'd be a reb colonel each time, and the Yankees never damn well won, either. Then fat Henry "Bawler" Johnson would start crying that we were lost. Or if the sun got below three o'clock, he'd start bawling for his mama. The boy had no sense of adventure. Funny how it's only Bawler I can re- call. He smelled funny. He had big ears, little eyes, and a fat belly, so fat that his pants never stayed up very long. He'd try to run. He'd try hard. . . . Hell, he's probably got another hardware store by now.

I wanted to be a soldier before I discovered the magic of the airplane. I was too young to go off to war, but Billy Taylor's brother wasn't. He'd joined the RFC over in England and Billy met up with him after the war. He never said much about it, just that something was missing from his brother's eyes—something important.

For a man who said he'd been married, Billy was awful shy around the ladies—especially my mother. He was back in the district the time Meg got sick. Only for a while—he was tying up loose ends before he went back to England to marry his new lady.

But I know he liked my mother—a lot. I know he sat with her till three in the morning the night of the day after Ed Maginley hit that pole. And I know he drove her to the hospital each day to see Meg, but he wouldn't go in. He'd sit outside for hours or however long it took my mother to finish. And he offered to buy Meg the wheelchair, but my mother refused, so he helped in another way. He sold his business to Bobby and me and he went back to England and the lady he'd met over there.

I remember going up to New York, watching the ship leave. I stood on the docks with hundreds of people, most of us pretending to be happy because someone we loved was leaving. And I walked away, wondering how that big hole inside me would get filled. His last words to me were, "Remember, Johnny . . . You can always replace a piece of machinery. You can't buy someone back from the dead. I know."

He shook my hand, hugged me, and nearly ran up the gangplank. I lost him in the crowd but waited until all those passengers were pinpoints before I walked away.

Billy had told me my mother needed a friend. In case I got the wrong idea, that's all he was to her. He didn't know I would have appreciated the wrong idea. Of all the things I should have said to that man, that was first on my list.

I never told anyone I cared about just how much they meant to me.

I took it for granted that they already knew.

SEVEN

●━●━●━●━●━●━●

I guess Thanksgiving has come and gone by now, maybe
even Christmas, too.

That time of year used to be important—opening gifts, eating
too much, my mother spending hours cooking for three, when a
passerby would have thought she was feeding Fort Bragg.
Christmastime held too many memories for her. It was around
Christmas when she first met my father and it was on a Christmas Eve when they got married.

The last few Christmases are only memories for me, but I
guess that's all the past is to anyone, a memory. I used to kid
myself by saying it was just another day. Back then, I never
thought I'd be without them—my family—at Christmas. Too
ridiculous to even consider.

For four years in a row, Bobby showed up on our doorstep
fully armed with gifts. Talcum powder for Lily, lace handker-
chiefs, a silver-backed hairbrush. Talcum powder for Meg, too.
Lace hankies. A Rudyard Kipling book she'd loved and lost.
Christmas 1923, he gave her a Walt Whitman poetry book,
Leaves of Grass. I wonder now if she still has that book, if she still
treasures it like she used to. Because a week later, Bobby was
dead.

It must be inbred in women, this knowing they all seem to
have. My mother didn't want him to leave. According to Bobby,
two more days of leftover Christmas dinner and he'd never get

his machine off the ground. And Meg just sat on the porch in her chair, hugging that book tightly, no doubt wishing it was him instead as she watched us ride away for Davis Field. Maybe she knew she'd never see him again. Maybe that was why she gave him piercing, long looks.

Looking back now, it seems to me that she was getting together her memories.

I'm trying not to look back, but the past, what used to be, is a magnet to me. Thinking if only I could do it all again is as futile as jumping a passing train.

So I guess I'll concentrate on today for a change. Because that's all there is.

There's a blizzard again, a howling northerly. Rain falling horizontally has to be seen to be believed. The winds are strong enough to put a three-hundred-pound man square on his butt and skidding backward or forward, whichever way he's pointing. It has a mind, will, and force of its own, this wind.

It rains here every two or three days, although sensing time is nigh impossible. The sun is ever-present in summer, and winter, which it is now, is ever-present night. It's a place of extremes, very little variation in weather, temperature. All I know for sure, if it's light, it must be summer.

And the people don't change much, either. They haven't for centuries. About the only gadget I've seen so far is Asuluk's spyglass. I still firmly believe that a Russian ship went down in the vicinity and the natives made use of whatever they could salvage, like they did with my plane.

But for now, there's nothing else to do except write this by the very dim light of the oil burner. Kioki is sleeping. For all I know, it could be 7:00 A.M. or midnight. The howling wind hasn't let up. It's so strong at times, I can feel its force vibrating right into the ground.

That's where we are now, living almost underground on the winter side of the island. The thirty-foot cliff's a stone's throw out of my door. Apart from the wind, it's quiet in here. Warm, too, I guess, though my senses about warm and cold have taken a new perspective. I reckon that if my teeth aren't chattering and I can still feel my nose and toes, it's not too cold.

Kioki told me a story today in her halting English. I'm getting better at anticipating what she's going to say. Sometimes I let her struggle, if only to watch her exasperation, her impatience. Mostly I help her out.

Our conversations would confuse anyone within earshot. She uses some of my English words and I use some of her Eskimo words. We were lying together under the skins and her head was on my shoulder and she was telling me one of her father's incredibly long stories, luckily without his antics. I've often secretly wondered if the medicine man could utter a word if I tied his hands behind his back.

Anyway, the story she told me filled some of the darkness. It was about the near death of the entire village some twenty-five years ago. The time's a guess of course—she was about five years old. The Bering had frozen over too early and the warmer waters of the Pacific had been cursed. There'd been no spawning; therefore, there were no seals or walrus and barely even a bird in the sky that autumn. Twelve of the village men were killed in a storm so hellish that "even the island shook in fear." I thought, Earthquake, and in my mind I saw high tides, king tides, maybe even a tidal wave.

With most of the men dead, the village hardly stood a chance of survival. Twenty more starved to death. She and her sister and two brothers were the only children left, and this was because Asuluk had seen it coming. And I guess, just like Noah, no one listened. He took his family to higher ground on a part of the island I haven't seen yet, and when the storm was finally over and the quake and aftershocks had subsided, survivors from other islands began the long, slow limp to Kulowyl.

And that was how this community was born—a gaggle of survivors and a new mix of fresh blood.

Asuluk has been called "the wise one" ever since, and she is proud to call him Father.

I could tell by the way she talked that she remembered some

of it, and I guess it was the howling wind that brought it all back, so maybe that's why she flinches so much when the wind is strong and unrelenting. Talking about it was painful but necessary. I think she needed me to understand, and to a degree I did. She faded off into sleep a little while later and I tried to imagine how I'd have felt if I'd been her. I tried, but imagination is nothing compared to experience.

Now if a gypsy had told me two years ago that I'd be here, I wouldn't have believed it. It wasn't part of the plan I had carefully laid out for my life. Most of it was filled with flying, and I never stopped to consider what I would do if I couldn't fly, ever. Because upsets to plans happened to other people, never to me or mine. But when I lie here and feel her hot breath on my neck and the occasional kicks from the baby ripening inside her, I wonder about plans, dreams, goals, ambitions. I think about how I always lived for tomorrow and never stopped long enough to savor what today tasted like. I know now that was my biggest mistake. I lived thinking it would never happen to me—my plans would all go perfectly, always.

When she's beside me in the winter's darkness, I should only think of now. Now is all there's ever going to be.

If I'd followed my plan and seen it through, I would have been too busy to enjoy what I had, when I had it. Bobby said it wasn't supposed to happen this way, but happen it has.

Lord, it sure feels like Christmas.

I know what kind of present I'm going to get this year and I don't care if it's a boy or a girl. I know nothing about being a father, but I guess no one does till it happens. All parents are learners at the start, and as with learners everywhere, there's always someone experienced who'll lend a hand before too much damage is done.

I've only held one baby in my life. I was eight years old and it was my cousin Brewster's baby half brother. Brewster and I used to play war games in the woods a lot. His father was my father's older brother. It was the first time since Dad's funeral that they came visiting—first and last. All I remember is meeting this new aunt, Lorena, for the first time. My original aunt had died. Well, she made me hold the baby and she took a photograph of the entire family. Brewster's in that photo somewhere. We looked so alike that folks used to say we could have been twins. I never saw him after that day. Last I heard, he had a couple of kids, had married his college sweetheart, and was living in Virginia.

Now it's my turn to be a daddy.

If it's a boy, I'll call him William Robert and I'll teach him baseball. I could make a ball, I guess, from bits of soapstone, cover it in seal hide. I can go looking for driftwood when the melt begins. I'll use my Bowie knife to carve a bat.

I'll teach him how to hit home runs just like Babe Ruth.

Till then, I guess I'll just have to wait, mark time some more. Hope something will happen soon, before I go crazy from the boredom.

Well, I guess it serves me right. There I was, hoping for something to happen. I've been here a year and a half, rough guess, and I have two wives. Came as a hell of a shock.

Her name is Tooksooks or something similar, but Tooksooks is all I can get my tongue around, and I wish someone had let me know what was going on.

I don't mind everyone else here having more than one wife. Who am I to complain about the way they live? Hell, it's taken me long enough to get used to living with Kioki; now her sister has moved in and it looks like it's permanent.

I hoped for a while that she was only here to help Kioki when it came time to have the baby, because the poor girl's as big as a mountain and whenever I try to help her, I get in trouble. Maybe she is here to help. All I know, she's living with us.

Now that Tooksook's found a new home, there's hardly any room left for me. Her brother, who has an extended family of his own, helped her move in. There's no way I can even begin to pronounce, let alone write, his name, but as he's the one with one eye and the one who helped beat me up that time, I call him Sinbad for short.

He came in one day, off-loaded Tooksooks's things, gave me a big grin, and left.

The last thing on my mind was the first on Tooksooks's. God help me, she smells pretty bad. Maybe I'm used to Kioki and she's used to me, but if I had one wish right now, it wouldn't be for a rescue or a way out of here. No. It'd be for a tub of hot water and fifty bars of perfumed soap. The most these people wash are hands and faces, and it sure gets pretty hot under all the clothes. I know I must smell pretty foul, too, but till now I thought we all smelled the same. Oh boy, I couldn't have been more wrong.

Kioki knew I was embarrassed by this new situation and she tried to explain what was happening. I wasn't concentrating. It was hard to. Tooksooks had taken my boots off and was rubbing my feet. She'd look up and grin at me. I can't remember what Kioki said, except something about "My sister is yours now." Then she lay down in the new bed she'd made for herself. She rolled the other way, faced the wall, and wished me a bountiful dream. Well, I think it was dream.

The hands were working toward my knees when I told Tooksooks to stop. Without turning around, Kioki rattled off something and her sister put my boots back on and spent the next hour or so staring at me from a far corner. I was pleased when the light went out.

Someone in the next house was laughing and from farther on I could hear someone playing drums and pipe. Then I heard weeping. It wasn't Kioki. When my eyes adjusted to the dark, I saw Tooksooks still in the far corner, wrapped in skins, cold, her head on her knees. She was trying not to cry aloud, but the more she tried to stop, the louder it got.

As I don't like being around anyone who's crying, I did what anyone would have. I got up, went to her, and sat beside her and asked as best I could why she was crying. Whatever I said made her cry harder. I wish their language was as simple as mine. I probably told her I hated her because she was as ugly as a walrus.

But when I said, "Come on, Tooksooks, don't sleep here," Kioki said something that must have translated it. I looked at her; she was watching. I helped Tooksooks up and I let her sleep against the wall beside me.

The weeping stopped, but damned if I could sleep. I felt her roll in close and curl behind me. Then the arm snaked over my side and rough, warm fingers found their way under my coat.

And worse, it felt really good.

It had been a long time since I'd felt like this, but it felt wrong with Kioki in the same room, too. To these people, it was right; to me, not so comfortable. So I rolled to my back, and all intentions were to tell her to stop. Stop, and just go to sleep. Leave me alone. Kioki was my wife; she was just . . .

Well, funny things these intentions.

Tooksooks worked some magic on me. Not that it was hard to do. When it was over, I faded off into the best sleep I think I have had since coming here. She was singing very softly, humming, chanting. I didn't even dream. And when I woke, I was still holding her.

That's the story of how I got myself a second wife.

I can only hope that no other lady decides she'd like to be married to me. It seems I have no choice in the matter. Maybe I shouldn't smile at them so much. They all get the giggles when I do that, even the old ladies.

Kioki doesn't seem worried about any sudden infiltration of her territory. After all, they are sisters. She's not jealous. In a way, I think she's relieved that some of the burden has been delegated. But I watch her closely and now and then a smile from each of us will meet halfway across the room. It's then I know where most of my heart belongs.

*

Asuluk brought me a torn fishing net a couple of days ago. Maybe he knew how bored I was, or maybe he was assuring himself that no harm had come to either of his daughters. And maybe I'll never know what or how this man thinks. He smiles at me a lot more these days, and his smile was worthy of a photograph the morning I took the repaired net over to his house. I'd fixed it with my right hand, the toes on my right foot, and a little bit of ingenuity.

It turned out to be a half-decent day, although it's not quite daylight yet. The girls bundled me up in pants, parka, and waterproof boots. I think they were pleased to see the last of me for a while, because I don't have much patience when things aren't working my way, and I guess I must have called that net every name I could think of, plus a few that haven't been invented yet, too.

In the dim light, I walked in a mild head wind and through three feet of snow with Asuluk to the summer side of the island. The sea was frozen solid. Out there on the pack ice was a circle of men I knew, waiting around a hole for a seal to rise for air. Patience isn't a word here; it's a way of life. I guess that's the only thing these people can't teach me, patience.

For a while, I thought we'd join them, then the medicine man led me directly west. He was in no great hurry. Over his shoulder was the net I'd repaired. We finally came to an inlet, a tiny bay, and farther out more islands appeared in the distance through the fog. There was a patch of water about the size of a football field where the seas met and battled to stop freezing over. His kayak waited. I wasn't invited in this time. I watched as he paddled out into the rough water, staked the net into the ice on the edge of the tiny strait that separated Kulowyl from the next island, and paddled back, throwing the net out as he went.

Without a word, he handed me the heavy mallet. A few minutes later, the net was secured and we were homeward bound, Asuluk dragging his kayak behind him.

It was a milestone for me. I had finally contributed after all this time, and Asuluk knew it. He probably sent someone else out to check the net, bring home the catch, because he never took me out that way again. But it didn't matter.

Before we'd reached the village, Tooksooks was waiting for me.

Kioki had gone into labor. I was allowed to see her for a little while. Then I got kicked out.

How long I spent in the cold is anyone's guess. My watch broke in the crash, too.

Sinbad appeared on the cliff, acknowledged me with a look, then turned to the boys who were hauling his catch up the cliff face. He sat beside me, heard the screams from inside the house, and immediately knew what was going on. He called out to the ladies inside and one of his wives came out. I listened to the conversation, didn't understand it. She went back in and he took from around his neck an ivory necklace and put it on me. Then he patted my leg and went home.

I still don't know what it is or what it does or why he gave it to me. Did it mean we were brothers because now I was married to his two sisters, whether I wanted to be or not? For a while, I sat outside my own house wondering if I should give something in return, but all I have is Bobby's St. Christopher medal, and I can't, I just can't be parted from that. I figured that when I was allowed back inside, I'd give him a pair of pliers. I have two.

I tried very hard to take my mind away from the sound of my woman. I felt useless, helpless, as if what she was going through was all my fault. I guess it was, but as far as I'm concerned, Kioki getting pregnant is nothing short of an accidental miracle.

I know now that I could have gone to anyone's house and stayed in someone else's warmth for the duration. I would have been welcome, but no one offered and I didn't know I could have asked, so I sat there huddled outside my house, protected by skins and wishing to God it could soon be over.

It was exactly how I'd felt that time Bobby and I did that Kentucky run. Impatient fear is a hell of a feeling.

EIGHT

⬤━⬤━⬤━⬤━⬤━⬤━⬤

THERE was a time when I ignored real beauty, when I took what was around me, everywhere I looked, for granted, when I cursed the mountains, the forests, and a clean freshwater creek across the only place to put down. Give me a hot day and a clean freshwater creek now, I'd know exactly what to do.

I know I appreciated nothing back then. Now all I have is memory of forests, of creeks, memory of beautiful things I used to ignore. And I know my memories would be clearer, cleaner, better if only I'd taken a little more notice of everything around me. The *if onlys* hit me hard some days.

What year did I go to Kentucky with Bobby? Was it the summer of 1923, '22? It was one of the few times we flew together in the same airplane.

"No questions," he said that bright summer day. "Just come for the run." At the time, I thought it a better offer than sitting alone, twiddling my thumbs in the office, worrying about how we'd pay the bills, and hoping Rosanna wouldn't visit, because she only came during a lull and then she'd spend two hours nagging me about getting a real job. Sometimes I'd see her coming and I'd lock up and hide till she grew tired of knocking and peeking in windows.

The location was east Kentucky, on the border, closing in on the Appalachians. Bobby had been assured that a strip had been cleared and we'd be able to refuel.

I had a fair idea what the cargo would be, and sure it would be safer flying it out, but some of the tales I'd heard third and fourth hand about moonshiners had to have some basis in truth, in fact.

The feds were at war with bootleggers, and those folk who had the recipe, the ingredients, the equipment, and the contacts were making a lot of money. Or at least that was the word. I know the reality of assumptions now.

Why I was there for the ride is anyone's guess. One of those fool things you do without thinking, I suppose. Why Bobby was involved, I don't know. It wasn't solely for the three hundred dollars plus costs he'd make picking up, delivering. I think it was part adventure. He thrived on living that way—when he couldn't find adventure or excitement close by, he'd go in search of it. Then again, he had nothing, really, to lose, or if he had, he figured it was a risk he wanted to take. *To hell with the world.* He never grew tired of saying that, always with a huge grin that overtook his whole face.

Sullivan and Shaw wasn't doing so well. We needed money bad. Maybe that's why I went against the urge to stay the hell away. Bobby had that look in his eyes again. And three hundred plus in the bank account would pay more than a few overdue bills. I even thought I'd be able to get Meg a new chair.

I also thought I'd be flying around the States one day. At least I can admit that my mistakes are really good ones.

Now, Dwight—whether that was his name or not isn't important anymore, and I have to call him something—had in fact cleared fifty feet by two hundred yards on the flattest part of his land. We came in low, both of us spotting for the strip—if it could be called a strip. Bobby saw it first and pointed. I hardly ever cursed, but I did that day. I shook my head. I didn't want to die, not in Kentucky. . . .

We had to put down at a forty-five-degree angle. But Bobby, always the adventurer, licked his lips, said a quick Hail Mary or whatever it was he said, and we circled half a dozen times till he decided it was now or never.

Jesus Christ, I was shaking. And I don't know how he did it, but we came down intact. I needed to shake out my shorts. Then we saw the welcome party and I needed to shake out my shorts again.

We were met by the old man, Dwight, and a herd of teenage boys, most of them armed with shotguns. Bobby never had to say aloud what it was we were picking up. But I knew that if we were caught, we'd both be peering through bars the rest of our lives—providing we survived long enough to get out of here in the first place. Bobby loved this. He lapped at it like a hot, thirsty dog with a big bowl of cool water.

I knew from that maniac look in his eyes that things could only get worse.

Bobby had said to let him do the talking. Maybe he didn't like my honesty or the way I stuttered with lies. Whatever, I didn't argue the point. I wanted to be elsewhere.

I remember staying well in the background, watching these hill people, these boys, boys with large shotguns. Watching while four crates of bottled moonshine were loaded. Half an hour at the most, Bobby had said. We would go in, load, get out again.

Half an hour became one and a half days.

Someone had forgotten the gas.

We couldn't get out. Without the load, we barely had enough fuel to make it to Huntington on a no-power glide. It would take a vehicle half a day to get to town, and it was mid-afternoon already.

I knew things couldn't get any better, so I started praying they wouldn't get any worse.

Dwight had no lines on his face to give an indication of his age. His voice was high-pitched and drawling and half the time I didn't understand a word he said. But he and Bobby reached some kind of understanding.

I didn't trust any of them, nor did Bobby, but he was master at bullshit diplomacy. He could talk his way out of anything, maybe even a firing squad.

112

The old man and his seven sons didn't want to spend the night by the plane, so in the end, after a long, hot verbal confrontation, an attempt to find an answer to our problem, we were invited—and not able to refuse—to spend the night back at the house while sons two and five drove off to town for a forty-four of gas. I was pleased to see two of them leave. I never liked crowds much.

It was a long walk, mostly uphill, through woods thick with snakes. And those five boys used those shotguns like toys. They shot at anything that moved. It took a couple of hours to walk to the house, and I have to admit that compared with time here, where one day feels like a week, those two hours took a fortnight to pass.

If Prohibition had made these folks wealthy, they sure didn't show it. How long they'd lived there was anyone's guess. They knew no better, certainly no worse, or if they did, they just didn't care.

And if the family survived by raising cattle, I saw none, just a couple of wormy horses in a yard that a light breeze might blow down, and pigs and chickens—chickens everywhere that hardly outnumbered the kids.

I saw two houses as we came closer. One house had stood there in a fashion for a hundred or so years. It had only one room, and the other was made of scrap—scrap wood, scrap tin.

If Bobby saw the things I saw, he hid his thoughts well. Safest place to look was at my feet, until a lady who looked eighty appeared on the porch, saw us coming, and retreated quickly. Another came out and called the kids for supper.

It would be a supper I'd gladly eat now, but back then I was close to puking just to smell it.

The girl calling the kids looked old, old before her time. It was hard to guess when she'd last washed or brushed her hair or taken a bath. She looked us up and down, ignored us, and called the kids as if she was calling the pigs. Kids swarmed in from nowhere, little ones barely walking, older ones fighting. Boys, mainly boys. None of the kids had taken a bath since they'd been born, either.

Dwight must have had a baseball team of kids. And they all looked the same. They all looked just like he did.

Bobby tried hard to smile at me. It was the smile born of a grievous mistake.

I didn't bother smiling back, and that, he knew, was not a good sign.

I made it as far as the porch.

I looked inside. Every kid in that one-room house was eating—a lump of bread, a bowl of stew. No spoons, no forks, no knives. And most of the eyes that stared at me were vacant.

I'd seen how and where Bobby had lived as a kid, but it was a mansion compared with this. There were about fifteen people living in a one-room house here, one room hardly bigger than my bedroom in Abbeville. Make that sixteen people; I didn't know there was a baby till a pregnant girl came in, sat down, let her dress fall, and, without saying a word, fed the baby. To me, it looked big enough to walk.

I looked at Bobby again; he looked at me. Maybe we had the same thought—that none of his charm would work on these people.

We were stared at a lot, stared at by a swarm of kids who probably hadn't seen any new faces in their lives. They ranged in age from the baby the pregnant girl was nursing up to a boy of about twelve who wasn't right in the head. And all he did was smile at me. He liked me. He liked me a lot. It sure was my lucky day.

And every one of them was barefoot and dressed in rags. Maybe they weren't staring at our faces; they were probably staring at our black leather flying gear instead—the caps, the boots, the jackets. We must have looked like a million dollars.

The old lady finished ladeling the stew out and then sat by the one window, picked up some checked cloth. She was making a shirt. She didn't say a word; she didn't look at us again. She was like me, watching the floor a lot. It was safe that way.

All I wanted was out.

Maybe that was all she'd ever wanted.

114

"See to us, woman," the old man said.

The old woman put down the shirt, picked up a wooden tray full of odd cups and tin mugs, and took them to the porch. When I stepped aside to let her by, she looked up into my face. I thought I saw shame there. Maybe it was my own reflecting in her eyes. She wasn't as old as she looked.

I took my cap off—one of those things I do automatically when a lady is around—and one of the boys snatched it from my hand. I opened my mouth to protest, caught Bobby's look, and decided I'd let the boy keep it. I had another three at home. If he wanted it that bad . . .

Well, it started a fight between four of the boys, which the old man settled by firing a single shell through the porch roof. I looked up. He had cured a lot of fights that way.

The old lady, the mother, she just rolled out a barrel of whiskey. Nothing bothered her, nothing.

"You give that back now. Ain't yours!" Dwight yelled.

The cap was thrown back to me. There was another fight, this time between Dwight and the boy. "I said give it back, not throw it!" The boy got a smack on the side of the head that would have stunned a mule. He took off into the sunset, with his father firing a volley of words this time. As far as I know, I never saw that boy again. If I'd been that kid, I'd have kept running till I got to Louisville. Maybe he'd have liked some company for the trip.

Three or four times, Bobby said how folks'd be missing us already, which was partly true. My mother would have dinner ready, but she was used to me coming in early, late, or never at all. I guess the last thing anyone wanted was trouble.

I didn't drink until that day. I'd heard so much about the evils of it; I'd seen for myself what it'd done to Ed Maginley. But there in the middle of Kentucky, I had no choice. I had to be polite. So I took a tin cup full of overproof moonshine whiskey and sat on the porch. I pretended I wasn't there, and whenever I thought no one was looking, I'd accidentally tip some out.

Bobby had gotten us into this, so he could talk us out. I was always quiet around people; I preferred to let others talk. This time, I hid behind my veil of shyness—that's what Rosanna called it—and before I knew it, I had kids around me, touching me. The spastic one sat down beside me, imitated what I was doing—swinging my legs over the end of the porch—and put his hand on my knee. I looked down into his eyes and tried to smile. For some unknown reason, I put my cap on his head. His grin nearly made the sun rise again. Then he held my hand. His grip was as strong as a boxer's.

I looked at Bobby; he was taking his second cup, being polite, if polite existed. Now and then, he'd include me in the conversation by saying, "Ain't that right, John?" and I'd agree for the sake of it.

The sun set; it came down quickly, and kids slept where they fell. We hadn't interrupted anyone's routine. I must have been sitting in the spastic boy's place, because he used my lap as a pillow.

I was half-listening to Dwight's high, droning voice, but the half cup of whiskey I'd already had was surely affecting me. All I wanted to do was sleep. But I woke quickly when I heard how the sheriff had been out three times in the past six months and had found nothing. Dwight related with pride how one day while they were out hunting deer, they found a truckful of federal agents. Lost. Most of them got lost in the mountains when they came snooping about, he said, and then more feds would come looking for the lost ones. He didn't say how many were never seen again; he didn't have to.

Now the boys were growing, Dwight had his own private army.

To me, it was his own private world, hardly touched by outside influences, and that's how it would always be.

Half the mug gone, I was beginning to doze off. I woke quickly when I heard the voice say, "Show 'em the badge, Willy."

A boy of about fourteen put down his whiskey, went inside, and reappeared with what had once been a deputy's badge. It had a .22 bullet hole in the center. As soon as I saw it, I knew it was being worn when it was redecorated.

The old man didn't sleep that night, nor did I, nor did Bobby. In Bobby's pocket was the money for the whiskey and in the back of our minds the knowing that there would be nothing to stop these people from shooting us down when we tried to leave.

But it never occurred to me that we were friend, not foe. Too much fear got in the way.

I wish I could forget the time we spent in Kentucky. The memory is screened by fear, and when there's fear bubbling below the surface, you don't remember very much except the things you see and feel because of that fear. But I do remember the kids, the old woman, the one daughter who came from a brother-sister union, the one daughter pregnant by a brother while she nursed the child of her own father.

Dwight told us all about it. And he was proud of it, too— proud he had managed to grow himself a good-looking daughter more useful and prettier than her mother had ever been.

But I remember most the vacant eyes of those kids.

And all it does is make me feel lucky. It did then; it does now. I was lucky to have been born to Lily and John Shaw; lucky to have had a kid sister to protect from other boys; lucky to have been to a school, to have had a decent, constant food supply, clothes, to have had a place to sleep that was my own, a family to talk to, to love, to be close to. I was glad to live on this earth like I was intended to, knowing what it was to live without constant fear. I still think if you're going to live like an animal, you would have been born with four legs and no conscience.

For the first time in my life, I was reassured to know that Bobby had that Colt .45 on him, that he knew how to use it and that he would, definitely would use it. Like I would have if pushed.

The rights and wrongs, the deep hatred I had for killing anything at all, they were buried that day and a half while we stayed with those hill people.

And that scared me more than the situation. I didn't know until then how circumstances could change a person.

Sons two and five came back just before dawn with the gas and we sat in the back of the truck for the trip back to the plane. The boys reloaded the cargo while I fueled up, and from the corner of my eye I watched Bobby complete the transaction.

I flew us out. That was all I wanted—out. Bobby didn't argue. He was still drunk. Maybe he saw something in my eyes that stopped his words before they hit his brain and he had sense enough to stay silent.

No one shot at us, but I expected it after the previous night—the longest night of my life.

It was a difficult takeoff. The plane was overloaded to hell, and we skimmed treetops at a steep, climbing bank, struggling, slow. Then the blue sky opened, and in the sky, that safe sky, with the long flight back home just begun, I started to rehearse just like Meg used to.

I never bothered to thank God for letting us get out. Not me. I rehearsed what I would say once we were back. But my anger drowned sane words, sane thoughts.

We were running on empty when I landed at Davis Field, taxied to the hangar, and shut her down.

And we stayed in the plane forever, neither of us game to move first. Some things you can forgive and be forgiven for. But that, no.

I guess I didn't have to say a thing to Bobby Sullivan. He learned by his mistakes, too.

I moved first. I climbed down. I walked away. I heard Bobby behind me. I felt his hand on my shoulder and I heard two words: "Jesus, John—"

It was automatic. I spun; I punched. I cracked bones in my knuckles when I contacted his teeth. He went down and lay on the grease-stained cement floor, one knee up. He was near crying, and it wasn't because of the punch, either. I can't remember what I said. I don't want to. Till that day, I thought I knew him. I thought he was my best friend. I didn't have many. I didn't have any. I treasured him—till that day.

For me, Sullivan and Shaw had ceased to exist. But somehow, someway, it was resurrected before it died completely. Maybe we talked. Maybe we didn't have to. It was one of those silent agreements that didn't need signatures on a piece of paper.

Bobby flew legal cargo from that time on. And I took up a mail service.

Now he's flying skies I can't see, but I know he flies by, close to me sometimes, because I hear his voice now and then....

Funny what I think about when I look up at the sky. There's nothing but vicious gray, and I wouldn't want to be up in that today. I guess I could still fly if I tried, if they made planes especially for one-armed pilots. What the hell. It's gone. It's gone.

So I'm looking at the sky, the clouds, streaks of quiet, dull gray in the half-light that signals a spring sunrise. A hint of a golden glow is streaking through the gray; shafts of gold light reflect off the water; the ice and the rock are mirrored on the horizon. Out there from where I'm standing is a lone man in a kayak, weaving his way through pack ice. The water looks still enough to walk on today. It's so quiet, so still. I don't like it when it's so quiet. There's no sound anywhere, not even a dog.

People will be out soon—boys in canoes, going out to find or make holes in the ice. See what they get this time. A couple of seals maybe, a net or two of fish.

This quiet is too unsettling.

Damn it to hell! Why does it always take so long?

He was standing on the shoreline, daydreaming, worrying, mind turning full circles too quickly, when the one-eyed Sinbad appeared beside him and nudged him with a sharp elbow to the ribs. John turned quickly. All he saw was the Eskimo's huge grin. Sinbad told him, slowly, a mixture of Eskimo and mime, that the baby was soon to appear. John pushed him aside roughly, and in the rush, he forgot his limp. He ran.

I've just held my son.

I can't describe the feeling; it's joy, despair, shock, and surprise rolled into one. And I cried again, quiet tears.

Maybe the emotion was just a release.

My son came out backward—just like me, doing everything in reverse. But at least he's here. He's okay.

Toward the end, Tooksooks and her mother sent for Sinbad to find me. They let me in only because Kioki kept calling for me. She was in another world by the time I skidded in, a world of unending agony.

I nearly felt it. I could taste it in the air, see it in her eyes, hear it in her voice.

I always thought ladies were frail, weak creatures, things to be owned, protected, cherished if you got the right one. But sitting alongside Kioki as she knelt, held upright by those two ladies, I knew she wasn't frail or weak, nor did I own her.

All I could do was let her squeeze the life out of my right hand. All I could do was talk to her. Every muscle she had was focused on one thing.

Then he finally appeared.

He came out feetfirst. He had big feet, big hands, wide shoulders. And if he wasn't a Shaw, my name's Myrtle.

There was a strip of dark hair down his back. But the hair on his head wasn't jet black like I expected it would be. And he had a powerful voice, too. It was his face I noticed most—squinting, confused eyes. The cry wasn't frightened, just bewildered, baffled.

I knew how he felt to wake, a stranger, alone in a new world, a cold, barren world. But like me, he'd get used to this world; he'd gradually accept it. He was lucky not to have known the other side of life, because it's easier to accept things that way.

Kioki lay down, exhausted. Her work was over for a little while. I looked down at her, caught a tired, happy smile. I said only one word: "Good."

She said in reply, "Show."

Tooksooks let me hold the baby. There wasn't a lot to see now; he was wrapped tightly in fur. She pointed me outside.

And I obeyed. The sun was almost shining for the first time in months, and Tooksooks ran about, yelping out long words I didn't understand but knew the general meaning of: Come! See! The one who fell from the sky now has a son!

They came from everywhere. Something else had happened to bring the people together in celebration. And the first to congratulate me was Asuluk. I'd never seen him smile like that before. He hit me on the back so hard, I nearly felt my ribs shatter again.

There I was, holding my son while these people swarmed me. And in the background, Sinbad stood grinning, his one eye squinting, arms folded across his chest in his stance of pride.

The little guy brought the sunshine with him. The sun was in his hair, and the sea in his eyes.

My boy.

NINE

EVERYDAY life took a dramatic turn from the moment the child was born. Unlike the other men and boys on the island, John found his usefulness depleting daily.

He was never invited to tag along on any expedition, never invited to hunt, fish. Nor could he successfully join in on the story nights. If he approached a group of men, he was largely ignored unless Sinbad was among them.

Kioki was too busy with the baby to give him much time, and her sister, Tooksooks, still had her own duties as part of the village. She helped educate the girls. As this was not man's work or expected of a man, for each day that followed the next, John turned more and more inward, looking for answers he knew he'd never find. His tatty, water-damaged logbook became his constant companion.

I'm not the world's best diary writer. Sometimes I don't think I'm a world's best anything. If I grew big tomatoes in my patch and took them into town to sell, someone else'd be selling bigger ones. For a long time, I thought I was a good aviator. . . . Deep inside, I know there's always someone, somewhere, who's better.

So I guess it helps to be as good as possible no matter what it is you're doing.

Just do the best you can.

My mother taught me that, and not by words. I learned by example. Whatever she'd do, she knew and we knew—Meg and I—that she gave it her best, even when she was sick. All those years I was a kid, I never stopped, never noticed. It's all there from hindsight, which I guess is better than having no sight.

Cooking, cleaning, sewing, gardening.

She baked the best pies in South Carolina; our house never had any dust in it or on it. Hell, even the henhouse was fit for royalty. She hand-sewed our clothes so well, it was hard to tell if the stitches were hers or from some sewing machine. And nobody's roses had the same smell as those yellow ones that grew on the bush to the right of the outhouse.

I see it so clearly. I can almost smell it.

And all that's left: memories of people I've left behind. My mother may as well be standing right beside me now, and I know she wouldn't be complaining. Maybe she'd be proud of me, proud that I never gave in, because for a long time all I wanted was to die.

When I think of her, it's as if she's here with me. Maybe I want her to be here—it's my imagination at work. Or maybe she's dead by now. Whatever, she'll never see this son of mine.

I've named him Billy in memory of the first friend I ever had, Billy Taylor. It doesn't matter if Billy's still alive. I'll never see him again. I knew that when he sailed off to England. Neither of us ever dreamed I'd be stuck somewhere in the Aleutians, living with Eskimos.

I don't remember the last time I wrote. It'd help if I knew the date, even the year. But what the hell, who'll ever read this, anyway? I sit here writing; sometimes my hand can't keep up with my brain, but mostly I can't think of a thing to write about. And I haven't been writing very much for one reason.

I'm so damned tired. The boy's either screaming, sucking at his mother, or sleeping. And he doesn't sleep much. Mr. Sandman's his main enemy. I was like that, too, or so my mother used to say. It was as if I couldn't wait to become a part of this world, that sleeping most of the time away was a waste, a sin. And after I crashed, I tried not to sleep—it brought in too many demons, nightmares. I'd do anything but dare close these eyes for too long after I went down. You can only crash the same plane once, but I was doing it over and over, and the end was always the same.

And now I'd swap the chance of touching some white Florida sand for a couple of hours shut-eye, uninterrupted. I'm so tired, I can't even think straight.

If this is parenthood, once is enough for me.

What's a father supposed to be, anyway? Is there anything he's supposed to do apart from not knowing what the hell is happening?

Kioki hasn't shared our bed since Tooksooks moved in. And I don't like that much. It feels as if we're becoming strangers again.

She sleeps with the baby. Times, I can't help the feelings I get, that maybe he's stolen her from me. I should know better. I feel left out, cast aside. It's as if that's all she wanted from me, of me—this baby. And often what I'm feeling must show on my face, because she gives him to me to hold.

And then I never know how I feel, because he takes one look at me and grins. So much for trying not to like him.

My God, I'm a daddy now.

The solo was my way of escaping all this family stuff, this married business, this raising a family. I'd see Rosanna and feel the terrible need to run. If I didn't want it then, why would a plane crash in the middle of a cold nowhere make any difference?

I don't know how old the kid is. I guess if I kept this diary every day, I'd know. But I never had a date to begin with, and days here aren't like days as I once knew them. Plus, I can't settle to it. There are times I want to, but I just sit here scratching my head, hoping something will come.

I'm missing civilization more than ever now, the small town I called home for so many years. I miss walking up Main Street, saying howdy to folks whose faces had been familiar to me since before I could remember. I miss the casual familiarity that was so comforting—so comforting, it became boring. I miss the picture shows at Columbia and hiking down to Calhoun Falls on a hot summer day. I miss Miami, too, but most of all, I miss flying. Even making it to Anchorage would be a dream come true.

Civilization—what does that word mean, anyway?

To me, it used to comprise two things: being nice to people you'd rather not know anyway and getting on with the job, trying not to kill or rob anyone in the process. If you did that, life in civilization was easy. Here, which is not really civilization at all, you get on with everyone because no one wants anything from you. No one's a threat. No one steals; no one kills except to eat. I haven't heard or seen a fight yet—except for the time I was beaten up. And I guess there're only two people here who don't like me much—my mother-in-law and one of Asuluk's nephews who's got a chip on his shoulder the size of Sumter Forest. He keeps out of my way and I his, and that's the way I hope it'll stay, too.

I guess the closest I have to the picture shows I'm missing are the storytellings at Asuluk's. Everyone comes along unless someone's sick, dying, or having a baby. I'm getting better at understanding the language and Kioki does her best to translate, using what few English words she knows. She never translates at the time, though; it's always later, at home, and so a lot of the magic is lost. But sometimes I come away with clear images of his meaningful stories. They're always meaningful, spiritual. But sometimes he'll surprise us all and tell the Eskimo equivalent of a joke.

I like watching the reactions of those folks sitting close to me. Sometimes it's better than the picture shows. I look around at all those round, red, Oriental faces, the eyes and ears and imaginations hanging on the medicine man's every word. He's a master at milking suspense, and these folks are like folks anywhere— they love a good story. And it often continues next time, just like the picture shows on a Saturday used to.

I often wonder how they'd react to seeing pictures on the wall instead of in their heads.

I guess the stories, the gatherings are the closest things these people have to schooling. And they also have very strong beliefs in spirits. They have a spirit for everything imaginable, while I still struggle with the notion of one God.

I often wonder what they would do if a preacher came along and tried to convert them to Christianity.

At times, I wonder, too, if I'm officially dead yet. I don't know how long it is before someone missing is listed as presumed dead. I wonder how many elections I've missed, if any. I even wonder if Calvin Coolidge is still President. It would be so strange for these people to come to terms with a leader they did not know. For that matter, what would these people know of any organized government aside from their own? Of civilization? Even if it's just a word. Of Seattle? Of Maine? Of the Nevada desert, of the Kentucky backwoods, of the sabal palms that line the streets of Miami?

Oh Jesus, I want to go home.

Kioki sat down beside him, lifted his face, looked into his tear-filled eyes, and asked what was wrong. He couldn't answer, so she took his logbook away and left him alone with the baby. It was the first time she had gone away with Tooksooks, left him completely alone, with full responsibility of a baby he hardly knew, or knew what to do with. But he knew, too, that all he had to do was call out and she'd be back.

I knew what she was trying to do. Trying to force me to leave the past behind and notice today before it disappeared.

I'd never been alone with Billy before, and after the *buts, I can'ts,* and *what'll I do's* had faded away, I looked at him as if for the first time.

His face is round and fat and his hair's gone dark again. His eyes are changing color, too. His little hands are fat and strong and he has a funny expression on his face, a mixture of curiosity and surprise. But that could be because he's half Eskimo, too.

I thought I saw the devil shining in his eyes for a minute, then it passed when he grinned at me.

I came to the conclusion that people are not meant to live here on this cold piece of rock. I told him so, but I don't know if he understood. "Billy," I said, "if babies were meant to be born on ice floes or on little islands of ice-covered rock in the North Pacific, they'd be born fur-lined, not clothed in bearskin. Where'd you get this, anyway? Is it your granddaddy's?" He just gurgled to himself and sucked on his fist.

I never thought any son of mine would be wearing bearskin and seal hide.

His skin was softer than the fur he was wrapped in. His eyes followed every move I made, and I made a few, just to make sure he could see okay, and hear. But when he looked at me— no, into me—it was as if he knew exactly who I was. He didn't stare because my hair was yellow, my eyes were blue. He didn't care that my beard was red, either. He grabbed a fistful of my nose and tried to pull it off. And when it wouldn't come off, he tried for the gold-capped tooth.

He knew me. He trusted me. He didn't have a choice, but if he'd had, I hoped he'd just lie there in my arms, comfortable, warm, afraid of nothing.

It came again, the feeling I had when I first saw him, touched him, showed him off to the village. It started in my belly and in an instant a warm wave of pure emotion was choking me. He grabbed my finger again; his entire hand closed around it tightly and we just watched each other some more. I felt fuzzy for the longest moments of my life and then he started yelling. Nothing I could do would stop it.

Kioki instantly answered the call, and I didn't mind giving him back. My eyes were stinging, and she looked at me strangely.

I don't think she'd ever seen a man cry until I came along.

Some great white hunter I turned out to be. Some fearless warrior who fell from the sky, who plaits strut wire and mends fishing nets. Some man I am. Some example I'll be.

Babies are for women, anyway. I'll have my say when he starts walking around.

That's if he doesn't die of smothering before then.

Kioki's going to pamper him to death. She talks to him constantly, and it only took a couple of days for him to recognize that voice, too. He's got the angriest scream I've ever heard. As soon as she speaks, he's quiet. Because he knows exactly what's coming next. Nothing beats being buried in layers of fur and the ultimate goal.

Sometimes she'll sing to him while she feeds him—the songs are more of a wail, a chant. Maybe it's sung as an assurance that he'll grow up strong, healthy, handsome, brave. Hopefully, immune to the cold.

And while he dines, he watches her face, the same way he watches me, but I can't do what his mother can. I think he knows that, anyway.

Soon—maybe a year, two, however long it takes babies to learn to talk, I'll have someone, finally, to talk to, someone who can understand both languages. I'll have my very own interpreter and there will be no misunderstandings at all. Then I'll be able to walk up to Asuluk's chip-shouldered nephew and say, "What the hell have I ever done to you?"

I know Billy's going to be smart. It's there in his eyes already. Who knows, maybe some of my father's brains would be inherited, passed down the line. And I wonder if this boy will ever have the need to find some wings. Maybe one day I'll see him standing on the edge of the ice, but he won't be looking at the sea. No, he'll be looking at the sky, wondering why birds can fly and he can't. If ever that day comes, I'll tell him about that kid who used to stand on the fence post, dreaming.

Could the need to fly be inherited?

I realize what I've done. I've helped create a new person who will spend his entire life in this hell unless . . . unless I can find a way out, a way home. Oh Lord, I don't want him growing up here. There's no dream here. There's no choice. There's nothing. There's no hope of anything better. I don't want him growing up here. If he does, he'll know nothing, and he'll experience less. There is more to living than simple survival. There just has to be.

Billy was seven months old before Kioki allowed John some freedom to take the boy walking. John would wait for a break in the weather—breaks lasted anywhere from half an hour to a full eighteen hours of clear daylight, although that was a rarity. The sudden storms were always a threat.

He'd always hated winter.

Whenever he could, was well enough and the weather allowed, he would escape with the boy. Gone the days of escape to the air, although he swore that he would fly again before he died, and it wouldn't be in dreams, either.

He dreamed of taking his son up in a biplane, proving to himself and his son that he was good at something, good for something.

With the baby on his back, the wild-haired white man would limp off alone to pick what few berries and seeds grew during the summer. He'd collect soft rocks, which he'd later polish or carve, and he'd often take the baby down to the beach in summer and search for shellfish, usually with a gaggle of Eskimo children three steps behind him.

John never fully realized the hidden talents that lurked, inspired to surface because of the unending sameness of daily life. The time he spent, once he was almost well again, was fairly productive, even if it was labeled "women's work." He'd adapted to the loss of the hand, found new uses for his feet, especially his toes.

But he didn't write as often. He was becoming forgetful of his language. Feelings were very hard for him to transcribe. Something intangible was always lost when words were written, because words described; words were not the true essence of thought, of feeling.

Occasionally, an unexpected smile was the only occurrence that altered the repetition. He didn't know whether these people—slowly becoming his people—had dreams, aspirations, goals. Mostly, he'd watch them and think they lived because of habit alone. To him there was no joy, no variety. Simplicity may have suited some people; to John, it was worse than prison.

Nothing ever happened. The rest of the world had forgotten about this place, if ever the world knew it existed.

The world had forgotten about him, too.

He always wanted more than what was available. Even when he was flying the mail and cargo and occasional tourist, he wondered what else life had to offer him. Impatience too often bred boredom. And when snow fell, he wondered whether this was his punishment for wanting too much, too soon.

Bobby Sullivan never wanted. He just took the opportunities that passed by; sometimes he reached, grasped, held, and experienced. Bobby had died the way all fliers wanted to, so what had John done so wrong that he still lived? Others received wishes fulfilled.

Ever since I was a kid, I knew there had to be a reason to be alive, a good reason. I'm here. They're here. They've been here thousands of years. They've adapted. They know no better, but I sure as hell do.

Miami to them wouldn't be heaven. It would be another world. It would be something as far removed from reality as a storybook is to a kid's imagination.

I wish I had some photographs with me, just to prove to them that I used to live in another world, another world situated a few thousand miles southeast of here, of nowhere. But show them California's surf beaches, or Monterey Bay, or Death Valley, or even the Everglades, they'd think it was some kind of spirit magic. Or Asuluk would point to the stars and explain it all that way.

Photographs—that's all my family has left, a few photographs. I bet the one of me and Bobby Sullivan is still sitting on my mother's mantelpiece, too. We both looked drunk, but we weren't—just being together did that. I had my arm around his shoulder and he was going to stand on a couple of tins so we'd be the same height. I was twenty-two, he was twenty-three when it was taken outside the hangar at Miami. It wasn't the photo that they put in the newspaper—that one had us both looking serious, businesslike. After all, we'd just gotten back from a search party, had found a lost fisherman. The photograph on my mother's shelf is my favorite.

But I guess I still have his St. Christopher medal.

"Take it," he'd said. "Take it. I don't need it no more. Don't need it where I'm going."

I still see it, feel it, hear it. It won't go away. It'll never go away unless I write it down. But that'll bring it back, as bad as it was, New Year's Eve 1923.

Maybe it was New Year's Day 1924.

I can't remember. Every day was the same, even then.

I didn't want to do any crowd-thrilling stunts. I wanted no part of his wing-walking escapade with that blond girl who also had a death wish. Hell, we had a business to run. Everything we had was tied up in our machines. I've said before how he liked adventure, how he came alive when he was playing games with death.

Even my mother knew. So did Meg. They knew what would happen if we went to Atlanta. But Bobby said too many times he'd rather die with an audience expecting it than go out flying boxes of Bibles to Salt Lake City. Said he wanted to die in the arms of a truly beautiful woman.

Bess never got there in time.

It was just me, me and about forty-five people all having a look. Curiosity brings out the worst in human nature. Maybe he was right. Maybe they only went to air shows hoping to see a real crash, see a man die.

Bobby wasn't the first to loop. He wasn't the first to take a spiral dive from fifteen hundred feet and pull out at a hundred. He wasn't the first to fly inverted at fifty feet. He used to say he could look up ladies' dresses that way. He wasn't the first; he wouldn't be the last. He'd come close to dying once before, and I thought then he'd find some sense after he shook out his shorts, but it made him more determined to try something—anything—different.

Maybe I was so safe that I was boring, but Billy Taylor used to say to me from the time I was a broken-armed, starry-eyed kid, "Remember, John, you can always replace a piece of machinery. You can't buy a person back from the dead."

And if I died, who'd take care of my mother and Meg? Frankie Dee? I never liked that weasel, never liked the way he'd bring Meg flowers, try to charm his way past my mother. I knew exactly what that bastard wanted. And all Bobby would say was, "John, it's none of your business." Maybe he thought that my trying to stop him from going up that day was none of my business, too.

But he damned well knew what would happen the moment we got to Atlanta and he joined Artie Best's Flying Circus for a day. Inverts at fifty feet past the crowd; wing walking; plane jumping; loops, double loops, triple loops; spiral dives—it all left more than just the crowd with hearts in ears.

I hated those damned shows. For a long time, I hated the people who'd go, too.

I tried to talk him out of it. I damn near sabotaged his machine, but the only time Bobby ever took any notice of me was after the Kentucky run, only because he knew he was wrong.

I knew he was as good as dead when he took off, banked over the grandstand, threw his flowers down, and had a good laugh while the girls fought for his yellow daisies.

I looked at Bess, standing there on her own, leaning against the pole. Above her head, Artie Best's faded banners flapped in the crosswind. I guess Bess knew, too. She knew she'd never have him forever; he was simply on loan.

And when Elsie the Wing-walker finally showed, it was too late, anyway. Bobby was already in the sky. I saw him coming in and rolling for the invert and I heard Artie's voice on the loudspeakers. I closed my eyes, hoping he had his harness on. I'd heard of one guy attempting a loop, forgetting to buckle his harness. Gravity isn't kind, and Bobby tormented me over and over about that. I hated his sense of humor. But he got through the invert without mishap. I opened my eyes when the applause came and he climbed and climbed.

And I knew if he didn't power on, he'd stall. But he didn't stall. The gods still loved this fool. He was barely fifteen hundred feet when he began the spiral. A few seconds later, I knew he was fighting for control. I could damn near feel the machine breaking up.

And the engine found life five seconds too late.

I was already running long before he came in nose-first at over a hundred miles an hour. I don't remember any sounds. I think I was screaming too loudly.

I remember most the stupid look on his face—he wanted to release his harness; he wanted to walk away. He wanted to crash in style, be some kind of hero for all those girls watching. It never quite happened his way.

I don't know how many people were crowding around and I didn't care. I released the harness. He fell out. The St. Christopher dropped to the grass.

I knew Bess was there somewhere and I heard later how old Artie had to hold her back while four or five guys tried to separate us, tried to take the body away. But I wouldn't let go, not even after I felt him die. He was alive and looking at me, saying, "Take it. Take it. I don't need it no more . . ." and then he was dead.

My buddy was dead.

I saw it happen.

But I still can't accept it. Two, maybe three years later, I still can't believe it.

The doctors said he'd broken just about every bone in his body, and one tried to tell me that injuries so bad are hardly even felt. How the brain reaches some kind of overload and there's no pain at all. But that had to be bullshit. It had to be.

I remember choosing the coffin and I remember what he looked like lying there in it, too. He was buried in his leathers and his hair was slicked down in a way he never wore it. And someone had put lipstick on him. I remember looking down at him, touching the face. I remember how it felt. And I knew that whatever had once lived inside, whatever it was that made up the essence of my buddy, it was long gone now, long gone.

I don't remember what the preacher said at the cemetery. What remains is walking into the Miami office and seeing Bobby's spare jacket hanging behind the office door. My knees turned to Jell-O and I cried for about an hour.

Then I went and sat in that garden for a long time, getting the courage to walk on in and tell his father.

John took his son for a walk and stood for a while on the rocks. The ice was still melting. Here and there, some grass struggled vainly to escape the mush, the squelch. By the time the ground dried, it would be winter again.

It may have been a landmass out there in the distance; it might have been Alaska, the mainland. It might have been clouds playing cruel tricks on a homesick man, too. John stood there with the boy tucked in under the coat Kioki had made him and he couldn't even pretend he was standing on Miami Beach.

Pretense didn't fit anymore.

Kayaks were coming in, and for a moment, the water looked still enough to walk on.

He was tempted to step off, fall into the icy, bottomless waters. He was tempted until the boy saw something in the distance and reached for it. John followed the small gloved hand.

Billy was trying to grab the moon.

TEN

✺✺✺✺✺✺✺

IT occurred to him one morning as he was lazily watching his son's vain attempts to walk that he was enduring the longest winter of his life, that he had been on Kulowyl for at least two years. What had he achieved in that time?

There was so much he could have taught these people if only he had some kind of proof that his world existed.

Proof in the form of photographs—of people, places, things, of automobiles, beaches, sun, fruit trees, a sack of corn seed, half a dozen sprouting potatoes. . . . If the people had been farmers, it wouldn't have been so bad—at least he'd have something constructive to do in teaching them, but growing corn on rock was impossible. Thousands of years of frost icing everything to a depth of two hundred feet left only a few inches of topsoil in the thaw, and a few inches were never enough.

They were people of the sea. And now, he was one of them.

There were times when he thought he understood the immense joy shared when an expedition returned safe and well. So many pleasures taken from such simplicity. Seeing, sensing the joy in a homecoming only brought the ache for home stronger than it had ever been. It was difficult to share excitement when he had forgotten what excitement was.

But his memory was soon jolted.

John had his first, and he hoped his only, fight.

*

Jesus Christ. I'm still shaking. I knew it was bound to happen. That nephew of Asuluk's just tried to kill me. Why? Hell, what'd I do? It's been a habit of mine to turn the other cheek, like it says somewhere in the Bible. And I've tried to ignore him for well over a year now, but some things just don't damn well go away.

I wish he would. I don't know what his name is—all I know is that it's long and starts with Zuk and eventually ends with ki. He looks more Indian than Eskimo—to me, anyway. The eyes are Eskimo, not the nose or the long face. And he's had a set on me since I came here.

I was taking Billy and most of the other kids for a walk across the beach when Zuk's favorite wife came along to collect three of her kids. They were all picking up soapstones or any small rocks or shells that looked different, because what I do lately is show them all how I polish and carve. They also collect bits of driftwood and watch me whittle.

The woman, a little older than Kioki, started talking to me and I kept the conversation going as much as I could. She wanted to know about flying in a soaring bird from the heavens. I'd seen her around before, talking to my girls and running off quickly whenever I appeared. But that's what happened just before Tooksooks moved in. She'd run away, giggling. How was I to know that this woman wanted to be married to me, too?

I didn't know why I was making her laugh—didn't know I was saying anything funny. It's impossible explaining aerodynamics to an Eskimo, especially an Eskimo woman who couldn't look me in the eye. When she'd stand closer, I'd move away a little. I didn't want her to get the wrong idea. In fact, I was praying for a miracle to get me out of this when Zuk came screaming down the cliff, and in his hand was the biggest knife I have ever seen.

I'd heard stories about this one's courage—to me, anyone who takes on a polar bear single-handed is plain stupid. I looked at him as he came hurtling down the incline and then I looked at her, his wife. Fear was all I could see in her eyes. She ran off, screaming for Asuluk. Zuk's elbow caught her in the face and she dropped. And I knew if I went over to help her up, he'd take my head off with one swoop of that hunting tool. They kept them sharp, very sharp.

Even the kids were wondering what was going to happen.

Billy was crying. One of the bigger girls was holding him tightly.

I said as best I could, using words I hoped he would understand, "I cannot fight you if the children are watching."

He smiled. Maybe he knew I was playing for time.

Jesus, he had that machete and all I had was a Bowie knife.

He stood ten feet away from me, put the machete down, and took off most of his clothes. I might have been two heads taller, but he had the strength. I could see it in his stumpy, muscled body.

My mind was blank. Sweat beaded on my lip. I wiped it away. The movement was enough to have him in a fighting stance, legs apart, knees bent, swaying side to side. All I could see was that damned knife.

I held my good hand up, shook my head.

It did no good. There was just hatred in his eyes. He needed a fight bad and I was it. What was he? Village champion?

I told him I didn't want his women or his children. It was a mistake.

A big mistake, because the men here shared their women around and declining an offer was considered an offense.

Asuluk called and I looked up. He was standing on top of the cliff, watching. There was a line of people with him. Everyone was quiet. I hoped he'd stop this nonsense, but all he did was nod.

This guy was challenging me for no reason that I could see. He indicated I take off my parka and undershirt like he had. God knows why, but I did. I said it was unfair, that he had the advantage. He had two good arms.

He threw the machete down and came at me, anyway—headfirst. He got half a breath away and I stepped aside, caught his pants, swung him around, and used my left arm, what was left of it, to hit him straight in the throat. He sat on his butt and gagged for a bit, then hate flickered in his eyes again.

He wouldn't be satisfied till I was dead. I just wanted to apologize and walk away. He took a smaller knife from a leather pouch by his right ankle. I reached for the Bowie and I knew if I stuck him with it properly, he'd probably die—because with a maniac like this one wanting to kill me, I wouldn't be trying to hurt. I'd go for a kill. I'd have to.

He stepped closer, throwing the knife from one hand to the other. My heart was coming out my ears. Timing here was important. If I could kick that knife away, maybe I could stand on him, put my hand up, and walk away. Forget it ever happened.

He was quicker than I was. I felt the cut, like I'd been burned. Then my anger got in the way. I kicked, once, twice. He went down. I stood on his hand, ground my heel into his wrist. He didn't utter a sound. He grabbed my leg, knocked me down. I hit him in the cheek with my sharp, hard stump and I felt the bones in his face crack. He cut me again. I didn't feel it. We rolled around on the wet ground. My anger had given me immense strength, and it didn't come in short bursts, either.

I winded him, used my stump, hard down on his chest—hard enough maybe to stop his heart for a bit. I heard and felt the air escape his lungs. I was within reach of the machete, so I grabbed it while he was trying to breathe. And I lay across him, staring down into his surprised eyes, holding his hunting blade across his throat. The slightest pressure would open his neck. More could cut right through, and I was angry enough to do it, too. Just put all my weight on it till I hit the ground.

And I would have. I would have if he hadn't smiled at me. There was no fear there in his face, none at all. Just a calm kind of satisfaction that said, You've won.

I took the machete away and got off. Then I stood tall.

I'd never been in a fight in my life, but did these people have to know that?

Sure, I'd stood by and watched Bobby a couple of times.

Seen a few street fights.

Seeing, though, was not doing.

I felt something hot trickling into my pants, running down my ribs, my leg. I looked down. Touched. There was a four-inch gash across my stomach, a smaller one up my chest. I looked up to the faces above, but everything was spinning.

Then I fell flat on my face.

Sinbad carried me home and sat by the bed while Kioki put a thick black ointment on the two gashes. Tears filled my eyes—the ointment hurt more than the wounds.

Sinbad scratched his face and told me I'd fought well.

I asked him why I'd had to fight in the first place.

He told me that Zukaniimaiki was tired of providing for a man who had done nothing to ensure the survival of the village. He was tired of providing food for one who gave nothing back. Someone had to prove him useless.

Kioki was translating what I couldn't grasp, but I knew she didn't tell me everything.

Sinbad told me again that he was proud of the way I'd fought. Who was my teacher? he asked. I tried to tell him I'd never had a fight in my life. He didn't believe me. He got up and sighed and looked down at me, saying it was good that I had proved myself to be a man; that I wasn't a sulky woman.

That little piece of information hit me harder than Zuk's right fist. Is that what they thought I was, a sulky woman?

Amazing what a couple of scars and a good old shiner can do for your image.

In the following days, before he took sick, John was treated with high regard and quiet respect. Zuk still kept his distance, but the antagonism was long gone. Zuk's wife still tried to talk to John whenever she could, but he made it clear that he was not like the other men, that two women were by far enough.

He told her that where he came from, in the land where the sky met sea and far beyond, where the sun shone hot, a white man could have only one wife at a time. She accepted this, and although she didn't understand it, she returned to her husband, returned to sharing the house with his three other wives.

John doubted that there would be too many others willing to challenge him ever again. His daily routine settled for a short time into its casual pace once more, but with increasing intensity his mind relived the fight just as it had the airplane crash. It wasn't so much the fight itself as the feelings John experienced. He'd never known that he could have killed another human being until that day, and the knowing led only to despairing thoughts of the monster he'd become.

He didn't realize that he'd caught a serious infection from Zuk's attack.

Kioki, who had long since stopped any physical therapy, relinquished care of her baby to her sister. She concentrated again on John. He was sicker now than he had been when he first arrived on Kulowyl. His Caucasian body was simply not designed for survival in Arctic conditions. His blood wasn't thick enough, nor did his body make its own vitamins as theirs did. For three weeks, it was clear that the white man she loved so dearly was going to die. She needed more than her father's medicine and spirit magic. What she needed, she knew was not forthcoming. Florida John had lost his will to live, and will was the only thing she could not give him. No ointments helped. Nothing she or Asuluk knew of would lower the constant fever. He could not eat. The Dark Wind blew across Kulowyl many times and called his name. She heard words from his mouth that made no sense, words of the places where he'd once lived, names of people he'd once known. And she knew those people were dead, because he would talk to them so much, as if they were in the house, visiting.

Kioki, Asuluk, and Tooksooks rarely left his side. No one had known a sickness like it. Then, toward the end, when both wives were preparing to mourn their inevitable loss, Florida John woke and said in their language, "I have seen the whales coming."

Asuluk, who sometimes flew in his dreams, ordered that a party of six investigate what Florida John had said.

And John, who found it hard to breathe because of the pungent smoke filling the house, wondered what was going on.

Whatever it was damn near killed me. All Kioki's done for the last hour is chant, thanking her spirits for my safe return.

Maybe I was just lucky.

Whatever illness or disease it was didn't come on suddenly. It crept up on me so slowly, I thought feeling weak, tired, and sick all the time was normal. I'd forgotten what it felt like to be well. And I'd never been sick a day in my life, either. My hair started to fall out; my fingernails were peeling and soft. Once, I'd needed heavy-duty scissors to cut them back. All I wanted to do was sleep. I couldn't look at raw fish, was forever hot, forever thirsty. And if I lost any more weight, my shadow wouldn't have known where to find me.

I don't remember much. I didn't know what was happening around me, but I do know that neither Tooksooks nor Kioki left me alone. In or out, I knew they were both there.

The dreams I had were like those coming out of a crazy mind, except for one—the one that woke me.

I dreamed I'd taken off from Anchorage, was heading for Prince Rupert. The sky was clear and fine; barely an updraft bothered me. The horizon was clear. But I'm damned if I know where I landed. I had two good arms and two good legs when I climbed out. Bobby was coming in right behind me and neither of us overshot the strip.

There wasn't a soul for miles. I remember thinking I shouldn't be in some desert; it was too far north to be so damned hot. Then through the shimmer of mirage, I saw the old house from Abbeville. It was painted white, so white that I had to look away.

There was someone waiting for me on the porch—my mother, her long brown hair caught in a bun. She was wearing a blue dress and a white apron, and as she called us in to supper, she wiped her hands on a towel over her shoulder.

I wasn't surprised to see her. It felt as if I'd never been away. She stepped aside and didn't say another word to me. As I walked by, I smelled lilacs and beef stew. The house hadn't changed, except that the door to my room was locked tight. There was nothing in there I wanted, anyway. Meg's room was open and bare. Not even her heavy rose-patterned drapes covered the window.

Gone the photograph on the mantelpiece; gone, too, the phone. The air-show banners lining the living room wall.

But I didn't question.

The table was set for two. My mother ladled stew into bowls, and a big fat dumpling stared up at me. But I couldn't eat. Bobby was talking a lot and flight-planning from maps spread across the gingham tablecloth.

Then he asked was I coming this time.

I could hear a baby crying somewhere far away and I knew that cry.

Then I was flying again, without an airplane. Flying fast, without a sound over a place that looked familiar. Ice. I was flying through heavy cloud, but it wasn't bothering me at all. I couldn't even feel the cold. Fog broke and I saw the biggest whale—as big as an icebreaker. And another. Another...

Kioki was shaking me awake, and I opened my eyes and realized where I was.

Asuluk was beside me, singing, and I was covered in ointment and thirstier than a gold miner's mule. I said something that had him skidding out of the house, but I can't recall what it was I said.

All I knew was that I felt fine.

What was the great problem?

Why'd everyone look so worried? What was Tooksooks doing holding Billy? How'd he get so big so soon? What was going on here?

I tried to get out of bed, but Kioki pushed me back down and offered me a bowl of blood. It hurts to admit it, but I drank it all and looked for more.

The girls were so happy. I even ate a little raw fish, then some dried fish. Kioki told me that the kids had been out collecting some shellfish for me. I ate them all. I was so hungry, I could have munched right through my own arm.

There was a celebration that night. In my stupidity, I thought they were celebrating my return. I was wrong, again. A party of hunters had found some whales off the northeastern tip of the island—it was a prehunt get-together.

Damned if I know why everyone was grinning at me.

Even Zuk tried to be friends.

Seems I've been accepted.

God knows why, I sure don't.

I still long to get a message home somehow, even a message to Anchorage. These days, I can only fly on some kid's story-book magic carpet. Even if I fly, I always wake and find myself damn well here.

I daydream about setting off toward the rising sun, but I can't row a boat, except in circles maybe. I can't go anywhere except in daydreams. I can't paddle a canoe; I can't navigate. My maps, what's left of them, tell me nothing anymore. Kulowyl isn't charted. For all I know, I could be fifty or five hundred miles from civilization, from the nearest white face.

I remember Anchorage, taking off, heading for home.

Four hours later, I was down.

Part of me, the practical part, has been telling me it's useless even to attempt escaping this prison. The other part, the part that's always wanting what it can't have, tells me there's still hope.

Hope of what, exactly, it never says.

I shouldn't bitch. I'm still alive after all that's happened. I have two girls who worship the ground I walk on, a little boy who looks a bit like me. But something's missing, and what I've got sure ain't enough to make me want to stay here. I just want my airplane back. Even when Billy sits in his corner munching on a bone and looking at me, grinning now and then, hell, even that's not enough to make me want to stay.

But thoughts changed, and moods changed erratically. As the baby grew, contentment took its lingering place. Billy spoke before he walked. He managed a few words—*aeta, naegaka,* but he also said "Dad" constantly. John spent the long, dark winter months of that year watching, learning, listening, just as the boy did. He managed to fashion a mono wing from sinew and bone, covered it with baby seal hide, but it was too heavy to glide and was no match for the boy's encroaching teeth.

One night as he lay between Kioki and Tooksooks, Kioki told him how she knew he'd come; how she'd told her father of the yellow-haired giant who'd be spat from the belly of a soaring bird; and how, soon after she'd told him, the entire village heard the howling bird and watched as it fell hard onto the ice.

Kioki had inherited her father's second sight.

She knows what's going to happen long before anyone else does, and she's hardly ever wrong, either. At times, it's a little uncanny. She never says much, unlike Tooksooks, who finds silence a real chore. We all get on fine. For sisters, the girls don't argue much, and the boy is allowed to do what he pleases. That upsets me a little, and if I try to interfere, I get in serious trouble. Kioki doesn't discipline him and he's turning into a brat. He's ten times worse than I ever was. I can tell from her eyes that she thinks he's perfect just as he is.

He's more destructive than the puppy I got when I was eight. He's being pampered to death and I don't like it. He's about two, but I'm only guessing, and Kioki is still nursing him, mainly when he starts yelling or has hurt himself. One screaming tantrum and he's at his mama's breast.

I know what I'd like to do and my hand itches because of it. I've been hit by one of her cook pots before, though. Don't want to risk it again.

Billy eats a little of what we eat, but mostly he drags around a seal bone, and Lord help anyone who tries to take it away.

I guess I was the same with my teddy bear.

Folks here call him Ignash. I call him Billy. The boy's name was the cause of the latest confrontation I had with Asuluk. He came in one morning, as he always did, a few days after we relocated to the summer bay. The girls had settled in; the boy was curled around my feet, chewing on his bone, talking to it, when his granddaddy came in, fully armed with a new jar of ointment. I could tell it was fresh; the smell is sickening.

I said no, no need, I was fine now, and Asuluk looked at me curiously. Once was never enough, so I had to repeat myself. He put the jar down, sat on the bed, touched the boy's head, and talked to him in Eskimo. I understood what he said, too. Ignash, the strong, healthy boy.

"His name's William Robert Shaw, not Ignash."

"Ignash, big."

"William Robert is big."

Exasperation flicked across the medicine man's eyes. "Ignash," he said in that tone he uses so well—I am the wise one here; damn well do as you're told.

"Billy," I said slowly.

"Bill . . . ee . . ." Asuluk grunted, then repeated, "Ignash." He put the boy on the floor and the little feller looked at us both and decided chewing his bone was more interesting—till his granddaddy called him in Eskimo.

The head went down, the butt went up, and he got to his feet. And, dragging his bone, he sunk down between his granddaddy's legs half a second before he tripped on something invisible. The medicine man looked at me; victory shone in his eyes, too.

"Come lie with Dad, Billy."

The boy climbed up his grandfather, kicked him in the nose on the way over his shoulder, and curled up next to me.

"William Robert Shaw," I said, victorious.

Asuluk studied me a long time before he tried to say William Robert, but Billy was easier. "Ignash Bill . . . ee."

"Billy Ignash Shaw."

He relented. When Asuluk smiled, it felt as if the sun had doubled its size. We may have compromised on the boy's name, but I couldn't escape the putrid ointment. He must have heard me wheezing or something. So he pushed me down flat, opened the layers of clothing, and rubbed that foul black stuff into my skin. It could clear anything—including a room. I watched his face. I always wondered about this man. He never got excited; he never got upset. He was gruff when angry, gruff when amused. If he was any drier, he'd crumble. If he had any personality, he kept it hidden. Now and then, something would flicker across his eyes, as if he had something he needed to tell me, something about me maybe, but he never did.

He told me in his curious mix of Eskimo-English that I'd be a daddy again fairly soon. If I was fortunate, it would be another son, and it was time that we both thought of Ignash's future—as a hunter.

I tripped him on the name.

He smiled at me.

Another baby. I knew it wasn't Kioki who was pregnant, because she was away for a couple of days, to the place she went every few weeks. Tooksooks and a few of the other ladies and girls took up food and drink every day to the little shack just out of the village, not far from the dog box, in fact. Past the burial ground. It was no place for any man up there, except for Asuluk, but he only went if he had to.

So it was Tooksooks pregnant this time. I had no way of knowing how far gone she was, and my curiosity got the better of me one night when she was asleep beside me. It was late, dark, and quiet. Billy was sleeping. I sneaked my hand up under her clothes and touched her belly. I took a guess: halfway, maybe. Then she woke and cuddled my hand between her breasts. She liked that, and so did I. I figured I had to take whatever I could whenever I could, because when this other baby came, I wouldn't be anyone's center of attention for a long time.

I've said before how time doesn't exist here. Well, neither does privacy. It used to embarrass me living in this little house with two ladies. Not anymore. Bobby used to say I'd never get anywhere being too shy all the time. If only he could see me now.

If Tooksooks got what she wanted from me, too—this baby—I can only hope that wealth on Kulowyl isn't measured by the quantity of one man's offspring.

They have new blood now, a little boy with sandy brown hair and bright blue eyes—a white Eskimo boy.

I often wonder what my mother would think of him. My sister, too. By now, they'd think I was dead. By now, Meg would be sole proprietor of Sullivan and Shaw Air Service. Meg, who would never go flying.

Everything I had, I left to her. Maybe it was a thought better left unborn, but I put a proviso in my will that two thousand dollars be invested as a college fund for her kids, if she ever had any.

I can see her sometimes in my head just before I go to sleep—Meg, filthy rich, with three kids of her own, two boys and a little girl who looks just like her. Seeing it is almost like being there and I feel good, but when I think of my mother, there's nothing.

I can barely remember what she looks like.

Maybe she finally died of that broken heart, worried herself to death about me. Maybe it was the sheriff, Fred Larsen, and Reverend Willis who knocked on her door, this time to say how her only son was lost, presumed dead somewhere between Alaska and Vancouver, that he'd never arrived. I imagine the sheriff's belly poking through his shirt while he's telling her. Maybe she just lay down and started to die after the door squeaked shut.

Maybe that look in her eyes, the one she kept for hungry, stray dogs, finally makes some sense to me.

She must have known. Lord, she must have.

It's the not knowing that eats away at me. I don't know if she's really dead. I don't know if Frankie Dee had his way with Meg. I knew after the night I threatened to beat his square-eyed face to a pulp if he ever touched my sister that my threat hadn't done any good; that he'd simply and patiently wait for me to leave, then he'd move on in, charm his way past my mother.

It was never that hard to do.

I don't know how Sally is. I don't know how Bess is. I don't know if Casey Sullivan is still staring at the walls of that insane asylum, either. I don't even know if Billy Taylor is still alive, or even if he thinks of me on occasion. It's the not knowing that feels as if someone's aimed a poison arrow at me and shot.

The only light that shines comes from my son's eyes when he crawls onto me, clings tightly, and baby-talks and gurgles into my ear. But I know there'll come a time when he'll go off with the rest of them and be taught how to hunt, to fish—be taught how to be an Eskimo.

I can never be that. I cannot become something I am not. I can't let go of the past. I can't pretend I had no beginnings, but if this is the middle, then, God, don't make me wait too long for the end.

It was during one of his worst suicidal depressions that he went to his father-in-law's house and took back the Colt six-shooter. He loaded it, returned home and kissed Kioki, Billy, and Took-sooks good-bye, and limped away, alone, past the burial ground, which was covered in three feet of snow. It was only visible during the short summer thaw. There were no crosses, just bodies wrapped tightly in skins.

They had their own Great Spirit watching over them.

John had neither. He'd never taken a fancy to the hellfires of Christianity; found his foot tapping too often to the rhythm of the Eskimo tambour. There were even times when he thought he saw their visions, their Great Spirit, but seeing was not feeling, understanding, or believing.

He made it to the inlet and watched the mirage of storm clouds defying common sense. It was the kind of mirage that would have a sailor call, Land ho!

Gray, scattered bergs below the horizon. In the distance, some drift ice.

He took Bobby's gun, studied it.

It would be such a short journey. No cold, no ice. No heartbreak, no loneliness. No more craning necks searching the endless foggy sky for the sight, the sound of a de Havilland. No more praying futilely for a search party to find him.

If he could do this, there would be nothing—a deep, peaceful nothing.

John sat.

The quiet was not broken by any sign of life. Even the water foaming at the rock made no sound.

It would be over quickly, that much he knew, providing he did it right.

He looked down at the gun again and knew he had the courage to continue.

John drew in a deep breath of the clean, icy air and looked out to sea one final time. The drift ice to the north, five, maybe six hundred yards offshore, was riddled with dark patches he hadn't noticed before.

His heart leapt to his ears.

He'd been here long enough to know what that meant.

He'd seen a herd of walrus at play.

He took the shortest possible route back to the village and didn't realize he was bawling the report in Eskimo till the entire population came out, understood every word he said, and took him at his word.

He didn't realize until later how he had ensured the village's survival for another season.

If they had a word for hero, he was made aware of it, and that night, after the unending celebration, he quietly gave the handgun back to Asuluk.

ELEVEN

———◦◦◦◦◦◦◦———

AFTER the walrus sighting, John found a more elevat-
ed degree of acceptance. The women and children
had never been a problem, mainly because he helped them skin,
stretch, and peg walrus, seal, and bear hides. He also tried to
teach the children a little English, some numbers, as well as attempting, however futilely, to broaden their limited horizons.
Sometimes, even a few ladies would sit in the circle around him.

But also, the menfolk now allowed him closer, a silent, unani-
mous decision among themselves that had nothing to do with
the elder's directives. The acceptance came as John wished,
from the heart. Where before he'd been largely ignored, he was
now beckoned to assist in building and repairing kayaks and
weapons and soon found that although he wasn't invited to a
hunt, he was still rarely home.

It was only during the extremes of foul weather that he had
the inclination, or chance, to write.

If the sun never sets from May to August, it must be June again,
and if I'm right, I'm about twenty-nine years old and it's probably 1931. I still don't know exactly where on this God's earth I
am. At times, I wonder if I'm near Attu. It could be Attu there to
the northwest, the southern tip of Kiska to the east, or just more
lumps of rock that no one knows exists except the folks and
wildlife that live on it.

As shaky as it is, I'm learning to call this place home.

I'm getting used to the tremors—my only assurance that yes, I am somewhere in the Aleutians. There's been no quake yet in the time I've been here, but some of the tremors are severe enough to still a heartbeat for a while. You see it on the faces, feel it on your own, a moment or two of fear, then it passes.

Asuluk explains it as angry spirit at work. Sometimes I believe him. Meg once built herself a volcano from paper-mâché—the damned thing worked, too. I wandered past her room, looked in, and asked the stupid question: What's that? She tried to explain to me the hows and whys of volcanic activity. I told her to impress her teacher for the A, said I had other things to do.

I guess I said that a lot to Meg when she was a kid.

Understanding the hows and whys of volcanic activity wouldn't make that moment of fear any less real. I was walking with the boy when I felt the first tremor—four seconds of the ground beneath our feet convulsing. Billy took fright and climbed up my arm, clung to my neck. "Dad," he yelled. "Dad, what's that?"

By the time I realized what it was, the tremor had passed. It's hard to explain to a little boy that his dad can't stop the ground shaking, when it's obvious to the boy that his dad can do anything.

The little feller is my shadow. No matter what I do, where I go, he's with me, chatting constantly in his English-Eskimo mix. He's learning both languages and can't differentiate yet. But I guess it's what he hears at home the most. And if any other kids laugh at him, he fights.

Not many kids, even ones older than he is, laugh much anymore. He's a fierce little guy, fights like his red-haired aunt.

As for me, I've learned enough Eskimo to get by without causing mass hysteria.

I still have dreams that a search party will find me. Sometimes they vary, not always, though. My favorite is the one led by a de Havilland. It lands on the beach and the American pilot is glad to see me. I don't look back as we fly out, but I know that Took-sooks and Kioki are standing there, crying as I go. Other times, it's a fishing boat, a couple of Alaskan fishermen sheltering from a storm on the northwest tip of the island. Other times, I just keep on walking across the ice.

The boy's with me, every time.

And every time, I wake and I'm still here.

Some of the disappointment is fading—only some.

Sinbad's made good use of the pliers I gave him so long ago—I've still to discover what his necklet means, but whenever we're together, he sees it hanging around my neck and the sight makes him happy. The pliers made him happier, though. I wonder sometimes what he'd think of my old workshop back home. I guess if I hadn't been an aviator or a soldier, I'd have been a carpenter—another of my mother's wishes unfulfilled.

A little while ago, Sinbad took me on a journey. He came to my house and asked if I would come. Just the two of us—another party had left two days before for a neighboring island. He knew I'd agree, because the canoe was already filled with enough food and water for an overnight expedition.

He dressed me in a layer of waterproofing—seal intestine—and the loaded two-seater kayak with both of us locked tightly inside hit the waterline immediately and made me a little apprehensive about the length of this "journey." I never was much of a sailor.

I soon discovered why we'd been waterproofed. My point of balance was opposite his—he'd lean right and I'd lean left. We'd barely moved thirty feet offshore when we capsized. I must have had my mouth open when we hit the water. We came up again, bobbed awhile. He was yelling at me. I'd just had my sinuses flushed with icy seawater, so I couldn't yell back.

Lucky for me he didn't hold a grudge too long. He just turned around, yelled some more, and gave me a look he inherited from his father.

I expected we'd head south to the winter side and the beach, where'd I let a few memories bury themselves alive. I was wrong. We paddled northeast, around drift ice, around islands no bigger than some Blue Ridge boulders, the canoe breaking through the glassy gray water with ease. It had to be the Bering Sea.

And suddenly, wide, open ocean appeared. To me, what seemed landmasses skirted us on three sides. Sinbad was singing to himself the entire time, a song I'd heard a hundred times in echoes of voices as they drifted back across ice and water—hunters departing. We'd all turn away only when we could no longer hear the voices and song.

"Great Spirits protect us, lead us toward bounty" is a loose and probably inaccurate translation, and singing English words to it would only kill the magic, because most of the time they all come back alive and with plenty of food. But I've also been there when fate dealt a bad hand, when the protecting spirits looked away for a moment or two and disaster struck. This unpredictable weather has killed too many experienced, strong men, left more than one family without a husband and father.

I felt safe with Sinbad. I guess I always will. But those thoughts weren't foremost in my mind as I studied this new, distant terrain. I was making deals with God again. Please, I begged, please, I will do anything just to see another white man's face. Is this the Alaska Peninsula? How far is it to Anchorage?

God wasn't listening.

We hit a stretch of rough water, skirted an iceberg that seemed the size of New Orleans, and paddled across toward the shelter of a treeless, rocky island inlet. And I was glad to have my feet on Mother Earth once more.

It was windier there than Kulowyl at its worst. Even the air felt different—brittle, if air can be brittle. The island seemed twice the size of Kulowyl and to me it seemed a far better location, a safer harbor—a natural harbor. As we dragged the kayak to higher ground, sat and nibbled on some dry, flaky salmon, Sinbad told me that this was "the place of my grandfather's birth."

I knew the story about the quake, the bad season, and the storm that wiped out the village, but as far as I could tell, Asuluk, Sinbad's father, and every one of his preceding forefathers for a century had been born on Kulowyl. So it seemed it was another story I had misinterpreted. I didn't argue that his story wasn't the same as his sister's nor did I say that they shared the same father, who just happened to be the chief storyteller. Storytellers exaggerated a lot, which made for better listening. Yesterday's tale was about the hunter who had no heart and because he had no heart, he was taken by something evil that lived out there on the ice.

I know they have a God; maybe they have more than one. They have a code of behavior but not written laws or rules as such. But for me, they're a tad too accepting of others' faults, too trusting that everyone everywhere must be like them.

There's no crime, no stealing because everything is shared. There're no murders that I know of, but there could have been that day I held that knife across Zuk's neck; that day I nearly beat Kioki to death. What would have happened to me if one of them had died? Will I ever know? I guess I could have asked Sinbad, but he never really tried to understand my language.

I remember seeing some Chinese in a newspaper once. They all dressed the same, looked the same. I wondered then how they could recognize one another. Now I know. I've been here God knows how long, I sure don't, and to an outsider these folks'd all look the same, too. Till you have to live with them, find they're all individuals—each one, from a newborn baby to an old man wandering off alone to die.

Sinbad seems content. If the belly's full, all's well. There's the occasional clown, the practical joker, the actor, the singer, the storyteller, the hunter who can bring home the catch of the day while everyone else's baskets are empty. There's one who's a faster rower; one who will not blink and who will jump into water colder than freezing, hold his breath for four minutes, and not be half-dead when he finds the hole in the ice again.

And the kids all dream about being better than one another

one day. You see it in their eyes as the hunting party leaves, comes home again, five, maybe six hours later.

Even a death here is a celebration, a sadness and joy, so I know that they believe in a better place afterward.

I can't remember when it was, but I saw an old man, so old he could hardly walk. He stumbled off alone and everyone watched him go. They had the same looks on their faces as they had when that old lady died in my arms.

He never came back alive. It wasn't till later that I saw his necklace hanging on a spear outside of his family's house. The village was quiet for a long time, till Asuluk had another vision, and I guess they all started to sing the old man's soul off to Eskimo heaven. Four men went out and came back with the body. It was wrapped in skins, a circle of stones put around it, knives, spears, the old man's bow and arrow, too. I guess it was to help him survive in the other world. He was carried off to the burial ground and just lay there in the thaw with everyone else. Snows will come, cover them soon enough. I looked at Sinbad when he wasn't aware and I wondered if he'd be like that old man when it was his time to die. The harder I watched him, the more I decided, yes. Yes, he'd do that. Probably without saying good-bye to anyone.

Sinbad was about my age, but that's about all we had in common. I didn't understand why he'd taken a shine to me. I did understand why he beat the shit out of me that day, and I'm glad he did. But he was friendly to me long before I had to prove myself worthy of survival. I know he was there when I lay on the ice, bleeding to death. For a long time, he ignored me, or that's what I thought. I'd taken it for granted they'd all welcome newcomers with open arms. I was mistaken.

We sat there in the sun, quiet, pensive. And this man of few words started talking in Eskimo, slowly. And he was as subtle as a shotgun blast, because the first thing he said was, "I wanted to kill you when you fell from the soaring bird."

The fish I was chewing on lost its flavor. "Why?"

"You are not like us. Stranger. Bad. Bad." He touched my

hair, my beard, and looked down at the length of my legs, which were stretched out. He was fully extended, too—but his feet ended where my shins began. Till then, I hadn't noticed how short he was.

"Strangers not to be trusted. Old stories say that strangers come . . . come and kill women, children. Steal men."

I told him how I'd heard that story already.

He looked at me and repeated, "We wanted to kill you. But my father said no. My father stopped us. He reminded us of the vision. His vision. My sister's vision. Of you. Falling from the sky." He sighed and looked at me. "I am glad I did not kill you, friend."

"Well, so am I, friend."

"Why do you call me Sin . . . bad?"

"You remind me of a pirate."

"Pi . . . rit?"

"It's good," I lied. "Friend." I smiled. He believed me.

"Come."

I followed him on the trek overland and carried his quiver over my shoulder, his hatchet in my coat. I lost most of his next story to the wind—it was blowing so hard, I couldn't hear myself think. We must have walked a good mile before we came to the other side of the island. I was about to ask Sinbad why we had to walk—because it would have been easier to paddle—when he pushed me down hard and whispered for quiet.

I looked over the rise, too. Below us, sunning themselves on a rocky outcrop, was a small family of seals.

I had the same feeling I used to get whenever I saw a new airplane—butterflies. My mouth watered. I couldn't remember the last time I'd tasted fresh seal blood. It felt like a lifetime.

It was at that moment I realized what I was becoming. The me that once was had finally disappeared—forever.

I never liked killing things, I'm a lot like my father that way. When I was young, I watched him kill a chicken—we always had roast chicken for dinner on Sundays. He never wanted me to watch, told me to go inside, help my mother instead. I must

157

have been about five. I hid behind the laundry door and peeked out through the cracks in the wood, watched the ax come down. I heard my dad curse because the chicken, without a head, got up and ran around. He had tears in his eyes. He never liked doing that, never. I know now it was just nerves that made the chicken dance, but what I'd seen haunted me for a long time—which is why he never wanted me to watch in the first place.

Before I came here, the closest I got to a seal was looking at a photograph of one balancing a ball on its nose. I remember thinking that was a neat trick.

I never knew they could scream.

Sinbad heard nothing, or if he did, he ignored it. He was like an African lion that day—he'd waited, chosen, and moved in for the kill. And I watched, just as I'd watched my dad chop that chicken's head off.

Questions rose from deep inside me. It was wrong to kill; no one had to tell me, because I couldn't fight off the innate feeling that contradicted what my eyes witnessed.

It felt wrong because I was watching it happen. It wouldn't be wrong tomorrow when the animal fed three families. But I guess not many folks apologize to a steak before they eat it, either.

I didn't like watching the kill, hearing the seal's buddies scream and panic, but I didn't hesitate when Sinbad and I shared its blood. I only got to thinking later about rights and wrongs. Here there're too many in-betweens.

My favorite story used to be Jules Verne's *From the Earth to the Moon*. I never wondered about other kinds of life before my mother gave me that book. I thought it incredible someone could think of an airplane that could travel into space like that. So now I'm thinking, What if there is life up there and that life is looking down on us the same way we had been looking down at that family of seals?

Frightening. Thoughts like those never seem to have a happy ending.

Bellies full, we were sitting together again, our backs against some more Blue Ridge boulders, sheltered from the wind. Not a storm cloud in sight. It was a perfect Eskimo summer day that had no end. I took my parka hood off and let the sun shine on my face. Sinbad finally asked what it was like to ride a soaring bird.

If I had a quarter for the number of people who had asked me that same thing, I'd have my own airline fleet by now.

I did my best to explain the feeling of flight more than the process involved. It was probably how he felt when he won his kayak races. I hadn't forgotten what it was like to fly, but translating feelings into English words was hard enough; searching for Eskimo ones was nearly impossible. I took him through a normal takeoff and a landing.

I doubt I succeeded in explaining.

Then he asked me to tell him about the far-off world where folks like me lived, folks with yellow hair and blue eyes.

I never knew how difficult the task was, because I had nothing here I could compare it with. He'd never seen a white man till I crash-landed. He'd never been to the mainland. Did he know it existed apart from his known world of islands and fish and birds and seals and whales and walruses? While I told him about my old world, I indulged. I told him about the woods near my old hometown; the creeks, lakes, waterfalls; the forests, Piedmont ranges; the up-country of South Carolina; the Savannah River; the towns and cities. I described how I grew up in the days when motorcars were replacing horse and buggies and wagons, how I missed the Great War. And when I'd done, I looked at him to see if he understood a word I'd said.

He was fast asleep, sitting there in the warm sun, catching a thousand z's. I wondered what he was dreaming about. Next month's whale, maybe. Or teaching his boys how to use a bow, how to be a champion like their one-eyed father. I'd seen him take two birds with one arrow, disappointed that it hadn't been three.

I must have slept, too.

Going home took half the time that arriving had, but any journey was like that for me, unless I was lost. And I'd been lost a couple of times, always in Alabama. But I recognized Kulowyl from a distance and was a little disappointed when Sinbad bypassed the island and took us farther west.

I speared my first fish about an hour later. He got half a dozen and gave two to me. I knew what that smile meant. Bringing home the fish would make my family proud of me.

They didn't go out for the sole reason of providing food; they did it for love, as well. And being invited along meant that at last I was one of them, no longer an outsider.

The best sight of all was coming in and recognizing the small greeting party long before I saw faces. My son was standing between my two wives, and he was holding hands, jumping up and down, excited. Beside Tooksooks was Asuluk and his wife, the one who always snarls at me and would harpoon me if she had half a chance, my mother-in-law. She looked disappointed that I'd survived the journey, so I met her with my best smile, considered giving the ugly old monster a kiss, too, but stopped just in time.

I didn't realize we'd been away close on three days.

The girls had a lot to tell me, even though nothing of great interest had happened in my absence.

Billy had cried the whole time I was away. I looked at him; he was sitting in his corner, trying to pull apart the shell counter I'd made him. Someone had slipped off the cliff and had broken his leg, and if it hadn't been for the little girls collecting shellfish, he would have lain there too long and died. Kioki had picked a full basket of *sue wuk* and had prayed for my safe return. A baby girl had been born and a polar bear was seen swimming toward drift ice. The gathering at Asuluk's had been postponed until our homecoming.

There were other items of interest—gossip—but I didn't hear them. It was so good to be home again.

Kioki took the boy to his grandfather's house while Tooksooks welcomed me back the only way she knew how.

I remember thinking, Hell, this should happen more often.

Later that long day, Asuluk came to visit. He stood at the entrance to the house, studying me for a little while. I was starting to wonder what I'd done this time, when he said, "Come."

I was playing with Billy. I was tired. I wanted some time with my family. "Now?"

"Come. We talk."

Kioki nodded. Tooksooks was smiling again. The boy thought he was going, too, and he helped me dress, then expected to get dressed himself. I could hear his angry screams as I walked out with his granddaddy. He never liked being left behind.

Nothing was said on the long, slow walk across the island. This time, we stopped on the south end, where the sea was always calm, smooth as glass.

Asuluk sat, folded his legs, and stared straight ahead.

I couldn't take any more. "What have I done now?" I asked in English.

"Sit."

When I sat, Asuluk turned to me and nodded. "You fish. Hunt now. Good." Something crossed his eyes. Was it affection? "No women's work. You man."

"Women's work is better than no work."

The old man grunted, yes or no—it was hard to tell which. Is this what he'd wanted me to come all this way for? To tell me I fish and hunt now, good? I tried to get up, but the medicine man grabbed my good arm and held tight. "We talk. You. Me. Now. Talk."

Something important was on the medicine man's mind; that much I could see and feel. I tried to get comfortable. If he was going to tell me another story, I knew it'd take a long time. I fished in my pocket, found the *sue wuk* Kioki had slipped me before I left. I held some out to him and he took it, sucked on it slowly. It tasted better that way.

Today he was thoughtful and agitated. From one of his many pockets, he took a handful of seal bladders and threw them into the water.

The spirits would allow more fish into the waters if they accepted this offering.

161

And I just sat there, watching the bladders float away until one by one they sank.

"You fish, hunt now. Good."

"You said that already."

Asuluk turned to me and said, "Ship come, long ago."

Here we go again, I thought. "Jesus, Pop, isn't there a new story you can tell me?"

"Pop?" he asked, fire in his eyes. So I lied, told him it meant friend. I don't think he believed me. I couldn't lie to him like I could to Sinbad. "No Pop," he grunted. I apologized.

Asuluk grew very quiet.

"How come I've been here nearly five years and now you talk to me in English? No Eskimo?"

Asuluk sniffed, blinked, and turned his expressionless face back toward the sea. "Ship come, long ago. My father take . . . no." He stopped talking and searched for white words. "Father leave with men in ships. Go. Trap. Trap for . . . for . . . bird." He imitated a shooter pointing a rifle at the sky first, then at something imaginary running around on the ground. "And seal. Not come back."

"So what? He went with Russian fur traders. I know. You've told me. Kioki's told me. Sinbad's told me. Asuluk, it happened a long time ago. Can't you forget it? Isn't there another story you can tell me?"

Asuluk was having difficulty finding the right words to use. His foot was jiggling; he was getting angrier, impatient. "The bird. Your bird. Like the ship, long ago. More birds fly. . . ." And he got up slowly and danced for me, his arms as wings, banking right, left.

I knew what he was trying to say. The gestures told me about another bird that had circled the body of its dead, mangled friend and had flown off again.

Tears filled my eyes. Too much desolation welled and found no outlet. The medicine man was telling me of the search party that came long ago, when I was fighting for life.

A search party had come?

A search party?

"When! Damn you! When!"

Asuluk turned to me, questioning. I'd gone and interrupted his story.

"When did the birds come?"

I wanted to take this man by the throat and squeeze and keep on squeezing until I got an answer.

The medicine man thought for a moment and held up his hand. Four gloved fingers and one gloved thumb indicated how many summers had passed since the roaring birds flew, circling their dead friend.

I put my head between my knees.

"Five years ago?" My voice shook. Five years ago? Jesus, I could have been home by now!

"Bird flies again, you go back?" Asuluk asked quietly.

How? Searchers had already come this far west, found the wreck. One look would have been enough. No one could have survived that. They wouldn't come back now, not five years on. It was too long ago. As far as my family knew, I was dead. I had to be.

"Ship comes, bird comes, you go?"

There was something in Asuluk's eyes that I couldn't read.

"What have you seen this time?" I asked.

"Ship comes, bird comes, you go?" he asked again.

"I tell you what, Asuluk. If a ship came by now, you'd never see me again. Yes, I'd go. Think I like it here? Fool—" I got up slowly and walked away. I had to. This medicine man had seen me crying too many times, too often.

He followed, repeating, "You fish, hunt, good," and he put his arm around my shoulder.

I couldn't take it. I pushed him away. "Don't damn touch me! Don't you touch me!"

Asuluk pulled a face and obliged.

A search party had come, and he thought he'd alleviate the

pain by telling me I was a good fisherman? Jesus. I wasn't even the one who'd caught the goddamned fish! I felt like punching the man in the head.

We walked back in silence. I was limping past Asuluk's house when he pulled me inside. We sat there in silence for a time, until Mrs. Monster handed me a bowl of warm blood. And she tried to smile in welcome, but it didn't work.

"Show you thing. Stay."

Asuluk brought out an old muzzle loader. It wasn't the Winchester repeater I'd imagined as the old man imitated the shooter, going off into the great unknown and never returning. And I knew what the medicine man wanted.

He wanted me to show him how to use it.

"No. There's no ball, no powder." I told him the only thing he could do with it was hit a polar bear on the back of the head and hope to stun it senseless. At that moment, I didn't care what he did with it. I just wanted to go home. Mrs. Monster was throwing me death stares from her corner. I hoped she chewed so hard on that mukluk that all her teeth would fall out in one hit.

"Ball, pow . . . der?"

"Yeah. Ammunition."

Asuluk's eyes widened. He stepped back so quickly, he fell over the earth table. I didn't know what I'd said, but he threw me out the door. I wondered if he'd just seen a ghost.

I made my way home, muttering to myself. I was still muttering to myself when Kioki sat beside me and asked what was wrong this time.

I told her, and the most she did was nod slowly. She explained as best she could in her calm way and looked to her sister too often for approval.

"Aeta have vision. Dream. Bad."

"Asuluk had a bad dream. So what?" I asked.

"Aeta have vision. Bad dream. Men come. You. Like you. Not me. Not us. Lots many die. Die. Die by . . ." She looked around, trying to see something that would explain. "Die by—"

164

"Bullets? Guns?"

"Yes. Bullets. Guns. Lots many die. Aeta have vision. Vision that you come in soaring bird. Vision that you go in bird boat with you men. You men."

"Men like me?" I asked. Excitement rose. What the hell was a bird boat? A de Havilland on pontoons?

"Bird boat come, you go?" Kioki asked. Her voice was shaking. I looked at her. She wasn't trying to hide the tears filling her eyes. I looked at Tooksooks, but she pretended she was very busy. Her face was about as happy as a dying seal's, too. And my son was trying to demolish the counter I'd made him. Bird boats, men like me. Men with guns . . .

"I don't know. Jesus, I don't know."

I had a lot to think about, and the more I thought, the worse it all got. I wanted out so bad, but part of me belonged here with Kioki, my son, Tooksooks, the baby growing inside her. I was turning into an Eskimo. I came to believe in Asuluk's visions like everyone else did, with reason.

If Asuluk dreams of a school of fish, you could lay a bet that within two days the kayaks would return full of fish. He even knew if someone would be sick long before the patient did. Sometimes he'd stop an individual from heading out to a hunt. No one questioned. Everyone trusted him. He was the closest thing they had to their Great Spirit and his word was law. Now it seems I'm alive because he dreamed of me crash-landing.

I don't know how he can tell the difference between a dream and a vision, and it's futile to ask. Now he's seen me leaving in a bird boat, of all things. A de Havilland on pontoons maybe? Men with guns? Lots many?

I guess it's a matter of wait and see.

What I'd like to know is why, after he's been talking to me, do I dream?

What he'd told me preyed on my mind for so long. I had known that a search party had been formed. Deep inside, I'd known that there was little chance of another, not after so long. It's been years. Bobby and I had been asked a few times to help

165

Miami police search for overdue boats, and a couple of times we'd been successful in finding wreckage.

Mostly, the sharks took care of the rest.

I guess the searchers—even if they'd seen the Jenny—would have listed me as dead.

God knows, I'd done it myself.

But I've been dreaming about blood on the ice—rivers of it, turning into lakes.

I usually wake screaming.

Tooksooks is quiet, too quiet. She's sick, too. If Eskimos can go pale, I believe she's ready to faint all the time. And even though she's sick, she can still manage a smile for me. Still likes to rub my feet. Still likes to be held all night long. Nothing makes her angry, nothing. It takes even less to make her happy, too. Just a look from me is sometimes enough.

And this damned nightmare—this blood on the ice—won't let me be. I keep asking Tooksooks if she feels okay. Lord knows, she doesn't look too good. Sometimes her lips go blue. Sometimes she can't move. She just lies there on our bed, staring at me. Her heart beats so hard and quickly, I can see it pulsing under her ear. Sometimes at night, I can hear it. All I can do is hold her hand and try to sleep without dreaming about rivers of blood staining the ice.

TWELVE

❦❦❦❦❦❦❦

PERHAPS it was the underlying fear in the medicine man's eyes that rekindled the recurring nightmare, or the way in which his second wife stared at him, as if she was getting her memories together.

Then Tooksooks went missing one biting autumn day, and Kioki would tell him nothing.

When she doesn't want to speak, she won't. She just sets me with that small, beady-eyed gaze and I'm sure that even Chinese water torture couldn't break the silence. Tooksooks had been gone two days and the days were growing shorter, barely four hours of light each. No one would tell me where she was, but I knew that I was the only person who didn't know.

And I was getting pissed off with all the secrecy. She was my wife. She'd lived with me for a couple of years and I liked her a lot, maybe not the way I felt about Kioki, but nothing could stop the worry. Even Billy was asking for her, because when he was in trouble with his mama, he'd run straight to Tooksooks for comfort.

I must have spent an hour trying different ways of questioning Kioki to get even a hint of where her sister might be. The most she offered was a shake of the head. Or she'd offer me food to change the subject. So when I said I wouldn't eat until Tooksooks was back, she sent me one of my mother's looks—the stray, hungry dog—and went back to chewing on her leather.

Because she damn well knew I'd eat when I got hungry.

So I copied what Freddie Larsen did that time the Milton's little girl disappeared. I did a house-to-house search. There were thirty of us searching the woods that time, and I realized who had the easier job when the Milton girl was found on the edges of the Sumter Forest, facedown in a shallow grave. We never knew how she got there, who had killed her or why. Things like that happened in other places, never in my hometown. The whole town went awful quiet for a long time after that child was murdered. It was the same kind of quiet that met me when I asked at each house where Tooksooks was, if anyone had seen her.

We'd just moved back to the winter side of the island and there weren't many places anyone could go, or dared go with winter so close by. I was feeling betrayed and angry by the non-committal faces, but most of all I was worried about my second wife.

Even Sinbad refused to help me, and I knew by the way he looked at me that he knew where she was and why. Stubbornness ran in that family.

I found out later that I wasn't completely shunned. I was sitting alone in the semidark, huddled on the top of the cliff, watching a storm building over the trench a couple of miles out to sea when Asuluk sat down beside me.

"Yes, I know. I hunt, fish, good now," I said before he did. He sighed and looked out to sea and started a story about life and death.

They really think that the stars are souls, waiting up there for a chance to be born. Now, their God, the Great Spirit, lives way up past the stars, and night falls when he throws down his skins and covers the earth. The story was about how the Great Spirit lifts his skins at night sometimes when a man and woman are together and by lifting the skins that cover the earth, he lets some stars see what's going on down below. And if he allows it, one will fall to the earth, to the man and woman, and it will become their son or daughter.

I thought it a different—and kind of nice—way to explain a shooting star, but I didn't have the heart to argue with him. I knew what conception was, how it happened, but never for one moment have I ever thought life was anything except a chance happening.

The story didn't end there. Now and then, Asuluk said quietly, the soul decides it made a mistake and wants to return home, back to the warmth and safety of the Great Spirit's skins.

Now when that happens, the woman is not favored anymore and she must stay away from the village until she's favored once again. To return too soon would curse everyone, and not even her name is thought, let alone uttered.

However, because I was still a stranger to the ways, the Great Spirit had forgiven me, had seen and felt my great concern of the heart. Therefore, I was allowed to see my wife.

The Great Spirit knew I had to see before I would believe.

It was the greatest load of crap I'd heard yet, but I knew better than to offend their Great Spirit and his middleman, Asuluk, so I let him put some safety necklace around my neck. Then he picked up his light and I followed him out into the darkness.

There were rules, of course, laws. I wasn't to look into her eyes or get close enough to touch.

Asuluk led me to a sheltered place about a mile west of the village. A sled dog was barking savagely from the end of a straining long rope staked to the ground. Asuluk threw him a piece of meat and it was gone in two seconds. I've always liked dogs, but I sure keep my distance from these half-wild wolflike critters.

Asuluk called out Tooksooks's full name and the soft wailing and chanting from inside the tiny shelter immediately ceased. He told her in Eskimo that her husband was here—the rest I didn't catch—and he threw some food in to her, then gave it a few seconds before he nodded to me and stayed out in the cold dark, alone.

She was on her own, facing the wall in the warm, dark shelter. One of her plaits was undone and greasy dark hair reached the skin she was sitting on. She didn't turn around. I wanted to sit with her but wasn't allowed to. She told me not to come in any farther.

The smell of blood was strong, which was the reason for the guard dog outside. It'd alarm the village if a bear came within five hundred yards of her.

She told me she'd be home soon, that I wasn't to worry. She said I had to go, that I had no place being there. She was trying not to cry, trying hard to be brave about it all when she said the little one had gone back to the Great Spirit.

Some things I can accept, but not this. She'd lost the baby, and no amount of stories could explain the reason for her exile. What if she'd bled to death? How would Asuluk explain that to me? I didn't understand why women came from far and wide for a birth but a miscarriage was taboo. Did they think it was contagious? Would I ever know?

When she returned to the village, it was as if nothing had happened—outwardly at least. Something passed between the sisters, something unspoken. Tooksooks, who chattered constantly, hardly said a word anymore. I didn't need anyone telling me that she thought constantly of what could have been. She'd sit quietly in our house and watch Billy playing by himself. Her eyes would glaze over and I could nearly feel the sting of tears she was trying so hard to hide.

All she wanted was to be a mother.

She lost the second one, too. I was away when it happened— out on a four-day expedition with Sinbad and seven others. I came home to a sleeping son and a quiet Kioki, who would not look me in the eye. And when I asked where her sister was, it all began again.

It took a long time, but she kept the third.

She even lets me feel the kicks from her belly and her eyes sparkle brighter than the moon's reflection off the still water when she looks at me.

170

Seems that this little shooting star was finally meant to be.

I want a daughter. And I wonder what she'll look like.

Because of some twist in the assembly line, Billy came out with blue eyes and light brown hair. I know he's going to be tall, like me. His legs are long from the knee to the thigh, where most of my length comes from. Billy's eyes are a different blue from mine—they're dark like his grandma's. And he got my square chin, too. I'm just hoping that if Tooksooks has a girl, the assembly-line workers will be kind to her. Eskimo ladies aren't the nicest-looking on earth.

I told Billy what will happen soon and he took the news of a brother or sister like he takes everything else—he looked at me and at Tooksooks and grunted his approval. I think it was approval. Sometimes I see more of Asuluk in him than anyone. It's as if nothing worries him unduly, or that nothing I say interests or surprises him—unless he's helping me make something or is watching me carve some ivory.

I can etch a '23 Jenny in about twenty minutes. Sometimes I'll etch a landscape—Calhoun Falls or sunset over Blue Ridge. Billy prefers the biplanes or the Harley I used to own. He likes machinery, and between us we've made a contraption that has no purpose, except that it works and makes interesting noises. It works on two pebbles and a windup starter.

It's my Gizmo Machine, twelve inches high by two feet long, with wheels, conveyor belt, traps, springs. I found a use for the Morse radio innards. We set the Gizmo up together now; he knows which piece goes where and why. I'd like to find something I could convert to a slate so I could teach him the alphabet, but I suppose if he knows how to speak and understand English it's the most I can hope for.

Things like this I can do, share with the boy, but what do you do with a daughter except hope she won't spend all her life chewing on leather and dying old, useless and toothless?

Bobby used to say I spent too much time worrying about things that might never happen. He never believed me when I said I was being prepared.

171

A little girl.

She'll be taught Eskimo ways—making clothes, jewelry, food preparation, how to skin a seal. When she's of age, she'll choose herself some boy, spend a long time making eyes at him, start sneaking off somewhere, and before I know it, she'll move out and become a wife. Probably to one of the babies born here in the last year. She'll make me a grand-daddy before I'm forty-five and life will go on in an ever-rising, ever-widening spiral.

I probably won't get to know her at all—not like I know the boy. And I'm not sure if that's the way it's meant to be.

Sinbad talks about his sons and there's pride in his voice when he does, but mention his two daughters and his eyes are kind of vacant, as if I've been asking him about a stranger or a new kind of critter they found on the beach.

Maybe Bobby was right. Maybe I do worry too much.

It doesn't hurt as much these days to think of the past, to remember things that weren't important then but are now. I wonder sometimes if everything I ever saw, touched, felt, heard, did, and thought has been recorded, like in the pages of that Walt Whitman book Bobby gave Meg, or maybe recorded somehow on an invisible phonograph record and it's all there, just waiting for me to find it, reach for it, touch it, bring it all back.

A lot comes back to me when I'm just sitting, doing nothing, thinking of nothing. Hell, sometimes a passing cloud will remind me of Miami's skyline or the monument in Abbeville's town square.

Nothing is the same. My life here revolves around Kioki, Tooksooks, the boy, and the baby that's going to arrive any old time.

I can't control this kid of mine. He bites; he squeals; he fights other kids. And if I say anything, I get in trouble. Kioki doesn't raise her voice unless he's going to do something that might kill him. Most times, he needs a good paddling. The only English word he likes to use is *no*. And he stamps his foot, like I used to.

I'd scream, pout, pound the floor and my father would give me a swift smack on the butt or the legs. My mother would just swing and hit whatever was there. Trouble was, all the paddlings and whacks and tantrums only made me worse, more determined that they'd never win.

I guess I had more paddlings than pancakes for the first seven years of my life. Then I discovered I could make them suffer in other ways, and mostly I used my kid sister to bait the hook. I still can't understand why that girl loved me, even if it was from a safe distance.

If Billy tries that with his new sister—or brother—I don't know what I'll do.

Damned if I know how these people teach their kids the limits of what can and can't be done. Back where I came from, it wasn't often anybody got to see kids except in parks, in school playgrounds at recess. People I knew who had families seemed to hide any children until they were walking around and being polite only when parents were looking. Babies were hidden, too, except when there was some kind of semi-official showing—like a baptism. A while after any birth, friends and relations would gather much like they did at a death. The body'd be on display in its casket; the baby'd be on display in its basket. Both were all prettied up for the occasion, shined and glowing like someone's new motorcar or airplane. And often if someone bought a motorcar or a new airplane, the occasion was a real celebration. At least there was something concrete and useful to display. What's useful about a newborn or a corpse? Dead people are dead people and are no further use. Babies are like slugs for months and months.

Seen and not heard seemed the best way to deal with kids. Maybe that's why civilized kids fight a lot, grow up with the need to prove themselves—because adults never let them be who they were or saw them for what they were, not kids but new people, learning to adjust to living on earth. It must be a different kind of life up there beyond the stars.

But that's just me. Maybe I'm wrong. I spent too long trying

173

to get my folks to see I was a person, too, even if I embarrassed them in public by asking stupid questions and doing stupid things.

Kids here don't seem to fight much, and if they do, no one steps in unless blood's going to be spilled. And it's usually one of the older kids who does that. If an adult gets involved, it's very serious indeed. Asuluk can stop a fight before it starts just by walking past, but other than that they wouldn't know authority if it bit them, and if it did, they'd just bite back.

I love these people.

It's this calm contentment that shines in their eyes that makes the difference. I guess that was the hardest thing for me to accept about them. They spent their life not knowing what warmth was, not knowing what real food was, not knowing what it was like to walk around half-naked and suffer serious sunburn, and not caring, either. Just this awful, dumb acceptance . . .

It must be something that's inherited and that's why Billy shows little contentment. I see myself in the boy, mainly through a thought lurking behind those eyes: What can I wreck now?

I say no all the time. He looks at me the way his granddaddy looks at anyone who questions his judgment. I've hit him a couple of times when his mother wasn't around. He hit me back. When I yell at him, his mother or aunt distract his attention, much like I used to divert course if I saw a storm on the horizon, a right-rudder slip. But attention and courses can only be diverted for so long. At times, he sees me as the enemy.

The little asshole's like me in too many ways—he loves fire. He gets his deafness from his daddy's sister. But when all else fails to satisfy that incredible curiosity of his, he'll come to me and for a while we'll be friends again. We'll go and do something.

If the weather's okay, I'll call the kids out.

I teach school now. I figured I wanted to teach my son, I may as well teach anyone else who wants to learn, too.

Billy and his swarm of friends, of all ages, can count to fifty so far. Next week, I'll take them to a hundred. Not that it will help much, because we're not living in white man's land.

I made them a counter that they can all use whenever they want. It's made up of fifty stones skewered on some strut wire, tied around two precious pieces of driftwood. When the weather clears or improves a bit, we can all go off hunting for more stones. Most of the kids learn fast, and some knowledge just isn't enough for most of them.

I guess I can take them into the mysterious world of arithmetic sometime soon. I was watching one day when the baskets came in, full. I heard the kids teaching their mothers how to count—in English.

Next, I guess, is a little more English. Times like this, I wish I'd paid more attention at school. Eleven grades, and I made it to the seventh. Spent more time staring out of the window, daydreaming about airplanes, than I did paying attention.

So I know the signs of boredom firsthand, and I try hard not to make any kid here fall asleep. Somedays my house is packed tight; others, only one or two will arrive. It all depends on what chores they have. If a hunting party has returned, everyone is busy till the work's done.

And sometimes I'm gone for a couple of days, too.

Billy strings a few English words together and mostly it's: "You go now, Dad?" I don't think it's because he likes to see the last of me. I hope it's because he likes to wave good-bye as his Uncle Sinbad and I set sail in the clipper in search of brave new worlds. And all we ever come home with are a few cod, the occasional seal, and once we nearly tangled with a fishing polar bear and decided he could win, no fight attempted.

Billy reaches my knee and I can nearly lose him completely in two feet of snow. His left arm must be stretched a foot by now, but falling in a snow hole seems fun, so he searches for another straightaway, and a hundred-yard walk turns into a mile-long trek. He walks about as fast as I do on a good day, but I have to stop him trying to imitate my limp.

One day, he'll be old enough to realize why I walk like this, why his is the only father in the village with blue eyes, a red beard, and blond hair way past his shoulders; the only dad with one and half arms and a bent leg. Till then, I guess he'll copy everything I do.

Maybe that's what makes me feel so special.

Sometimes I lie awake while everyone else is sleeping and I look down at Billy lying there with Kioki, Tooksooks, and me and I wonder what my mother would have thought of him, what my sister would think if only she could see this now. And I often wonder what sort of father Bobby would have been. It's occurred to me that in all the time I knew him, he never talked of any future except to say, "I'm gonna have my own airplane." It's as if he got what he wanted, he flew the skies and loved it, and then he died the way he wanted to, but not before he left a mark on everyone he ever met—good or bad mark, so what, Bobby was Bobby and will never be easily forgotten. But me, I knew there would be more to this life than just flying.

I wanted it all, a job, money, a house, a wife, a family one day. Not necessarily in that order, but you need it all for a complete picture of normal life. About the only thing I never wanted was to be President of the United States, because I never was that good at bullshit.

Now, whether the wife would have been Rosanna is a futile guess. I think I would have liked to court and marry a girl with green eyes and long hair—hair she'd let me brush for her. She'd have been a girl who wouldn't care what I did, only how I did it—someone who didn't need to change anything about me but wouldn't mind if there were things about me I needed to change for myself. I always thought I'd settle in a place like Atlanta, Georgia. And on my wildest days, I wanted a farm in Montana, or maybe Iowa.

But the only green-eyed girl with long hair I ever met was Sally with no other name. She lived somewhere in Washington State, forty-two miles from Seattle. She had a voice that sounded like honey tasted. She wanted me to stay, and for a while, maybe five hours, I wanted to stay, too, but that damned dream got in the way again. And I suppose it was a could-have-been option that simply wasn't, a chance not noticed until it was long gone.

But I do have a family, and its boundaries are limited only by the size of this island. I'm closer to some folks than others and I have trouble with the mother-in-law. Everyone's different, but we all seem to fit. Life could be boring as hell, but somehow it isn't. I'm finding joys in the simplest things. If someone takes hours making a new kind of harpoon head, or knife, or spear, it's a cause for a get-together. Everything that is done is appreciated—large or small.

A birth is a time for mass celebration. When my son was born, everyone, I mean everyone, was as happy as I was.

Sinbad's the brother I never had. In Asuluk, I have, nearly, the father I lost. The strong man of few words, but what he has to say is respected.

The home's got no picket fence and it's nowhere near an airfield, nor does it have fifty acres of wheat out back. There's no sink, no bath, no outhouse, and no gingham curtains. But when the ladies are away, it's not a home at all. There's always a soft, warm body curled into me at night and the food I'm given tastes better these days because it's served with a smile. And a smile takes all the bitterness away. But I still miss the talk, the conversation, the friends, the sun.

Bobby and I used to sit on Miami Beach and talk—mainly about nothing—and he'd whistle if he saw a nice-looking girl walk by, then he'd turn to me and blame me for it. But the girls always knew, always. And he'd drag me off to dances, pick a girl for me, ask her to dance with me. I loved him too much to take any notice of the occasional urge I had to kill him. And I suppose we both could have been forty and he'd still behave like a sixteen-year-old let off the leash for the first time.

I miss hearing my mother worrying about where I'd be sleeping and what I'd be eating should something unplanned ever happen. Take an extra this, an extra that in case I was caught overnight or the weather turned. Ha, the weather. Oh, Lily, if

177

only you could see me now. She didn't want me to catch cold, said I had a weak chest. Maybe I did. But I never used anything she ever made me take.

I broke her heart when I told her I was going to fly from Miami around the States. She knew she could nag as much as she liked, cry as much as she had to, but I wouldn't change my mind. And maybe I never had a weak chest at all. Maybe it was just a weak heart, because if I was tougher, I'd be accepting of all this, not holding out for a miracle, hoping for a search party finding me, thinking I'll be back in Miami before I know it, sitting in the sun, watching the girls go by. And I'll look at the lady sitting on the sand beside me and I'll know what Sally's other name really is.

Maybe that was why she wanted me to stay.

Maybe she'd seen it, too—the Florida she'd seen in picture books, that new land of opportunity, a tropical paradise that reflected itself once or twice in my eyes.

I'd like to know what should have been as opposed to what now is, but thinking like this only causes problems. So I just hurt myself by keeping it all inside, because no one here would understand what it is I am missing the most—my own kind.

I should have known better. Something always happens when I get the miseries bad. A handful of kids came through my door, expecting it to be a school day.

I couldn't remember what we were up to, so I unwound the bull seal's hide I've been using for a blackboard and hooked it on the wall. I'd been using body paint for chalk, and Kioki must have cleaned it off in the last couple of days.

It's no use giving these kids American names. I spell out theirs as best I can by how the name sounds, it didn't take long for each to recognize his or her name. I teach more girls than boys, but Sinbad's youngest, Eennali, is always here, sitting up front, eyes shining. He's a year older than Billy and they're best friends when they're not rolling around fighting. Sinbad doesn't mind, because what Eennali learns, he teaches his father. Before I knew it, Sinbad was saying a few English words to me.

Asuluk has sat in a couple of times, probably to make sure I'm not doing anything damaging. I don't know what kind of teacher I am, but we sure have some fun.

Whenever the sun shines and it's almost warm and the ice isn't too thin, we all go out across the pack ice and play baseball. There are no rules to this game, just a gaggle of kids trying to hit a misshapen, splitting ball with a bear's thighbone.

They like gymnastics, not that I can do much to help. I used to be pretty good at handstands and walking on my hands, crab walking, fence walking, cartwheels.

It was during one of these outdoor gatherings that I thought of Elsie, Bobby's wing-walker. Maybe it was the little girl trying to master cartwheels that made me remember.

I started laughing so hard, damned if I could stop.

It all came back, as if it'd happened half an hour ago, not years.

THIRTEEN

●◆●◆●◆●

I been thinking."

I looked at Bobby. Something in his voice set my red light flashing out a big warning.

"Why don't we go to Jamaica?"

"What for?"

"I need a vacation. What else you go to Jamaica for?"

Oh, sure. Vacation. Six days a week flying two mail services with a staff of three: Bobby, me, and Sam, our mechanic. The contract was coming up for renewal and apart from the occasional passing sightseer joy flight over the Keys, the mail runs were our only income. Now he figures it's time for a vacation? "What's the matter with you? Been sitting on your brains too long?"

"I need a change."

I looked at him. "So go on up to the Seaview for an hour."

"Jesus, John. I'm bored!"

I thrust the books at him. "Be my guest."

He scratched his nose. "You don't want to go to Jamaica?"

"Of course I want to go to Jamaica. Just can't do it, is all." He reached for the telephone. "Who you calling?" I asked.

"Chuck. I just had an idea."

"Chuck? No way. No way in hell I'm letting that crazy touch my airplane! I said I ain't going to Jamaica, all right?"

"This's got nothing to do with Jamaica. I want to try some wing walking."

Jesus Christ, was he trying to kill me from a heart attack?

"We can't afford it."

"Afford what?" Bobby asked.

"To pay for some dope to risk killing himself because you're bored!"

Bobby sat on the edge of the desk and swung his leg. I knew from the far-off look in his eye that he was dreaming again, thinking. "Won't take much to refit the de Hav. Reinforce the top—"

"Don't you read the papers?" I yelled at him. "There've been six folks died from wing walking in the Midwest this month alone! One was a lady!"

Ladies wing walking? Something gleamed in his eye. "Ladies, huh? Sure would bring the crowds in."

I stopped him getting to the phone this time, guarded it with my body. "No. I won't let you do it. I won't let you kill Bess!"

"Why would I wanna do that?" he asked.

"We don't need money this bad."

He wasn't listening, so I threatened to punch his face in if he didn't get out of my sight. Bobby looked out of the window—the mail was finally loaded for his run. "Don't wait up," he said as he left.

I waited till he'd taken off and circled the field before I rang Bess and told her what Bobby was up to this time. But she didn't believe me. She didn't even know what wing walking was. "Bess, he's got that mad-dog look in his eye again."

"But you're the only person he listens to," she said.

News to me. I thought she was the only person he listened to. "I got a bad feeling about this, Bess. Like you had that day the oil line ruptured and he damn near killed us all."

"Oh. What's wing walking?"

I told her. "Don't let him talk you into it, Bess. I know what he's planning."

But he never asked Bess. There was another friend of his, an adventurous girl with short blond hair and big blue eyes who made her money in the red-light district of downtown Miami.

She got off the back of his motorcycle the next Sunday afternoon. I thought, Not here, Bob, not here. This is the office. He could pick them a mile away, anywhere, anytime.

"John," he said. "This is Elsie." He slid his arm around her and she giggled. "She tells me she's an acrobat."

She whispered something to him and he said, "In bed, on a wire, no difference. You know she can walk a fence three inches wide in her high heels?"

"I'm not gonna let you do it."

"Do what?"

"It's gonna be outlawed soon!"

"We got four months till Atlanta. Law's not going through that quick." He walked off with her. God knows what he was saying to her; she was a terrible giggler.

"Bob!"

He looked back. I knew he'd been drinking. So had she. Sunday was the only day off unless there was a special charter. I was working on the books, the only day I had with a couple of hours straight. That day, I let the books slide.

He was walking this girl, this Elsie creature, toward his plane and I was being a nuisance by following him.

"You fly today, I'm gonna report you!"

I wouldn't of course, but maybe the threat would be enough. He helped the little floozy into his plane.

She was a tiny thing, thin, not so tall, and maybe she was an acrobat. She got up on the top wing and I saw Bobby rubbing at his eyes.

Well, she did a cartwheel across the top.

Her dress fell down over her head. She didn't have any underwear on.

Even Sam stopped work; he couldn't believe his eyes.

Here was this pretty girl of dubious background doing cartwheels, headstands, and my Lord, backflips across the top wing of the grounded de Havilland, and I was there, too, watching.

Then, at that moment, Rosanna arrived.

I didn't know she was coming. Sam saw her, tried to get my attention. Nothing worked till I heard her call my name.

I just wanted to be struck by lightning.

Rosanna came four steps toward me, saw the show, and promptly fainted, as all good southern ladies tended to do—last century.

I reached down, grabbed her thin arm, and pulled her till she was sitting up, then squashed her head down on her chest with enough force to break her spine.

She came to, saying, "Ooh—"

Ooh, be damned. Bobby had seen Rosanna. He knew what she was like and he didn't care one hoot. All he was interested in was enticing Elsie to do another cartwheel, this time facing the hangar. Rosanna opened her eyes this time, to see a little more than a curvy butt shining white in the sunshine. She screamed and clamped her hands over her eyes, expecting me to, as well.

"Jesus, Bobby! Get her outta here! Someone's gonna call the cops!"

I looked at Sam for some help, but I could have knocked his eyes off with a stick.

Bobby got Elsie down.

"You're no fun," Elsie said as Bobby wheeled her past us. Rosanna was still spluttering, her face as red as a glass of cherry soda.

"Water," she said. "I need some water—"

I took her inside the office.

Bobby and Elsie were in a corner, against the wooden filing cabinet, kissing. For a minute, I thought Rosie'd faint again. I got her a cup of water and came back.

She was hitting Bobby with her new hat.

Elsie pushed her away.

"How dare you talk to me like that, you no-good piece of white trash!"

Elsie let out a scream that crumbled my spine.

It was on.

I should have been shocked at what I saw. Rosanna was one hell of a fighter. She was kicking and scratching, tore a chunk off Elsie's red dress. So Elsie ripped a sleeve off Rosanna's. Rosanna slapped her face. Elsie came back, screaming some more, and clamped her long fingers around Rosanna's neck.

Bobby got smacked in the mouth by a high heel when he tried to pull the girls apart. I didn't know what else to do, or where to look, so I drank the water. Wondered what would happen next.

"Would you two cut it out!" Bobby was still in there, trying. No good. I went out the side door and dragged in the fire hose.

That stopped them, pretty quick, too.

All was quiet except for the sound of these two so-called ladies on the floor, wet, exhausted, breathing heavily.

I looked at Bobby and he looked at me, but the grin appeared on his face first. I laughed so hard inside, I nearly wet my pants trying to keep it all in.

Bobby took Elsie away to dry her off somehow and I got rid of the hose and tried to stop Rosanna from crying and myself from laughing.

She had a huge scratch on her cheek, there were finger marks around her neck, and her hair was standing on end. Her left eye was already starting to swell up.

And I still thought it was funny, but I tried hard to cover it and be serious.

"Rosie, you should have told me you were coming down here. How'd you get here, anyway?"

"I . . . I . . ." She tried to stand up. I helped her. I would have held her, too, but I didn't want to get my leather coat wet. "I . . . I . . . haven't seen you for so long. I thought I'd . . . I'd surprise you, but you weren't home, so I . . . I . . . I drove here and then I saw you and her and . . . Oh Lord . . . I thought, Is this what he does when I ain't here?"

"Rosanna, that's no reason to pick a fight with another lady." I said it as straight as I could, but I had to keep biting my lip hard.

"When I came in here, she looked at me and she said . . . she said . . ." She burst into tears and couldn't tell me what Elsie had said. Every time she tried, she cried some more.

I drove her back to her hotel in the new Ford automobile her daddy had let her drive all by herself and I told her I'd see her real soon. That we'd have a real nice dinner. I had to tell her I loved her before she'd let me leave.

Bobby was sweeping water out when I got back.

"Nice automobile," he said.

"Where is she?" I asked, inspecting every room of our little office building for more surprises.

"Sam's taken her home."

"Sam?"

"Yeah. I think he fell in love." Bobby kept sweeping, tried not to laugh.

"You gonna tell me what happened in here?" I asked.

"You used the fire hose, Johnny."

"No. I mean, what started that fight?"

"Oh, that. What'd Rosie say?"

"Nothing. She can't talk about it."

Bobby started laughing to himself. "Let's see if I can remember right. . . ." He rested the broom against the wall and reached in his pocket for a cigarette. He lighted it and took a deep breath.

"Well, Elsie and I were getting acquainted. Rosie comes in and you was out getting some water for her. Elsie says, 'What's wrong with you? Ain't you never seen titties before?' I guess that's when it started. Maybe it was the way Elsie looked at her. You know. Rosie sure ain't top-heavy. I tried not to smile and then she starts slapping into me with that damned hat of hers. Like it was my fault she's got no, you know."

"Oh," was all I could think of to say.

"Books got wet," Bobby said offhandedly, that smile still stuck on his face.

I looked down at my desk, at the books and papers. Wet.

"Bobby?"

"Hey—"

"I don't want you wing walking."

"I'm not gonna. Elsie is. John, it's all right. I'll get her to wear something underneath next time. Okay?"

"It's not that. Well, sure it is. But it's—"

"Look, buddy. If I'm gonna die, I'll die my way. But I'm not going to die. You have to trust me on this one. We're gonna give 'em something to remember over there in Atlanta. Right?"

I watched the little girl still trying to get a cartwheel right. So I walked on over and helped her out. It was almighty cold, even in the sun, but somehow inside, I was feeling very warm. For a minute, I thought I could feel Bobby's presence very close, then it faded away. A storm was coming in, so I herded up the kids and we all walked on home.

John wondered whether the Eskimos were like Indians, with their dreams, their visions, their spirits. The longer he was there, the more he thought he understood. At times, the survival of the people depended on the power of Asuluk's medicine. He knew it was faith alone that kept hearts beating, sustained the light of contentment that forever shone in those dark eyes.

And not a lot could surprise him anymore.

When Asuluk came to visit and asked me to go walking with him, I wondered if he'd had another vision. Maybe his dream had repeated. I hoped it hadn't because mine would surely come back, too. But he never asked if I'd seen what he'd seen. I was glad. White men with guns. All I ever saw was blood on the ice. I never liked real guns much, just pretend ones. I had a slug rifle when I was a kid, but pointing it at something alive seemed wrong. Especially when I got a good paddling for shooting the rooster in the butt—Mom never knew till one Sunday when she

186

broke off some of her tooth on the slug. I used to read Westerns, cowboys, Indians, but I never related well to the tales of gunfights and showdowns, dead bodies that never bled. I always wanted to read about the freedom of those open plains, and I found it for myself in the skies.

Men with guns. The closest I ever came to a soldier was Rosanna's father. The main strategy of the time was making it in and out of Rosanna's house alive and unharmed. I was never that scared of the colonel; I just didn't like the old bastard very much. I heard how the Negro gardener found the old boy hanging. He was in uniform, too, and that was all Rosanna could say, or so it seemed. I remember sitting on the porch swing with her for hours the night of the day they buried him. She never cried aloud, just sat there whimpering into my shoulder, leaving lipstick stains on my white shirt. I can still hear the porch swing creaking. It was a cool night, stars so bright, so close I could have reached out and tasted them. Staring at a night sky, especially a South Carolina sky, was always a good way to let go of the cloudy, misty thoughts that tend to tangle a mind with things I know now weren't worth worrying about.

Rosanna's father had just committed suicide, and there I was, a real comfort, secretly worrying about how I'd pay the fuel bill due three days ago.

Something about the way the stars meet the horizon on a black, black night makes you mellow. Makes you think how nothing really is important. Makes you feel like some insignificant flea-sized piece of some jigsaw puzzle a larger hand is trying to finish on time.

I'm wandering again.

Asuluk didn't want to tell me about dreams or visions or even ask me questions. He wanted me with him awhile. Apart from my family, there's only been one other I don't feel uncomfortable sharing silences with, but Bobby never was that thoughtful. He'd enjoy it till he noticed the silence had crept up and grabbed him. Some folks hate it. But Asuluk appreciates a good quiet, like me. And a good, long silence—one of those where the entire world's been hushed by a magic lullaby—is as scarce here as it was back home.

All we did was sit on the rocks. Asuluk watched the northern sky for a long time and so did I. Anyone's guess what he saw. I know I saw a moose and a lady with an upperdown umbrella, among other things. Then the sky cleared. Maybe Asuluk's humming chased the clouds away.

It was timing. Absolutely. We'd sat there, the medicine man and I, for a couple of hours—so long, my ass was sore—and when the time came, he spoke.

I don't know what he said; he didn't know the English equivalent of the northern lights, the Aurora Borealis. That magnificent magnetic phenomenon that can last for a heartbeat, ten minutes, or a few hours. Sometimes the light's so good that they go out seal hunting.

Summer must have been ending, because it was dark enough to ease the squint and see the colors.

He'd been waiting for this a long, long time. Maybe he thought that when the lights ceased, so would his people. Maybe there was some kind of strange magic for him. Whatever, he was spellbound as I was.

For me, it was magic because it was color and it was flooding me. Too long, I'd lived in gray, white, brown, with the occasional spill of red—like make-believe blood staining the ice, the snow. The tears in Asuluk's eyes weren't for the same reason as mine.

I felt like a blind man with sudden, unexpected sight for the first time. I'd forgotten what bright green was. What a true blue was—not the blue-gray excuse for the sea up here. There were pinks, golds, red, orange and purple, too. Blue. Bursts of color were caused, according to some long-winded scientific explanation, by the position of the sun, the change in magnetic poles, atmospheric pressures. But sitting there watching those lights Asuluk knew were going to come, all I felt, deep down, was that Asuluk's gods and my God were working together on this one.

Showing off maybe.

And a mile away, there they were, some hunters out waiting over holes in the ice. No one wasted any kind of light.

I knew then that Asuluk wasn't just my father-in-law. He was a friend and he was becoming more than just someone to talk to, to smile at, to argue with. I felt as if I'd been sitting beside him doing this forever.

Then he went and asked me what I felt about fatherhood.

But I never could put feelings into words, so I said, "It's good."

He looked at me awhile and told me he'd had four women in his house but one favorite—Kioki's mother, the only one left. My enemy. The old lady who kept hitting me that day so long ago. He had four wives, eight sons, three daughters. Sinbad was the eldest son.

So I sat there and calculated. If Asuluk had married at about eighteen, like most of the men did, and Sinbad came along soon after, it would make him forty-six, fifty at the most. And all this time I'd thought he was an old man. Maybe I thought he was old because of his eyes, the gray in his hair. His skin was toughened from cold, that incessant biting wind, and not from age. I had thought of and treated Asuluk as if he was older than my father.

But he wasn't.

And then he told me another story about the trees he remembered when he was a child. Tall, tall trees. Grassy plains. Mountains and valleys. But it was always the aurora that took him back to a campfire, to his grandfather's knee, his grandfather's stories. He explained how he hadn't wanted to leave his grandfather behind, how he'd sat in an umiak, a long, cold journey, tears and confusion his companion.

Even sitting on his butt out there on the edge of the rock, he was poetic. I only got pieces; his English is as pitiful as my Eskimo.

I've deduced these people are a mixture of Indian and Eskimo, and once upon a time, God knows when, someone came along who spoke English. Traces of it remain in this one man, Asuluk. I wasn't the one who taught him at all.

But I think that probably about 1890, he was amid a handful of survivors from a skirmish between Eskimo tribes and Russian fur traders and it's here that some survivors escaped to and stayed. It's about the only conclusion I can come to. I doubt God would drop anyone here on purpose.

He's seen things that the dwindling number of older ones have seen, that the younger ones only hear of secondhand in stories passed down generation to generation. And I had a hand in the next generation. Maybe that was why he told me. Who knows.

The story didn't end there. Along came the Russians again to this island, captured most of the men, including Asuluk's father, and they were never seen again.

I suppose he was afraid when I crashed, when the search party came. He remembered too much of a past he couldn't forget. And I can't blame him for that, even if I should be angry.

When he's telling his stories, I can see what he remembers. Maybe he tells his tales so well, they become a part of my mind. I see it happening, just as he must. I can see his people being herded together by the Russians. I can see those trying to run away, shot. I can see those fighting back, shot. I can see those trying to defend themselves, too, the chaos, the fear. And I see a boy, no more than three or four, staring down at his grandfather's body, hearing the women crying, howling. He's grabbed by his father and they hide. And eventually they escape.

There are times when I wish I was like Meg, Meg, who has no imagination, because it wouldn't hurt as much if I didn't see and feel and hear. Damn imagination. Damn this ability to feel other people's pain as much as I feel my own.

I wanted to ask why his people never went back to the place of trees and grass, because surely to God it was warmer there, and there was a better variety of foods to live on. But deep down, I knew why they'd made Kulowyl home—they wouldn't risk it happening again.

I wanted to tell him things had changed since the last century, but I was in no position to know if I'd be lying or not. I never had any interest in Alaska or Eskimos. The last I heard, the States and Russia had been allies.

So I said nothing. I wasn't the only one who'd had to brave a new world. Maybe that was why he was so tolerant of me.

He was still watching the lights when I touched his hand and pointed. "Aurora Borealis."

He said it, eventually—at least he tried to—and then he said something that I translated to mean: "The light of we the people."

"We the people. *Unangan.*" And he looked at me when he said it.

We never argued much after that night.

He wanted me to tell him about Florida again, so I did. I told him about Abbeville first, the airplanes, my family, Bobby, Billy Taylor; the weather, the Miami skyline at night, flying above the keys midsummer. I don't know how much he understood; he just listened to strange words about strange places, worlds suddenly removed of ice and Arctic winds. It was beyond his imagination because he'd never experienced it. But he didn't doubt that it existed. And that's what I liked the most about Asuluk. He was open-minded, considerate of anything new or even impossible.

"You go back?" he asked.

I shook my head. I was better able to handle the realization I'd never see home again. Years of hoping for a miracle had dimmed any chance I'd had of getting out of here alive. "My family thinks I'm dead." I said it in Eskimo. He likes it when I talk Eskimo. Unlike the others, he doesn't laugh if I get it wrong.

He squeezed my hand and words weren't needed. But he knew as I knew that if a plane came searching again, I might look back with a tear in my eye, but I would most definitely return.

We lapsed into another silence until he reached into his coat and withdrew a warped red leather book four inches long by three inches wide.

"This yours, Floreeda John."

I opened it. The pages had stuck together; most of the ink had run. It had been water-damaged. The pages were brittle, fragile.

But I recognized the copybook handwriting after I gently unstuck the first pages.

It was Meg's writing. My heart hit my ears, I wanted to throw up. The copybook writing said, "One day you will understand the rainbows."

Typical Meg. I never understood a word she said when she was in a philosophical mood, which, after her illness, lasted forever.

I stared at the book. I'd never seen it before. I'd pretended not to see her slip a Bible into my bag, sure, but not this. I hadn't seen her hide this.

Every page I dared look at had been handwritten, something deep and inspirational on each. Well, it would have been inspirational to Meg. But glued to the final page was a photograph. It was discolored and peeling, but the faces were recognizable.

It was a sepia-colored photograph of my sister and my mother.

I stared at it until I couldn't see it anymore. I was blinded by tears.

"Your family?" Asuluk asked.

I turned to Asuluk. I could hardly see his face. "My mother. Sister."

He was more interested in Meg's wheelchair. He asked me what it was, why she couldn't walk. I tried to tell him, but words wouldn't come.

Oh, that photo. Those words she'd written. What did Meg know? What had made her compile this for me? A book of hope, of bleeding ink, and some pages wouldn't be separated.

I've tried to work out how long it had taken her to write this for me. I never took any notice of what she was up to. She was just there, the quiet intellectual fixture, always with her head in some book because her feet could no longer wear ballet shoes.

Only Bobby knew how deep she ran. I'd lived under the same

roof all my life and barely scratched the surface of this being, my sister.

And damn it, I still don't know what the rainbows mean.

The words I can read make little sense.

But the photo . . . the photo. The faces in front of me now are different from the faces I see in my mind every day. I remember my mother as young, not gray-haired or faintly stooped from the pressures of life. Where's her smile gone? There're hands on my kid sister's shoulders, and on the left hand is the wide wedding band she'd wear to the grave. But they're not the hands of the lady who served me, smacked me, comforted me. They belong to an old lady who looks like a stranger. This is not the lady I see when I dream, when I remember.

And that little girl whose stockinged feet kept our porch in a deep shine, she's a woman now. And she looks a bit like me.

I've read some of the words she wrote for me—not a lot make sense—but right in the middle of that little red book I found this. I don't know who wrote it; maybe Meg did when she was eighteen and the doctor told her she'd never walk again.

I am hurt but I am not slain.
I will lie here and rest awhile
before I rise and fight again.

I can see her when I hold the book. I can see my sister. She's twenty, her hair's the color of a roaring fire. She's sitting at the table by the window in her room, gently biting that fountain pen I gave her when she turned nineteen. It's night in Abbeville, but she's not looking outside; she's looking inside herself again. She's thinking about me, flying tinned food and mail to Alabama. She has to get this page done before I get home, before I accidentally see what she's up to this time.

My mother taps on the door and comes in. A cup of tea is rattling in its saucer and Meg takes it before it spills.

"What's this?" my mother asks.

"It's for John."

My mother smiles. "He doesn't read."

She looks at Lily and there's a sparkle in her eyes when she says, "He will one day."

And one day always comes.

I closed the book and put it in the inside pouch of my overcoat. I kept my hand on my chest for a long time, too.

Then Asuluk spoke. He'd given me enough time to remember. He took something else from his coat.

Bobby's handgun, the one I'd given him so long ago.

He passed it over. I was going to tell him it was useless, as much use as the old muzzle loader he'd shown me once. A six-shooter without bullets. Something to hang on the wall. I didn't get time to open my mouth. The bullets appeared on my lap, wrapped in skin.

I thought I'd thrown the damned things away. I must have given them to him.

"Show me," he said.

I put only one bullet in. I had fifty more in my lap. But I didn't want to know if it fired. I saw that deputy's badge again. This would make a hole twice as big. I didn't like what it reminded me of.

I knew what he was afraid of.

He touched the bullets on my lap and said, "*Am . . . u . . . nee . . . shun.* Show me."

He wanted me to shoot and he'd sit there forever until I did. For a moment, I considered the possibility of putting it at my forehead. But the suicidal days had long since died.

That was why he'd held back until now. All these years, he'd had this stuff in safekeeping, this book, this weapon. Apparently the time was right to return it.

"Show me." He was getting impatient.

"No. No, I won't use it. You have it, Asuluk. Please. It's yours now. Remember, I gave it to you."

He didn't have anything to trade, either that or he didn't want it. It was mine. He was no thief. God help me, I thought. I can't have this close by—not when I get remembering, when I forget I'm here forever, when I think of Florida or my mother or sister, or that I'll never fly again.

"Show. Now."

I cocked it, aimed at a lump of ice a few yards away, and shot. The noise echoed forever; the hunters waiting for a seal all jumped ten feet in the air and turned our way, quick.

Asuluk thumped my chest and said, "Good." He had faith in me. I'm glad someone did.

Then he went back to the sky, but the clouds were coming home again. And in the distance, we both heard the cries, the usual hysterical screams that signaled someone was down. There'd been a spate of sickness and injury lately.

Asuluk looked at me, more despair than anger in his eyes.

"No peace," he said in Eskimo. "No peace." And he dragged his tired bones to a stand, offered his hand to help me to my feet, and I took it.

It was Kioki coming. Each step took her two feet into the snow. No Eskimo names this time. She didn't want her father. She wanted me.

For the first time in God knows how long, I sure don't, I actually ran.

FOURTEEN

⚬━⚬━⚬━⚬━⚬━⚬━⚬

A thousand tragic possibilities vied for supremacy as he ran home, Asuluk one step behind, and, closing in, a distressed Kioki.

The greeting party of four women were holding lights aloft, all shouting, crying, and Billy's grandmother had a death grip on the screaming toddler.

I knew she was going to die. I knew she was bleeding to death and everyone else packed into the house did, too. I would have given all I had and more to have a real doctor there, to get her to a hospital.

Kioki was on her knees beside her sister, howling. Tooksooks was naked, shining from sweat, on her back, knees up and parted. I watched helpless while Asuluk did what he could. But he couldn't stop the bleeding. And with each contraction, more blood came.

All I could do was watch.

Asuluk grabbed hold of the tiny head and he pulled. My daughter came out headfirst and quiet.

There wasn't a sound; even the dogs had ceased the racket outside.

Tooksooks raised up on her elbows a little to see what the baby was and she looked at it. She looked at her father and she smiled at me.

And Asuluk gave the baby to Kioki and he fled, ordering me to go, too. But I couldn't move. My legs wouldn't work. Nothing would.

The baby wasn't crying or breathing.

And this was supposed to be third time lucky? Why wasn't anyone doing something here? It was the worst moment of my life. I made another deal with God but can't recall what it was I promised this time, maybe my life if only she'd cry, if only she'd live.

Tooksooks asked to see the baby and Kioki put it on her belly. The little thing was still blue, lifeless, covered in white slime and blood, and those few seconds of silence were the longest I've ever known. Then Tooksooks started crying, too, in her soft way. She looked up at me and said she'd failed me.

Again.

Like hell.

I saw fear in Kioki's eyes when I picked up the baby. She was slippery, hard to hold, and everything I'd read, that first-aid test I'd done so long ago came flooding back. I held her upside down by her legs, shook her a little. For a second, I wondered if I should swing her around, like Denny Jones used to do to kid goats if they were born lifeless. He'd stand up, swing them around and around above his head, but something in me said no. Just talk to her. So I did. Come on, baby, wake up now. You're gonna die some toothless old lady, not now. Not now before you've even begun living. No Shaw's ever given up before and you ain't gonna be the first, you hear me?

Stupid things like that came pouring out. I begged; I pleaded; I got angry. I shook her some more.

And there was nothing, until I half-screamed, "Please, God, please!"

She started crying, once, twice. Startled, angry, then confused. And I started crying, too. Everyone was staring at me, horrified, afraid. Everyone except Tooksooks. Tears mixed with smiles, exhausted, weak smiles.

As the baby breathed, her color got better. The thick cord

stopped pulsing, so I cut it with my Bowie and told Kioki to tie it off as close as she could, but she sat there staring at me as if she'd never seen me before. So I tied it myself, teeth and fingers. And angry again, I grabbed the soft, furry skins that Tooksooks had been keeping especially for the baby and I wrapped her in them and slipped her down beside her mama. And while I stood there shaking, everyone in the house fled.

And I wondered what the hell I'd done this time.

I sat down beside Tooksooks and I lied. I told her everything would be just fine now. Just fine. All was quiet except for the sounds the baby made, little squeaks and gurgles muffled by fur. And I watched Tooksooks with the baby, the way she was gazing, how her eyes were misty.

She was fine when I left to go for that walk with her daddy. She and her sister were sitting up at the table there, sewing tiny boots for the baby. They'd both looked up and smiled good-bye when I left. Billy was already asleep. I couldn't have been gone more than an hour, two at the most. It had taken Kioki nearly two full days to have Billy.

I knew I was losing Tooksooks and there was nothing I could do to stop it. No more than nineteen, this girl with the round, squashed face and laughing eyes. So I lay down with her and put my arm around her. Touched her face, talked to her in the language she never tried to understand. I told her I loved her and I always would, and I think she understood. There seemed no pain left to feel. Her breathing went light, uneven, and I can't describe the softness in her eyes when she looked down at the tiny baby, a part of us both.

Then she just sighed and slipped away, peaceful, quiet. She died the way she'd lived. I put my hand on her chest but couldn't feel any heartbeat. I listened, too. Nothing.

It wasn't supposed to be like this. I'd promised my life for the baby, not hers. It wasn't supposed to end like this.

I think I cried. I know I let loose every imprisoned agony I'd never paroled since 1926, and when I'd done, all I heard was quiet, broken only by a tiny squirming against my stomach, squirms and squeaks and half-coughing cries.

So I took her away from her mother, wiped my face so I could see—really see. I'd never seen anything as small as this little girl. My thumb seemed as big as her hand, and she looked up at me, squinting. So new. Helpless.

What was I supposed to feel then? If it was love, it shouldn't hurt so bad. I don't know how long I sat there holding that baby, looking at her. It felt like forever, until Asuluk came back in. What had he done? Where had he gone? Off somewhere, to cry alone? Was it taboo for the medicine man to shed a tear others could see?

"Spirit of Wind come," he said quietly.

I'd heard about that too many times. Spirit of Wind was the death collector for these people.

"Spirit of Wind come. Take," he said a little louder so I'd hear.

"No."

"Yes."

"No!"

Admittedly, the baby was tiny—too small. She wasn't fat and heavy like most of the babies born here. Was it imagination, or was this baby's grandfather telling me to put her down, walk away, let her die?

So many things here don't need words for full understanding.

I denied the possibility that anyone could even consider this tiny baby was as good as dead. Dead is not good, not to me. She was alive. I'd make damned sure she stayed alive. I wished him to hell. I wished them all to hell. If I was some anomaly in this world where only the healthy and strong survived, if I'd cheated death, so could my daughter.

Sad and confused, Asuluk retreated again. I heard him outside, talking with Kioki, with his wife, with Sinbad and God knew who else crowded around out there in the cold dark.

199

Then he said that Tooksooks had been taken on the wind but that I wouldn't let the girl child go.

The people outside, the friends and relatives, made more noise than the dogs ever knew how. And I tried to ignore it.

I sat in my corner with my baby. The blue had faded and a tiny hand was clamped hard and tight to my finger. She couldn't have weighed more than four, five pounds at the most. I'd flown smaller packages heavier than she was. She knew how, but she wouldn't cry. She just lay there, balanced in my half arm, looking up at me in the dim light. I don't know what she saw, but I know what I felt, and if the Spirit of the Wind wanted her, it would have to blow this house down before I'd ever let her go.

Folks came in to take Tooksooks away. They wrapped her up tight, carried her out. Sinbad's wife looked back at me and didn't speak. She didn't have to. I read her face—pity. I hate pity. I hated the way no one said, Show this baby to the village. I hated the way they would have buried her without even giving her half a chance at life.

She fell asleep, sucking on her fist, pulling faces, squeaking. Then she cried, short, sharp bursts that brought my heart to my ears again.

And from the darkness, I heard a soft voice say, "Give."

Kioki was crouched in front of me, watching me carefully. Beside her was one of her cousins, an older woman who'd had a stillborn son about a week before. But there was something in her eyes I didn't like. That little voice inside my head kept repeating, No. Don't. No.

It's never been wrong yet.

I shook my head, thanked the woman for her kindness but said she wasn't needed here.

Kioki thought I'd gone crazy. She tried to tell me that the baby would be well cared for in that family, but no matter what she said, I couldn't let go. Did she know what a promise was? If she had any love for her sister, she'd care for her sister's baby, for her husband's baby as she'd cared for her own son.

I have never known Kioki to take so long in deciding what to do. Then the little one helped me—she started crying, an all-out effort this time. Over the baby's cries, I reminded Kioki that she'd been nursing Billy far too long. Was this because she knew her sister would die in childbirth? Hadn't she dreamed of having a daughter to call her own? Hadn't we been trying and trying for so long now for another baby? What was this, then, if it wasn't a gift from the Great Spirit? Here was her chance to prove her love for her dead sister.

I don't think it was my speech that worked. It was the baby's crying. She held her hands out and I gave her the baby. She looked at it, touched it, hushed it the only way she knew.

And it worked. Thank you, God, it worked.

It was another day before the weather cleared enough to allow us to bury Tooksooks. She's in the graveyard under four feet of packed snow now; come the summer thaw, she'll be buried with whoever else never survives. I didn't attend the celebration, nor did Kioki. I couldn't have listened to the superstitious crap without crying, so I kept well away. Said my good-byes in my way.

Hours passed into dark days and, one by one, folks happened by with a gift or some food for us.

The one who fell from the sky now had a daughter who was strangely missed by the Spirit of the Wind. And to be missed, bypassed by the Spirit of the Wind—to cheat death, to survive when the odds are against you—makes you someone very special here—magic almost.

The one visitor who surprised me the most was Sinbad. He came in, sat down, and I knew he was uncomfortable, because he wouldn't look me in the eye. He eventually peeked over at the baby Kioki was nursing and he grunted his approval. I think it was approval. Then he looked at me with a pitiful expression in his eyes, as if he were sorry she wasn't a boy. So I smiled at him as best I could, fluffed my own feathers, and told him she'd be more beautiful than any of his daughters. He grunted again and left, a little happier to know I was back to normal again.

Any fresh seal blood is first offered to Kioki now.

It took me a long time to understand that under similar circumstances, a sick, weak baby is simply buried with its dead mother and life continues until some other couple is chosen by a bright shooting star.

Billy returned to our household about a week later and found it a little too easy to adjust to his mama nursing a new baby.

I recall what he said when he came in holding his grandma's hand. His big blue eyes widened when he saw his half sister taking his favorite place. His mouth opened wide and he looked at me, surprised. "What's this, Dad?" he asked in his combined southern-Eskimo accent.

I told him and he crawled onto his mother's lap and peered into all that fur. Satisfied, he climbed down, took up the Gizmo pieces in the seal hide wrapper, and put each piece on the earth table. He looked at me and said, "Come on, Dad. Gizmo."

My son never asks. He orders.

With the death of his aunt and the birth of his half sister, Billy was the least affected of us all. I was afraid of jealousy, but again my fears weren't real and I was ashamed for a while at how I'd underestimated my own son. I became aware of how different he was from me.

Traces of Tooksooks remain, a lingering, painful memory. For a long time, I blamed myself for her death. No one else did, but my conscience had a field day far too long.

Kioki has gone quiet and won't talk of her sister, nor will she express any kind of feeling in words. Tooksooks's overcoat is still hanging on a peg over the bed where we all slept. No one wants to take it down yet.

Sometimes it's as if she's still with us, especially when we're together, eating, talking, laughing. Then we'll remember she isn't with us anymore and the laughter dies as quickly as it was born.

I'm missing the way she used to rub my feet. More often than not, I'd drop off to sleep, all light and fuzzy. And I miss the way I'd curl into her at night, how she'd reach for my hand and hold it tightly all night long.

She made me a pair of boots that never fit, but if I didn't wear them, I'd break her heart. I hardly knew anything about her, so why is it she is so important now she's dead?

Why is it that something tragic always has to happen before you realize how important some folks are to you?

Billy knows his auntie's dead; he knows the difference between life and death. I just hope he never learns just how fragile that difference can be. One moment alive, next . . .

It can happen here to anyone at any time. Maybe that's why tomorrow is never that important to these folks.

Maybe they've learned the value of now. Maybe that's why they're so damned happy all the time. "Lily," I said in reply to Asuluk's question. He'd come by to watch me mend another net. "Her name is Lily."

"Lill-lee." He sang it three times before he considered it, then eventually agreed with a nod of his head. "Lill-lee. Good, Floreeda. Good."

I looked up at him. "My name is John. John Robert Shaw. Not Florida. Not Florida John. All right? You got that yet? John. Not Florida. I am from Florida; it is not my name."

"Floreeda."

"John."

"John," he mumbled, and spat. "Floreeda." He thumped my head and wandered away, still mumbling to himself. I had to laugh. He'd repeated my name as he ambled away, spitting each time. No, I was definitely Floreeda to him.

Will nothing ever change here? I wonder what he'd feel if I called him Kulowyl.

FIFTEEN

●━●━●━●━●━●━●

IT was a warm, clear day today, so warm that when I first went outside, it was like walking into a different world. For a while, I thought I'd died and this was heaven, but my idea of heaven right now would be flying with eighty feet between me and the Appalachians, so I figured I hadn't died.

The sky was blue, blue as it should be. There was no fog, no mist, no rain, nor was there any forty-knot head, tail, or cross-wind. I wasn't getting hit in the face by sheets of ice or rain that felt like razors.

It was what I call a good day.

No wind, not even a breeze. Just blue sky, a semipermanent nine o'clock sun, and Anchorage somewhere to the northeast, maybe a thousand miles, or maybe just a day's paddle. Maybe two years of paddling for a one-armed white man who rows in circles.

It had been too long since the sun touched my face, so when I have the chance, any chance, I take it. I pulled my hood off. It felt kind of strange at first. It had been a long time since I'd gone bareheaded, or bare anything else outside in the fresh air. I pulled the coat open and there was no immediate numbing, so I took it off and stood there, outside my summer house, not looking out to sea, but looking down at my right arm.

A lifetime ago, the skin there had been brown. Now it looked paper white and felt soft, as soft as Lily's, Kioki's. I looked at my fingers as if I'd never really seen them before—my hands were getting older. I hadn't noticed before.

I wondered what my face looked like these days. Sometimes I've tried to see how a blind man would, by touch, but all I feel is the hook on my nose, and this beard. I'd like to get all my hair cut properly instead of having two kids watch while I saw it all off with my Bowie knife. Braids don't suit me at all.

I guess if anyone saw me lately, they'd think I'd been lost in the mountains for the past ten years—at least I don't feel as wild as I must look.

I know I'm thinner than I've ever been—no matter what I do or what I eat, I just can't put on any weight. And a little extra fat would sure help keep out the cold.

I haven't written since Lily was born for a couple of reasons. I've been busy, either making things, mainly weapons, or drawing things, or I go out with Sinbad. There hasn't been a lot happening I could write down, either. Maybe things will come as I go along.

I guess I've nearly given up the search for answers, the whys, wherefores, mainly the why me's—you know, what'd I do to deserve this? Once I decided to stop fussing, stop thinking about what I can't have all the time, once I accepted this lot, things have been okay—till I look to the northeast and wonder how far away the mainland is.

A part of me will never belong, but when I think of it, I never belonged anywhere, anyway. That part will never be satisfied. Because I know that even if a miracle occurred and I got out of here, got home, it still wouldn't be enough.

Meg used to call me a wandering, free spirit. And now that I've lost my wings, I'm still restless.

The Jenny went down for good about a year ago during the summer melt. This time, there was no ledge of ice fifteen feet below the surface to break the descent. She went straight down, God only knows how far—I sure don't.

That skeleton's finally been buried.

A group of us were watching her go down and the faces

around me were mostly cautious, fearfully curious as to how I'd react. But I didn't do anything—just stood there with the rest of them, watching the ice crack, hearing the roar as she went down for the last time.

I didn't feel a damned thing.

RIP, old friend. We sure had some good times together.

Billy was with me at the time. He looked up into my face, grabbed for my hand, and gave it a squeeze. He must have known what that old wreck once meant to me. Maybe he saw it in my eyes whenever I'd tell him about flying.

He'd be five or six by now. Speaks fluent English and Eskimo. He's better at math than I ever was. He can write a few words, and Meg's Bible has come in useful when I teach him reading. If I could remember how I was taught, it'd be easier. Keeping his interest was the hardest part, because I believe I started him too young. He knows his alphabet and sounds, but I can't help him spell because I never was that good at it myself.

He's a funny-looking boy. His skin has an Asian glow—not dark, not red, not yellow. But he's not white, either. He has my hands and feet and he'll be over six feet tall, the rate he's growing. His eyes are magnets. They're not pale blue like mine; they're not dark blue like his grandma's. The color is neither blue nor green. He has Oriental brows and can lift one when he's questioning something. Damned if I can do that, nor can his mother. I've seen her try when she thinks I'm not looking.

He acts no different from the other kids he plays and fights with, and occasionally I've watched him from a distance when he's rousing around with his friends. He reminds me of me, the reb soldier in the woods by the lake, the only time I've ever successfully bossed others around. He has the quiet, amused patience of his mother. Thank you, God, for giving him that. And he's the best exaggerator I've ever known, since Bobby at least. I guess if one grandfather was a poet and the other's a storyteller and medicine man, imagination has to be inherited somewhere along the line. That boy of mine could bullshit his way out of a polar bear's stare.

And I'd willingly die for him. Till Billy was born, I never understood why my own dad swam that flooded river. Now I'm just like him—I wouldn't think twice.

I guess it's got to be 1934 or 1935 by now, and I'd be thirty-two or thirty-three—just numbers. Inside, I don't feel any older, and not having seen my face for nearly ten years is probably a good thing.

If Billy's six, Lily is about two.

I remember betting Sinbad she'd be prettier than any of his daughters and I've surely won. Two years old, and I'm already grinding my teeth and wanting little boys to stay the hell away.

Picking the boys from the girls here is mighty hard sometimes—the little round, red-cheeked faces all look the same, neither boy nor girl when they're all playing together—except my two.

The children don't notice any differences. I like that kind of innocence.

Where I grew up, there were more blacks than whites and no in-betweens, and I doubt it'll ever change. I grew up with the notion that black folks didn't have a soul, that they were less human than the rest of us, like a horse or a dog. But I'd seen black kids cry when they got hurt, and I'd seen them bleed. I never understood why my daddy tried to stop that fight down behind the mill that day. Mom used to say, "He was one of a kind, your daddy." I wonder if she understood herself. She was afraid of Negroes. I didn't care either way. Didn't trust them much. Maybe it was because I never really knew any.

Being here's made me a lot more tolerant because the coin fell on heads, not tails. And while I felt I was different, I was treated just as I expected. When I learned to fit in, I was accepted.

The folks here didn't change; I did.

It's all perspective, I guess.

Lily kind of grew into her name. Maybe I should have called her Annie, after that fat girl I went to school with. Her skin's paler than her brother's; her eyes are light brown—or the color of dark honey; and her hair's the color of her eyes. I know if the sun touched it more often, it'd be the same color as mine used to be. She has Meg's heart-shaped face, Meg's nose, and Meg's laugh whenever she decides something is funny enough to laugh at, and that doesn't happen often, unless she's watching me trying to dress myself in a hurry or when she hears me arguing with myself. She never says very much to anyone, but on the rare times when she looks at me and smiles, all I ever see is her mother, Tooksooks.

She's like an oil painting of everyone I have ever known and loved.

And she's a stranger.

This little girl has to be the best escape artist since Harry Houdini, especially when she was a baby and had finally mastered the art of walking. She never crawled; she just up and walked. Her brother was the fastest crawler I've ever seen and he never knew what his feet were for till he was about two. Clumsy as hell. Not Lily. She could disappear so fast, it was incredible.

I kept promising myself I'd make some kind of babyproof gate just to keep her in. Kioki can do four things at once, like any woman I've ever known, but all it ever took was thirty seconds of Kioki's attention elsewhere for that little girl to vanish.

Straight to her granddaddy's house.

She was about a year old when she cheated death for the second time. I wasn't there when it happened.

Kioki was working with the other ladies, filleting salmon for drying. It wasn't a lengthy job because the catch wasn't so good, and when she left home, Lily was sound asleep.

A party was returning across the sea of ice and somehow three of the dogs pulling the main sled got loose and bolted.

I heard three versions of the same story, but basically, Lily woke about the time the dogs got loose and was toddling off to visit her granddaddy when the dogs rampaged through the village. She got in the way. One of them set on her a few seconds before Kioki got there and pulled this half-wild dog off with her bare hands.

If it hadn't been for the overcoat, the dog would have ripped the baby's throat apart. Kioki had her hand and arm badly chewed before anyone could get the other dogs off her.

I returned a couple of hours later and both Sinbad and I knew something had happened while we were away because of the lineup of people waiting for us.

Sinbad came home with me, and I'll never forget the sight. Kioki's forearm was still punctured and ripped and she had a smear of blood across her face. She'd been crying a long time. She wouldn't look at me; she was frightened of what I'd do or say. But I'd already been told what had happened and how she'd bravely fought the dogs to save the little one.

Lily seemed unhurt except for a bite on the side of her face, and she was asleep at Kioki's breast. Sinbad left when he saw for himself that neither was badly hurt. But all I could think of was rabies. I hadn't seen any signs of it in all the time I'd been there, but I still thought about it.

She'd been telling herself she didn't deserve to be a mother, and once Kioki had decided on a certain course of action or thought, nothing, nothing, could make her change her mind. If I could give anyone an award for stubbornness, first prize would go to my wife.

She just wanted to sit there, basking in her shame, and she wouldn't put the baby down to sleep, either. There was shame on her face—shame and worry.

I knew better, so I said nothing. I searched around till I found my old cotton shirt and I tore it up into long pieces. Then I found the black ointment that's used for everything from frost-bite to toothache and I wrapped her hand and arm and spent the rest of the evening assuring her I wasn't angry.

And I made that damned gate out of anything I could find, then watched my daughter try to figure another way out of her prison.

I decided then that I'd take notice of these "things I'd better do." I never think of them without reason—these early warnings I get and never take any notice of. I've had them all my life—images, pictures of things happening either moments or hours before they do. I don't tell anyone about it; I never did when I was a boy, either. But I always know when someone's lying, and I know when someone's going to get hurt or die, too.

It hardly ever works for myself. But it's hardly ever wrong for other folks, even strangers. Most things I see when I'm drifting off to sleep or just before I wake are the most reliable, but sometimes I get pictures when I'm out fishing or waiting for a seal on the edges of an ice hole. It happens when I'm not thinking of anything else.

I've seen Asuluk looking sick and weary and I've asked him to be truthful with me, but the most he does is grunt at me as if it's none of my business.

Lily's been scared of the dogs ever since that day. It happened a long time ago, sure, but I can't blame her, either. I never went near a horse after Rosie's dumped me on my butt and kicked me for good measure. I wore the hoofprint on my back for three weeks after that and never forgave her for laughing at me. I never trusted her or horses after that.

Lily's like me in that respect. Her feelings get hurt far too easily and she holds it all in, just like I used to. She likes her granddaddy's company more than mine. I tell myself it doesn't matter, but the lie doesn't sit well, because when I see them walk off together, I get upset. Jealous. Like I've lost her already.

Probably what my mother felt every day when she watched me walk across the field toward Billy Taylor's magical airplanes.

Strange how it all turns circle. Lily will usually come to me if I ask her, and then she sits on my lap and won't look at me. I know I wanted a daughter and I've tried hard to make friends with her, but it's as if she wants to be as far from me as possible. I wonder if she's upset that this crippled man, so different from everyone else, as luck would have it, is her father. I often wonder if she knows how much I love her. Is she the only person here who can't accept my difference? Why is it that when I have convinced myself she just doesn't like me, she'll sit down beside me, look up at me, and put her head on my shoulder?

And she never says a word that isn't necessary. She's so much like Meg used to be. She runs way too deep. A little stranger, this girl of mine, whose face matches her name. She won't ever know that, though. It's too cold here for lilies to grow.

So I guess I just have to sit back and watch her grow prettier each day. I'll give her fifteen more years. It won't matter if it's here or Main Street in Miami—some lucky guy will grab her before she gets away.

And she's not old enough for schooling yet. Her mind's quick and sharp, so I can't postpone the inevitable forever. If I could teach my son and most of the other kids on the island, I can teach my daughter, too—if she'll let me.

Since Billy has gone off learning Eskimo ways, she's taken to a new friend and protector. He, she, or it is invisible, and I'm always in the can for standing or sitting on it. She talks to it for hours on end; they huddle together under the skins in the winter dark. Billy's taken to tormenting her about it, but she just fights back.

Lord help anyone else who torments her, though. I've seen him fight a boy twice his size for his little sister's honor, and the kids were separated by Asuluk before Billy won. He never forgot what was said or done that reduced Lily to tears, and he never forgot the boy responsible, either. I think they'll be enemies to the grave now. Once, they were inseparable.

It's a shame that he just happens to be Sinbad's youngest boy, Eennali.

I don't know what sort of father I am. Too soft, I guess. I still remember what being a kid was like.

I watch them all at play, practicing for adulthood. And I watch my son playing at being a champion hunter, my daughter playing Eskimo house with older girls, and I ask myself why, under ordinary circumstances, she would have been allowed to die.

I never get an answer I like.

My son can take four birds midflight with his bow and three pointed arrows, and soon he'll be going out with the older boys to learn more. In a couple of years, he'll join Sinbad and me. Lily spends so much time with her granddaddy. I think he's teaching her about Eskimo medicine, because he comes to get her if he has to treat someone.

One day soon, I'll have to take her walking, and we'll sit on the rocks and I'll point to the sky and tell her about the world I came from and will never see again.

She's already accepted what I've told her about her grandma and aunt and she often takes down that red book and stares at the last page, touches that photograph and looks at me. "Gran'ma Lily, Auntie Meg," she sings softly, and gives me a huge toothy grin.

"Yep," I say.

She grins wider and says, "Yep," just like my sister used to.

I've used the gun three times since Asuluk decided it was safe to give it back to me. I've brought down two bears and one walrus so far. Till I arrived here, I never could get used to killing. I knew it was a case of kill or die and I know that sometimes it's necessary. Sometimes it's defense. I wasn't the world's best shot when I had two good hands, but me shooting one-handed is a case of either God's will or pure luck—or some animal's misfortune to be in the wrong place at the wrong time.

I only use it when I really have to—I don't have an unlimited supply of bullets, nor do I lend it out.

One of the men who always looked more Indian than Eskimo to me—Zuk's younger brother—recently got himself killed by a polar bear. He wasn't trying to prove how brave he was, either.

It happened just after a whale kill and everyone was busy, including me. I was helping by slicing off blubber. It was a cold autumn evening. Outside, oil lamps were burning, and no one noticed he'd gone till we heard the screams coming off the ice.

Maybe it was the smell of hot whale blood that had drawn the bear so close. Now, if I said a polar bear was fierce and aggressive, I'd be making an understatement. Polar bears do to me what snakes used to do to Bobby. He'd climb up a brick wall in two seconds to get away from one. With hungry bears, there's nothing in the eyes except this maniac kind of hatred.

All I know is what I heard, what I saw that day. With one swipe, the poor bastard was ripped open from his throat to his hip. And half of him had been eaten by the time I could get there and unload four bullets into the bear.

It took four before it went down. I felt nothing except a hot, sick pity for this poor bastard who'd sing funny songs about me, the one-armed hunter, because he must have been taking a piss in the fog when the bear saw him and attacked.

Where there was one bear, there were bound to be more, so everyone went about in groups for a short time. You'd be out on the ice, one thing in mind, bear, bear, bear, and some fool would creep up behind you and . . . Sick jokes.

These people have a real sense of the ridiculous, and at times I don't understand it. What I think is hilarious will be met by stony faces. They can roll about laughing at God knows what, I sure don't. And if my legs wandered as much as my thoughts do, I'd have been lost on the ice years ago, snap-frozen forever.

They gave me the polar bear's skin, mainly because I'd killed it. Not that I needed a reminder, but I couldn't say no. I'd be insulting someone if I did, insulting tradition or some spirit. Some of the skin keeps my children warm at night; some of it frames my wife's face. She wears it like a moving-picture star wears a mink coat. The rest of it, I don't want to know about. I can't remember what I did with it—all I know is, I got the bit with two bullet holes.

The other bear was shot during a hunt. It was taking too long to die, so I did what is laughingly called "the humane thing to do." I stood five feet away and shot it between the eyes.

I know what the twenty-two other guys here want, or would like—my firearm. And I know that firearms would make life a

213

lot easier, but so would wood for building, for fuel. If these people were farmers, I'd be happier. I could teach them so much,
but they're people of the sea. I know about the air, about the
land. I was never meant to be a sailor or a fisherman.

Maybe they weren't always people of the sea; maybe their
ancestors did come from the mainland, where there was fruit,
honey, seeds, deer, and birds. But they live here now, on a
rocky, treeless island, almost marooned, dependent on whale,
on salmon, on cod, seals—and on their myriad gods, spirits, and
spirit magic. Yes, they're primitive, but they're also people, and
people, I've come to realize, have certain needs—food, clothing,
shelter, companionship, and something else to believe in. I came
as a stranger, a different color, a different race, from a world they
can't believe exists. Either I'd live or I'd die. Either way, it was
up to me, and they let me and my God decide.

So here I am living with Eskimos somewhere off Alaska,
maybe in the Aleutians, on a piece of rock the world doesn't
know of, or if it does, it doesn't care. People die or are accidentally killed; babies are born to compensate. The cycle continues
despite incredible odds.

If I could leave, I probably would, but I'd like to take these
forty-seven other people with me. Show them this other, better
world, this easier world I used to live in, show them how easy
living can be.

It wasn't supposed to be this harsh, unforgiving, but if I had
the power to take them away from what they know, from what
they are, I think the contentment would die. I think they would
die. They'd lose who they are, unlike me, who never knew who
I was till I crashed my plane and found this instead of death.

So if my family thinks I'm dead, then I hope they let my
memory rest in peace and I hope they find it, too—peace.

But I doubt a day will go by when my sister won't wonder
what happened to her only brother and vice versa. At times, I
wish Asuluk had never given me her little red book. Sometimes
it'd be easier just to forget I ever existed. Other times, I wish I
could pretend I was an Eskimo, that I was born here, raised here.

214

Then I'll see that photograph of my mother, my sister, and all the pretense dies.

The sun didn't last very long. Clouds built across the southern sky; the wind howled in from the west. What John thought might have been the Alaska Peninsula turned out to be a huge, encompassing storm front, bearing down quickly on Kulowyl. He covered his head again, tied up his jacket, pulled on his glove, and waited for Sinbad to return. For a moment, he was afraid—afraid that he might lose this other friend to the weather. But deep down, John knew that Sinbad would be watching the sky, too, because sunny days brought out the seals on the tiny rock outcrop to the southeast, and they all mated at that time of year.

Within a few moments, he sighed, relieved, because rounding the tip of Kulowyl was Sinbad in his two-seater kayak, a bull seal his dead, limp passenger.

He saw John waiting, whistled at him, and pointed with his paddle toward the encroaching storm front. John gave him the thumbs-up in return and waited a few minutes until his friend docked. They walked home together, carrying the heavy seal between them.

SIXTEEN

●━●━●━●━●━●━●

SINBAD and I were repairing his canoe one day, and neither of us had much to say. I was on my butt, pulling with all my might on some new waterproofing that he was securing with all his might, and using my old pliers, too. He was tired of getting wet in rough water because his old skin was leaking and holed, so he had asked me to help.

It was one of those days when nothing was going right. Murphy might have invented his law, but O'Leary knew that Murphy was an optimist. Even I was getting pissed and impatient. Damn skin wouldn't stretch far enough.

Nearby, Eennali and Billy were fighting to the death—two thirteen-year olds trying to kill each other, until Eennali got hurt and Billy was horrified at what he'd done. Watching, too, was Lily—she wasn't helping her mother stretch the skins. Her eyes were on Eennali. I knew that she wanted to run on over and kiss him to make him better.

It seemed to me that Sinbad and I would be related by marriage one day, probably as soon as Lily became a woman and went off to spend some days in the exile hut with whoever else was unfavored by pregnancy that month, too.

Any old time now. She was growing real tall, getting prettier each day, growing breasts. Yep, any old time.

Well, Sinbad nearly had it secured when the edges of the intestine snapped. The whole thing whizzed back and hit Sinbad in the face. He landed on his butt, cursing in Eskimo, which for a while had everyone out, curious.

I started laughing.

He wanted to fight me, too. He had no sense of humor. I had to turn my back so he wouldn't see my smile. No offense eventually taken, but his face was bright red from the sting. It would have hurt, too. We had to start over again.

I asked him how he'd lost his eye. I used the wrong word for *lost* and he was confused, as if he'd lost his eye like he'd lost his best throwing spear once. So I asked how it had happened.

He told me in Eskimo, in between his curses and grunts and groans.

"When I was small," he said, "like Eennali, my uncle taught me the ways, for my father, busy with his medicines, could not. I had no gift of sight or healing. A better hunter, I would make. My uncle was teaching me the arrows. My string pulled back and I shot and missed. My string came back once more with such power that it snapped and struck my eye."

He said it so offhandedly, then he stopped awhile and showed me where his eye had landed. I nearly threw up. Apparently, the eye had split and hung on his cheekbone.

He said he never cried.

Now it made sense why he never pulled back at shoulder height, but always low across his chest or waist, like a gunfighter in a Western storybook, shootin' from the hip.

I told him I wouldn't like to lose my sight. Sinbad laughed at me and said it was better to have one eye than only one arm.

It was the first time he'd ever been sarcastic. Funny, but he never seemed to take any notice of me being a cripple. He might have waited up or slowed a bit when we were walking because I couldn't keep up, but he never got upset or impatient with me. Probably because he knew I was trying hard.

Here, trying is as important as doing.

Lily was still watching, not working. I was back on my butt, pulling one-handed on the waterproofing that just wouldn't stretch that extra half inch needed, when I yelled at Lily to get back to work and stop looking at Eennali. If she didn't do as I said this time, she'd be in deep trouble.

She stuck her nose in the air and turned her back on me.

Damned girl, I thought. Everyone else's daughter does what she's told. Not mine.

Till then, I hadn't known either of my kids to get in serious trouble. And the one who did was the one I least expected trouble from—Billy.

I was still teaching school, now with Lily's assistance. She kept the smaller ones in line more easily than I could. We were on the beach one biting autumn afternoon, just finished a history lesson. I'd let the youngsters go off to play. Most of the girls were with us that day, and three boys. I hadn't seen Billy all day. I wasn't sure where he was, but I wasn't that worried, either. I'd only worry if a storm came up and he wasn't back. I'd been caught once before, and once had been enough.

Lily heard something from the southeast and caught my attention. She pointed. My sight wasn't as good as it used to be, but about five hundred yards out, two people were approaching on foot. They were stranded, calling out, waving. I sent Lily to fetch her granddaddy. By the time Asuluk came down, the two were close enough across fifty yards of rough water to yell at us the cause of the trouble. Names were screamed out, including Ignash's.

I closed my eyes as more of the tale unfolded.

Asuluk looked at the sky as he stood on the beach beside me, yelling at the kids to be quiet while he considered—a little too long.

Till he heard that someone had been speared but was still alive.

I immediately thought of Billy. I saw the weather. I also heard how far away the boys were.

Asuluk turned to me. He looked tired, sick, old. His eyes were expressionless. "Come," was all he said.

He got his pack ready, and some food. I was waiting by the

rocks on the summer side, ready to load the twelve-seater, when he finally appeared.

He rowed us over to the two stranded boys. I recognized them: my son's friends. They traveled together in a group of five, learned together, fought together. The oldest was sixteen—sixteen and stupid.

Asuluk wanted to know exactly what had happened. So did I. And when I discovered it wasn't my son who was injured, I breathed again. But Billy had stayed behind with his friends, sent these two to get help. Neither of the two boys wanted to say much else, until Asuluk backhanded the closest, set him on his butt. It wasn't hard to do; the boy was exhausted, physically and emotionally, and getting punished by the wise one was not a commendation. Asuluk and I were told the full story.

The group had slipped out to prove their collective courage. The expedition had ended in disaster. Eennali had been speared but was still alive. The kayak had sunk. Most of the boys' weapons were lost and there was no sled to bring the injured one back in. The ice was breaking; he couldn't be carried very far. So they built a snow house and were sheltering in it.

Asuluk got the directions, got back in the umiak, and left the two boys pondering the near future, which wouldn't be so bright once the wise one returned. Even I knew that. Last I saw of them, they were waiting for someone to collect them.

We headed east toward territory only the most experienced would dare venture into. I kept watching the sky all around us. So far, clear enough.

Asuluk was quiet, angry. It took a good hour before we found the three boys. Asuluk saw the snow house long before I did and turned us toward it. At least the boys had had sense enough not to build it on the edges of the drift ice. The wind was howling and blowing sheets of ice horizontally, so strong and fierce, I damn near got blown over a dozen times. I kept my eyes on Asuluk as he walked, head down into the blistering wind, one objective in mind—kicking two of his grandsons in the butt for being so stupid.

219

The three boys huddled in the snow house were scared to death. I'd never seen my son as terrified. He was crouched, holding his friend's head.

Eennali had a ten-foot-long spear through his right leg, just above the knee. He was in and out but mostly quiet. There was a large pool of thick blood under his leg; steam was rising from the wound.

Billy wouldn't look at me and I sure didn't feel like looking at him, either. If I did, I'd knock him halfway to Siberia. Jesus, these boys, what the hell were they trying to prove?

The other boy, Menak, I knew all too well. I ignored the little bastard.

Asuluk told me to check the weather. I went out and looked, shielding my eyes from the terrible glare. It was hard to tell direction here. For as far as I could see, we were surrounded by sea and drift ice. I couldn't see Kulowyl. The current had acted as a tailwind getting us here; it'd be a head wind getting back, take twice as long. If I said we were clear to leave, we'd probably be caught in a storm and all die. If we stayed here, we'd probably die eventually—unless the boys had caught some food, and I hadn't seen any. I went back in. It'd be dark by the time we got back if we left now, so I shook my head. We'd have to stay overnight in the snow house, the house of ice bricks, twenty degrees warmer in than out.

Menak didn't want to stay. Asuluk trusted my judgment; this boy did not. I remembered him well; he'd come to one of my school lessons—once. A true leader, or he'd like to think he was. He told Asuluk we could go, that we could leave Eennali there. He was going to die, anyway.

That proved to me this boy had no brains at all. If Asuluk hadn't hit him, I sure would have. But he beat me to it. He moved so quickly, I nearly missed it. I thought he'd hit Menak hard enough to break his jaw. He went down on top of his buddy. Billy heaved him off, and that's where Menak stayed, unconscious.

Asuluk said one word: "Children."

And he spat and glared at Billy.

Tears formed in my son's eyes. I was pleased to see them, too.

Asuluk told me to get his pack, find the lamp, and light it, which is something you need two good hands for. Here, they use flint and spark. Billy lighted the lamp for me. So far, he hadn't said a word. He was too scared, scared of the trouble he was in, scared for his buddy. He did ask if he could help, but Asuluk pretended he wasn't there. That hurt him more than anything. Tears rolled down his cheeks and he sat by his buddy's head.

I knew this boy, my friend's son, my daughter's beau. He lay quietly on his side, cold, teeth chattering, sweating, talking to himself, now and then mentioning Lily's name. He was upset that he'd never see her again. My son kept telling him that he would. But I doubted it. He was in shock. I thought of infection. And I knew if Asuluk pulled the spear out, he'd probably bleed to death unless the artery was stitched up. I looked at Asuluk and asked what he was going to do. He sent Billy out to gather up some fresh snow, some "burning ice." He gave the boy something to chew on and looked at me.

"Hold," he said.

"What?"

"Hold!"

He put my hand on Eennali's leg, mainly to hold the spear steady. Asuluk chose his sharpest knife and sawed through the spear. It was made of bone, long, shaped for less wind resistance, and as thick as a quarter. I could feel the spear vibrating. I tried to hold it steady and felt nauseous the whole time. Eennali, though, made hardly a sound. Asuluk cut through halfway, told me to hold it real tight. Then he cracked it off and threw the triangular head over his shoulder.

I damn near passed out. Blood was pouring now. "Asuluk?"

He looked at me.

"Don't take it out here. Not here. He'll bleed to death." He took no notice of me. Was he going to push it through now? Or crack it off again? He looked through his pack, couldn't find what he was looking for. I took my pliers and cutters from my pocket.

He looked at me, at the boy. Eennali wasn't looking so good. There was a hell of a lot of blood now.

Asuluk took the cutters, whacked off the spear an inch from the pants, and pulled them down. I got the intestine bandage ready. It was strong, elastic, waterproof, but I knew the artery was hit. This kid would keep bleeding, into his own leg. Asuluk would have to cut the leg open to find the artery and sew it back together. He knew it, too.

And Eennali just lay there, not making a sound.

The snow was ready, some lumps of ice. Asuluk told Billy to hold Eennali's head, tight.

I couldn't watch. I heard the spear slip through and I looked back. Asuluk was packing snow and ice on the boy's thigh, then putting on the bandage, but it didn't work. Eennali's eyes were rolling. He threw up and felt nothing else. For a horrible moment, I thought he was dead.

Asuluk rolled him onto his face, cut the leg open. The artery was pumping hard. He was on his stomach, too, sewing it together, until the spurts eased up. Then he asked me to hold the muscle together while he sewed it up again. There was still blood, but not as much. He watched for a long time before he touched. And I heard one long sigh. Asuluk sat back and chanted while he wiped the thick, cooling blood off the bandage and wrapped Eennali's entire leg with it.

The bare butt was covered with the hunting pants again and Asuluk took off his outer coat, the bearskin. He covered Eennali with it. And he looked at me. I tried to smile. He ignored it and turned to Billy, who was still holding his friend's head.

Billy knew he was so far down the outhouse, he'd probably never see daylight again. Personally, I thought witnessing this was enough to make him obey the rules for the rest of his life.

Asuluk didn't say a word. I think that was a worse punishment.

Two feet away, Menak was still in never-never land, missing all the fun.

Asuluk started chanting, using his magic stones again. There was something about that bearskin, about those special stones that aided the magic. I joined in the chant, and so did Billy. I put my hand on Eennali's neck. The chanting was in time to a heart-beat and I could feel a heartbeat growing stronger. Maybe it was my imagination, but the pulsing grew steadier, stronger, little by little.

Asuluk knew what I was thinking. He smiled at me, then went back to concentrating on his work—the magic part, the part he thought worked best of all.

This old man had just saved his grandson's life and he hadn't batted an eyelid. There'd been no sign of fear, of impatience, no sign of doubt.

Unlike me.

Menak eventually woke and remained very quiet as he sat, huddled in a corner, holding his face tightly.

Outside, darkness had come. I hadn't noticed.

The dark lasted eighteen hours this time of year; just before dawn we headed home, Eennali stretched out on the bottom of the umiak. He was weak, feverish, but at least he was alive. Asuluk made Menak and Billy row us back and for two long hours he death-stared the boys.

No way in hell would I ever have wanted to be those two boys, or Eennali when he got better, or those other two who'd spent twenty-four long hours waiting for the inevitable—the wise one's wrath.

Eennali lived, but of course he had one special girl tending him constantly. For a long time, I suppose he wished he'd died. He acquired a limp like mine after that ordeal and punishment for them all was the dog box, at different times of course. When one was ostracized, the others were at women's work.

The five of them were banned from attending any kind of hunt for a full season, until summer turned summer once again.

By the time their punishment was done, they were all men, not just boys playing games.

Billy never mentioned it again, but he never forgot the experience, either. I could see the memory in his eyes each time he was with his best friend. They'd learned a lesson the hard way, but at least they'd learned.

It took me a couple of days, and Billy almost a year, to convince Kioki that nothing like that would ever happen again. The worst thing that can happen to a woman here is to lose a son.

The ordeal only gave Lily the opportunity to exercise some of the spirit medicine her granddaddy had spent years teaching her.

She was eleven before she believed me. Those times we were together and alone and it felt right to tell her what her daddy really was didn't come by as often as I'd have liked. And when I got her alone, I knew she always wanted to be somewhere else.

I never once translated from Eskimo to English. I never once described my 1923 Jenny as a soaring bird falling from the sky. I never talked in symbols, used pretty words or phrases. I just told her truths as I saw them, and they lacked her granddaddy's pretty style. Bored her senseless. She'd tell me which disturbed spirit was creating the white blanket and I'd call it plain old fog. She knew numbers, but they had no meaning. A 1923 Jenny had no meaning. The year I crashed here meant nothing. Fourteen ninety-two and Christopher Columbus and sailing ships did not have a place in her world. Her spirits meant more to her than her daddy's God. Her mind seemed as closed as a sprung rabbit trap until she was eleven and her granddaddy told her about me. Only then did she want to listen, believe, imagine.

Once, she asked me how the spirits put Gran'ma Lily and Auntie Meg into that flat, peeling photograph. I didn't have a mirror to show her her own reflection and I didn't have the words to explain images and photography. She wasn't like her brother, who contstantly questioned why, who needed to know how things worked. He's nearly a man now, and he still asks his daddy why. Even if he asks in a different way.

At times, I want to pretend Lily isn't a part of me. We have nothing in common. Gone now the rare times she'd sit with me voluntarily. She spends her time helping Asuluk, playing her role in life here, a life I'm not a part of. I feel as if I'm nothing to her, never have been, never will be. Maybe I should have called her Meg, not Lily.

Maybe I tried too hard. Maybe I thought that if Billy was eager to know and learn about life, places, and ways far removed from this one, it naturally followed that she would.

It breaks my heart that I was wrong. Breaks my heart that she chose to believe I was just like everyone else here.

Till that get-together not so long ago, that is.

I have Asuluk to thank. Again. He must have been running out of stories to tell, so he decided it was time to tell about me, rekindle the memories for those who were here when I came, give understanding to those who weren't born then.

It's been seventeen years. The longest winter of my life.

Having someone tell your story while you're in the audience is a strange thing. And not once did I feel the need to amend anything my old friend said. I realized as I sat there, quietly listening to his magical voice, that he had heard every word I'd ever told him, that he'd seen in his mind some pictures as I talked, just as his words built pictures in my mind. He had a far better way of describing his mind pictures. The most boring story on earth only he could make interesting.

Asuluk, over a series of nights, told everyone about the new, other world, Floreeda's world, a world that one day might become their world, too.

And listening to his words just brought it all back again, fresh, new, more painful than ever because I'd deluded myself all these years by thinking I could be who I was without having to acknowledge where I'd come from.

I can't lie to others, just myself.

Only after my daughter heard her granddaddy tell the story

of the stranger who fell from the sky did she believe it was about me. I should have been glad—far better late than never, but I felt betrayed, hurt. After those story nights, she'd come and sit by me, pick up the model I'd made for Billy so many years ago, and ask in English what made it fly.

She'd pretend she understood when I told her what I remembered of aerodynamics. Or she'd ask, "What's a tree?" And then she'd pretend she understood when I'd describe one. "What is cotton?" What is this? What is that? Never once did she feel the need to ask why. She hardly ever asked questions about me; they were all about her grandma, especially when she was studying the photo.

She'd look into my eyes, touch my face, and say in Eskimo, "I have a grandmother, your mother?"

"Yes, and you have her name. Lily."

If only she could see a lily, she would know how much she means to me.

She only took an interest in English after Asuluk told his stories. Coming from him, all was believed. It was real. From me, it was fantasy. Now she's decided she wants to read like her brother can, and as he's never home, I am approached. She sits opposite and spends her time staring at me. Now and then, she'll break concentration and smile, always after being caught for not paying attention.

I keep telling myself that it doesn't matter. She's come to me of her own choice now. Does it matter that she's almost a woman and that it might be too late for her truly to understand or benefit?

Why didn't she believe me? Why did she have to hear it from her granddaddy before she recognized the truth?

She's breaking what's left of my heart.

She's so pretty, so alive.

She already knows who she's going to marry—Sinbad's youngest boy, Eennali.

Forty-one years of my life have flicked by as quickly as a sneeze.

Forty-one years, and what do I have to show for it?

Where's my dream gone? What happened to it? Is it waiting in a box under the lost-and-found booth at the Abbeville County Fairgrounds? Has anyone I ever knew missed me? Do they wonder why I never called, never wrote, never came back?

Eternity is so long a time. Maybe my dream lies a little southeast of eternity. Or is it just a cobweb now, not freshly spun and glistening with dew, but old and sagging and gray from dust? Dust of shattered dreams. Lost in the nowhere zone on the other side of eternity.

Forty-one years.

If I went down in 1926, the year's 1943.

I just want to know where the hell it has all gone.

I've spent nearly as long here as I did in Abbeville, South Carolina. My first eleven years of life were spent in a dreamland mixed with reality, and when you're a kid, time goes by very fast. I hated having to wear shoes to school. I hated having to go to school, until Billy Taylor told me I'd be nothing without an education. He was the only person who ever thought I was halfway bright. God knows, having to show my reports to my mother made a liar out of Billy Taylor. So what if Paris wasn't the capital of Spain? Would that help me get my license to fly? I flew for nearly four years without one and I flew a hell of a lot better than the dense bastard from Virginia who tested me.

Pieces of paper meant nothing to me, anyway. Certificates and framed diplomas on a wall still mean nothing. What good did lots of study do for Meg? The more she learned, the less she could experience, and she just got lonely and bitter and disillusioned.

She accepted pity more easily than I did.

I wonder sometimes what would have become of me if Billy Taylor hadn't put his flying school five hundred yards from our house. Where would I have ended up? I wasn't much good at school, and I swore I would never, never pick or farm cotton, so I suppose I would have worked in a factory or a mill somewhere.

Jesus, that would have killed me quicker than this place ever could.

Seventeen years I've been here. Some days feel fifty years long; some days take five minutes to end. Some days I'll wake disoriented, lost again, nearly crying, expecting my mother to come in holding the lamp in the darkness.

"Are you all right, son?"

Sometimes I can smell her—lilacs. It comes; it goes just as quickly—as if she's walked up to me, touched me, and walked away again. I see nothing, but I know it's her. Then it's gone and I'm left with the sight of the walls of this summer house, the smell of the dried fish, the salmon shards, the blubber. Here I am, forty-one years old, wanting my mama. As if she could wave her magic wand and I'd wake in Bertuse Street, Miami.

If I do wake in Bertuse Street, Miami, I know it'll be a hot day, a free day. Bob and I'll check out the newest private hotel, where the rich tourists stay. It's always called something stupid like Seaview or Paradise End.

Bob used to like the rich girls—especially the ones from New York or Chicago, the daddy's little darlings. He liked to give them a taste of the other side of life—our side.

So what we'll do on this free day is sit on the hotel's private beach till the management realize we aren't who we pretend to be and make us move on—politely, of course. It won't be like the dance halls in the rougher quarters. Bob went out through a window one time, lay bleeding and laughing on the pavement. All it did was add another scar to the face that attracted girls like bugs to light. I've been cursing Bobby for dying when he did. I've been cursing myself for letting him have his way. If only I'd said, No, we can't go to Atlanta, maybe he'd still be alive.

And if he'd lived, we'd have done that flight together, that trip across America, Florida to Alaska to Maine to Florida. We'd be home by now, after a hero's welcome, maybe even a ticker-tape parade. Our pictures in the paper again. And on to bigger things. The publicity would have been good for business. Sullivan and Shaw would have grown, too. We'd probably be employing two, three, maybe four pilots by now. Bob and I would take to the air when we wanted, not when we had to. I'd be living in a nice house with Sally as a wife, a couple of kids I wouldn't see very much or know that well. I'd be driving around in the latest automobile; I'd be wearing expensive clothes, too, and smoking Cuban cigars. I'd take my family to California for vacation twice a year.

Might even have had my own flying school.

As for Bobby, who knows. He might finally have settled with Bess. If he had married her, that forever-frightened look might have faded from her eyes.

So I curse him for dying. I curse him for not being with me when I crashed here.

Then I get pictures. I'm back on the ice with Asuluk. I see what is left of the Jenny. And whoever would have been sitting in the front seat would have been pulp.

I wish I'd been more like Bobby. At least I would have experienced something of life before this jail sentence hit.

Defendant, please rise. John Robert Shaw, the court of life has sentenced you to ninety-nine years in an ice land time forgot.

Forty-one. A wife, two kids. I work; I pay no taxes. I'm learning every day. I might teach, but I'm also a student. I should be used to the cold, but I'm not.

I can't take it like I used to. Last time I spent too long on the ice with the northeaster howling across the flats, I got so sick that I damn near died again. Pneumonia, I guess. It felt like someone was driving red-hot pokers into me with each breath I took.

Asuluk won't let me out when it's windy. So these days, I have to stay home with the women and kids. I'm back to square one.

Billy goes out instead of me.

I can't keep up with them anymore. I think I might be excess baggage and they don't know where to put me. If it was an airplane I was flying, I'd just say, No. Sorry, we're overloaded. Best leave it behind.

I can shoot a bow and arrow if I sit and use my foot and right hand, but I'm still not as fast as Billy. He can off-load six arrows before I've shot two.

No one's asked me to go hunting for a long time now. If I'm up to it, I help the ladies and kids with skinning, pegging, drying. I can make a good triple-hooked harpoon head and I can sharpen an arrowhead so fine, I could nearly shave with it if I wanted to. But the beard keeps my face warm.

I made Lily a necklace from walrus ivory—it was a heart on some beaded sinew—and I inscribed her name on it. She watched me making it, never said a thing. When I gave it to her, tied it in place, she looked at it, at me, thanked me quietly, and walked away. The limit of her affection.

I guess she likes it; she hasn't taken it off yet.

She's still quiet, never says much, but I know she was worried last time I was sick and couldn't breathe. I barely remember her sitting there, holding my hand when she wasn't rubbing in that putrid black ointment, chanting me to sleep, chanting me awake.

While I was sick, she never left my side. But once I was a little better . . .

She spends too much time with Eennali's mother these days. Too much time. I wonder when she's going to move in with them. I can't forbid it, either. That's how life is here. If she does leave us for Sinbad's boy, it'll be her choice.

Other boys look at her and fluff their feathers, but she never looks back. She's fallen in love with her brother's best friend. I should have called her Meg.

But I catch her sometimes, sitting on her own, staring at nothing, thinking. I'll sit with her and give anything to know what's on her mind. Is she wondering now if there isn't more to living than this cold, barren, unending routine? Is it the "I know better" look that ran so strong in the Shaw blood that I see now and then flicking across her eyes? Or is it my own imagination?

She'll look at me and smile as if she's answering my silent question and she'll hold my hand and tell me without words that she'll always love me, then ask me why I worry so much about nothing.

My sister has a nephew and niece she doesn't know about. How many have I got that I don't know about?

What would I do if Meg appeared here now? What would I say? I couldn't offer her a cup of tea. A bowl of seal blood maybe? What does she look like now? She'd be thirty-nine, probably married, still in Abbeville, when all she wanted was to practice law in Chicago. She'd cook and clean and sew and have some hot chocolate and biscuits ready when the kids got home from school. Her future was wrecked because of a polio virus, mine because of a plane mishap. Never will we two meet again. But where there's life, there's hope, they say. I can't picture it in my mind anymore—me going home. Limping up the front path, taking those stairs, knocking on my own door. Hearing the squeaks of the chair coming down the hall, seeing the doorknob turn. Seeing my sister's face. I can't imagine her older than twenty-two.

And I can't read her pretty words anymore. I've tried so hard to understand them. Damn her and damn Walt Whitman, Matthew, Mark, Luke, and all of them. My brain doesn't think that way. All I've ever known is what I've felt, seen, heard, touched, and tasted. I guess I'd always envied her way of knowing hidden meanings behind a tree branch waving in the wind.

All I'd do was wait for it to snap, land on my head.

A pile of yellow, stained, torn paper is all I have to show for seventeen years of life here. And it's fast running out.

I had a dream last night. It haunted me so much, I went to Asuluk and told him about it. He listened until I was done. He didn't look at me as if I was crazy. He studied his fingernails, scratched his head, pulled a face, and looked me in the eye.

"You say we would go? Leave this, our home?"

"That's what I saw."

"No. This. Ours. Yours."

"Asuluk, I know you've seen this happen, too."

"Dark Wind," he said softly, fear in his eyes.

"No. No, it's not the Dark Wind playing games."

"Yes." He turned to me and asked, "Bird boat?"

"Yes. Bird boat."

Just what I'd seen in my dream—a huge flying boat, floating on the water in the summer bay.

"My dream say you go, we stay. You go home. To Carolsville. To Lily. Meg. The soaring birds—" There were tears in his eyes. "You see fire sticks? Fat canoes? Many men?" he asked.

I told him that all I saw was a huge bird boat, some kind of four-engined seaplane, floating in the bay. But I knew when I saw it, I had a ticket out of here. I wanted these people to come with me.

"This our home." He was getting angry, adamant.

Then we both heard it from afar—far, far away, probably the north-northeast. Storm clouds were too low to see much, but I looked up to the sky anyway, straining hard.

The noise, a low but booming hum, seemed to still all life for miles.

And before much longer, Asuluk and I were joined by fifty-three others. Everyone had come out, wondering what was going on, and they mostly looked to me for answers I didn't want to provide.

I felt my wife's frightened touch, saw the look of confusion, of wonder in my son's eyes.

Then I knew why Asuluk had gone to such trouble to tell these people about the world I came from, because an airplane that big would have to come into sight soon.

And I wondered as I held my wife tightly what else he knew.

I couldn't believe what I was hearing.

SEVENTEEN

◦◦◦◦◦◦◦

THAT distant hum remained far off before it disappeared. Four days passed. No planes came near Kulowyl, and with each day that drew to a close, John convinced himself that both he and Asuluk had been wrong; that for him, it was only a dream born of wishful thinking, no more, no less.

Until the fifth day.

Spirits had accepted the seal bladder offerings and had supplied the village with a school of fish two miles to the southwest. Every man had gone except John. Billy took his place, and it was the first time in years that Asuluk had joined the hunt, too.

John was alone with the women and children when he first heard it. It was more of a familiar feeling at first—déjà vu. Instead of standing on the Abbeville field waiting for Billy Taylor to land, he was looking to the northeast when, from the building cloud bank, it appeared—a dark pinpoint, slowly enlarging as it came closer.

A plane, a huge plane. It had to be to make that much noise.

John's initial reaction was disbelief. As he watched, the pinpoint suddenly disappeared from sight. The plane had landed. John waited for it to reappear. There was nothing. He went back to the women, to his daughter, whom he was helping stretch and peg a bull seal's skin. He said nothing, although she sensed something wrong. Any questions, she kept silent, continuing with the task at hand. Her father, though, was like a dog sensing danger long before it was apparent. She didn't like it when he acted this way, but he had very good hearing, far better than his sight.

And so it was that the dogs finally heard, too. From the distance, it came—just as her grandfather had decreed—a huge dark bird, screaming thunder, breathing smoke. It swept low over the village, still screaming, and turned back to attack again. If it weren't for her father so close, holding her tightly, she would have run in terror as everyone else did.

I told her there was nothing to be afraid of. She had to go find her mama and grandma and they had to sit in the house very quietly till I came back.

I went across to the summer side and stood on the rocks, and through the thick blanket of fog, I tried to get a good look at this gigantic seaplane. It had to be huge from the noise it made reversing thrust on touchdown.

Storms were boiling in the cold sky, barely a hundred feet above my head, and I knew that if I was the pilot, I'd be wanting out of there, fast.

It was my dream all right. But it had nothing to do with salvation, with rescue.

The rafts came in and I counted the heads as they closed in, coming straight for me through the fog. Twenty of them, and they weren't dressed for the climate, either. One raft, the first, was loaded to the waterline with long steel boxes, rifles, ammo, tents, tinned food. Then the plane took off, tried to escape the brewing storm. It had four engines, and it needed each one, too.

I didn't know what to do or say, so I offered my hand to help the first man out. He was a sergeant, about as old as I am. He was an American; I heard him cussing.

He didn't even look at me until he was standing on the rocks. He looked up, because I was a head taller, and he looked at me twice, surprised.

I didn't say a word. His boots were wet and I knew if he didn't do something soon, the soles of his feet and his toes would get frostbite.

The first white man I'd seen in seventeen years and I took an instant dislike to him. He gave me the rope to hold the raft while he helped the others to shore.

"Hey! Lieutenant! We got ourselves a wild man here!"

They thought I was an Eskimo? With my face covered in hair, my eyes the color of a summer sky?

I stood there, stunned, sucking air like a dying cod. My voice and any English words were stuck halfway between my throat and the foggy air.

The sergeant came back, grabbed the rope from my hand, and pushed me out of his way. I never liked being pushed. All I could see for a while were his overcoated butt and wet trouser legs as he unloaded the boxes onto the rocks. I resisted the terrible urge I had to kick him right in the ass as I heard him muttering to himself and cursing, using language I only thought, never voiced. Cursing the cold, cursing the fog and rain and storms and wind and more Eskimos. Who in their right mind would live here, anyway? . . . On and on and on. Instead of kicking that ass pointed right at me, I said, "*Unangan* live here, buddy."

He froze for a while, then looked at me, upside down, face under his arm. Then he rose and took a good look at me before he called out, "Hey, Lieutenant! We got ourselves a real live English-speaking Eskimo over here!"

A dark-eyed youngster loped over, his boots slipping on the wet rocks. More frostbite, I thought.

"You speak English?" he asked slowly, and loudly too, in case I was deaf as well as stupid.

"Name's John Shaw," I replied, watching the way he was staring at my red beard, my eyes, my half arm. "Don't camp here. Tents are no good, either. Storm'll blow you halfway across the Bering. Best you come with me."

But the youngster, this Lieutenant Morrison, Seventh Division, just stared at me. "You're an American?"

He wasn't telling me anything I didn't already know. "Yeah. I sure enough am. You better come with me, quick."

I was watching the boiling sky and I'd been caught in storms like this three times too often to risk a fourth.

"Where are you from?"

I wanted to get out of harm's way and this idiot wanted to talk. So I said we had time for that later, all night if he wanted it, but if he didn't get his men into shelter now, most of them would be dead by morning.

I guess it was my worst mistake. I should have pretended I was an Eskimo and let the bastards be. But I had no reason to act that way. I told them to bury their weapons and stuff in the snow and mark the spot, but they couldn't leave it, so I let them drag it all across the island without any help from me, any sled I could have used, half a dozen dogs eager for a little exercise. The wind was fifty knots and a headwind, too, and I asked that the Spirit of Wind hold back the storm. Till then, I hadn't known how much of an Eskimo I'd become.

As I led the twenty soldiers into Kulowyl's winter village, we were met by the dogs, tethered, of course, and very aggressive, worse because of the new human scents, which must have been very offensive to them.

I led the young lieutenant into my house and the sergeant followed us in. I told Kioki, her mother, and Lily to go to Asuluk's meetinghouse and stay there. I said the soldiers would be staying in our house.

I saw the frightened look in Lily's eyes as she darted out and I heard the lieutenant say quietly, "Branson, don't even think it."

I'd recognize the tone anywhere. I looked into that sergeant's eyes and what I saw there I did not like. Nor did I like the series of wolf whistles from those gathered outside, either. I knew who they were whistling at and so did the lieutenant. He went outside and I listened to him warning of charges if they didn't leave well enough alone. The kid had the bars and the rank, but he had as much authority as me telling the sled dogs to sit up and beg.

It was then I started praying for Asuluk to bring the others home quickly.

"Sorry about that, Mr. Shaw, but this is the twenty-third island we've evacuated and they're tired—"

"Evacuated? What's happening?"

He looked at me as if he'd never heard anyone talk before. I didn't know I was talking half Eskimo, as well. All those years of needing someone to talk to, now my prayers were answered and he didn't understand a word I tried to say.

"Dutch Harbor's been bombed, sir, and we've orders to secure the peninsula and the islands across to Kiska. The Japs have taken Attu."

The Japs have taken Attu?

"The Japs?"

"Japanese, sir. We think they're coming in from the north to take us."

They what? What the hell was happening?

"What year is it?" I asked.

"Don't you know, sir?"

"I've been here since April 1926," I said very slowly.

"Holy shit," he said, giving both words an emphasis I'd never heard before. "Sir, it's May 1943."

Hell, I thought. I was right. It *was* 1943.

He didn't know why I was so happy. "Where are you from, sir?" he asked.

"South Carolina."

"Wheeling, West Virginia," he said, a genuine surprised smile on his face, and he shook my hand. "What the hell are you doing here?"

I said that it could wait. I told him that if he put his men nine to a shelter, they'd be warm enough to sleep—the wet blankets from their packs would be no good, only freeze so hard that they'd crack. So if he could organize his men before too many of them got frostbite or crotch rot, I could go on over and calm the womenfolk down till the others came back. He asked how many of us there were. I told him fifty-five. Maybe.

My son was out there on a hunt, and the storm was closing in too fast. Unless they'd taken shelter on another island somewhere and were waiting it out, I knew the chances of them making it home in kayaks in this weather were not good.

I tied up my parka hood and walked out.

All the women and children were confused and frightened and they had all gathered together in Asuluk's meetinghouse. No one was missing. I asked them to stay until their husbands and sons returned, saying that then we could all talk, the visitors, the elders, everyone.

The storm hung overhead, not yet breaking, but not moving, either.

It was coming on summer, but the winter had been a bad one, sleeting, snowing far too late. We hadn't moved yet and wouldn't until the thaw began.

When I got back to my house, the sergeant had disappeared and a medic was tending the lieutenant. Some of the skin on the bottom of his feet was burned, peeling. And I knew how it felt. So I gave the medic the bowl of black ointment, told him to use it. I said it was the only thing that worked.

The medic touched it, looked at me, and asked what was in it. I lighted the lamp because there'd be a few hours of darkness soon. Then I told him if he didn't use it, the lieutenant would lose his feet. His choice.

I sat down, took my parka hood off, and scratched my head. My hair was past my shoulders again. I pretended I wasn't watching the pain on the youngster's face as the medic dabbed the putrid potion on his frostbitten toes. I looked at the boots. They'd be frozen by morning, too.

"How'd you get here, sir?" the lieutenant asked again.

I told him about the solo, about leaving Anchorage, the storm, coming down.... He was going to put his wet boots back on, so I threw him my spares.

"Well, thank you, sir, thank you."

And as he put the boots on, the dogs went wild again. It was the sound I was so used to—the men were back.

238

"Let me tell them first."

They had baskets and nets full, half a dozen seals, as well, and they were singing their thanks still. By the sound of it, they'd spotted a colony of whales and would head out again as soon as the storm passed.

Asuluk saw the huddle of soldiers and held up his hand for immediate silence. I walked to him and told him quietly that the women and children were all fine, safe in the meeting place. I asked him if he would calm his people, because these men had fire sticks in their hands and fire in their eyes, too.

I knew how I'd feel if this was my twenty-third island to evacuate.

Three families, including mine, were ousted from their homes and the soldiers moved in. The storm opened up and I thanked whichever god was responsible for seeing everyone home safely.

It was only then that I could talk freely with the young lieutenant, but even then I was constantly distracted by the others in my house, touching things that weren't theirs to touch—my son's bow and arrows, harpoons, spears, his waterproof. I knew if he came home now and saw this, there'd be hell to pay. I hoped that for a change he'd do as I'd said, stay with his mother and sister.

"Is there anyone you want to get a message to, sir?"

"My mother. My sister. They think I've been dead for seventeen years. You know?" He said he did, but how could he? I gave the address at Abbeville and the lieutenant wrote it down. Then he looked at me again.

"You'll be home before you know it, sir. The boat'll be here before dawn to take you all to the mainland." He got to his feet and, still wearing my boots, limped outside again.

Those words repeated in my brain: You'll be home before you know it.

The medic started fussing over me. "Where's the lieutenant gone?" I asked.

"To radio in, sir. Just sit back for me. . . ."

Next came a lot of questions. As he looked into my eyes with a little light and listened to my heart, he asked how old I was, what I'd been eating all this time, how I lost the arm, what caused me to limp so bad. . . .

"Shut it a bit, son."

He looked at me, surprised.

"You got an orange in that bag?"

"An orange? No." He reached into his pocket and brought out a chocolate bar instead. He unwrapped it for me and handed it over. I touched it, smelled it. I hadn't tasted anything sweet for God knows how long. The medic watched me eat it. Suddenly, I was back on Miami Beach, chewing on sweets, whistling at pretty girls going by.

"It's been a long time, huh," he said, and it wasn't even a question.

"Where you from?"

"New Hampshire."

He told me about his hometown, but I was too busy savoring the taste of his chocolate to be bothered concentrating on two things at once. It wasn't till he asked what I flew that I heard him again. *Fly, plane, sky,* always the words to get my attention.

"A Curtiss Jenny," I replied.

"My old man flew biplanes in the first war. Lost his arm, like you. I was just a kid, of course, but I remember one day he took me to this airfield and he let me sit in this biplane. Pointed out some things to me, you know, the stick, the throttle—"

"Mix. Spark advance . . ." I was thinking aloud again. Thinking how I had my name in gold leaf under the cockpit rim— John Shaw, in Old English lettering. You never forget, never. Bringing her down, pulling her back to idle, a full-rudder slip to scare the pants off any passenger, round out . . . Touching down on grass, it's a feeling you never forget. "Thanks for the chocolate bar."

"Yeah, well, maybe you won't thank me tomorrow, sir."

Sir. No one had ever called me sir before. It felt strange.

"Who are we fighting this time?" I asked, wondering what else I'd missed in seventeen years.

He told me about the war in Europe, in the South Seas. Just about every country he could think of was fighting. It had to end soon, that's all he knew. And they couldn't let the Japs take America by coming in from the north.

I remember thinking, They have to be kitted better than you people. Because neither side would survive up here in the ice too long. Bullets wouldn't kill them; the weather would.

The lieutenant came back in, limping. He looked sick to me. Sick, tired, worried. "I got the message through for you. You'll be met at Anchorage tomorrow. Someone from the War Department'll be there waiting."

"I don't think these people will want to go. They've been here a long time. It's all they know."

"Sorry, sir, but every inhabitant of this island is being evacuated at first light, whether he agrees or not. I have my orders."

"You're gonna use force?"

"I'm hoping you'll make that unnecessary. You'll help them see reason."

Oh sure. Reason. I'd been there seventeen years and was still learning about these people—my people. I felt more a part of them than these bad-mannered, foulmouthed American soldiers cursing the cold.

Later that night, the lieutenant and I sat with the elders. It was up to me to tell these people they had to leave their island or be caught in a battleground and die. Whether they liked it or not, they were American citizens and their island home was now under military control.

Halfway through the meeting, we all heard the commotion—screams, shouting. I didn't know I could move so fast.

Outside, in the dark, Eennali was fighting that sergeant. A group of soldiers were standing in a circle, watching, yelling. A wider circle of my people were also watching, stunned, confused, horrified.

241

The lieutenant pushed past, took a gun from his belt, grabbed Eennali by the hair. Eennali had his fingers locked tightly around Branson's throat. He was turning blue, his tongue sticking out.

"Tell him to get off or I'll shoot him!"

Eennali's mother was screaming.

Sinbad came from nowhere, pulled his son off, and held him firmly. The medic came and tried to help Branson breathe again.

I pushed through the crowd to where my daughter stood with Kioki and Eennali's mother, but she clung to Kioki. When I touched, she screamed and jumped a mile. I asked her what had happened.

And Kioki, angry, confused, told me what Branson had tried to do. But Eennali had heard the screams. Eennali had taken revenge. I looked back at Branson, sitting up now, spluttering. He was saying, or trying to, how he only wanted a bit of fun. It got out of hand, was all.

Billy, who had more sense than I did, tried to stop me. I pushed him aside, kept throwing his hands off. The medic saw us coming and leapt out of the way. I kicked Branson in the face and put my foot across his throat. "She's my daughter, you bastard! My daughter!"

The lieutenant managed to calm me down enough to stop me from killing the man. He led me away. I remember telling him to keep that bastard out of my sight.

It took me a long time to calm down. I never heard a word the young officer tried to say. I sat in my house with him a long time till I decided I couldn't spend the night there. I wanted to be with my wife, my son, my daughter.

I got up and left, walked straight to Sinbad's house.

Lily was huddled in a corner, crying quietly, shaking. Her clothes were torn, her mouth bleeding. I'd told her to stay with her mother, but no, she had to sneak off to be with Eennali.

"Lily?"

She looked up at me and, just as she used to do when she was five years old, she put her arms out. I held her close, told her how sorry I was. I said I knew that these men were from the land I came from, that they were supposed to be my people. I tried to tell her that not everyone acted as these did, but any words were wasted, even on myself. If they were my people, I didn't want to know them anymore.

Then she started crying for Eennali. I looked up at Sinbad. He still had a tight grip on his son, who had sworn death to the one who'd touched Lily. I beckoned the boy to come and the young man took my place.

Sinbad stared at his feet. No one would look me in the eye, not even Asuluk.

Was this an example of what my people were like?

All faces turned when the young officer knocked on the door. He stepped inside and asked, "Is she okay?"

He was met with a lot of vacant stares, mine among them. No one slept that night. When dawn finally came, it brought with it no joy, no laughter. We were all packing to leave.

I wrapped my journal, made of two logbooks and the wads of yellow notepaper I'd used to record happenings and expenses on the original trip. I had Meg's red book with me, my Bowie knife, the handgun, and ten bullets. Seventeen years of my life lay in a one-foot-square sealskin package tied with sinew.

At sunrise, we were evacuated by boat. I looked back at my island until it became a spot on the misty horizon. Twenty soldiers were watching us go. The fog rolled in from the north and that was it. It was over, done, gone.

Then I looked at the faces around me. Asuluk, sitting as if this was the end of life as he knew it; his old wife beside him, crying. Sinbad was quiet, holding one of his grandsons as we all sat crammed on the crowded deck of the old whaling boat. Any life that was once there had disappeared from his eyes. No one was laughing; no one was singing. No one was telling stories. No one understood what was happening, and to a point, I didn't, either. I'd lost something, somewhere; I didn't know what it was, let alone how to find it again. Where the hell were we going?

Where would they take us? All my questions had been answered with, "You'll be fine, sir." Sure, I'd be fine. What about the others?

Kioki was with her mother. Now and then, she'd look over at me, at Billy, and at Lily, who was with me. I didn't have to hear her speak to know what was on her mind.

Lily was terrified of what would happen if she let go of my arm. So I just sat there, holding her tightly, trying not to tell any more lies, because I wasn't sure myself what lay ahead for any of us.

Billy was on my left, staring up at the blue sky, the patches of sunshine. But in his eyes lay the hatred that hadn't faded from the night before. We tried to sleep on deck, fifty-five Eskimos all huddled together, five babies crying, old women crying. My woman was crying, too, because she'd always known this would happen. Just like her daddy.

I didn't sleep. Maybe I knew that it'd be the last time I had all my family close to me. My wife, my kids. And fifty others that may as well have been family, too.

It was the hardest day I've ever endured.

I remember trying to eat my first tin of meat. It stayed down about two minutes before I was over the side, barfing so bad, I thought I'd go overboard, too. Kioki waited till I'd sat down again before she offered me a salmon shard she took from the depths of her coat. Then I saw what she'd packed. I thought the bundle contained extra clothing, a few cook pots. It was all food.

I suppose I will never forget the look in the children's eyes when they first saw trees. I suppose it was like the look that must have been in my eyes when I saw the Atlantic for the first time. I'd turned to my father and said, "Hey, that sure is a big lake there, Dad."

I'd told them about this. Some of them could speak passable English. But even though they'd been told, it was still a journey into the unknown—an unknown that they feared.

I was no exception.

What I saw as we came in was not the Anchorage I remembered. I guess a lot changes in seventeen years. I was coming in by boat, not from the air.

Most of the folks who met the boat were in uniform—army uniform. There was someone there who spoke Eskimo, but it wasn't the language my people understood. Maybe these Americans didn't know that languages differed as much as locations did.

If these people were American citizens and evacuees from a war zone, then I wondered how prisoners of war were treated. I guess they were Eskimos and that was the excuse. No white face, no white treatment. Not a lot changes.

They were herding us into groups, groups that weren't made up of family, either. I tried to tell them not to separate families. No one listened.

There we were in a world of boats, with planes flying overhead, trucks, cars, buses, houses, hotels, wharves, and civilized white people screaming in frustrated anger.

Jesus, it was chaos. And no one heard a word I tried to say. This was not my people's world or even a world they could adapt to. Or myself. That's how I felt.

The last I saw of Kioki and my daughter, they were being pulled into the back of an army truck and no one would tell me where they were going. I was screaming so hard, I thought my lungs would explode. I kept saying, "No! No, that's my wife, my daughter! You can't take them away from me!" And someone yelled to someone else to shut that noise up!

I'd even lost Billy in the roundup. That's what it felt like—a Wild West roundup.

"Someone here called Shaw? John Shaw?"

I pushed through, still yelling for them to stop that truck. The man in uniform with papers in his hand stepped back quickly when he saw me coming.

"My wife is on that truck! My daughter!"

"What?" he yelled back. "What?"

The stupid bastard couldn't understand a word I was saying.

"You speak English?" he asked.

245

"Jesus Christ—" I saw over his head that the truck was disappearing fast out of my sight.

"My wife—"

"Your name John Shaw? John Shaw from South Carolina?"

I started crying. I was shaking inside. I was trying to talk to this stupid little man. Why couldn't he understand me? At least try? What was wrong with these people?

I felt Asuluk's touch to my shoulder, heard his words, "You go to Carol, to My." And I looked at him, wiped my eyes on my sleeve. He nodded. "Yes, you go. Floreeda. You go." And as I stood there, getting pushed this way and that, they herded Asuluk away. Last I saw of him, he had picked up someone's little boy who had gotten lost in the mayhem.

Billy? Where was Billy? Where was Sinbad?

"John Shaw! If that's your name, would you move it! I don't have all day. We got more Eskimos coming in. Would you move your ass!"

I got pushed forward so hard, I tripped and fell down the ladder and onto the docks.

I saw Billy in the crowd there. He was fighting his way toward me when a soldier grabbed him and threw him into a truck. I saw his head surface. I saw who was putting an arm around him: Asuluk.

"Let me go—"

The uniformed man with the papers was pulling me to my feet, saying things I never heard. That truck was driving away, too.

I heard my son call, "I will find my mother and my sister and I will care for them! I will protect them!"

I heard someone else call, "Will someone shut that little sucker up? Where'd he learn English, anyway?"

"I've got to go with them! That's my son! You can't do this! He's my son!"

"Someone help me with this asshole, for Christ's sakes!"

The truck drove off one way; these soldiers took me another. I wish I could remember more, but after that, all I recall is a room, an office in a log-walled building. There was an American flag, a telephone, and a wireless. Music—the Andrew Sisters, so the man on the radio said.

Then an army captain came in. He had this look on his face as if he'd just trod in dog shit and couldn't get it off his shoe fast enough.

"You have no identification at all?"

I showed him my log.

"And you flew out of Anchorage . . . when?"

"Nineteen twenty-six. I don't remember the date exactly. April, I think. You gotta bring my family back here. You gotta."

"And when did you leave Miami, Florida?"

"I don't remember exactly. You promised me you'd get them back!"

"Calm down, Mr. Shaw. First things first. Do you remember your aircraft's registration?"

"Where're my wife and my children? Why won't anyone tell me where they are?"

"Mr. Shaw, there is no need to get upset. Your . . . family is fine. But as for your . . . well, your other family, we are trying to contact your sister, but the only Shaw at the address you gave, a Lily Margaret—"

My heart rose. My mother?

Maybe it was the hopeful look on my face that made the captain move. He rose, defied the stench, and touched my shoulder, saying, "Your mother has been deceased for twelve years, John. However, a friend of mine at Fort Bragg is doing all he can to locate your sister. But seventeen years is a long time to be missing."

"My mother's dead?" My voice was nothing more than a squeak.

The captain said nothing. He sat down and looked at his fingernails. "Nineteen thirty-one, John."

"You have to find my family. I need them here with me. Please."

247

"Be assured that we will take good care of them until you're ... until you're well again. Have faith in that."

"I want to see them. I have to see them right now. You don't understand. They need me. All of them. They need me."

"That's not possible, Mr. Shaw. They're already on their way to a government reservation on one of the Pribilof Islands. Now, I understand how you must feel. Please understand our position. These native people are far better off with their own kind, doing whatever it is that these people do. They keep their ways, their culture, everyone wins. Trust me."

They'd be living on a government-controlled reservation?

I wanted to cry, but I couldn't raise enough emotion to help me lift a finger. I was tired; I was sick. I just wanted to die. Then everything went gray.

I woke in a hospital. Some smells, you never forget.

Betty-Sue, the first white girl I'd seen in seventeen years. She was about twenty years old, and the only one, they said, who could calm me down. She took me away in a wheelchair, ran a big, hot bath, and added half a bottle of antiseptic to it. Then she undressed me and helped me into the bath.

I was too confused to be embarrassed.

I remember her sitting on the other side of the bathroom, talking to me. I remember her shaving my face, my neck. She scrubbed my head, washed my hair four times. And me, too, of course. I let her bathe me. I'd forgotten what soap was, what hot water was, until I smelled it, until I felt it on my skin again.

I just lay in that tub for too long listening to her sweet little voice droning on and on ... while in my head I could see Kioki, standing in the back of that truck, her hand reaching out, grasping at thin air. Grasping for me.

"Aren't you cold yet?" this pretty little nurse kept asking.
Cold? "No."

"I'm always cold here," she said. "I'm from Louisiana. It's way too cold here for me. . . . Is it true?"

"What—"

"That you lived with Eskimos for seventeen years?"

248

"It's true."

"Will you tell me about it?"

"What, now?"

"No, not now, silly. Later. Come on, you'll have to get out of the bath soon, Mr. Shaw. You'll be just like a prune if you don't."

A prune? I tried to recall what a prune was, then I looked at my fingers. They were wrinkled from being underwater so long.

"You better get out now, Mr. Shaw," she said, standing there beside the tub, a big towel stretched out for me.

"Don't call me that. My name's Fl . . . My name's John."

"John," she said, and smiled. "Doctor wants to see you, and we can't keep him waiting too long."

While she was drying me, she asked if there was anything special she could get for me. I thought about it. "An orange. Or maybe some bread, and honey so thick, I have to lick it off my fingers. That'd be . . . that'd be . . ." What was the word I wanted? What the hell was it again?

"Nice?" she asked.

"Yeah. Nice." I turned to her and smiled and she tried to smile back. I didn't know why.

Once she'd shaved my face, she couldn't look at me for very long.

"I'll see what I can do," she said as she helped me into some pajamas that were way too short and then into the wheelchair again.

I asked for a mirror as she was wheeling me down the corridor to the ward where I was to stay for a while. Stay and get better. She said it'd take a long time because I was so sick and all. I had to ask for the mirror again because she pretended she didn't hear me. Again, she said she'd see what she could do. And I had to call her Betty-Sue when the matron wasn't around.

I liked her, a lot.

The bedsheets were clean; the bed was soft. I hadn't felt a pillow under my head for too long. She covered me up, but I said I wasn't cold. She thought that was funny until she looked into my eyes and said, "Are you sure you want a mirror, John?"

Of course I was sure. I told her I hadn't seen my face since I was twenty-four years old.

She pulled the blankets to my shoulders, drew the curtains around one side of the bed, and went away. I couldn't see who was snoring beside me, but Jesus was watching me from across the room. So I watched him back for a while, not knowing what to think, hardly knowing where I was, or who I was. At any time, I expected Kioki, Lily, and Billy to come through that door.

They didn't.

When this pretty little girl came back, she handed me a mirror.

And I wished she hadn't.

A stranger was staring back at me.

I didn't know the crash had mashed me so bad. The left side of my face was full of old, ridged scars, so many that one side looked like a grid map of the Appalachian Mountains. My cheekbone must have shattered in the crash; my left eye had sunk down and the pupil was dilated. No wonder I couldn't see that well. I put my hand over my right eye and when it was covered, I couldn't see much at all; there was nothing except some foggy haze and the outline of Betty-Sue's watch pinned on her uniform.

I touched my face. It definitely was my face looking back at me. But it wasn't the face I thought I had. It sure wasn't the face I was born with, the face girls used to look at, smile at.

I put the mirror down and looked up at this pretty little girl. She asked me if I was okay, but I turned my head away quickly. And she sat on the bed and stroked my hair while I cried.

EIGHTEEN

❊❊❊❊❊❊❊

COMING back from the fog and realizing where I was took me a long time. I keep slipping back to what I was when the plane went down. I still can't think straight. It had to be the pills doing this to me. Betty-Sue says I've been here four weeks, that I sleep a lot, and that sometimes the medicines I'm on make me hallucinate.

I keep having waking dreams where I'm back on Kulowyl and nothing's changed till I get out of the kayak and no one's there to meet me, and I'm running through the village, but all the houses are empty. I'm screaming, but there's no sound; my voice won't work. So I run across the snow, fall into holes that shouldn't be there, and I see the summer side, but when I get there, everyone is dead—everyone.

And I wake, but I wasn't asleep.

Betty-Sue is always there by my bed, telling me it'll soon pass. She says the medicine is too strong, that it was just another hallucination and soon, very soon, the doctors will get the dose right.

I sure hope so. I don't want to go crazy again.

All those X rays they took and tests they've done haven't told me anything I didn't already know—a severe vitamin deficiency, old, healed fractures of the skull, ribs, leg, collarbone. One doctor in particular found it amazing that I survived my mishap at all. And when he was poking and prodding me one day, he asked what that scar was—the one across my gut. I told him about the day I had to prove myself to the village, how it had been my first and last fight. He didn't believe me. But I guess at the time I didn't believe it, either. Then he told me I was lucky to have escaped with so little brain damage. He asked how often I felt angry or depressed, felt like killing myself.

I asked him how he'd feel if he was stuck on an island in the ice for seventeen years. He just huffed, told me if I wanted to feel normal again, I had to be taking those pills for the rest of my life. Then he walked away.

I kept asking Betty-Sue if someone from the War Department had come by, maybe when I was sleeping, but she said no one had yet. She was sure that if they had any news, they'd tell me right away.

That pretty little girl had to teach me how to eat again. I couldn't keep much down for long, and damned if I could stop a fork shaking long enough for it to reach my mouth. I wanted to stop the pills. It was the pills making me shake. But she wasn't allowed to. She told me that "the drugs to stabilize the chemicals in my brain also interfered with my coordination." I wanted to feed myself and couldn't. I wanted to find my own log and start writing again and couldn't. I tried hard a couple of times— at least that's how I acted—and before I knew it, Betty-Sue offered to write down anything I wanted to say. I didn't mind.

At the end of her shifts, and sometimes on a free day, she'd sit by my bed or with me at the window if it was a sunny day, and she'd write down what I said. The more I spoke, the more she understood, or tried to. Now and then, an Eskimo word slipped out and I had to search for the English one to fit.

I liked her from the moment I first saw her, not because she was pretty or young. There was something about her that calmed me down the moment she looked at me or touched me. She was the only nurse I wanted to tend me, the only nurse I'd let anywhere near me.

Sometimes I'd call her Kioki and she'd look at me and remind me silently that she was someone else.

252

Every day when she came to work, I'd ask if there was any news and every day the answer was the same. There'd been no word from the Pribilofs or the War Department concerning either of my families, although at one time, someone from the War Department heard that Kioki and Lily had been shipped out to Saint Lawrence. No one really knew or cared where they were. It was always Betty-Sue who'd quietly explain that the country was at war and often no one had the time or the inclination to find one man's sister or his Eskimo family. I wasn't in the armed forces, either, so my request wasn't considered a priority. She didn't think I understood, but I did. I did. It made me all the more determined that I'd find them again, someday, some way.

The doctor's just been again. My left lung doesn't inflate like it should and he expects me to spend my time blowing into a tube all day. If it wasn't for Betty-Sue here all the time, I know exactly what I'd do with that damned tube, and the doctor would surely need another doctor to have it removed.

Eight ribs have broke and healed, and if I wanted one, I could have an operation to rebreak my left leg and my right arm. Trouble is, there's already been nerve damage and there'd always be pain when I walked; my right hand will never work properly, anyway. Plus, Betty-Sue said the operations had about a thirty percent chance of success, so I decided not to. And nothing will give me the sight back in my left eye.

No one wants to operate on me, anyway. I overheard a doctor say how I wouldn't survive on the table. Hell, I don't feel that sick.

I can't look into mirrors very long because it's someone else looking back at me, someone I don't know. By the looks of him, he's someone no one would want to know—except the nurse, Betty-Sue.

I look forward to her visits, and I always think up something else to keep her nearby, writing. The more I talk, the more she stays close. She has the best smile I've seen yet and she says I

253

have a wicked sense of humor. So I tell her she must have one, too, if she recognizes mine.

Asuluk used to say that what you see in others is only that same part of you shining back from their eyes. He said it a lot prettier of course.

There's still no word about my sister, but someone came in yesterday with some news—five thousand Canadians had landed on Kiska, but no Japs were there. So I guess that means the evacuation wasn't necessary after all.

Eskimos are still coming in and they're running out of places to put them, so they're being "interred" as "government wards" in abandoned fish canneries down in the southeast. Now they're getting sick and some are dying, too. I hear things like this or read them in the newspapers and I itch to get out of here, to find my family. Somehow, some way, I damn well will. Why won't anyone even try to help me?

It seems my marriage to Kioki was never legal and because of that everyone thinks it's best I forget the past and look ahead to what they call the future. What I think doesn't count around here. I'm tired of people making decisions for me. I just want to go home, but these idiots say I'm not well enough yet to travel so far south. At times, I just want to hit someone, because I don't want to go south at all. Damn government's gone and lost my family, but I've promised myself I am going to find them— whenever I can escape out of this place.

I'm stuck with timetables again. They wake me up to give me something to make me sleep. My butt's a pincushion. Breakfast is always at the same time, and so is lunch, and dinner. Going back to regular food was harder than I thought it'd be. Not a lot stayed down, either. Eating a moose steak is like chewing on boot leather. I had cravings for dried fish for a long time—it was a damned nightmare and I swear if I see one more orange, I'll hit someone between the eyes with it. I've thrown three against the wall so far; one hit Jesus in the face and Betty-Sue got mad at

254

me, real mad. Told me she just couldn't get any *sue wuk*, that I had to make do with oranges and if I didn't keep eating them, then she would make my butt a *real* pincushion, find the biggest needle yet and make it hurt bad.

But I still pitch the oranges pretty good when she's not around. My aim's gotten better with practice.

This place is ticking me off, but I can't get out till the doctors say I can. I tell them I feel better than ever now. I can eat okay without throwing it all up again and they don't take blood from me all the time now, either—looking for levels of this, levels of that. I'm alive, aren't I? I can go to the john now without someone holding my hand, seeing what I've done.

Today, Betty-Sue came in late and told me that a Catholic priest she knew was going back to Seattle, that he had room in his car if I wanted a ride, because the hospital needed my bed. Betty-Sue was sure there would be somewhere in Seattle where I could find a telephone directory to help me find my sister in South Carolina.

The War Department's not much help. They keep saying they're working on it, but all I see when I close my eyes is my name on a piece of scrap paper in the bottom of someone's out basket.

I was feeling really pissed one morning when Betty-Sue came in wearing regular clothes. She looked so different, I hardly knew who she was until she took her woolly hat off. "What'd they say?" I asked.

She shook her head and put a heavy suitcase down.

"What'd they say?"

"Captain Carnes isn't sure now whether that intake of evacuees was sent to the Pribilofs, Saint Lawrence, or both. John, no one really knows. It'll be months before a mail plane goes out to either island. Don't get angry. I've had an idea. Will you listen to it?"

I looked at her, sighed, and stared up at the ceiling. "How

come you spend all your time here with me, anyway? Haven't you got a boyfriend or something else to do?"

"My husband got killed in the war."

I looked at her. She was studying her fingernails.

"We were married six months when the army took him away. He never came back. Day after I got the telegram, I decided I'd go somewhere else, start over again. I got as far from Baton Rouge as I could. Now will you hear what I've got to say? Or you just gonna lie there and sulk 'cause you can't get your own way?"

Fighting words. If she were a man . . . "What—"

"I came north because Charlie's brother works up here. He's offering us a lift to Seattle and he's leaving today. Now, you have to get out of here, John. But you can't go find Kioki till the mail planes go out again. I'm taking my annual vacation and I thought that we could travel south together. We can get the train from Seattle. I'll go as far as Little Rock with you, for company, and you can go on to Abbeville and I can go on to Baton Rouge. You listening to me?"

Seems she had it all planned, anyway. "I don't have any money. I don't have any clothes."

"Well, I do."

She opened the suitcase. There was a lumber jacket, a blue checked shirt, and long pants, too. I noticed she'd even let the hems down. She'd packed underwear and socks and cowboy boots the size I used to wear. It'd all belonged to her husband, she said. After he died, she never could get rid of them. But she wanted me to have them now. Best they got some use.

Before I knew it, Betty-Sue's brother-in-law, the Catholic priest, picked us up from the hospital. He was young and cheerful and didn't seem to mind that I wasn't a Catholic, but most of the time I was hoping he wouldn't try to convert me. Mom used to drag me off to the First Baptist Church when I was a kid.

But I only had one religion now—my own.

As he drove us down through Canada's Yukon in a black Buick that made me seasick, I never said much, but I never had to. He was a real chatterbox. He didn't talk about God; he talked about everything else, though, mainly politics.

Now and then, I'd look back to see what Betty-Sue was doing. She slept most of the way to Seattle—or at least pretended to. I think she was used to her brother-in-law.

I asked if he'd try to find my wife and family, because sometimes people felt they had to comply with a man wearing a collar. No one said no to a man of God.

He said he'd do everything in his power to have us all reunited but that I wasn't to expect an overnight miracle. One of his buddies was a missionary-teacher on an Eskimo reservation in Canada and he described the Eskimos as a kind, happy, generous people who were accepting Christianity without too many problems at all.

His buddy had never met Asuluk.

At Seattle, where he lived next door to the church, he made a lot of phone calls for me. He discovered things Captain Carnes could not. I remember thinking that God really is powerful.

All those evacuated from Kulowyl were happily settled on Saint Lawrence Island, had been so for the past eleven weeks, but it would be difficult, if not impossible, to get a message to them. Until it was possible, would I be satisfied knowing that on Saint Lawrence they were being taught the new way of life by modern Eskimos?

Well, I didn't have much choice, did I?

At least I knew that they were all together again, not torn apart and fretting themselves to death, because they were able to do that, fret so much that they made themselves sick.

I don't know what I would have done or where I'd be now if I hadn't met Betty-Sue. She'd sit with me for hours after she should have gone home. She wanted to hear everything—where I'd been, what I'd done, how I felt, how I came to fit in with the Eskimo people who saved me. She didn't seem to care what I looked like, or that when I told her something I'd start at the end and finish in the middle, or that I'd start on one story and finish on four others.

I told her I'd written it all down and if she could find that bundle I had with me when I arrived, she could read all about it. If she could read my writing, of course. I guess she did find it, because she walked into the hospital room with it one day. She said she'd type it all up for me if I wanted. But I think it was she who wanted. She kept saying things like, "John, others really should know about this, about what happened."

I'd change the subject to something else.

Hell, I only wrote it all down to save me from going crazy. From Seattle to Portland, I kept wondering about Sally. I had it bad. I kept imagining walking up that narrow muddy road, going up those stairs, smiling at that old Indian with the cracked face. I'd knock on her door and the wind would push me inside again. And she'd be there, saying how mighty windy it was that day. . . . I had it bad, real bad. But I couldn't remember exactly where she lived, because I'd been trying to outrun a storm and went off course a way. I could hardly remember her face. My memory of her has been reduced to a girl with her head between her knees, brushing out long flaming-red hair. She'd be nearly as old as I am now, if she's still alive. If she didn't go to God the way her mama had. It's hard to pull up a train if you think you see a landmark you recognize, even if it's from the wrong angle. I only ever noticed things from the air.

Soon it was way too late to do much about Sally except wonder. So I decided I'd wait till I came back this way again. I'd have more time to find her. . . .

We're in Omaha now. Everywhere the train's stopped, I've seen posters about the war. Soldiers, sailors, marines are everywhere. Ladies wait on train station platforms, hope in their eyes. Hope turns to tears when the train pulls out again. Sometimes it's pretty bad if a coffin gets unloaded—someone coming home from the war, and not the way he or anyone else wanted him to, I guess. I used to be able to feel other people's sadness. I think I've lost it now. I don't feel much of anything these days.

Whenever we stop, I keep hoping for Kioki and the children to walk through that door.

But they never do.

I guess they're settling into their new kind of life, with new people around, new things to do, new ways to do them. Billy will take it all in his stride—he has a good head, that boy. If only he could control his temper better . . . Give him a year or two and he'll be running the whole reservation.

Lily. Not a day goes by I don't wonder if she's still having nightmares about what happened to her. Has she married Eennali yet? Is Kioki missing me as much as I'm missing her? I miss her soft chatter in the dark. I don't like sleeping alone.

I guess when things change, they change slowly, so slowly that you barely notice. Twenty years later, you can say, I remember when . . . I haven't been around to see these changes, to live them, to feel them. They're everywhere I look—clothes, buildings, motorcars. People aren't polite anymore. If you smile at someone, they just look right through you, make you feel you have no right to do that. Or they get confused and you see the question in their eyes: What you smiling at me for?

Moving-picture shows aren't silent these days and there's no need to read the words, either—which is good, because the actors talk. Betty-Sue and I saw a moving picture in Oregon, at Portland. It was some love story, and just when it got interesting, just when I thought I could follow what was happening, they'd burst into another damned song and start dancing, and I'd be back where I started. We walked out halfway through—it gave me a headache, it was so damned loud. And I think that the couple kissing so much reminded her of her dead husband, Charlie. She said it was the first time she walked out of a Ronald Colman picture show.

Everyone's talking about Ronald Colman. Betty-Sue thinks he's great. I saw a picture of Ingrid Bergman pasted up on the theater wall and I told Betty-Sue how much she looked like her. She thought I was joking. I wasn't.

Prohibition must be over. There're bars everywhere, dance

halls. Ladies dressing up, looking pretty. A lot of men in different kinds of uniform. Rum and Coca-Cola is supposed to be pretty good stuff, or so Betty-Sue says, but I can't try it, not with all the pills I take. One day, I might sneak myself a beer when she's not looking.

She keeps asking me why I've stopped talking about Kulowyl. I've told her a hundred times it's all there, that all she has to do is read it. Then she asks, why I don't want to tell her. She wants to know so much, so soon. She'll even wake me up when I'm asleep to ask me something, or nag me senseless.

"I need to know, John. I need to know what it felt like to be missing so long."

"I wasn't missing, Betty-Sue. I got found. By me. Can I sleep now?" I said once, and that shut her up. I knew she'd figure it out for herself if ever she read all that stuff I'd written down so long ago.

"Have you ever made a deal with God?" I asked as we were coming in to Topeka.

"A deal with God? I don't think so. I never step on cracks in the pavement. Is that the same thing?"

Down on the platform, I was watching an old lady embrace her uniformed son. "That old lady down there, she made a deal with God. I can tell by the look on her face." Betty-Sue looked, saw what I saw, and squeezed my hand. "She's dead, you know. I never said good-bye."

"Who's dead?"

"My mother. I never got to say good-bye."

"Of course you did. You said she was there at Miami when you left."

"No. You don't understand. I never got to say good-bye. Not just, I'll see you soon, Mom. No, I mean the good-bye you say when you know you'll never see that person again, ever. I took it for granted I'd be back, that she'd be old and I'd be there holding her hand when she died."

"Don't think that way."

I couldn't help it. I was still looking at that old lady and her boy. "She must have died the year before my daughter was born."

"How do you know that?"

"I smelled her a lot, the perfume she used to wear—lilacs. She always used to say that when there was a death, there was a birth to compensate. Someone'd come take their place. I think Lily took her place."

I looked at Betty-Sue. She didn't know what to think.

"Do you know what a shooting star really means?" I asked.

"No. What?"

I told her about the Great Spirit lifting his skins, and by the time I'd finished, the train had pulled out of Topeka.

"You ever made a deal with God?" I asked again. "A real one?"

"No," she said.

"I did. All I wanted was to get home again. Now I'm scared because I'm going home. Am I crazy, Betty-Sue? Am I crazy thinking there's nothing there for me now?"

"No," was all she said. I reached for her hand but kept my gaze on the window, the passing scenery. I didn't care what the man sitting opposite us thought.

"Is your mother still alive?" I asked.

"I don't know," she said quietly. "I haven't spoken to her in two years. When I left Baton Rouge, she said she didn't want to see me again, ever."

"Why?"

"Charlie and I had to get married."

"Oh."

"But it turned out I wasn't having a baby, anyway. He went off to war thinking he was going to be a father but . . ."

"Do you love your mama?" I asked before she started crying, because she sure was close to it.

"Very much."

"Tell her. Promise me you'll tell her. Knowing just ain't enough, sometimes. I want you to remember that."

She kept holding my hand.

In St. Louis, I learned that girls are going to play baseball now so that the game won't die from everyone being away at the war. The man sitting opposite us named a lot of players I'd never heard of—the only ballplayer I ever liked was Babe Ruth. I didn't like what he had to say about Babe Ruth, and I wished he'd just shut up so I could get some sleep. But when the man said they were going to make these girls play in skirts, I woke up real quick. I thought that was a good idea. I guess I'd like to see girls playing pro baseball. I wonder what they'll call them—the Dodgettes? I told Betty-Sue she should try out. She laughed at me.

The girls I've seen so far are just as pretty as ever, but I don't look that much. I can't. It hits me pretty hard when I realize I'm old enough to be their daddy, that I have a daughter of my own. Then someone called us father and daughter by mistake and Betty-Sue got real mad. I thought I'd have to hold her back there for a bit, told her it wasn't enough to get upset about.

It was me calming her down for a change.

Betty-Sue became very thoughtful and quiet a day out of Little Rock, Arkansas. When we left Seattle, she said that Little Rock was as far as she could go with me. She had to continue on south to Louisiana. But as we got closer, she got really scared, started chewing on her fingernails, the way Bess used to when she watched Bobby flying at an air show. I asked what was wrong and, like Bess, she said nothing, but soon enough I knew she'd tell me.

And she did. It had all been brewing inside since that love story moving picture we saw in Portland. She was like me, scared stiff of what lay ahead once she got home.

We were having some sandwiches and coffee at the railroad station when she said, "I can't."

"Can't what?"

"I have to make sure you get home first, John."

I looked at her awhile and said, "Oh great. If it works out for me, it'll work out for you?"

262

"Don't say no, John. Please."

I couldn't say no to her big, pleading eyes. I didn't say how her sitting next to me all the time gave me the strength I needed to keep going, or how it was like being out on the ice alone with Sinbad. Sometimes we really hated each other out there in that white, wet cold—so white and wet and cold that at times it was hard to tell which way was up. I'd only stop if he did, and he'd only stop if I did. So we'd push on, constantly, not stopping, never stopping.

I can't count the times I wanted to get off the train, find an airfield, maybe steal a plane and head back to Alaska, because this place, this country I once called mine, doesn't fit anymore. It hangs off me like an overstretched pullover. Everything once familiar is gone. So many changes in so short a time. Seventeen years is barely half a lifetime, but right now, to me, it's eternity.

God, I do not belong here. I just don't belong.

I miss my wife so much, my heart is aching. It hurts worse than pneumonia or that broken leg ever did. Why wouldn't the War Department help me? I didn't have to come all this way by train. All that damned captain had to do was find out where my family went. I would have waited in Anchorage and hitched a ride on the next plane or boat. After all, it was a government reservation. Surely they sent some kind of official out there, two, three times a year? If they never needed me before, they sure as hell need me now. I didn't get the chance to pay that debt because some official red tape never recognized my marriage to Kioki. Part of me went to Saint Lawrence with her, because there's a hole in me that's so big, it echoes. And all Betty-Sue can say is that she's sure I'll have my family back one day.

The farther south we go, I'm finding some people who talk to me ask if it happened in Europe or the South Seas. "It," of course, means my mashed face, my missing arm, my limp. I just smile and say I'd rather not talk about it. They must think I'm some kind of war hero. The eye patch I wear must look pretty convincing, too.

Betty-Sue said I should have gone into the movies, that I could even fool her sometimes.

The farther south we go, I'm starting to look forward to getting home. People are friendlier; they talk the way I'm used to. But when we got to Atlanta, I didn't know what I was feeling.

Atlanta, Georgia.

Georgia in the rain. I must have been here a thousand times, and whenever I arrive, it always starts raining.

It always was a big city, and I had to stop walking a lot to get my bearings again, find familiar landmarks, buildings, parks. I got lost in a maze that had tripled in size since 1924, and Betty-Sue had never been here before, so she wasn't much help. We had a couple of arguments. She wouldn't have known where true north was if it bit her. I was lost in Atlanta with a girl who had no sense of direction.

I didn't want to stay overnight, but there'd been a delay, some kind of track problem. I could get to Charleston, then to Columbia if I wanted to wait a day, but straight to Columbia meant a two-day wait.

I hated being so close to home but so far away, as well.

Betty-Sue and I found the main post office in the city by mistake and we spent a long time trying to find my sister in the phone directory. She wasn't listed. I damn near looked up Rosanna but baulked straight away. I hadn't considered meeting up with her again. I wanted to take this one day at a time. I wanted family first.

I was thinking about calling my cousin Brewster in Virginia when Betty-Sue suggested I talk to Abbeville's county sheriff. It was a good place to start. Someone there had to remember me.

The sheriff was the other side of fifty-five when I was ten years old and I knew that Freddie Larsen hadn't stood for election again in 1926—he'd wanted to relocate his family to Alabama. All those I knew who'd remember me were a lot older, and I guessed most of them would have died in the meantime, too.

Except Bawler Johnson. Damned if I could remember his real name, though. He'd taken over his daddy's hardware store, and I knew he'd never forget me—how could he? I beat him up every time I saw him when we were kids, but we were polite to each other in passing as we got older. So Betty-Sue called the store for me. I was so nervous, I'd already walked a mile standing in one spot.

I let her do most of the talking because sometimes I just can't talk very well and people have to strain to understand me. I knew by the way she said, "Oh, I see" that Bawler had gone, too. Sold out and left for San Francisco. And no, sorry, the lady who answered at the hardware store had never heard of a Meg Shaw or a brother who used to fly out of Davis Field.

Betty-Sue called the Abbeville County Sheriff's Department and handed me the phone. The lady who answered said the three deputies were all out and the sheriff was in Columbia till Thursday. I asked the lady on the phone what had happened to Freddie Larsen, but she'd never heard of him. She'd only been in town two years.

I hung up. I knew that Betty-Sue was starting to believe none of this was real. I had to prove it somehow.

I took the phone directory back inside and looked for the little lady who worked the post office counter. She always used to talk to me whenever I came in. She was so short, she had to stand on a box to see over the counter. We became acquaintances in 1920, and I recall what she said the day she first saw me. "Lord in heaven, you'd be the tallest person I ever done seen!" She came out from behind the counter, stood beside me, and everyone had a big laugh. She hardly reached my waist; she was so tiny, I could have put her in my pocket.

But she wasn't there anymore, either.

I looked at Betty-Sue and wondered if she'd believe me when she saw Bobby's grave. That couldn't have disappeared, too, surely.

We were walking out when I heard an old lady's voice: "Oh, my Lord, where you been all this time?"

Betty-Sue and I both turned around, and there she was, the short lady. She knew me but not my name.

"You're the pilot. You come back. Lordy, what's happened to you?"

Just like yesterday, I was looking down at her and grinning as hard as I used to at a blanket toss. Then I turned to Betty-Sue and said, "She remembers me. She remembers me." Then the old lady said something that took me by surprise.

"Mighty pretty wife you have there."

It felt as if someone had punched me and everyone in the post office was staring at us.

Well, I lied, told her I'd come back. She watched us walk away. She even waved good-bye, happy that a little of the past had come back to say howdy.

Betty-Sue got upset at being called my wife, too.

So we sat in a diner awhile. From the window, I could see the Atlanta Police Department, cars coming and going all the while. It hadn't changed much; if anything, it'd just gotten bigger.

"It isn't that I didn't believe you—"

"It doesn't matter. I was wondering myself if it hadn't all been some kind of bad dream."

"People think I'm your daughter or your wife. I'm twenty-one years old. Either I look old or you look young." She was really ticked off.

"If people are gonna think I'm your daddy or your husband, they will no matter what we say."

I kept looking at the police station, and it took me back to December 31, 1923. I had to look at Bobby in the hospital morgue, a formal identification. Bess and I. I didn't want her there, had a fight with some barrel-shaped cop over it. We hated each other on sight and the bastard kept me too long asking questions, as if I'd been responsible for killing Bobby. He had nothing better to do, I guess.

In that diner, I tried to let the thoughts go, but they wouldn't. And the hatred I had in 1923 came back as strong as ever.

The blueberry pie tasted a little like *sue wuk* but sweeter. Instead of coffee, I wanted a bowl of warm seal blood. It's better when it's hot.

Betty-Sue had to do a lot of fast talking, because the waitress nearly fainted when I told her what I wanted. Hell, when she said, "What can I get for you, sir?" I just told her outright.

Betty-Sue just about burned my ear off after that one. Told me I'd have to stop saying what I was thinking. I was back in the real world now. I told her what I thought of her real world.

And when I said I was going to the graveyard and did she want to come or not, she looked as if she was going to cry. It was raining again. She was worried I was too tired, till I said it wasn't far. And she believed me. She bought an umbrella—didn't want to catch cold—and I wondered how long she'd last on Kulowyl, because to me the July rain felt warm, not cold.

We walked through the cemetery gates and I turned right. In 1924, Bobby was buried on the outskirts, the first in a new row between two old trees, and one looked like a giant W. All it was then was a hole in the ground. I never went back to see the headstone I'd paid for. I found the trees eventually and there were fifty more rows of old graves. He wasn't on the outskirts anymore.

Beside Bobby stood a cement angel covered in bird shit. It made me laugh—an angel beside him now?

And I looked down at what I'd paid so much money for— gold lettering on black marble.

ROBERT FLETCHER SULLIVAN

AUGUST 9, 1901–DECEMBER 31, 1923

And the stonemason had done a fine job on the gold biplane banking into infinity there below the dates. But I couldn't tell what kind of airplane it was. I told him I wanted a de Havilland. Maybe he didn't know what it was.

And Betty-Sue, sheltering under her umbrella, went very quiet when she saw the grave. She watched my face carefully. No tears. Not anymore. Nevermore.

Pretty white pebble stones bordered the concrete graveside, black marble tiles in a narrow strip down the middle—exactly what I'd chosen. On a ledge below the biplane sat a glass bottle and in it was a handful of wilting yellow daisies.

Yellow daisies.

My eyes stung. If he couldn't buy them, he'd steal them. He'd throw them out to the girls in the crowds at the air shows.

So someone else hadn't forgotten, either.

Twenty years almost. Six more months and he'll have been dead twenty years.

I knew that Betty-Sue wanted to leave, but I sat down and talked to him again in my mind like I always did, and all I got was the feeling of a smile—the feeling of someone close by.

Around my neck, his St. Christopher medal. I touched it and heard him gargling—"take it, buddy. Take it. . . ."

Twenty years, and I cried again. Betty-Sue let me. Then I heard someone coming, so I stood up and tried to hide my face. It wasn't right here to let anyone see a man cry.

I'll never forget what happened next.

A voice I knew and hadn't heard for twenty years said one word: "Johnny?"

A thousand caterpillars raced up and down my spine.

"Johnny Shaw? Is that you?"

It was Bess. I wanted to walk away. I wanted to do something, anything. I was frozen to the spot, staring at the cement angel.

"Johnny Shaw?"

I turned around. It was Bess, sure enough. Her eyes hadn't changed one bit, but the rest of her sure had.

"Hi, Bess." But my voice didn't work that well. It came out a croak.

Her bag dropped and so did the bundle of yellow daisies that she was carrying, wrapped up in wet newspaper. "They said you were dead."

"They were wrong." I smiled at her and she ran to me. Next thing I knew, she was in my arms. I couldn't believe it. She still reached my chest. She was fatter and older, but she was still the Bess I used to know.

She didn't know whether to laugh or cry and neither did I, so we did a bit of both. Then she grabbed my face, looked up into my eyes, and she was damned near crying when she asked, "What has happened to you?"

I didn't know what to say.

"All these years . . . What happened?"

I couldn't say a thing. I just held her again, this girl, my dead buddy's best girl, the one who still put yellow daisies on his grave, probably every day.

"I had to come here early today. I didn't know why. I just had to come early today. . . . Where are you staying?"

"I don't know."

"How'd you get here?"

"Ah . . . train."

"Train? From where?"

"Seattle."

"Well, you're coming home with me. Your daughter, too."

I looked at Betty-Sue and shrugged. But she didn't mind. She had big tears in her eyes.

I watched Bess as she emptied the old daisies, took a bottle from her bag, tipped water into the vase, and put in the fresh daisies.

"Do you do this every day?" I asked.

"Every second day," she said, then she grabbed me again.

I swear to God I felt Bobby laughing at us both.

NINETEEN

●━●━●━●━●━●━●

I wasn't in Bess's car long enough to get seasick. If there had ever been a familiar kind of strangeness, I experienced it that summer afternoon. She still lived in the same house she'd grown up in.

"Mother and Dad died within six months of each other back in '35," she said quietly. "Dad went first. But I always knew they'd never live without each other." She gave me one of her sad smiles. I'd forgotten about that smile till I saw it again. "That has to be love. True love."

And I wondered what Betty-Sue was thinking. She'd been awful quiet ever since the graveyard.

While Bess rattled on a little more about true love and what it was supposed to be, I looked at the house. It was hers now. It was the only one in the street without a fence. Plants and flowers hung from the ceiling of the porch; a gray cat was waiting near the front door.

We all got out of the car. Betty-Sue was having trouble keeping her dress down in the wind, so I let her walk behind me while I followed Bess up the path. Bobby had walked these steps a thousand times—Atlanta was never too far to visit his lady.

"How come you never married?"

She put her key in the lock, turned to me, and answered as she always did—directly. "I never found anyone I could love as much as I loved Bobby. I still teach grade school, Johnny. And it's all I need now. I get by."

I didn't know she taught school. Bobby never told me, and I never thought to ask what it was she did when she wasn't with us.

More changes reared up at me. Locks and keys? In days gone, in yesterdays, you never had to lock anything.

Her house was dark inside and smelled of lavender. I'd only been here once before, after the funeral. I took her home, sat with her awhile, then ran when she needed me the most. I was hoping she wouldn't remember, or if she did, she'd forgive me for being such a coward.

She never mentioned it.

"Would you like some tea? Coffee? Something to eat?"

"Coffee'd be good." I looked at Betty-Sue; she was busy with the cat. She'd told me about hers and how it had run away the day her husband died. It never came back. But I'd seen how a lot of animals followed her around. We had a Siamese cat follow us for a full two blocks barely an hour before we met up with Bess.

"You still don't like tea?" Bess asked, surprising me. Why would she remember something like that?

She filled her kettle with water from a tap over the sink and plugged it into the electric socket. The kitchen had changed from what I recalled. There was an electric stove now—a housewife's helper, guaranteed to give the lady of the house some more time to herself.

Bess took some milk in a bottle from a refrigerator. Gone the days of the cow in the backyard, the jug of milk in the meat cooler, the fights over who'd be first to scrape the cream off the top.

I didn't realize just how many changes I'd missed out on. It wasn't the inventions so much—the things to make life easier. It wasn't the trains, the buses, the cars on the road. It was the people mainly. No one smiled much anymore, and certainly not at strangers. No one trusted anyone anymore. Bess locked her own door when we all came inside. A precaution, she said. A precaution against what? I wondered. What kind of neighborhood had this turned into?

My hand was shaking again. I had a terrible need to run away, head north, go home—home to what I knew, what I wanted most. Coming back wasn't anything but a huge mistake. Then Betty-Sue put her hand on my arm. She always did that to calm me down, let me know everything was fine, or that it was time to take my yellow pill. That always worked. Calmed me down. I sat down and waited, quiet. Waited to feel the calm descending, waited for someone to say something to break the silence.

The kettle whistled when it boiled and it had the same effect as a school bell ringing for recess. Suddenly, there was life.

Betty-Sue was helping. She put a blue checked cloth on the table, was pointed to the cups and saucers. I nearly felt at home, nearly. Bess put a full plate of cookies in the center of the table. Something else I'd forgotten—this girl baked better cookies than my mother ever had. She'd load Bobby up with enough to last a week.

Between us, sitting under a fabric wing in an open field, with a pot of coffee within reach, a week's supply of Bess's cookies lasted half an hour.

Sights and smells can bring back memories. So can tastes.

"You're still very quiet, Johnny."

I looked up. I couldn't talk with my mouth full of cookie, could I?

"But I never knew what you were thinking twenty years ago, either."

"Habit," I said eventually. "Say nothing no one misunderstands." Hell, I thought. I said it. I actually said it, *misunderstands*.

She pulled the same face she always pulled when she didn't believe a word you said. "Misunderstandings, my foot. You're just shy." She pushed the plate of cookies closer. "You always were. Kept too much to yourself."

But that was my business. I looked at Betty-Sue. The cat was on her lap now. I looked back at Bess. Her fingers were short, her nails short. She didn't bite them anymore. All she ever did when she watched us fly was stand there biting her nails down to the elbows. She only went flying once, but she made the mistake of flying with Bobby and that's why she never got into another airplane ever again.

She picked up her cup of tea, looked into it, and finally asked, "What happened to you?" I knew she couldn't hold that question back any longer. I had seen it in her eyes for the last hour, how anxious she was to hurdle the small talk.

So I told her what I thought she needed to know, and Betty-Sue, who must have heard it a hundred times, just sat there, listening again. The cat was asleep on her lap, asleep and purring loud.

"My Lord, really?"

I excused myself and left the room. I heard Betty-Sue explaining how we'd met, why she was with me, and soon enough the kitchen was filled with lady talk.

In the bathroom, I saw the hairbrush and the gray hair caught in it and I looked at the mirror. A lifetime had surely passed, and there we were, pretending otherwise.

She was glad to see me again. No pity. Just concern. Especially when I told her about Kioki, and Billy and Lily. I even told her about Tooksooks and how she'd died. Asuluk, Sinbad . . .

There was concern sure, but not understanding. I'd told her what it was like up there on Kulowyl, having only a few shattered memories to keep me going, to give me something to live for, how I sometimes thought of her, too.

If I ever felt Bobby Sullivan closer than ever before, it was in this house. If she put flowers on his grave every second day, then surely she'd known how I felt about missing people bad.

But it wasn't her stuck on that island for seventeen years, so how could she really know? How could anyone?

I went back out, and there was immediate silence, which meant they'd been talking about me. So I had another coffee and pretended I was dumb when Betty-Sue said she'd like to take a walk around the block, alone.

We watched her walk off, the cat following, up trees, over fences. It was coming on sunset and Bess and I sat out on the porch, on the swing, among the plants and pots. A canary in a cage started whistling. I looked around me and wondered just how many times she and Bobby used to sit here, arms around each other.

"What are you going to do?" she asked.

"You asking what I want to do or what people think I should do?"

Bess said nothing. She looked uncomfortable.

"I want to go back where I belong."

"And if you go back and find you don't belong?"

It had crossed my mind, but I didn't need her telling me.

"Johnny, you haven't gotten home yet. How do you know you don't belong?"

"I know."

"It's never too late to start over. Pick up the pieces."

"Experience talking now, Bess? Huh? Looks like you picked up the pieces and got on with living. Yep, sure does look like it."

She looked down quickly.

"What can I do?" I asked. "Look at me, girl. I'm forty-one years old. I've got one eye, one arm, and I can't walk without a stick. All I ever knew was flying. There're no pieces left to pick up, and even if I did, it'd be like putting a jigsaw together when half the bits are missing."

"You could teach. Instruct. Have your own flying school."

She was talking crap now. Crap. Plucking stupid thoughts out of the air. "Don't say it, Bess. Don't. Ain't no way I can teach somebody to fly if I can't fly anymore. And I can't. I know I can't. You need two good arms for that."

We were quiet. I wasn't angry with her personally and I hoped she knew it. She must have. She reached for my hand. Didn't pat or squeeze, just put her hand on top of mine.

"Betty-Sue said you've had no end of trouble trying to contact Meg."

What was in her voice now? Was Meg dead, too? "Is she alive?"

"You don't know?"

Oh God, no. Not Meg, too. My heart was tap-dancing.

"She's chairman of the South Carolina School Board these days. Lives in Columbia now. She married. . . . No, you wouldn't have known him. A university professor, Gordon Meschers. They have two sons and one daughter."

"Yeah?"

"Oh yes. I hope you didn't spend seventeen years worrying about Meg."

"I was thinking of her a lot. You, too."

"Thinking and worrying—with you, it's the same thing."

That little girl shy look spread over her face, so I picked up her hand and held it tightly.

"And my mother? It's okay, I know she's dead. Do you know how she died?"

"Cancer. It spread after the operation."

"Oh."

"I saw her at Meg's wedding. I wasn't invited, but I went to the church on North Main. I had to see what Meg looked like. Your mother saw me standing there while the photographs were being taken, and she came over and we talked a long time."

"She always liked you, Bess."

"Yes, I know. I liked her, too. We talked about you. I remember what she said. How one day you'd just knock on her door. She never gave up hope and she never believed you were dead. Said she'd know if you were. In her heart, she'd know. I left soon after because she was needed for the photographs. I promised I'd visit her, but I never did."

I let her talk on about search parties finding no trace of me, how she'd been in contact once a year with Meg ever since I disappeared. They exchanged a card at Christmas and a letter and that was the limit of their contact. But something told me that it was always Bess who sent the card or the letter, always Bess who received no reply. Meg never liked her much, because of Bobby, I guess.

"Why don't you call your sister? It's almost six. She should be home by now."

Why don't you call your sister?

The question froze my soul.

I followed Bess into the next room and while she called my sister, I looked at the mantelpiece over the fireplace. Photos of her family.

And there was a photo of Bobby standing in front of his de Havilland soon after it had been refitted to carry cargo. The Sullivan and Shaw emblem on the leather pocket, the fur collar, the right arm resting on the cowling, and that damned grin on his face a mile wide. I was there the day it was taken. He was grinning at me, something stupid I was doing behind the photographer's back. The very next photo taken of us both made it into two newspapers—Miami and Columbia.

While Bess was calling Meg's number, Betty-Sue came back from her walk. She took the framed photo from the shelf and studied it closely. "Is this Bobby?" she asked.

I nodded. I'd talked so much about him, I guess she knew him as well I did.

I heard Bess say, "Joshua, I don't care what time it is when she gets home. You tell her Bess Muller called and it's very, very important she call me. You write it down...." She even sounded like a schoolmarm. I could picture this kid in my mind, tongue out, scratching down the message for his mother—my sister.

The phone eventually went back in its place and I was relieved I didn't have to talk to Meg, because I didn't know what I'd say. "I'll lend you my car. You can drive up to Columbia tomorrow. I'd like to come, but I have to work."

"It's summer."

"I'm teaching math at summer school."

I saw the way she looked at Betty-Sue, who was still studying Bobby's photograph. Then I saw the tears in Betty-Sue's eyes, too, and I asked what was wrong. She put the photo back where it belonged and said in a whisper, "He looked so much like Charlie."

"Her husband," I said to Bess. "He died in the war."

Bess took her away, busied her in the kitchen, making supper,

276

and I settled down into a chair in the living room and listened to the wireless. Above the music—another thing I couldn't adapt to—I heard Betty-Sue apologize for acting silly and soon after I heard her laughing again.

I've never been comfortable when women are crying or upset.

I kept staring at the telephone, hoping it would ring, praying it wouldn't.

The three of us gathered in that house couldn't let the past be. I knew Betty-Sue would be okay. I knew that one day she'd find herself another man and have a family, move on with her life. Hell, her life had hardly begun. And she was a pretty thing, too. I'd seen the looks she'd gotten and I knew all too well what those looks meant. Sometimes I looked at her that way and told myself not to be a fool. Betty-Sue had herself a future, that much I knew. All she had to do was reach out and grab it.

But Bess? I'd look into her eyes and I'd know that she couldn't let the past die, either. And there she was, not long before, telling me to get on with life?

Why is it you never really recognize the best times of your life while they're happening, that instead it's all known in hindsight? Bobby died and I went missing and she was left with nothing but teaching school and memories and thoughts of what might have been. And that's all she wanted now. And I just couldn't understand it.

Gray hairs in a hairbrush.

Twenty years of her life had been wasted for the memory of a dead man she'd once loved. Now what was she, a lonely middle-aged lady who could never forget, who had no belief in a future, who lived each day as it came and not a day went by when she didn't remember.

I wanted to give her a good kick in the butt till I realized it was too late for that. She'd had enough kicks already.

She'd go and die like my mother, old before her time and lonely.

After supper, we talked some more—mostly the do you remember whens—things I'd forgotten that she hadn't and vice versa. Twenty years ago, I never let her know that Bobby had different girls scattered over three states, and I sure wasn't about to let her know now, either. I always felt she knew, anyway, but chose to ignore it. Because if he'd been going to marry anyone, it would have been her.

I would have killed him if he hadn't.

"Bobby visits me sometimes. Usually when I'm lonely."

I knew what she meant. I'd lived it myself, and I figured Bobby visited her a lot. "He used to visit me, too," I said.

I'd forgotten that Betty-Sue was in the corner, listening to us. She must have thought we were both crazy, and I think she decided that maybe she should have taken the train south from Little Rock after all.

The phone rang at 11:15 and Bess moved to answer it. Then she stopped and said it'd be for me.

I heard a woman's voice say, "Bess?"

It was Meg. God help me, it was Meg. Tears filled my eyes; my voice wouldn't work.

"Bess?"

I handed the phone over to Bess. I couldn't say a damned thing. I heard her talk to my sister, explaining that there was someone there who wanted to talk to her, asking if she could hold a little while. Betty-Sue was yapping in my ear, but the only thing that would have seemed real at that moment would have been snow. But it never snowed in Atlanta in summer.

"She's waiting, John." I looked at Betty-Sue. She said it louder.

I didn't want to be called John or Johnny. I wanted my old name back. I wanted them to call me Floreeda. I wanted to see my wife, my kids.

"John, for heaven's sakes! You are here now! Here! Do you understand where you are? Who you are?" Betty-Sue was yelling at me. I stared at her, blinked a few times. "Don't you think your sister wants to hear your voice as much as you've wanted to hear hers for the last seventeen years?"

Meg? She had to be kidding. She didn't know Meg like I did. "She'll think it's a joke, a lousy, rotten joke."

Bess held the phone out to me again and I had to take it. I could hear chipmunks on the line, my angry sister.

I cleared my throat and said one word, "Meg?"

"Who *is* this?"

"Meg, it's me."

"Who the hell is me?"

"John."

"John who?"

"John Robert."

I have never heard a silence so loud.

"If this is a joke, it's in mighty poor taste."

I covered the phone and said, "I told you. I told you."

Two voices at once: "Talk to her!"

"John. Your brother. I'm back, Meg. I'm back."

Well, I heard a bang and a thump and footsteps in the distance, then an angry man's voice, so loud that I had to hold the phone away. Who the hell was this! And other things I better not repeat, because there might be ladies around.

"No, it's no joke. Really. I'm her brother. I swear to God it's true. Will you just tell her I'll see her tomorrow sometime after noon!"

Her husband kept me talking for about five minutes before he was satisfied, and when I finally hung up, I saw the two ladies, both staring at me, silent questions filling their faces.

"I think she fainted," I said.

It was midday by the time we got to Columbia, a hot stinker of a Carolina day, too. And I endured seventeen years of freezing my butt off longing for this swelter? I must have been crazy.

Columbia hadn't changed much except for more paved streets and stop signs. The airfield I once knew blindfolded was now an airport. No tin shed these days—there was a brick terminal. I was glad Betty-Sue was driving. She knew where to go. She could read Bess's map; I sure as hell couldn't.

The car stopped outside a two-story house with a high white fence, pillars beside the front doors, and shutters beside the windows. It was so white in the blazing sun that it hurt my eyes.

Even Betty-Sue checked the directions four times and then the street sign before she was certain this was the house.

My sister lived here?

"Taken your medication?" Betty-Sue asked.

I sure had. I'd taken a double dose just in case. I didn't know how Meg would react, or how I would, for that matter.

Betty-Sue rang the bell and a Negro lady answered the door. "We're here to see Mrs. Meschers," Betty-Sue said, so sweet, so nice. I looked back, wondering if I'd make it down the path and over the fence before Meg came out. My wondering didn't get me very far.

We were shown into a huge white room with shiny black-and-white tiles on the floor, a big bookcase along one wall, tapestry-covered chairs, and a table so shiny, I saw my face in it.

French, antique furniture. I was standing in the middle of my kid sister's dream. Apart from the ballet and the law, she wanted a big house with pillars at the front and French antique furniture inside.

And she'd gotten it. Meg always got what she wanted and to hell with anybody else. Seemed she hadn't changed with age, either.

"Ma'am's coming," the dark lady said, and Betty-Sue thanked her. But no one came in for a while, so I looked at the bookcases. Only one book caught my eye, drew it like a magnet—*Leaves of Grass*. Now I knew that my sister lived here—for a while, I thought we'd gone to the wrong house.

I thought it was strange that we had to be shown into a room first, to wait for my own sister's arrival. I didn't like that much. I was her only brother, for God's sake. I wasn't seeing the governor.

Then I heard a *clack, slide, clack*, and I turned around quickly.

My sister was standing in the doorway. I didn't know what to do except stare. I knew it was Meg standing there; it just didn't look like her. I guess I didn't look like her brother anymore, either.

We stared at each other for too long, then a hand lifted from the walking frame she was leaning on and a gloved hand touched her mouth. Tears filled her eyes and her voice shook when she said, "John? Is it really you?"

"Who else would it be?"

"They told me you were dead. That your plane ditched somewhere between—"

"Anchorage and Prince Rupert. I know."

"They said you couldn't have . . ." She looked at me as if she'd never seen me before. "Survived. God help me. It is you?"

I grinned at her. "Aren't you even gonna say hello?"

I don't know what ran through her mind. Seventeen years later, here he was, a one-armed, scarred cripple, her brother.

"Introduce me to your . . . your friend."

"Oh, sorry. Betty-Sue, my sister, Meg."

They touched hands and Meg said, "Margaret Meschers, pleased to make your acquaintance."

Betty-Sue was polite, too, and explained quickly how she had to return Bess's car and catch the four o'clock train. "Here's my mother's number in Baton Rouge, and mine in Anchorage. Call me. Please." She picked up her bag and left before I could even begin to thank her for coming all this way with me.

When Betty-Sue had been shown out, my sister and I were alone and the real Meg, the one I knew too well, reared like an angry stallion.

"Where the hell have you been for seventeen years!"

And we were kids again. "Sit down, shut up, and let me tell you."

For the first time in her life, she did what I said.

I remember telling her about the crash, but I knew it was futile trying to appeal to my sister's feelings, so I outlined the situation in as few words as possible. But after that, I don't recall what was said exactly; maybe it was a lifetime of words that

281

should have been said too long ago. We both softened, let down the barriers as much as we could.

Her mind was always on now, now and later. She always said the past couldn't be changed but that the now could. Before I knew it, I was booked to see a doctor friend of hers about my eye, another doctor about the rest of me. I tried to tell her what the Anchorage doctors had said, but when Meg was deaf, she wouldn't have heard the roof falling in. My kid sister was still bossing me around, but now we were taking turns. I wondered if the school board wilted when she entered the meeting hall. Damn, she would have been one hell of a lawyer.

"Eskimos?" she whispered, and sipped the iced tea her housekeeper had brought in. "Eskimos. My brother, the Eskimo." I guess it was funny in a strange kind of way. I always hated winter, the cold, the ice and snow. I'd never go outside to play with snowballs. My skin had been a deep brown from the time I was a small boy in baggy short pants and bare feet. Skin brown, brown hair turned blond from the sun. It wasn't blond anymore; no sun had turned it gray. Gray and brown, like I remembered my father's, but I didn't feel old. I still felt like the twenty-year-old flying deep blue skies, delivering the mail to Alabama.

Meg. She was more beautiful than anyone I had ever seen except for my daughter. Her hair was the color of firelight still, but short now. Her face was painted, too, and the clothes she wore looked expensive. But so was this house. And there I'd been, worrying about how she was, what she'd be doing.

I should have known better.

She didn't need me to play any part in her life. We were only kin; we weren't each other. We might have been born to the same parents, but we weren't attached by any invisible, unbreakable rope. But I felt that maybe, just maybe, we might be friends now.

"I thought about you a lot," I said.

She looked at me, never had to say, I thought of you, too.

"So much happened. You and Mom, that's what kept me going. Gave me something to live for. Years of hoping I'd see you again, then the captain told me Mom was dead. They couldn't find you, either. For a while there, I thought you were dead, too."

Meg did what she had never done before; she took my hand and she held it tightly. I could see the lines on her face, the lines that the war paint wasn't covering as I suspected it was meant to. Then again, she was thirty-nine years old.

"Mother died in August 1931. It was lung cancer. By the time the doctors found it, it had spread too far, too fast."

Mother. I'd forgotten she called her that.

"Where's she buried?"

"Abbeville. Next to Daddy. Grandpa John, Grandma Ellen."

"You go there much?"

"No."

"You're walking now."

"Some of the paralysis lifted."

Lifted enough to use a walking frame. But she'd never dance again. Just like I'd never be able to fly an airplane again.

"We'll have to get you decent clothes—"

"No. I like these clothes."

Then we were arguing, until she said I needed decent clothes and that she'd pay for them. I didn't have any money left and I owed Betty-Sue a hundred dollars, too. I was back in South Carolina, hardly half a day gone and the old ways returned. Money worries again.

"What on earth is that?" she asked, pointing to my package— the one-by-one sealskin, tied with sinew. I gave it to her, told her she could open it if she wanted. She saw the little red book, the pages still stuck together, a few torn from shaking fingers. I never said a word, nor did she.

And there was the wad of typed paper, stuff that Betty-Sue had already typed up for me. Meg flicked through it, looked up at me, and I didn't recognize what was in her eyes. "Like I said, you two kept me going."

She looked at the tattered photograph she'd stuck in the last page. She looked at all those pages I'd written on, but I doubt

283

she was able to read the writing. Now and then, I'd looked back over it, read it from memory, drove myself crazy trying to understand a scratch or two meant to be a word, one word to make the rest understood. And I'd looked at those words and I'd see Kioki. I'd be back on Kulowyl. She'd be lying with me, tickling me. I always knew what she wanted when she did that.

"Gordon's coming home for lunch today. He never does that." She pushed the journal away, half-afraid it might bite.

"Gordon—"

"My husband. The one you spoke to last night."

"He sounded pissed."

"Please don't use that language in this house. And he's a very gentle man."

Sure he was. She'd need someone gentle to boss around. "How long you been married?"

"Twelve years."

"Did Mom go to the wedding?"

"Yes, she did. We were married in June; she died that August."

"She'd have liked that. She loved weddings."

"Have you tried to contact Rosanna?"

"Nope."

"Good. I never liked her."

"Well, she never liked you much, either, Meg."

"You could have done way better than her."

"I did. Her name's Kioki. She's four foot eleven and—"

"I don't want to know."

I'd figured that already. "I had two wives. I could have had as many as I wanted."

"John! No!"

Forty-one and still tormenting her. So I let her see my little smile and she softened. She knew I was only teasing. "Where is Rosie, anyway?"

"She married Frankie Dee," Meg said, half a smile on her lips. "Two months after you left Miami."

284

Well, I sat there, stunned. I tried hard to imagine it, but all I did was grin. A large weight lifted.

"John, what are you going to do?"

"I don't know."

"Are you staying anywhere?"

"I was going to go home."

"Home?"

"Abbeville."

"There's nothing there for you now. There's nothing. Do you understand?"

Now she was talking to me as if I was a retard. I understood all too well. I got up off her French antique chair. "Sorry to come home like this and embarrass you, sis."

"Oh, for God's sakes, stop it!"

I sat down again and she sat beside me, closer this time. "I had to sell your business, John. I waited seven years. I tried to keep it going, but I had no choice. Sonny Milligan bought it. He gave me a good price."

I knew what Sonny Milligan's price would be, too.

"I couldn't stay in Abbeville. I was offered a good job in Columbia. I had to get out. There were too many memories for me there."

There was nothing she could tell me about memories I didn't already know. "I still want to go back to Abbeville."

"Why? The old house is not there anymore. The place has changed."

"Every damn thing has changed. But I never thought you'd sell me out."

"Did I know you'd magically reappear after seventeen years? Be reasonable!"

"You wish I wasn't here, don't you? You wish I'd never come back."

"I won't have you saying that! I just need time to adjust."

"Bullshit, Meg. You've never needed time to adjust to anything. Just tell me if there's anything of mine still left."

"Can this wait until Gordon comes home?"

"No. This is between you and me, not him."

"You don't know him!"

"I don't think I want to."

"What did you come here for?"

"I came to get what was mine before I went back. Where I belong. For good."

"And where's that?"

"Place called Saint Lawrence Island. In the Bering Sea. Off Alaska."

"You're going to go back to Alaska?"

What was it, surprise or relief in her eyes now?

"What can I do here now, Meg? Get a job? How? What do I do? Sit around railroad stations holding a tin so folks throw me a spare dime? I can't do a goddamn thing and you know it!"

"What the hell do you want from me!"

It was a scream and she had tears in her eyes again. I'd never seen her so upset before and I needed another yellow pill. I took it. Okay, okay, she'd sold the business. My airplanes to the opposition. Put myself in her place, what would I have done? Kept someone else's dream alive and neglected my own?

Now she was crying, crying and angry and confused. But I didn't say I was sorry, because I wasn't. I felt cheated. All those years of working, for her, for my mother, for myself, it was all gone. She'd gone and sold everything.

"What do you want—"

"What I want is to go back to my family. That's why I came back here first. I tried to find you, call you, but nothing worked the way it should have. . . ."

"Mommy? Who's that?"

Then I saw a little girl peering around the door, afraid to come in, afraid to stand outside. She'd heard us arguing. I knew who she was. One look, I knew. I'd seen her before.

"Rachel, come and meet your uncle."

She came in. I swear she was the little girl I had seen a hundred times when I thought of my sister. Bright red hair, huge green eyes. She looked about five. Just woke up. And as she came in, holding a teddy bear by the leg, I heard my sister say, "We'll talk about this tonight, when Gordon's home."

Talk about what? I wondered. Two more people planning out what was left of my life?

The little girl stood in front of me, looked at my face, looked at the shirtsleeve pinned so it wouldn't flap in the breeze. She reached out and touched, like my own daughter used to. Then she looked into my eyes. "Where's your plane, Uncle John?"

I looked at Meg. I'd been gone, presumed dead all this time, but she'd kept my memory alive. I wondered what she'd told this little girl about me. I looked back at her. She didn't seem scared. She didn't run away squealing like most kids when they saw me coming. She stood there, swinging her bear and waiting for me to say something.

"I crashed it, honey."

"Why's your face like that?"

"I got hurt in the crash."

"Is it still sore?"

"Sometimes."

She went to the bookcase, took out an album of photographs, came back, sat down beside me, and flicked through the pages until she found *the photo*. Bobby and me, together and grinning. She pointed to me, on the left, looked at the photo closely, then at me. "I can tell it's still you."

She cuddled into my arm and swung her legs midair. God had given Meg a child just like she had once been and I don't think she liked it much. "Tilly had an accident, too."

I looked at Meg for help, but she was staring into space.

"Who's Tilly?"

"Back in a minute. Don't go nowhere."

"Anywhere, Rachel. Don't go anywhere. . . ." But the girl was gone, up the stairs, and I heard the bear thumping on each step, too.

Meg sighed and looked at her watch. Rachel came back down with a porcelain doll that had been glued back together. "Daddy ran over her with the car and Ella put her back together. Who put you back together?"

"An Eskimo medicine man called Asuluk."

"Wow." Her eyes filled her entire face. "They kiss funny, don't they?"

"Thank you, Rachel, that's quite enough. Go and tell Ella we'd like some more drinks."

Off she went, calling for Ella.

The housekeeper brought in a lemonade for Rachel, an iced tea for Meg, and an iced coffee for me. And while we were all politely silent, the little girl heard a car door slam and she sprang to her feet, threw the doll and bear on my lap, and ran out, squealing, "Daddy, Daddy!"

"Gordon's home for lunch," Meg said.

And I could see Kioki, with Lily beside her, waiting on the edge of the rock for Sinbad and me to come in. Lily would do that sometimes. No, Lily would do that most times—run to meet me, to see what I'd gotten that day.

"I've got two kids up there, Meg. A boy of fifteen and a girl who's eleven. And I miss them like hell," I said quietly, watching for Meg's reaction. She pulled herself into her walking frame, turned to me, and said, "Well, I've got three."

But her smile said it all.

It hadn't been as I had dreamed it would be, but I suppose nothing works the way some dreams do, the wishful kind. I thought I could go home; I thought I could be me. But the me I'd become just didn't fit anymore. And as for Gordon . . .

I liked him.

I always thought I'd hate anyone Meg ever liked.

I was wrong. He was a little guy, about five eight, receding dark hair, gold-rimmed glasses, the three-piece suit, the brief-case under his arm. He had a good handshake; he didn't study me as he would a new kind of bug crawling out from under a rock. And he took the whole afternoon off, too. He'd canceled three lectures because his sister's brother had reappeared after seventeen years. He wanted to meet the man he'd only heard so much about.

I didn't want to admit it, but I liked the guy, even if he occasionally dropped words I'd need a dictionary to understand. And throughout lunch, the suit gradually disappeared. First went the jacket, then the vest. After lunch, the little girl who'd sat beside me decided it was better to sit on my lap and cuddle in, make sure I had a heartbeat, make sure I was real.

That's when I really missed my own daughter, and I think Meg knew it, too.

After lunch, Gordon took me outside. He led me into the garage, turned the light on, took a cover off something lying in a corner.

"I told her I'd divorce her if she sold this little honey."

My old bike. My Harley-Davidson. It brought tears to my eyes. Gordon looked at my face and said five magic words: "Anyplace you'd like to go?"

TWENTY

●━━●━━●━━●━━●━━●━━●

GORDON opened an old closet and in it hung three leather coats. He gave me the one with a fur collar and I held it awhile. The leather was crinkled and peeling and above the left pocket was a faded red patch with black lettering: Sullivan and Shaw.

My spare coat. Meg had kept it.

Gordon helped me into my old uniform coat, opened the garage doors, and pushed the Harley out into the sunshine.

"I ride her sometimes, John. Didn't think you'd mind."

Dead men don't mind. Even if they did, there's not much that can be done. I was itching. Itching to get back on my bike. My left arm from the elbow down seemed to be alive again, till I tried to touch.

My bike was clean, polished. Gordon had taken better care of it than I had.

"Meg doesn't like surprises. Surprises upset her plans," Gordon said. "Life's a box to her, you know. Anything that doesn't fit doesn't stand a chance, if you know what I mean."

What was he saying? I shouldn't have come home, upset my sister's life?

"Damn thing never starts. . . ."

"Ah, no. Not like that. Here, let me." I turned the fuel on, gave her three bursts of throttle, let her sit there five seconds, and Gordon kicked her over.

First time, every time, but the idle needed some adjusting. Sounded like she was crying for a new plug, too.

I sat behind him, no good me even trying to ride one-armed. "You all right back there?" he called. Whether I was or not wasn't the point. I realized that this brother-in-law of mine needed a little freedom, too—leave it all behind, and riding the Harley was the second-best way either of us knew how.

He rode the bike like I did, fast. Any misgivings flew when we hit the open road, heading west. I didn't have to guess about destination or ETA. I'd ridden this bike along this same road two thousand times. I'd known every bump, every curve, every corrugation. But the road was sealed now, sealed and wide, and there was no chance of coming off at fifty miles an hour on dead man's curve, sliding a hundred yards on my butt.

Cotton fields, orchards, factories, houses where farmland used to be. The only things that hadn't changed were the mountains in the distance and the blue of the sky; the pines, the forests, the way they blanketed the sunshine.

Abbeville might have been the town that time forgot, but I sure hadn't.

I'd seen it last in 1926. Now it was 1943. We rode on, crossed Blue Hill Creek, down Main Street. Even the air was different here. I guess it always had been. We rode by the Thomas D. Howie Monument. It probably hadn't changed, this town square, but it looked so different to me. Down East Greenwood, over the Seaboard, into West, and out toward Calhoun Falls.

And Davis Field.

None of the people out walking looked familiar to me. Then Gordon turned a sharp right and for a bit I was lost, till I realized he was heading for Rosanna's place.

He never slowed at her house. It looked the same—the gables, the covered porch, the overgrown garden.

One fading FOR SALE sign on the fence.

I always avoided going to the field this way, in case she saw me. For a second, I wondered if she was happy, then the moment passed right by.

On we went. Past the hospital. Denny Jones used to farm this land with corn, corn and pigs. What had happened to Denny Jones's pigs?

Davis Field, finally. A sealed strip, wind socks indicating a southerly. And all I could see were single-engined mono wings.

Not a biplane in sight.

Gordon parked the bike. I didn't realize my knees were Jell-O till I tried to stand, but he was walking his own race. He headed straight for the hangar and was inside it before I'd made it across the grass.

It took some time for my eyes to adjust from daylight to dark, then I heard a voice I hadn't heard for too long—twenty-one years to be exact. "Jesus Christ on a tricycle, Johnny Shaw?"

This old man came toward me so fast, I stepped back. He reached out, grabbed my head, and said, "Johnny Shaw!"

Billy?

"What happened to you? What happened to my boy?"

Billy Taylor was still alive? This fat, bald man with trousers hanging below his gut was Billy Taylor? I just stared, heart in mouth.

"You're supposed to be dead."

"Ah, yes, I know."

"Did an aircraft do that to you, son?"

This old man was still calling me son? "Yes, sir, sure did."

"What aircraft?" he asked.

I told him the story. I was saying it so much, so often, I was boring myself.

"So you tried to do it solo."

"I tried."

"Fool. That's what you get, chasing dreams. What'd you think you'd be, some kind of hero?"

I laughed at him. And he laughed at me. He touched my face again, looked at me, and he hugged me, tightly. I think he even cried. Then he cast a look toward Gordon, a conspiracy smirk. What was this? Suddenly, it was clear. Sure, he'd canceled lectures. He'd spent all day tracking down Billy Taylor.

And I was back where I'd wanted to be for so long. Davis Field, with Billy Taylor, still alive after all these years. I wanted to tell him about his namesake, my son. I wanted to ask about his rich wife. I didn't get time. He put his hand on my shoulder, looked at me, and said, "Still want to fly, son?"

Oh Jesus, how? In what? "I can't."

"Do you want to fly?"

"God, yes, yes."

"Follow me."

I looked at Gordon on the way past; he was in deep conversation with a mechanic. I wanted to thank him. I wanted to say so much. I just grinned at him instead.

Billy opened the door to the next hangar.

"Just like old times, Johnny," he said. I was staring at the machine I'd learned to fly in—*Gloria*. The one he'd ditched into the water hole when I was a kid. The one I thought he'd died in. She'd been rebuilt, restored to her former beauty.

Gloria. Still whispering to me after all this time. I touched, just as I had that day when I was nine years old.

I helped push her out, watched the tail as she came off the cement and on to the grass. I felt like a kid again. If I let the tail drop, my butt would get kicked good. How many times had I cleaned up someone's puke? How many times had I sat in the cockpit and flown the Atlantic in twenty minutes? The dog-fight champion who polished wooden propellers for ten cents an hour . . . Just a kid who learned mechanics by watching, listening, doing. A kid taught to fly by a would-be father who was taught by Orville Wright himself.

I was stepping back into a yesterday I thought I'd never have again. And I looked at my brother-in-law, and I knew he was responsible for this.

I stood back while the aircraft was fueled. My heart was caught in a fire, couldn't find an exit. Feeling returned to my left hand; it seemed so real that I touched. There was nothing there. No way I could fly with one arm. No way. At that moment, I didn't want to fly. I didn't want to be a passenger, either. If I couldn't ride my own bike, what use was there in flying my very first plane again?

My own fear was taking over—fear that I'd crash again, that this time I would die, that I couldn't die yet. I had to see my family. From wanting to die for so long, now, facing it, I was finding excuses not to.

I must have been crazy.

"I can't do this, Billy."

"Sure you can. Gordon'll take you up. I can't fly anymore, son. Disqualified. Too damn old." He touched his chest. I guessed it was his heart. He looked at my face, my arm, my legs.

He couldn't fly anymore.

Nor could I.

Then he helped me into the front seat.

Dual controls?

Refitted, rebuilt. It wasn't the same machine—it could probably do more than the original.

I stretched out, leaned back. No, I didn't want a cap. I wanted to feel the wind in my hair. Someone said I'd better, that it might get cold up there. I fell apart laughing. These people had never been touched by cold in their lives.

After awhile, my heart stopped looking for an exit.

Lunch needed a way out instead. Meg's chicken salad was going to be a joy for that freckled-faced boy to clean up. I knew it; he knew it. He went back to sweeping the hangar floor.

Gordon climbed in behind me, touched my shoulder. He ran his preflight check, which I checked, too, and a heartbeat later, we were hurtling down the strip. I was waiting to lift. Now, damn it. Now.

Three seconds later, we lurched into the air.

Gordon flew like Bobby. I screamed at him, asking who'd taught him to damn well fly, and he screamed back, "Sonny Milligan! Where do you think I met Meg?"

We reached six hundred feet, according to the altometer. It felt like five hundred to me, still climbing. We were heading northeast into North Carolina.

It took awhile to relax, feel almost safe, look out, look down.

Oh boy, this was better than good, better than best. I was flying again. God had given me back my wings. I looked around at Gordon. He had his fingers laced behind his head and his eyes said, Take it. I'm bored.

So I took the stick; the machine was mine. I had twenty minutes, which felt like twenty seconds.

Time nearly up, I banked her right, a full-rudder slip, descended back to five hundred, and took her home to Abbeville. Closing in, I found the square, the monument, the county sheriff's office.

And I did what I'd always wanted but never had the guts—I buzzed my hometown's main street.

Hell, it felt good.

All I needed was a boxful of yellow daisies to throw down at all the faces staring up in disbelief.

I powered on and took her up, straight up, guaranteed to a near stall, put her into a spiral, and pulled out at 250 feet, then gradually descended, skimmed the airfield fence by half a whisker, and let Gordon put her down.

We landed, taxied in, and shut down. My heart was still at twelve hundred feet. I was invincible, complete, and I didn't want to get out.

Gordon was white, shaky, and I could have knocked his eyes clean off with a stick, they were protruding so far.

I pretended I didn't understand why.

He left me at the airfield after Billy assured him he'd see me home. He never told Gordon exactly when that would be and by the time the cops arrived, the three of us were long gone.

Twenty-one years we hadn't seen each other—it could have been last week. Billy was an old man now, the body slowly giving in while the spirit, that light in his eyes, remained stationary at thirty-five. He told me doctors had given him five years to live twenty years ago. England had been too wet and cold for him, the people too stuffy. He'd never known what they were thinking. If he had his time over, he said, he'd have waited until

295

the ship's journey was done before marrying Elizabeth. If he'd waited, he never would have married her.

He told me the hardest thing he'd ever had to do was say good-bye to me that day in New York, how for a year nothing could fill this empty space inside him—not even a new life, a new wife. It was as if everything he loved had been left behind. But not forgotten, never forgotten. He told me how much he'd loved getting my letters. And he took something from his pocket. It was old. Old and yellow and the ink had faded. It was the last letter he ever got from me. I looked at it. I hardly recognized the handwriting. It was legible, almost neat, written with a left hand that no longer existed.

I'd written it to him three days before I left Miami on that solo run. By the time he'd gotten it in England, I'd been presumed dead.

Billy said, "I got your letter one day and a telegram the next. A telegram from Lily. I came back to the States the very next day."

He looked at me, then back to the road again.

"I loved your mother. You know that, don't you? I loved her the first time I saw her. You remember that? It was the day you broke your arm."

"The day after," I said.

"That's right. The day after." He was driving, thoughtful. "She sure had one temper. I tried to tell her how I felt, but she didn't want to hear. Didn't want to know. She wouldn't marry me. Said it wasn't right. I asked her five times."

I thought of all those times I'd prayed he would marry my mother, anything to stop her from sitting alone in the dark.

"I came back as soon as I heard you were dead. Your mother and I never believed it, though. Never."

Damned if I could say a word. My eyes were stinging.

"I was with her when she died, Johnny. I was holding her hand. Meg had slipped out to get some lunch and as soon as Meg left, your mother gave up the fight. She opened her eyes, she looked at me, and she whispered your name. Then she just ... It wasn't me she was looking at. I felt it. She wanted me to be you so bad, Johnny. I think she was seeing you there, not me. When Meg came back from grabbing something to eat, I was sitting by the bed, still holding Lily's hand. I said, 'Honey, she's gone.' And, well, Meg hasn't spoken to me since."

I didn't know what to say. I didn't know what to feel, either. He was talking as if my mother had died yesterday.

He stopped the car at the Long Cane Cemetery.

I didn't know where my father's grave was—Lily had forbidden us to go there ever. Life wouldn't have been worth an ounce of racoon crap if we'd done the unthinkable. That was probably why I went through life not believing he was dead, or a hero.

Before he got out of the car, Billy found his wallet and took a color photograph from it. "It was taken three months before she died. At Meg's wedding. I gave the bride away. Did you know that?"

I shook my head. No, I didn't know.

I looked at the photograph and saw an old, thin lady in a blue dress, a white hat, white gloves, bag, shoes. She was standing beside Billy Taylor. He was either being friendly—I saw a hand on her waist—or he was holding her upright.

"You have it, son. I have another. Come on."

As I stepped from the car, I smelled lilacs. I damn near called out my mother's name, then it faded away. I put the photo in the wallet Betty-Sue had given me and followed Billy across the graveyard. It was small, but so was Abbeville.

The town never appreciated change that much.

I guess that's why my mother never left. She was born there; she died there. Her grave proved it.

I stared at it a long time, that lump of concrete poking out of the ground. One inscription was twenty-two years older than its partner's.

JOHN ELIAS SHAW
1885–1909

297

Too many *should haves* started running amok in my brain. She was forty-four when she died? My daddy was twenty-four? He was twenty-four? Jesus, I was twenty-four when I crashed. . . . My eyes stung. I stepped away.

But in that photograph she looked sixty! Why hadn't I been there? I wanted to punch Billy for being with her when it should have been me. And I didn't care what he thought she saw; it was *not* me.

He let me walk off alone. Then five plots down, I found Freddie Larsen. So much for Alabama, I thought.

I looked around at the graveyard on the outskirts of town, the town that meant nothing to me now. It was only a place—it'd remain here long after I was gone. So would Atlanta, Birmingham, Miami, Hialeah, the Appalachians, the Blue Ridge Mountains, Calhoun Falls, and the Savannah River. I only wanted this when I couldn't have it.

Billy gave me some time. Even when I was a boy, he knew how much time I needed—time to work things out for myself. It seemed as if he still knew me better than I knew myself.

When he finally came over, I asked, "Gordon had this all planned, didn't he?"

Billy leaned his butt on a gravestone and grinned. "He called me at home. Told me an old friend was back in town. Wanted me to be at Davis Field by half past three. Damned if I knew who it'd be."

"Yeah?"

"Yeah."

"That means you carry my letter everywhere you go?"

He stood up, sighed, and slapped me on the ear. "Yeah."

I saw him four more times during my stay in Columbia. And one day, I actually saw Rosanna in the Belmont Inn in Abbeville. I was walking by the inn and looked inside, saw a familiar profile, and backtracked. She was sitting by herself, having a coffee. I stood outside, looking in for a long time, wondering if I should.

And the wondering got the better of me.

I was walking in as she was coming out. She crashed into me, mumbled an apology, then turned and walked out the door, leaving me still holding it open, watching her. And she came to a sudden stop, the bag of groceries she was holding dropped to the sidewalk, and she turned around.

She looked up at me. She was older, but still pretty in a dragged-out, tired way. Still thin, but her clothes weren't spiffy. Her skirt had a patch on it. I guess it was her eyes I saw first— lost eyes, sad eyes.

Maybe she only half-recognized me because of my glasses, because of the walking stick I have to use these days. But her mouth opened to say my name and nothing came out. I closed the door, took a couple of steps toward her, and picked up her groceries. But she stepped away, quick. So I handed the bag back to her. Then I was on my way, down the street.

I looked back as I passed the tailor shop, but she was running the other way. I figured it best to leave well enough alone. But it hurt just a little to see her step back from me like that.

No, it didn't hurt a little. It hurt a lot.

The weeks I stayed with my sister were the longest of my life yet. She expected I'd stay. She expected I'd resume my place in the family tree. I tried to tell her that someone had sawn the branch off, but she wouldn't hear me. She talked of her family being my family. She didn't understand that it wasn't.

Gordon sensed my feet were stuck on flypaper, but she wouldn't listen to him, either. We didn't go flying again—he wasn't home that much. The university took up a lot of his time. He had degrees in science and philosophy. I never made it out of grade school. But we had two things in common, a love of flying and being connected to my sister.

The boys looked like their father. Steven and Joshua. Steven kept his distance, was polite and quiet, and Joshua knew more about Alaska than I did.

I liked Rachel most of all. She knew who I was, this uncle she'd never met. She'd sit on my lap and ask unceasing questions, not just about my time on Kulowyl but also about the people. And she'd sit in the bathroom and watch me shave my face. I taught her how to plait rope with her right hand and her toes.

And she cried when I told her I had to go.

Meg was too distressed to consider the possibility of sending the kids so far north to visit. She had a hard time letting them stay with Gordon's parents in Queens. I figured it best that I take what Gordon and Meg offered and leave.

Maybe I'd return one day, but most likely I would not.

There was nothing for me anymore. I couldn't fly like I used to, and flying was all I knew—except for Eskimo ways. And Eskimo ways wouldn't carry me very far in South Carolina.

So I got a cross-country ticket on United Airlines and decided to worry about what came next when it came and not before.

Betty-Sue had been right. I had to slip back into what was before I knew where I'd be heading.

I felt a strange kind of sadness when I walked on board that DC-3, took my seat, and looked down at my family in a group down there behind the fence. Gordon was holding Rachel, and I could tell she was crying. Billy Taylor came, too. I'd promised him I'd write him as soon as I got to Saint Lawrence. I begged him to come visit, even though I knew the cold would probably kill him.

This time, Meg waved good-bye. I don't know whether I will ever see her again, or any of them. But I don't worry about them anymore.

My mind is all right now. I know what I want. I know who I am and where I should be.

I don't know how I'll get to Anchorage from Seattle yet, but I know what I'll do when I get to Washington State. First is find that trading post in the middle of nowhere, and the second thing I'll do is get to Anchorage somehow, repay Betty-Sue, maybe take her to dinner if she will come out with me. I want to give back a little of what she gave me, if anything is enough.

EPILOGUE

———◦◦◦◦◦◦◦———

A T ten o'clock on a cold autumn morning, I was steril-
izing pans when Margo told me I had a caller who
didn't understand what no meant.

I saw brown pants, a leather coat, polished shoes, and when
he turned, he had a bunch of flowers in his hand.

Flowers and a smile, just for me.

I hadn't seen John or heard of him for so long—his promise of
writing to me had fallen short, like most men's promises. Nor
did he call me, and I'd given him two numbers—my folks at
Baton Rouge, my home in Anchorage.

Maybe I hoped he'd need me or something silly like that.

Only a faint echo of the wild man remained in his voice and
all the worry and confusion had disappeared from his eyes. He
no longer attempted to hide his face. Even with those scars, he
still looked handsome to me.

His hair was tricolored, goldy-brown, blond, and gray. I saw
traces of the face he'd had for twenty-four years before the
plane went down, and my knees went weak. How handsome and
sweet he must have been when he was young.

I didn't know what to say.

He returned the clothes and the cash I'd forgotten all about
and he waited patiently for four hours until my shift was over.
We had dinner in the fanciest restaurant we could find and we
danced until midnight, and just when I was hoping he would ask
me out again, he told me he was leaving at six in the morning.

He was flying out to Saint Lawrence Island, a special charter. He'd been officially informed that his family had been relocated from the Pribilofs to Saint Lawrence. He also told me I'd probably never see him again. But if he wrote to me, would I answer? I said I would.

I didn't go home that night.

We talked for a long, long time. He told me the trip back north had been a lot quicker and better, too—he'd flown to Seattle. He'd even spent a lot of money in cab fares and a lot of time, too, trying to find Sally and that trading post. He searched for two days before he finally came upon it—at the end of a road no one had used for a long time. But the trading post was a ramshackle old joint, falling down. No one had lived there for many a year. He hadn't the heart to go on in.

And he'd flown from Seattle to Anchorage, too. Said it took too long any other way.

I didn't want him to go and I think he knew that.

The charter plane left ten minutes late—it took us that long to say good-bye—and I stood there in the chilly air, waving until the aircraft was out of sight.

He left me his journal—the past was done; he was looking forward to the future now. He didn't care what I did with it. He said he wouldn't need these memories of yesterday anymore.

Well, the mails came in twice yearly from Saint Lawrence. This time, his promise was kept, and he kept it for eight years.

There's only one letter I feel is important enough to include, just as he had written it. It was his first letter, which I received six months after I waved good-bye.

Dear Betty-Sue,
I'm home. The stink hit me first—rotting seal carcasses. It's an untidy place, Saint Lawrence, and it's flat except for a two-thousand-foot hill they call Kinnipaghulghat. Don't try to say it, trust me. The place is treeless and just as windy and, I guess, colder than Kulowyl. The weather's worse, but you either acclimatize or die.

I bought a lot of things with me—tinned food, kerosene, antiseptics, bandages. Hell, you saw the crates, I forgot.

No one knew I was coming, but everyone was out waiting as soon as they heard the plane coming in. It's the only contact they have with the mainland. I guess you know that, too.

Sinbad was the first one I saw. For a while, he didn't recognize me without the beard and long hair, which I know I'll be growing again. Maybe it was the glasses that confused him.

Soon as he realized who I was, he started yelling, "Floreeda is back!" It was a happy riot, I guess.

They haven't changed. It was like stepping into yesterday even though I felt like I'd been gone forever. I can't really tell you everything or even how coming back made me feel. Words aren't right. It's like describing something worth a million dollars when you've only got five-cent words to use.

Kioki was washing clothes with soap when I found her. She was singing to herself, the same song she always sang when she was sewing or stringing ivory flakes. No need to tell you how she reacted. She had so much to tell me, she didn't know where to begin or what to do. First, she showed me the house—it's a one-room wood hut with real furniture. It's rough, but it's guaranteed to last forever. Oil lamps, kero lights, a table, and four chairs. Real plates, knives, forks. She's a little scared of the fuel stove, though. Seems other ladies had to teach her how and what to cook. She even had a crate of oranges that had been flown in at the beginning of summer. No pallet of skins these days; there are beds to sleep on.

She wouldn't let go of my hand, and it wasn't until the plane took off that she realized I was back to stay. I can't tell you any more about that—I know how shy you get sometimes.

The kids were all in school. Kioki and Sinbad showed me the way. I stood at the door and listened to the teacher covering some basic arithmetic—stuff I'd already taught them—and it was awhile before he noticed me.

I guess it was another million dollars with five-cent words.

To think how scared I was about coming back. It was easier than seeing Abbeville again. But I told you all about that, didn't I.

Seems that Asuluk died ten days after they were relocated. Kioki won't talk about it, nor will Lily. Losing her grandfather wasn't the best thing that could have happened to her, and for a while she didn't believe I was back to stay, either. Billy told me how she prayed to the Great Spirit for her father to return. There I was praying to my God to get me back here in one piece. I tell you, Betty-Sue, we came through one hell of a storm to get here.

Tonight, there's another blanket toss to celebrate my return.

I wish you were here, Betty-Sue, but I know how much you hate the cold. One thing I learned, girl—once I stopped hating the weather, it stopped hating me. Try it.

The mail plane's due in two days, I have to write to Meg yet. Write back to me, okay?

I'll never forget you.

Someone like you is hard to forget.

John.

We corresponded for the next eight years, sharing thoughts, news, experiences.

I met Kioki and Lily when he brought them to Anchorage in 1945. Kioki was tiny and quiet and frightened the entire time, scared almost to death by the plane trip, poor thing.

Lily was perhaps one of the prettiest young girls I have ever seen. She married her first love, Eennali, in 1947 and John became a grandfather eight months later.

Kioki died in her sleep three weeks after she helped her first grandson into the world.

John still came to the mainland once a year, bringing his son each time. I met William Robert Ignash Shaw in July 1950. He was tall, handsome and serious, highly intelligent. He was just as I'd pictured him as I'd read through John's journal or listened to him talk with that faraway look in his eyes. Billy's English was fluent and impeccable—when he chose to speak, of course. When I met him, he already had two wives and four children.

It was Billy who came to the mainland in May 1951. He knocked on my door and, with tears in his eyes, told me how his father had died as his mother had, peacefully in his sleep a few days before.

John was forty-nine years old.

When Billy left, I closed the door and I cried and I cried . . . and then I realized what that silly dream I'd had really meant.

It was April 26, 1951. It was so clear, so real, that I wrote it down the moment I woke.

I was standing on a cliff, near a lighthouse, the sea breeze tossing my hair. I felt a hand on my shoulder and I turned. It was Bobby, as I had seen him in that photo on Bess's shelf. He was standing beside his best friend and both of them were in their pilot's uniforms.

John was six feet four, with spiky blond hair, goggles in his left hand. He was smiling at me as he leaned against a bright red Curtiss Jenny biplane. He winked at me, said he'd see me later.

He had two good arms and a perfectly featured face.

I wanted to cry, Don't go! but nothing would come. They both waved to me and they both climbed up into the plane and I watched it take off. And out over the ocean, it banked right, then it climbed, and climbed. . . .